STORM CROSSED MAGIC

WHITE HAVEN WITCHES (BOOK 10)

TJ GREEN

Stormcrossed Magic

Mountolive Publishing

Copyright © 2022 TJ Green

ISBN eBook: 978-1-99-004743-5

ISBN Paperback: 978-1-99-004744-2

Cover design by Fiona Jayde Media

Editing by Missed Period Editing

Contents

Chapter One

Alex Bonneville leaned back in his chair and closed his eyes, enjoying the caress of warm air on his bare skin.

He could hear the sound of the waves breaking on the beach, and the odd scurry of night creatures around him, but it was otherwise quiet and still in the walled garden behind the house he shared with Avery. It was as if the huge storm that had battered the coast the night before had never happened. When he opened his eyes again, he found Avery watching him from across the garden table, her red hair appearing golden in the flickering candlelight, her face etched with concern.

"Stop worrying," he instructed her. "I'm fine."

"I can't help it. You haven't had a vision in weeks, and last night... Well, your shout terrified me."

"Sorry." He leaned forward and took her hand, giving it a gentle squeeze. "I'm sure it was just the storm. All that electrical energy must have invaded my dreams."

"Liar." She pointed at the silver bowl filled with water that was placed on the table in front of him. "That proves it."

"A precaution. Just like the cards." He nodded to her pack of tarot cards.

"I always read them, you know that. Especially on a night like tonight."

He smiled at her. "Liar."

Avery laughed and pulled her hand away, picked up the cards, and started to shuffle them. "Tell me what you saw again."

He took a moment to recall the vivid imagery that had invaded his sleep. Avery was right. He hadn't had a vision for months, but last night something had broken through his carefully prepared defences, shredding his equilibrium. "I heard screaming. Actually, more like a wail. Bloodcurdling, horrific. But it sounded..." he paused, uncertain if what he felt was correct. "Lonely. Distraught, perhaps. I was lost in a wood and I was running. Branches caught my hair and scratched my face." He ran his hands across his cheeks, as if he would actually feel scratched skin. He'd even inspected his face in the mirror that morning as it had felt so real, but of course all he saw was his tan and usual stubble. "Something was chasing me, and I couldn't run fast enough. And then I saw huge eyes—red, bloodshot..." He shuddered at the recollection. "It was a jumble after that. Darkness, branches, eyes, the scream. But what was worse was how I felt. I was just so depressed. I felt like I had nothing to live for. It was horrible. I think it was that feeling that woke me up more than anything. The need to escape feeling so aw ful."

Avery nodded and placed the cards in front of Alex. "Split the deck."

He did as she asked. "You're doing my reading?"

"It was your vision." She started to place the cards out, her deft, practiced hands moving swiftly. "We'll try and find what caused it."

"This was how I found you last year, remember?" Alex smiled at the memory of when he had pushed through the gate into this garden and found Avery reading the cards under a full moon. She hadn't been that pleased to see him, but he'd been captivated by her, and was determined to prove her beliefs about him were wrong.

"How could I forget? You were cocky and annoying." She shot him a cheeky smile. "But you looked hot. Bastard." He laughed, throwing his head back, but before he could respond, she added, "Now start scrying, bad boy."

"Yes, ma'am."

He took a few deep breaths, bent his head above the bowl of water, and stared into its depths. He focussed on what he wanted to know. *Who had screamed and chased him? And where had he been?*

It didn't take long for the cool, clear water to start swirling and darken, and suddenly it was as if he'd plunged head-first into a dream. He could smell damp earth, rich with detritus and leaf mould, the peppery scent of blossoms, and then the stench of death and decay. He reeled, barely feeling the coarse wooden surface of the table gripped beneath his fingers. It was so dark he couldn't see anything around him, but he felt smothered by the close proximity of the forest again—sharp branches, and something scratching his feet. And then a scream shattered the silence and his control. He lurched forward as the feeling of loss stabbed him like a blade.

Alex took a deep breath, struggling to regain his composure, and forced himself to look around again. He needed a landmark. *Anything*. As he stumbled forward, a dark pit opened beneath his feet and he fell, the scream echoing around him.

The shock was so great, he jerked backward, slamming into the chair's back as he gasped for breath. With relief he saw the candle flame flickering in front of him, and incense smoke snaking between him and Avery.

"It's okay, Alex," she murmured gently. "You're back in the garden. Are you okay?"

He exhaled. "I'm fine. Wow. That was too real. I normally hover over my scrying visions, but that one sucked me right in."

"Anything new?"

"A pit. I fell in it, but otherwise, the same. Branches, the feeling of being trapped and chased. The scream." His heartbeat was slowing and he took a few more deep breaths before noticing that Avery's Celtic cross was complete. "What can you see?"

Now it was her turn to sigh. "A crisis, loss, desperation. Swords are everywhere, as is The Tower. A powerful woman lies behind it all, The Empress, and I sense a cycle that has been played out before is once again repeating."

"A cycle?"

"The past is manifesting in the present, Alex, and it brings death."

Avery lifted the hair from the back of her neck to allow the fan-cooled air to play across her skin, and turning her back to the shop, uttered a spell that would bring the temperature down a little more. Within a few moments, she felt its effects and sighed with relief.

"Thank the Gods," Dan murmured. Her friend and shop assistant reached for a leaflet on the counter to use as a fan. "That was you, wasn't it?"

She nodded. "I love the heat, but yes, this is a bit too warm for my liking. I thought Saturday night's thunderstorm would break the heatwave, but it hasn't made the slightest difference."

"Man, that was huge! It woke me up. Shook the whole building."

"It woke us up, too," she said, wondering how much to share with Dan. However, she hated lying to her friends, and they always offered her invaluable advice. "It wasn't just the storm, though. Alex had a terrible vision and woke up shouting," Avery confessed. "It scared the shit out of me, and combined with the lightning and the thunder, I couldn't work out what the hell was happening."

"A vision?" Dan knew what that meant. Alex usually kept them under control, but they could be devastating when he had them. "Is he okay?"

"Shaken, but fine." Avery was trying to make light of it, but Dan saw through it.

"Avery!" He frowned, staring at her accusingly. "We've been here all morning, and you only think to share that now?"

It was mid-morning on a Monday in late July in White Haven, the morning after Avery and Alex had sat in the garden at midnight reading the cards and scrying, and two days after the storm that had rattled the coast. Cornwall was three days into a massive heatwave, and the heat and the storm were all anyone could talk about that morning. Customers had reported fallen trees, damaged roofs, and campers had been battered in their tents and caravans. Now, however, it was as if it had never happened—other than the destruction that had been left. The sky was bright blue and cloudless.

Avery and Dan were both behind the counter at Happenstance Books, wilting on the stools while they kept an eye on the customers who were also affected by the heat. They moved sluggishly around the shop, pausing every now and then in front of strategically placed fans.

The entrance door was wedged open, but seeing as there was hardly any breeze, it was virtually pointless.

Avery leaned against the shelves behind them and lowered her voice. "Sorry. I wasn't sure what to say. 'How was your weekend? Oh, yes. Alex had a vision of doom and gloom again.'"

"That bad?"

"I'm afraid so. I read the cards last night—his cards. He scryed and had a really strong response." She sighed, recalling his expression as he emerged from his vision state. He looked appalled. Scared. "The cards showed me a powerful woman emerging from the past. A return. Or even a homecoming. I think it's a repeated cycle."

"That doesn't sound good. As if something is unresolved, perhaps?"

"Maybe. I sense conflict, loss. Nothing specific." She decided not to mention her belief that she also saw death in the cards. She might have been wrong, after all. "Don't worry. We'll monitor it. It might turn out to be nothing. Let's talk about the crazy weather again."

Dan grunted, pursing his lips. "A safe English subject. But don't think for one second that I won't come back to this issue, Avery Hamilton." He gestured to the window and the deep blue sky visible above the street. "According to the news, this weather will last at least a few more days. I might be dead by then."

"Idiot. It's good for sales." The beaches were packed with tourists and books were flying off the shelves as customers settled under umbrellas to rest and read. "It will be lovely if it lasts for the Lughnasadh celebrations."

"Maybe. At least there's no parade this time." Dan laughed. "I think they'd overheat in their costumes."

"True. But the heat will bring the crowds, which means Stan will be happy." White Haven's Lughnasadh celebrations were only a few days away, and although there was no parade through the town this time, as usual there would be a bonfire on the beach, and fire-filled braziers would line the streets, along with a handful of performers.

"We don't need any more crowds!" Dan pointed at the presently crowded street. "I've never seen White Haven so busy. It's freaky."

He was right, Avery reflected as she watched the groups of families and friends meander in and out of shops. "That's Ghost OPS's fault."

"I saw Ben on the news again last night. They're getting a lot of publicity lately. I knew posting those videos of the ghostly giants on their website was insanity."

"That is what their website is for!" Avery pointed out, quickly changing the subject as a customer brought a couple of books to their counter. With a cheerful smile and polite chat, she completed the sale and waved her through the door. "And to be honest, all it's doing is adding to the White Haven mystique. It just means that more of Cornwall is affected now, too, and that's great for everyone."

Dan scratched his head, perplexed. "I suppose so. Cornwall needs the cash the visitors bring, but the roads are jam-packed."

"Can't have one without the other, unfortunately. And besides, the visitors love it. It must be working well for Rupert's business, too."

White Haven Occult Tours had increased the numbers of groups over the past few weeks with the arrival of the summer holidays, and now most days, especially evenings, Rupert and his wife, Charlotte, were seen escorting their patrons along White Haven's streets.

"And how's it going with your *group* now?" Dan asked, emphasis on the word 'group,' and she knew he meant the Cornwall Coven.

"To be honest, I haven't heard anything from anyone for a week or so. I think we're all just glad to return to some sort of normalcy. Besides, we'll catch up next week for Lughnasadh at Rasmus's. We're all keen to move on after the solstice celebrations." She didn't need to elaborate. Dan knew exactly what she meant after Maria, Zane, and Lowen's deaths from a few weeks before. "And," she forced a smile at Dan, "I am enjoying normal life, with no weird occurrences."

"Yeah, yeah. Apart from Alex's vision and your ominous card reading."

"Oh, shut up! We changed the subject."

"It's hard to forget, Avery! I was hoping for an uneventful summer."

"So was I. I didn't even want to read the cards last night." After the horrible betrayal in the Cornwall Coven, Avery wanted to live in ignorant bliss. "Of course, I had to, and I'll read them again later." She changed the subject again. "Oh, Sally is back!"

Sally, the bookshop's manager and Avery's oldest friend, arrived at the counter looking flushed as she placed their iced coffees and cakes on the counter. "Bloody hell, it's barely eleven, and it's boiling. I'm not sure how iced those coffees will be anymore."

Dan was already lifting his to his lips. "It's the caffeine and sugar I need."

Sally rolled her eyes. "Some things never change."

"No, they don't. Avery," he nodded at her over his cup, "had a doom-laden tarot reading, and Alex has had a harrowing vision. She's intending to read the cards again, but is clearly putting it off!"

Avery's lips narrowed. "Tattle-tale! It might just be the heat."

Sally's eyes widened with worry. "Oh, no. And I've been enjoying the peace and quiet, too."

"Honestly, Sally, I'm sure it's nothing."

"How's Alex?"

"He seems fine. It was a shock to have a vision, but he dealt with it. He's at work now." He was at The Wayward Son, the pub he owned, and would have already opened up for the day.

Sally thrust her cup at her, along with one of the cakes she had bought. "Don't put it off, Avery. Go and read the cards again."

Knowing they were both right, but resenting them for it, Avery glared. "Fair enough. But it's just the heat, and probably the after-effects of the storm."

They didn't answer, instead just looking at her knowingly, and she felt their eyes on her back as she left the shop and entered the stuffy back room. She opened windows as she progressed upstairs to her attic that doubled as her spell room. It was even hotter than the rest of the house, and she repeated her spell to lower the temperature.

At least it was blissfully quiet. The street sounds were muffled so high up, and she felt a calm steal over her. Once again, she questioned her reading. Was she imagining things? Had the weather affected Alex, and actually nothing was out of the ordinary?

Avery looked out of the rear dormer windows at the view of White Haven and the tumble of roofs heading down to the sea. The colour of the sky matched the sparkling blue of the sea, and it all melted together, becoming a milky white hue where they met at the horizon. But she was procrastinating. She sat at the worn wooden table and pushed the grimoires away, as well as bundles of herbs and candles, to make space for her tarot cards. She opened the box they were stored in, eyeing them warily before picking them up. Immediately, she felt a tingle of anticipation, as if they guarded secrets within.

The scent of incense wrapped around her, and she closed her eyes. Already the feeling was intensifying, and she couldn't put it off any longer. She started to shuffle the cards.

Chapter Two

B en Carter frowned as he consulted the map on his phone and then looked around him. "It says it's right here, but I can't see a thing!"

"Maybe the navigation is off," Dylan suggested. "The back lanes confuse Google."

"Bollocks. We could be going around in circles for hours."

Ben and Dylan, two of the three members of Ghost Objective Paranormal Studies, were on their way to a potential new job, but if they didn't find it soon, they would be horribly late and it would be embarrassing. They had virtually pulled into a hedge in a passing bay on a narrow lane high on the hill behind White Haven, and the leafy green hedges towered over them.

Ben clambered out of the driver's door. "I'll get on the roof to see if I can spot anything."

They were in their old van, and without waiting to hear Dylan's response, Ben climbed up onto the bonnet and then the roof, wincing as the hot metal burned his extremities. "Bloody hell! It's boiling!"

Dylan climbed out of the passenger seat, battling with the hedge as he did so. "We could just call them."

"We might have to." The sun penetrated over his sunglasses, and Ben shielded his eyes as he swung around, his eyes adjusting to the light. "I feel like a twit, to be honest. I know we're close."

"It's an old estate, right?"

"Something like that. The woman said she'd been renovating it, but the grounds were unkempt." The heat was making the air shimmer, but as Ben turned, he saw a chimney and the curve of a roof to his left, just visible above a high wall and a mass of trees. "There it is! Well, I think it is. We need a left turn."

Trying to avoid touching the hot metal with his hands, he slid off the roof, batted away some flies, and clambered back behind the wheel. Within minutes they had rounded the corner of the winding lane, and Dylan spotted a turn off, just as they were virtually past it. "Down there!"

Ben wrestled the van down the rutted track, branches whacking the vehicle as they progressed. The hedges were a mixture of hawthorn and blackthorn, effectively blocking anything else from view until they rounded another corner. Ben gasped as he pulled to a halt. "Holy shit! It's a bloody mess!"

"That might be a slight exaggeration," Dylan said, peering at the rambling building ahead of them. "It's certainly interesting. So that's Stormcrossed Manor."

"Looks ominous, right?"

"Very. It's sort of gloomy."

Despite the bright day and the cloudless blue skies, the house seemed draped in shadows. It was a long, two-storied building with a low-pitched roof, constructed of differing styles. A higgledy-piggledy mass of chimneys staggered across the skyline, and old nests were visible on the top of some of them. Trees crowded in on either side, and the windows seemed to absorb all light, offering a blank, shuttered front as if to repel all newcomers.

Dylan shuffled in his seat, reaching for his camera. "Let me grab some first impressions before we get any closer. It's nothing like Reuben's place, is it?"

"No. But that's because Reuben's place has been looked after over the years. This seems abandoned." He looked uneasily at Dylan. "I'm not sure we should be filming before we introduce ourselves. I want to make a good first impression."

"I won't be long."

Ben waited, feeling uneasy as he recalled the conversation he'd had with a woman called Rosa. She'd phoned him a couple of days before, saying she wanted their opinion on the old family house, but beyond that hadn't been forthcoming.

"Are you sure we haven't been invited here for a ritual sacrifice?" Dylan asked as he stopped filming. "It looks like a murder house. They could bury us on the grounds and no one would ever find us."

"It does have that look about it, doesn't it? At least Cassie knows we're here." He flashed a grin at Dylan. "*If* she ever finds the place. Or misses us at all." Cassie had been put out at not coming to Storm-crossed Manor, but she was covering the office and taking phone calls. It wasn't as if they'd relegated her to office duties; they'd drawn lots, and Cassie had pulled the short straw. "We'll take her some cake as a peace offering. Are you done?"

Dylan nodded. "Yep. Let's see what secrets this place holds."

Alex finished serving an early customer with coffee, watching them head to The Wayward Son's small courtyard that was currently bathed in sunshine, and put their breakfast order through to the kitchen.

It was promising to be another hot day, and once the lunchtime crowd hit, it would be very busy. Marie, one of his regular bar staff, was teasing Zee as she restocked the condiments on the side tables, and he was taking it all in good humour. Alex shook his head as he watched them, glad that he could count on both of them to look after his holiday staff.

He grabbed a cloth to wipe over the bar, and then took a deep breath as his vision swam. *Not again*. He probably needed to drink more water. Then pain shot through his head, and he leaned on the counter for support. *Shit*. He knew exactly what that meant. Before it got any worse, he ducked into the staff room behind the bar. Glad that the room was empty, he sank onto a chair, taking deep breaths in an effort to quell waves of nausea. However, Alex's vision darkened, and with a horrible certainty he knew this wasn't brought on by dehydration.

Pain rocketed through his skull again, so severe that his vision completely blackened and he fell forward. A wild, keening cry blocked out all other sounds, and the scent of rotting flesh swept over him before he passed out.

Newton's mouth settled into a grim, hard line as he surveyed the two dead bodies sprawled on the floor in front of him. This was the last thing he needed. It was the last thing any of them needed, with the holidays in full swing and Cornwall teeming with visitors. This would create panic.

"When's the doctor getting here?" he asked Detective Sergeant Moore, who stood a few feet away, his sharp eyes travelling around the small courtyard.

"Shouldn't be long, now, Guv."

"Good. These two are already smelling ripe." Detective Sergeant Kendall was standing next to him, silently taking everything in. "First impressions?" he asked her.

"There are no obvious signs of trauma, except for their horrible, bloodshot eyes, but that could be a medical condition."

"Both of them dying at the same time of the same medical condition?" Moore asked, sceptical. "That's too weird."

She looked up, eyes wide. "I know, but there are no obvious marks on their bodies. I guess it could be poison."

"And what else do you think is unusual?" Newton pressed.

Kendall looked down at them again. "The woman's hands are clasped around her ears, and she's curled up in a foetal position."

"Which suggests what?"

"She heard something horrible?"

"Perhaps. Which probably means this is another bloody paranormal death," Newton complained.

He had arrived on the scene only a few minutes earlier, after receiving a call from Moore. Newton had been tied up in a meeting with his superior officer, Detective Superintendent Trevena, updating him on the latest paranormal activities in the area. Trevena normally left him well alone, glad to wash his hands of paranormal issues, but the events with the Cornwall Coven, and the number of deaths and publicity they had caused, had unfortunately meant he was more than usually interested in Newton's activities, and that was annoying. He had hoped that with recently quieter few weeks, his interest would wane, but it hadn't. Now, with these potentially paranormal deaths, his interest was likely to increase.

The bodies were those of a middle-aged couple. It looked as if they had been seated around an outdoor table. Glasses of half-drunk wine were still on the table, but one of the chairs had been upended, and both bodies were on the ground.

"So, this is a holiday home?" Newton asked, his gaze traveling around the small garden surrounded by hedges and flowering plants, the quaint old cottage behind them.

"Yep," Moore confirmed. "The owner was dropping by with some fresh bread and eggs when he found them."

"Fresh bread and eggs? Nice!"

"It's part of the deal, apparently," Kendall explained, eager to help. "Homemade bread, jams, clotted cream, and eggs are part of the rental fee. It's a nice, local touch."

"I guess it is. And he found them like this?"

Moore nodded. "Retreated to the front path to wait for us to arrive."

Newton remembered seeing him before he entered the house. He was sitting on a bench in the front garden, looking shell-shocked. The DC who had arrived first was standing next to him. Newton had swept past them in his eagerness to get inside, but now he asked Moore, "Have you interviewed him yet?"

He shook his head. "No. I wanted to see in here first." Moore nodded at Kendall. "We've checked the entrances. There's no sign of a break in, and the garden is secure. Well, unless someone got over the hedge, but it's high."

"And there's no sign of battered branches or breaks in the hedge," Kendall put in.

"What's beyond the garden?" Newton asked.

"Not sure yet," Moore said. "But the owner will know."

The sound of a door slamming interrupted their conversation, and they all looked round as Arthur Davidson, the Medical Examiner, arrived. He frowned as he reached the patio doors, nodding at them and sniffing the air. "Hmm. This heat really doesn't help." Flies had already settled on the bodies, refusing to move even when Davidson crouched down to examine them. "Visitors, I presume?"

Newton nodded. "We'll get their details now. Could it be natural? A massive heart attack, perhaps?"

"Both of them at the same time, and with those bloodshot eyes? Unlikely. Grasping at straws, Newton?"

"Hoping not to ruin my day, more like."

Davidson settled back on his heels. "Impossible to say right now. Their bloodshot eyes could suggest strangulation, but their neck shows no obvious signs of trauma. I won't speculate. Keep an open mind, and all that." He looked up at Newton, raising an eyebrow. "We'll analyse stomach contents in case of poison. I'll run a tox report, but I wouldn't get your hopes up. First impressions suggest this is very odd indeed."

"So, what do you think?" Reuben Jackson grinned at Caspian Faversham, not in the slightest bit put off by his perplexed expression.

"Do I look like the rowing type?" Caspian asked.

"Well, yes actually. You have the build for it."

"Let me rephrase that. Do I look like the *outdoors* type?" He gestured down to his tailored suit. "I haven't rowed in years."

"But you run and go to the gym, and besides, rowing is like riding a bike. You never forget. And," Reuben added, his grin broadening, "that's why we're starting to practice now—well, when we have the whole team."

Despite Caspian's reservations, Reuben could see that he was weakening. His lips twitched with amusement, and he wasn't outright refusing. "But I live in Harecombe, not White Haven."

"Have you got your own gig team?"

"Well, no..."

"Exactly. And neither have we yet, so you may as well join ours."

For the last few weeks, Reuben had been obsessing about a new venture, triggered by a conversation with Nils, his Swedish friend who was the tattoo artist who owned Viking Ink. Nils loved being out on the water, and owned an old fishing boat that had seen better days, but over a pint, he'd suggested that maybe they should get a gig team together, purely because it sounded like fun. Gig racing was very popular in Cornwall, and there were many regattas held during the ye ar.

Nils had already bought a gig, and Reuben had brought Caspian to the old harbour shed to see it. It was upside down at present, being repaired and varnished, and they were surrounded by the smell of paint, varnish, and brine.

Caspian folded his arms across his chest. "Six rowers in total, plus the cox, if I remember correctly. How many do you have so far?"

"Me and Nils, Nils's mate, Rory, maybe you, maybe Alex, and we need one more."

"*Maybe* Alex? Isn't he keen?"

"Says he hasn't got enough time, which means we need two people because I don't think I'll change his mind." Reuben wasn't altogether surprised. Alex's business demanded a lot of his time, unlike Greenlane Nurseries that Reuben owned, because his manager dealt with most of the day-to-day tasks. "But you said that you wanted to get away from your business more, and this is the perfect opportunity!"

"I suppose I did say that." Caspian ran his hand across his smooth, shaved chin, obviously perplexed. "How often would we need to practice?"

Reuben shrugged. "We haven't really thought it through. Maybe two or three times a week, initially. More pre-race. It will be fun! And if you hate it, you don't have to do it again." Reuben regarded Caspian hopefully, knowing it was just what Caspian needed. It would be a complete change from being CEO of Kernow Industries, and would hopefully take his mind off Avery. It was hard to feel sorry for Caspian because he had so much going for him, and yet, his confession weeks prior that he didn't have many friends had struck Reuben as horribly sad. However, that wasn't strictly true. Gabe, Shadow, and the Nephilim were his friends—loyal ones, too.

"All right," Caspian said, relenting. "I'll give it a go. But if I hate it, I'm out."

"You won't, I promise. It's purely brawn, us against the elements—no magic allowed. Besides, you run a shipping business. You should love everything sea-related."

Before Caspian could retort, Reuben's phone rang, and he frowned when he saw the name. "Hey Zee, what's—"

Zee cut him off. "Thank the Gods I got you! I can't get hold of Avery. Alex has had a weird, psychic episode. Can you get here?"

Reuben was already moving to the door of the dockside shed, summoning Caspian with his free hand. "Is he okay?"

"He's awake again, but I don't know if I'd say he's okay. Briar is coming, though. Try and get hold of Avery, please?"

"Sure. On our way."

The first thing that struck Dylan as they entered Stormcrossed Manor was the scent of must and things long forgotten. The hall was dark, the wallpaper faded and peeling in places, and the worn stone flags that lined the floor were uneven and needed a good scrub. Cobwebs hung from the ceiling, and dust lay thick in patches, as if someone had tried to clean it and then given up.

The woman who had let them in, Rosa Davies, looked almost apologetic as she led them past open doorways that fed into dimly lit rooms, finally stopping in the old-fashioned kitchen that stretched across the back of the house. Here the light flooded in, illuminating old cupboards and work surfaces, and tatty-looking vinyl on the floor. But it was at least clean. Dylan, for all of his lack of domesticity, was thankful that his and Ben's flat was nothing like this place. It looked like it hadn't been updated for years.

Rosa had been silent as she led them to the kitchen, but now she sighed, as if relieved to be out of the rest of the house, and urged them into seats, thrusting a plate of digestive biscuits at them. "Sorry," she started, "when we agreed to move in here, I had no idea what I was getting myself into. The whole thing is a nightmare."

Dylan wasn't sure if he should agree, therefore admitting the place was a wreck, or just smile politely. Fortunately, Ben answered. "It has a lot of charm—good bones, as they say. Lots of hard work is needed first, though."

Rosa put the kettle on and prepared cups before sinking into a seat in a patch of sunlight, and Dylan could see how tired she was. She looked to be in her forties, with streaks of grey in her fair brown hair, tied up in a messy knot on her head. The light revealed a smear of dirt across her cheek and the faint lines around her eyes. She laughed. "You're very kind. A lot of hard work doesn't even come close." She closed her eyes briefly and sighed again. "But it's not the dirt that worries me, it's the odd feeling that descends here at night."

"Perhaps before we dive in, you should give us a bit of background," Dylan suggested, opening his notebook. "Context is everything. Ben said you didn't reveal much on the phone."

"No, I didn't. I thought you might turn me down if I did. I wanted to get you here first."

Ben shrugged. "Our job is to be open-minded. It's what we do."

She smiled and swallowed. "Let me get the tea first." She stood and quickly poured hot water into the teapot while Ben and Dylan exchanged curious glances, then carried it over to the table where it steamed in the sunlight. "We moved in about a month ago. Me, my twelve-year-old son, Max, and my six-year-old daughter, Beth. My grandmother owns the house. It's been in our family for generations, but as you can see," she spread her hands wide, "it's seen better days. I feel guilty, actually. We've been living in north Wales for years, and I haven't visited since I was a girl. However, I've recently split from my husband—rather acrimoniously—and I wanted to get away. My mother," she rushed on, as if speed would give her courage, "said that Gran was struggling on her own, so coming here seemed like the perfect solution. Except..." She trailed off, obviously overwhelmed, tears pricking at her eyes.

Unusually chivalrous, Ben rushed in. "It's not what you expected."

"Not at all."

"Where is your grandmother?"

"There's a wing to the left," she gestured vaguely around to the side. "She lives in there, and it's barely more habitable than here."

Dylan peered out of the window, able to see a grey stone wing off to the side, most of it covered in Virginia creeper, which was why he hadn't spotted it straight away. The place was curiously quiet, though. "Where are your kids?"

"Max will be exploring the garden, and my daughter is with her Great-grandmother, Tamsyn." A frown creased Rosa's face, and her fingers rubbed the mug her now cooling tea was in. Dylan thought she was going to add something, but she didn't, instead taking a deep breath in and out. "Anyway, that's why we're here. I'm now trying to clean the place and restore some sort of order. We've moved in for the foreseeable future. Tammy is far more fragile than I realised. In body, I should add." Her eyes darkened. "In spirit, she's as strong as ever."

There was tension in this house. Dylan could feel it. Something beyond the shadows, decay, and dirt. Something that lurked beyond the sunshine that fell in the cobbled yard beyond the kitchen window. *A restless spirit, perhaps?*

"So, what's worrying you, Rosa?" Dylan asked, his voice gentle.

Her fingers played with the mug for a few more seconds before she looked up at them. "I hear things at night. Odd bangs in the house that I try to believe are just the house settling. I thought I'd get used to it, but it's getting worse! When I phoned you, it was just the bangs and thumps I was hearing, but after Saturday, it got worse." She swallowed, clearly summoning her courage. "I now hear screams on the wind."

"Screams? Are you sure it's not foxes?" Ben asked, leaning forward. "They make the oddest noises."

"That's what I thought, at first. But then they become long and drawn out, like a wail." Rosa shuddered. "It's unnatural—unearthly. And it seems like no one else hears them! I need you to tell me what's out there."

21

"Hold on," Dylan held up his hand. "You said after Saturday. Do you mean after the storm?"

She stared at him, her lips trembling. "Yes. The storm woke me up. It was terrifying here. It's so lonely. So remote. The whole sky lit up, Beth screamed, and we even lost electricity." Rosa sipped her tea, her hands shaking. "I thought I was imagining the first scream...that it was the wind whipping through the trees or down the chimneys. But when the storm passed, I still heard them!"

Her hands were still shaking, and Dylan eased the cup from her white-knuckled grip and placed it on the table. "Do you hear the screams in the day, or just at night?"

"Just at night." She closed her eyes briefly. "Last night seemed to last forever."

"Just to clarify," Ben asked, "you've heard odd noises for a while, but screams started with the storm, and even though there was no storm last night, you heard the screams again?"

"All night."

Dylan exchanged a worried look with Ben, who nodded, all business. "Okay, Rosa. Don't worry, we'll find out what's happening. We'll get the details first, and then set up some cameras and recording equipment, if that's okay. In here and outside. We can monitor them every day, or even live stream it. It's whatever you're comfortable with."

"You believe me?"

"Why wouldn't we?" Ben smiled. "Just because no one else hears it doesn't mean you're going mad. Sometimes spirits—if that's what they are—can only be heard or seen by certain people."

"And," Dylan added, "our equipment can pick up lots of things that can't be seen by the naked eye. Whatever it is, we'll find it."

Or them, he thought. He had a feeling this house was hiding lots of secrets.

Chapter Three

A very emerged from the trancelike feeling that reading the cards had brought on, blinking as the sunlight that reached across the attic registered in her brain.

She sat back in her chair, regarding the spread in front of her. It wasn't often that reading the tarot had this effect. She always stilled her mind, letting her breathing settle and her mind empty as she placed the cards out in the Celtic cross, but this time, as her vision narrowed, everything else had disappeared into darkness.

The cards seemed to take on a life of their own, their colours shimmering, and the images seeming to move. The spread contained so many potential omens. There was the Three of Swords—a heart pierced by three swords—telling of heartbreak and grief, as well as the Five and Eight of Cups. There was a lot of loss in these cards, an end of things, and an inability to move on. Again, the reversed Empress seemed to be directing the action, sitting alongside a reversed Death and Wheel of Fortune. The whole reading signified change. But more ominous was The Tower heralding the future. Something was manifesting.

Avery took a few deep breaths, and then the muffled peal of her phone shocked her out of her reverie. Startled, she headed for the sofa and dug it out from her bag, noting she had missed a few calls from Zee. "Reuben!" she said as she answered, already starting to worry. "Is everything okay?"

"I'm fine, but Alex has had a weird psychic episode, according to Zee. You'd better get to the pub. I'll see you there, but don't panic. He's okay!"

He didn't wait for her answer, instead ringing off, and Avery didn't hesitate. They hadn't told their coven about Alex's recent visions, and she knew they'd be annoyed as well as worried. She summoned air, intending to use witch-flight to arrive in Alex's flat, and hoped that none of the bar staff were in there. With luck, no one would notice where she'd emerged from, either. Right now, she really didn't care anyway.

In seconds, she was striding down the stairs of The Wayward Son and nodding at Marie, who looked puzzled as she passed by, but Avery refused to be waylaid. The fact that Marie wasn't looking panic-stricken was a good sign, and she took a deep breath as she pushed the staffroom door open, relieved to see Alex sitting on a chair in the corner of the room, sipping water. Briar Ashworth, the earth witch, was sitting next to him.

Both of them looked around as the door opened, Briar's worried eyes meeting her own. Alex smiled wanly. "You got the message, then?"

"I'm so sorry I didn't get it sooner. I was reading the cards and they sort of sucked me in." He'd know exactly what that meant. She glanced over to Zee who was at the kitchen bench making tea. He dwarfed the counter, but his smile was dazzling as he acknowledged her arrival. "Hey Zee, thanks for calling."

"No worries, Avery. I honestly wasn't sure what to do. I settled for making tea like a good human does. Strong and sweet, that's the rule, right?"

"You should all stop fussing over me," Alex remonstrated. "I'm fine."

"You are now," Zee corrected, "but you had me worried for quite a while!"

Briar's lips pursed as she looked between them. "I think it's a bit too soon to be saying you're okay. Your energy levels are all out of whack!"

Avery calmed herself now that she saw Alex was all right, and she sat next to him, noticing that Briar had already opened the box of herbs and crystals she used for healing. Small jars were spread across the closest table, and the scent of herbs hung on the air.

Avery reached for Alex's hand. "Do you know what triggered it?"

He shook his head, and a lock of his hair tumbled across his too pale face. "No idea. I'd just finished serving a customer when I had a splitting headache. I just about made my way in here before I collapsed."

Zee carried over the tray with the teapot and mugs. "Fortunately, I saw him stagger in here, and followed him in. He landed on the floor in a heap. I managed to keep the other staff out." He pressed a cup into Alex's hands. "You were out for a good ten minutes."

Alex nodded and sipped his drink, wincing slightly. "Bloody hell. That's sweet."

"It's good for you—or so I'm told."

Avery accepted her own drink gratefully, feeling a little lightheaded herself. "Cheers, Zee. I was reading the tarot when you called, and I'd completely zoned out."

Briar looked startled. "Does that normally happen?"

"Not often. I entered this sort of fugue state."

Briar looked between them. "This does not bode well. You had an intense card reading, and Alex has a vision...something he's been able to control for months! This is eerily reminiscent of last year. What did you both see?"

Avery exchanged a guilty glance with Alex. They hadn't wanted to alarm their coven if their experiences had been only temporary, but now... Before they could answer, Reuben barrelled through the door, Caspian behind him, both bringing the scent of the sea inside. Reuben dragged a chair to Alex's side, sitting astride it with his hands on the backrest. "Well, you look about as shit as I imagined."

"Cheers, Reu. Always so comforting." Alex's eyes narrowed with pain as he nodded at Caspian. "Don't tell me Zee called you, too?"

"No. I happened to be with Reuben talking gig teams, but let's leave that for another time." He settled next to Briar. "What's going on?"

"They're both having weird premonitions again, and the last time that happened, well..." Briar trailed off, looking guilty.

Reuben, however, sniggered. "Oh yeah, the last time that happened was when your family targeted us, Caspian." He pursed his lips. "Are you up to something dodgy again?"

"I can assure you I am not," Caspian said loftily, and not the slightest bit offended.

It was a sign of Reuben and Caspian's friendship that they could refer to last year's events with humour. But Briar was right. That was a very ominous time.

Zee interrupted the banter. "Will you lot explain what exactly you're talking about?"

Avery turned to him. "Last year, just before the midsummer solstice and before I was part of the coven, me and Alex both had omens of something dangerous coming our way. We saw death and bloodshed.

It heralded the arrival of demons in White Haven, sent by Caspian's cousin—and Gil's wife—Alicia."

She quickly summarised what had happened and Zee nodded thoughtfully, a hint of a smile appearing as he looked at Caspian. "I get it. When you were the bad guy." Caspian rolled his eyes, but Zee continued. "And now you're both having ominous premonitions again. What did you see?" he asked, repeating Briar's earlier question.

Avery took the lead, plunging in. She quickly described Alex's experience during the storm, and then what had happened overnight.

Briar, usually so calm, erupted with anger. "You should have told us!"

"We didn't want to worry anyone. It could have been an anomaly."

Reuben snorted. "Well, it obviously isn't. What happened today, Alex?"

He grimaced. "As usual it was a jumble of images, and none of them really make sense right now. The thing that really stood out was a scream again—horribly blood-curdling." He shuddered. "I felt it right in here." He tapped his chest. "I saw bloodshot eyes, and felt a horrible loss and loneliness that cut through me. I've never felt so alone."

Avery groaned, rubbing her hand across her face. "The feeling you experienced the first time. Damn it. That echoes my second reading, too. The cards showed loneliness, an inability to move on from loss, and I've been carrying this horrible sense of foreboding all morning. Well, since last night, really."

Reuben shook his head as the rest of them looked on, alarmed. "Yippee! More death and mayhem to look forward to. Just what we didn't need."

"It may come to nothing," Avery said, trying to sound hopeful. And then her phone rang, and she saw Newton's name. "Oh shit. Maybe it already has."

Caspian wasn't sure if he was grateful or not to have been included in the trip to Newton's crime scene, although he had sort of invited himself when he heard what Newton had relayed to Avery.

He'd followed Reuben and Avery to the small holiday cottage in his own car, intending to return to the office as soon as they were done, and parked on the narrow lane behind Reuben that was already crowded with police vehicles and the coroner's van. They had left Alex at the pub with Zee and Briar. Although frustrated, Alex admitted he was too ill to go with them.

Moore and Kendall were sitting on a garden bench tucked under the shade of a tree, talking to a man who looked pale and sweaty, and a DC stood at the gate at the end of the drive, his face impassive.

Newton was waiting for them, smoking a cigarette, although he said he'd given them up, a grim expression on his face as he leaned against the wall next to the front door. "Thanks for coming so quickly. I didn't expect you, Caspian." He ground his cigarette out on the wall and then pocketed it.

"I was in the neighbourhood, and I'm curious. Do you mind?" He glanced at the small, holiday cottage with its picturesque garden and tiny leaded windows. "It looks too quaint a scene for anything violent."

"*Quaint* means nothing in my business, and no, not at all. I'd appreciate anything you can tell me." He quickly summarised what they'd found. "I'll warn you, the heat has made things tricky, and the bodies are already...*ripe*."

Avery shuddered. "That's okay, Newton. I know you wouldn't ask unless it was important."

Newton handed them paper shoes to go over their own, watching them carefully to make sure they had them on correctly before escorting them through the front door. "Don't touch anything! Although, to be honest, nothing seems disturbed inside." He grimaced. "Arthur wants to take the bodies, and he's not impressed at having to wait, so I'd appreciate you being as quick as possible."

"But you obviously think this is unnatural," Caspian said, as he kept in step with Newton, Reuben and Avery just behind them.

Newton nodded. "Blood red eyes, and the woman is clutching her ears. It's weird."

"By the Goddess!" Avery exclaimed behind them.

Newton turned to look at her. "Is that significant?"

"It might be."

Newton scowled. "I suppose I should be pleased that we might already have a lead on this."

"I wouldn't go that far," Reuben remonstrated. "We'll explain later. Does Arthur know who we are?"

"You're my expert consultants," Newton explained. "He seemed happy enough with that." He slowed down as he led them to the patio door leading outside, and Caspian caught a glimpse of the bodies on the floor, a small-framed man next to them. "I know you don't want to be too obvious with your magic with him here, but do what you can." Without waiting for their response, he led them outside and made brief introductions.

Arthur grunted. "You guys better make this quick. I need to move these bodies ASAP."

"Let's check these first, then," Caspian suggested, biting back his distaste and crouching by the woman. Reuben crouched next to her husband.

Newton was right. She was curled up in a foetal position, hands clamped tightly over her ears, and even in death they remained fixed in place. Her face was scrunched up, as if whatever she'd heard was unpleasant. Caspian forced himself to ignore the odour and the flies, instead feeling sorry for them both. *What on Earth had she heard?*

He looked up at Avery. "You're thinking of Alex's vision, aren't you?"

Avery was walking slowly around the outer perimeter of the garden, and he could feel her magic as she explored her surroundings. She paused, looking over to him. "Of course. It's too much of a coincidence."

"He heard nothing last night, though? Nothing woke him?"

She shook her head. "No. Just the exploratory session we had," she added vaguely, and Caspian knew she meant when Alex scryed.

Reuben was holding his hands a few inches above the man's body, and asked Arthur, "Do you know what time they died?"

"I suspect close to midnight, but the autopsy will tell me more." He cleared his throat and gestured at Reuben's hands. "What exactly are you doing?"

"Er, it's a sort of energy reading." He raised his eyebrow, more of a question than a statement.

Caspian suppressed a smile. It was as good an explanation as any, and he extended his hands, too. But there was no sign of any lingering magic on the bodies. "I can't detect anything. You?"

Reuben shook his head and straightened up. "No. In fact, everything feels very normal. Avery?"

Avery was now by the high hedge at the back of the square garden, and she paused before she answered, lifting her head as if sniffing at the wind, but then she shook her head, too. "No, nothing here."

"Damn it," Newton muttered. "I don't know whether to be annoyed or relieved."

"I admit to being plain old confused," Davidson said, rising to his feet from the patio chair. "Can I take them now?"

Newton nodded. "Yes. Thanks for your patience." He herded the witches to the side of the garden and lowered his voice, while Arthur called in his team. "Seriously? *Nothing*? No sign of curses or weird magic?"

Caspian exchanged an uneasy glance with Avery and Reuben, but they looked as puzzled as he felt. "No, nothing. As you know, magic leaves signatures, like faint perfume. This place just feels normal—apart from the dead bodies, of course."

"Poor buggers," Reuben said, studying them again. "They must have been enjoying the balmy night with their wine. The fact that they were still sitting suggests that whatever it was happened swiftly. It's not like they were running to the back door or anything."

"Excellent point," Caspian said, impressed at his logic. "And their deaths must have been quick, too. They've both fallen where they were sitting. He's not trying to protect her."

Avery cocked an eyebrow at him. "Or, she's not trying to protect him!"

Caspian grinned. "Or that."

Newton lit up another cigarette and Avery grimaced. "Newton! You said you'd quit."

He shrugged. "I relapsed. Besides, I gave up for a reason, a reason that no longer applies."

"Your health is a good reason, and that always applies!" she shot back.

Caspian knew exactly what that 'reason' was. *Briar.* Perhaps Newton thought he stood no chance now. Or perhaps it was his acceptance that he was investigating the paranormal on his terms now, and resuming his smoking habit was part of it.

"Avery is right. Your health comes first, but it's your choice. You're an adult," Caspian said.

"Exactly. Now, can we get back to the job at hand?" Newton watched as the team loaded the victims into body bags and carried them away. "You're telling me there's nothing remotely magical or paranormal here at all?"

"Not obviously so," Reuben said. "Is there anything magical about *them*? Do you know anything about them? Who they are, where they're from?"

"I have names, but that's it. I'll do some research on them. And now," Newton nodded as the SOCO team entered the garden, "we need to get out of here and let them do their thing. For all the bloody waste of time it will be."

Caspian took a final look around the small garden, wondering if he was imagining the gloom that seemed to have descended, despite the bright day. They'd had a quiet few weeks since the events at the solstice, weeks in which he had started to reorganise his working life, and Estelle's. Reuben's invitation to join his gig team was generous, and he thought he probably would accept. Something different to fill his newly carved out time. The thought of going back to his office that was no doubt baking in the midday heat was unappealing, but Caspian had to tie a few things up.

As they all turned to leave the garden together, he suggested, "Perhaps we should meet again tonight, or tomorrow, to hear what you've found out, Newton. You could all come to mine, if you want. We'll have a barbeque in my garden."

"Great idea, mate," Reuben said cheerfully. "You know I always enjoy a meat fest."

"Tonight sounds good," Newton agreed. "I'd like to start discussing ideas sooner rather than later."

"Excellent." Caspian pulled his phone from his pocket, thinking he'd like to question Avery and Alex further, too. "See you at seven."

Chapter Four

"I wish you would have called me," El Robinson remonstrated to Briar and Reuben as she drove them to Caspian's place on Monday evening. "I feel I've missed out on all the excitement."

El had only found out about Alex's visions and Avery's tarot readings when Reuben had met her after work, and now he rolled his eyes. "It wasn't a conspiracy. I think Zee phoned me in a panic, and called Briar for her healing skills."

Briar nodded in the back of the car, meeting El's eye in the mirror. "It's true. I was going to suggest lunch, but then Newton called, and three of them rushed off to that cottage. I was very glad I didn't have to go there."

"Yeah, it wasn't pleasant," Reuben admitted. "In fact, it was horribly sad. At least they went quickly, with a glass of wine. That's the best anyone can ask for, right?"

El snorted at Reuben's assessment of the best way to die. "In your forties? I hope I'm a bit older than that."

"Well, me too, obviously, but if I had to go, having a fun time with my missus in the back garden would be it. Well," he paused, giving her a rakish grin, "maybe during sex would be the best."

Briar sniggered in the back. "There we go. I knew you'd think of a better way."

"Don't encourage him!" El glared at Briar in the mirror. "I wouldn't want to be found naked, halfway through sex. How demeaning!"

"Yes, but you'd be dead, so you wouldn't care," Reuben pointed out. "And then they'd take your clothes off and examine you anyway, so what's the difference?"

"I would like to die with some dignity! Ugh! *Men*."

El wrestled her Land Rover around the bend, not caring that Reuben crunched aggressively into the door. As much as she loved him, she sometimes marvelled at the way his mind worked. El took pride in her appearance, from her makeup, to her piercings, to her clothes. She intended to sail gracefully into death, too.

As if he'd read her mind, Reuben squeezed her knee. "You'd look just as fabulous dead."

"Yes, I would. Piss off."

Briar giggled again. "As charming as this is, do you think you can save this discussion until you're alone?"

El swung the car onto Caspian's drive, and pulled up a short distance from the front door, noting that Newton's car, Gabe's SUV, and Avery's van were already there. "Avery should have asked me for a lift."

"She thought they might have to leave early if Alex wasn't well," Briar explained.

El sighed, worried about his recent visions. "I didn't know Gabe was coming, though. That's great. I haven't seen him and Shadow for a couple of weeks. It will be good to catch up."

In seconds they had exited the car, grabbed the bag with the wine, beer, and salad they were contributing, and headed around the side of the house to Caspian's broad patio, drawn by the sound of music and voices, as well as the scent of charcoal.

Their friends were seated around a large table, chatting animatedly, and a chorus of greetings rose as they joined them. El was relieved to see that Alex looked fine, despite his morning vision, and she kissed his cheek. "I'm glad to see you look okay."

He laughed. "Don't you start. I'm fine!"

"He just likes the attention," Avery said, teasing him. "Glory seeker."

"Funny!" he shot back.

Shadow was already rising to her feet, and she hugged El as she said, "I can always rely on you guys to keep life interesting here."

"Like you don't have enough going on!"

An impish grin graced Shadow's face. "I guess so, but we can spare a night for friends." Shadow, as usual, was an arresting sight. Her tall, slim figure, was dressed in black, and her hair cascaded down her back. Despite the fact that she kept her Otherness under wraps, she still emanated an Otherworldly glamour.

Gabe raised his beer in greeting, and winked at El. "Before we have to race off again."

He was seated next to Newton, his long legs outstretched in front of him. He looked relaxed, far more at ease than he used to be, as if he'd let down his guard. A result of his relationship with Shadow, perhaps. *Good.* El liked her friends to be happy.

Reuben headed to Caspian's side, next to the barbeque, no doubt to pester him about the proposed gig team, while El and Briar settled around the table, helping themselves to drinks. For a while they chatted easily, making conversation about anything and everything, all of them seemingly avoiding the recent news of the deaths and the ominous premonitions. However, as soon as Caspian and Reuben carried the meat to the table and they loaded their plates and topped up drinks again, the conversation turned to their problems.

Newton, for all of his chattiness, seemed distracted, and El asked, "What did you find out about that couple, Newton?"

"It's tragic, actually. They were a very normal couple with two adult kids, but only a few months ago one of their children died in a car crash. They'd come to Cornwall on holiday in an attempt to lift their mood. Their surviving daughter, Samantha, encouraged them to. She, as you can imagine, is devastated."

Briar was staring at him. "Did you tell her about her parents over the phone?"

"No! I'm not a monster! Local police told her. I just spoke to her this afternoon." Newton looked shattered. "She couldn't stop crying. It was horrible. Anyway, Tim, her dad, was an estate agent, and her mum was an accountant." He huffed as he loaded his burger with toppings. "There was nothing remotely paranormal or weird about them at all."

"So, just wrong place, wrong time?" El asked. "How awful."

"Yeah, but the wrong time or place for *what*? SOCO confirmed that there was no sign of anyone else being in that cottage, and there were no signs of a break-in—whether through the garden or the house. It's uncanny." He squashed his burger so it was easier to eat with a little too much aggression. "And annoying!"

El looked across to Alex. "I gather you heard screams in your visions?"

"More of an unearthly wail, actually. It didn't sound human." He frowned. "I've been trying to sort through the jumble of images that I saw. There were trees, and what felt like abandoned grounds—don't ask me why I think that. Also, a sense of suffocation, and as I mentioned earlier, a feeling of loss."

"Which is what I saw in the cards," Avery added. "Loss and an inability to move on."

"And a cycle, you said," Alex reminded her. "As if something was being repeated."

"But," Shadow said, her finger drumming the table, "what does that point to?"

"Too soon to say," Reuben said. "It could be anything. Unsettled spirits, trapped spirits..."

"Or," Caspian suggested, "something not spirit-related. Maybe another Cornish *something* that's been stirred up."

Newton grimaced. "I'd like more than *something*!"

"I'm just thinking out loud," Caspian pointed out. "We shouldn't jump to conclusions."

Briar picked at her salad, only a small portion of steak on her plate. "Maybe we should look at where it happened. Is there something unusual about the place?"

"Not really," Newton answered. "It's a holiday rental, a private one, but advertised through one of those sites that list a few places. The owner, a man called Guy Rogers, has been renting it out for years. There's nothing unusual about the land. It's just a cottage with a small garden, just outside White Haven. The post-mortem is tomorrow, so I don't have any more details on their deaths yet."

El needed to narrow things down. "Why don't we start a list? Not right now, but we'll look at what could make odd screams and wails. Dan could help, surely, with his local knowledge of folklore?" She looked hopefully at Avery.

"He could. I'm sure he'd love to. And maybe we should include Ghost OPS—see if they have picked up anything in the area."

Briar nodded. "I know they're busy. Cassie hasn't been able to help me for days. I'll call her tomorrow."

"But what else could cause sudden death?" Gabe persisted. "A curse? A cursed object? You're all witches. What other magic-related things could do this?"

"You think a witch could have done this?" El asked, surprised. "I never even considered that. I guess it's possible. Maybe a hex?"

"It would have to be a very powerful one," Avery said. She reached for her wine and took a sip. "I don't like to think we have another witch causing problems here, especially after our recent events, but it is possible."

"Perhaps," Alex said, leaning forward as excitement kindled in his eyes, "they were targeted by someone from where they live, and it's only happened now."

Reuben raised a sceptical eyebrow. "Like a spell on a timer? Please!"

"Like a cursed object they brought with them!" Alex suggested, refusing to rise to Reuben's sarcasm.

"But surely," Avery said, "that object would have been close to them, and we found nothing remotely magical in that garden."

"True," Caspian agreed. "It can't be that."

Alex sank back in his chair, deflated. "Damn it."

"But this is an interesting line of enquiry," Newton said. "Cursed objects, hexes...family curses, perhaps? Spells from a distance?" His voice rose with excitement. "Poppets?"

El groaned as images flooded her mind. "Oh, no. I have horrible memories of the last time we used poppets."

"I don't think your encounter was anywhere near as bad as ours," Reuben pointed out, including Alex in that statement.

They had both been caught in the blast of power from Mariah's death when she had accidently set fire to her own poppet during the fight in Reuben's cellar. Although both of them had fully recovered, El remembered the aftermath with horror. She'd had to help Moore and Kendall by moving Mariah's burnt remains. *Ugh.*

Alex answered Newton. "You're right. A poppet is a possibility."

"Of course," Newton went on, "if the PM points to poisoning, we're all wrong. This death could be utterly unrelated to your vision, Alex, and Avery's tarot reading."

Caspian shook his head. "I think we all know it's not. And unfortunately, despite all of our suggestions, we are none the wiser. Let's hope," he raised his glass to Newton, "that this was a one-off."

El raised her glass, too. "I really hope you're right. However, I have a feeling this is just the start."

Alex was running through a wild landscape, branches thrashing around his face and catching his legs. Something was chasing him.

It followed steadily, relentlessly, always out of sight, and he couldn't outrun it. Alex knew that if he stopped, it would be on him. And yet, he didn't know what it was. There were no sounds from it. It wasn't like a wild animal. It was a presence, like something stalking his soul. It was lonely, and it grieved, as if all the love in the world wouldn't be enough to comfort it.

A wild, keening sound enveloped him, and Alex crashed to his knees, hands over his ears. It wouldn't stop, and it was getting closer...

"Alex!" Avery's voice broke through the horrendous screaming. "Alex! *Wake up!*"

For a horrible moment, the scream and Avery's voice mingled together. He tried to move, but he was powerless. *Something was coming for him.*

"Alex!" Avery once again shouted. *Where was she?* He could see nothing but darkness.

He felt a wave of freezing cold air wash over him and the scream receded. He became aware that something was shaking him, and he opened his eyes to find Avery leaning over him, her eyes frantic with worry.

He struggled to sit up, feeling as if something was on his chest, and he took big, gulping breaths of air. "I'm okay!"

She pulled back, her expression just visible in the low light of the room, her hair a tumble of waves around her shoulders. "You really don't sound okay!"

He squeezed her warm hand that rested on his arm. "No, I guess not." He looked around the room, as if something lurked in the shadowed corners, but as his panic eased, he realised the room felt just like always. It was safe. *He was safe.* "Shit. That was intense."

"A dream or a vision?"

"Hard to say. It felt like a dream, but..." He rubbed his face, feeling his stubble and a light sweat on his face. "Did you hear a scream?"

She flicked the beside lamp on with magic, and it illuminated her tight-lipped expression. "No. There was no scream. Tell me what happened."

He related his experience, because he wasn't sure what else to call it. "I don't know where I was."

"And the scream? Human or not?"

A cat settled on his lap, and he dug his fingers into Circe's thick fur, comforted by her solid, warm presence. "Not human." His heart still thudded in his chest, and he placed his free hand over it. "I don't think my body knows I'm okay yet. Whatever it was, Ave, I felt utterly powerless."

"Did you sense magic? Like someone was directing something at you?"

"Nope. It felt kind of wild and abandoned." A horrible thought struck him. "I'm not sure what would have happened if you hadn't woken me."

Avery scooted closer, wriggling into his chest, and he lay back against the pillows. "You weren't there. You were safe and sound in bed. It was just a horrible dream. Or vision."

"Did you do something with cold air? I felt freezing cold as I woke up."

He felt her nod, rather than saw her. "I wasn't sure that disturbing you would be a good thing, but I had no idea what else to do. I thought a jolt of cold might shock you out of whatever it was. Sorry."

"No. Don't be sorry. It worked." He squeezed her. "As to whether it was dream or vision, I have no idea. Let's just hope that nothing weird has happened overnight, and it was just a dream."

However, even as he was saying it, he was thinking of the two deaths, and El's words earlier. Whatever was happening, this was just the start.

Chapter Five

Cassie Davis looked at Dylan's preliminary footage of Storm-crossed Manor, and her mouth fell open. "Wow. Look at that place. It's amazing!"

"Amazing? Look at how much work needs doing!"

"But it's wildly romantic!" She brought her chair closer to the screen, her imagination already working overtime as she envisioned clearing away old wallpaper and scrubbing the slabbed floors. "I love it!"

It was Tuesday morning and Ghost OPS were in their office, talking over current cases, while Dylan showed Cassie his footage from the day before. Now, more than ever, Cassie wished she could have gone to the manor.

"The next time you go, I have to go with you," she insisted.

Dylan nudged her aside as he manipulated the mouse to bring up other shots. "You'll change your mind once you're there."

Ben drew his chair closer to Dylan's screen, too. "No, she won't." He winked at her. "It has good bones—under a lot of crap, admittedly. But the house has an odd feel to it. More than just neglect."

"Haunted?" Cassie asked, intrigued.

Ben's face screwed up in thought. "Not sure. Anyway, we're going back today to set some cameras up, if you're interested?"

"Of course!"

"Anything interesting come in on the phones yesterday?"

"A few queries as to the type of work we do, a couple of prank calls, and a few calls from people wanting to send us their own footage of spooky activity." She rolled her eyes as she considered the odd conversations she'd had. "I think that TV interview with Sarah Rutherford came with a sting in its tale."

"The loony sting, you mean?" Dylan asked, finally pulling away from the screen to face her. "It was always likely. Any publicity brings a mix of good and bad." A grin flashed across his face. "But it's making us money. Or it will."

"Apart from this case," Ben persisted, "is there anything we need to follow up on?"

"What sounds like a haunting in Mevagissey." Cassie stood and walked to the pad of notes on her desk in the corner—a desk that was considerably cleaner than either Ben's or Dylan's. Ben's space in particular was littered with coffee cups. So far, she was resisting cleaning up his mess, but she felt her resolve weakening just looking at them all. She grabbed her pad and scanned her notes. "Here we go. A Mrs Robertson who owns an old cottage on the edge of the moor says she's been hearing odd noises lately. I've arranged to go around midday."

Ben frowned. "A recent haunting? Has she disturbed something?"

"I don't know yet. She said *lately*, but to be honest, she sounded old and infirm. I figured I could get more information when I arrived. You know that some people aren't good on the phone."

Ben stood, draining the dregs of his tea. "I'll come with you. We can go to Stormcrossed Manor with Dylan, and leave him to set things up."

"Sounds good to me," Dylan said, rolling his shoulders as he walked away from his bank of screens. "It will take me a while. As long as Rosa consents, I want to put up quite a few cameras."

"Cool." Cassie grabbed her bag, making sure her notebook, pens, and phone were inside. "Let's hope it's another case!"

Briar propped the door of her shop open and wished there was more of a breeze wafting through it.

It was only halfway through the morning, and it was already hot. The lane her shop was on had no direct sunlight at this time of day, but the heat was already intense, the sky above deep blue.

Taking advantage of the fact that the shop was empty, she blew the flame on the cedar-scented candle burning on her counter, and the scent magnified, along with a cooling breeze that carried around her shop. She smiled, feeling like she'd been transported to a mountain meadow.

Eli emerged from the back room carrying a watering can, and he paused, sniffing the air. "Nice! It reminds me of the Taurus Mountains in the spring." He continued to the front of the shop. "I thought I'd water the plants before the sun hits them later."

"Good idea." Briar returned to the shop entrance with him, nodding in greeting to the passers-by, and glad that Eli was so practical. And glad that she didn't have to lug the stepladder around to water the hanging baskets outside. Eli's height and strength made her life so much easier. "What do you think about those deaths in that cottage?" She hadn't had a chance to discuss it with him earlier, and she valued his opinion. It had been all over the news, and the Nephilim and Shadow would have undoubtedly discussed it.

"Not sure, to be honest. It could be something quite random. Maybe they *did* eat something odd. Maybe they'd been picking mushrooms and managed to poison themselves." He lowered the watering can, his muscles flexing in his arm. "It happens."

"But Alex's visions?"

"Might be related to something else." He moved to the next basket as water streamed from the plants he'd just watered. "Maybe it was heat stroke. It *is* bloody hot!"

"And maybe the heat is making us all paranoid."

As they talked, Briar noticed a woman heading down the lane, checking all the shops as if she was looking for somewhere in particular, an air of determination in her stride. She looked to be in her thirties, fit, with well-defined arm muscles, her brown hair tied up on her head. As she reached Briar's shop, she met her eyes briefly and then studied the name above the window.

"*Charming Balms Apothecary,*" she read with an indeterminate accent. "Do you work here?"

"I own it," Briar told her. "And this is Eli, who works with me. Can I help you?"

She studied them both intently before answering, her eyes narrowing with suspicion as she took in Eli's size before turning back to Briar.

"I hope so. I need candles and some herbs, some hard to get ones, too. I gather you have a good selection."

Briar bristled under her stare, as if the woman was accusing her of something, and she was particularly annoyed with how she looked at Eli—as if she suspected him of doing something terrible. Briar decided she didn't like her, and then immediately felt guilty. She forced herself to be polite. "I have a good selection of candles and herbs, but only a small amount of herbs on display. What do you need, and I'll see if I have it?"

The woman had already entered Briar's shop, heading straight to the candles, and exchanging a wary glance with Eli, Briar followed her in.

The woman studied the selection before saying, "Parosela, Mistletoe, Wolf's Bane, and Edelweiss. Have you got them?"

Briar's prickle of unease intensified and she didn't answer her question. "Those are quite powerful. What do you want with them?"

The woman looked over her shoulder at Briar, eyebrows raised. "I have a few herbal concoctions I need to make. They're not illegal."

"No, they're not." Briar shook off her worry. She shouldn't judge the woman. She knew nothing about her. "Yes, I have them, in small quantities." *Liar.* "I can give you an ounce of each."

The woman turned to face her fully, a smile playing about her lips, as if she knew Briar was lying. "That will be fine."

"Good. I'll leave you to browse the candles while I measure them." By now, Eli was inside and behind the counter. "Ask Eli if you need anything else."

As soon as she shut the door to her back room, Briar placed her hand against it and closed her eyes, feeling for the woman's presence on the other side. She sensed no magic about her. She wasn't a witch, and she was pretty sure she wasn't any other type of paranormal creature, either, but there was a knowingness about the way she carried herself, as if she knew of the paranormal world. *However*, Briar reminded herself, *there was nothing wrong with that, and no reason to distrust her.* Still, the quicker she prepared these herbs and got her out of the shop, the better.

A few minutes later, the herbs carefully weighed and wrapped in paper, she entered the shop to find the woman at the counter, a range of coloured candles in front of her. Some were scented, others plain. Eli was chatting to her as he wrapped them. "No, I'm not from here," he told her cheerfully. "But it's my home now. I like it here. What about you? You're a visitor, I presume?"

"First time here, but I sense I'll be back." Her gaze flicked to Briar as she joined Eli behind the counter. "It's a haven for the paranormal, isn't it?"

Briar forced herself to laugh. "I don't know if I'd say *haven*, despite the town's name, but this place certainly has had some interesting things happen in the last few months."

"Interesting is one word. I would say that it's a place that courts the unusual, actually."

"To be fair," Eli said, as he finished wrapping the last of her candles and placed the herbs in the bag with them, "all of Cornwall embraces its myths and folklore. It's why I love it here—especially the celebrations."

"But the deaths?" The woman stared at both of them, all amusement gone. "Surely that's unnerving?"

"Of course they are," Briar said abruptly. "Only a psychopath would like that. But that's what the police are for."

"Of course." The woman gave them an enigmatic smile as she paid and took her bag. "I'll see you around."

"Look forward to it," Eli said, his usual, easy smile on his lips as he watched her go.

Briar, however, said nothing until she'd left. "I did not like her."

Eli's smile disappeared as he sat on a stool. "No, nor did I. If I had to guess, I'd say she's a hunter."

"Like Ghost OPS?"

He nodded, absently rubbing the back of his neck as he stared out of the window. "Yes. Actually, no." He finally looked at her. "Sorry. I'm being confusing. A hunter, as in a killer of paranormal creatures. They don't film them, catalogue them, or even just investigate them as curiosities. They kill them. And that puts me and you firmly on their list."

"*What*?" Briar's voice rose in alarm. "Are you kidding me? I'm a harmless witch and you're a harmless Nephilim. We work in a shop!"

Eli sniggered. "Neither of us is harmless. Yes, you perform positive magic, but you are still considered dangerous by some. And you have been known to use your magic violently—"

"To protect others!" Briar said, interrupting him.

"And yourself. And I," he continued, undaunted, "am most certainly very dangerous when I choose to be. I killed Lowen only weeks ago. And I have no regrets about doing so, either."

"He was dangerous."

"To us. He might not have been considered so by others." Briar stared into Eli's beautiful brown eyes, her thoughts reeling. He, however, still looked amused. "Plus, you date a shifter, and to be fair, he's a very violent man when he chooses to be, too."

Briar sat on the other stool, her legs suddenly weak. "We keep White Haven safe. Our actions are justified."

"But to someone who dislikes the paranormal, and finds everything about them abhorrent? Well, we're just part of the problem."

"She came into my shop for supplies. She's clearly not *that* bothered. She must be using some kind of spell or potion. Anyway," she studied Eli again, "how do you know she's a hunter? You seem very certain, and she said nothing."

"I've been around a long time, Briar, and seen many things. I have a sixth sense for things, too. She knows I'm different—you, too. I think she was sussing us out as much as topping up her supplies. I don't know what's brought her here—us or the deaths—but I have a bad feeling about her. And I doubt she's here alone, either." He regarded her steadily, a hint of regret in his eyes. "I think life here just got a bit trickier."

Avery's shop had a special visitor that morning. The pretty young woman with light brown hair and an intelligent expression smiled at Avery, her hand outstretched. "It's good to finally meet you. Dan has told me so much about you. Both of you, actually." Caroline extended her beaming smile to Sally. "Just call me Caro."

"And you have no idea how pleased we are to finally meet you!" Sally said, clasping Caroline's hand in her own. She narrowed her eyes at Dan. "We thought he was making you up!"

"I'm not a sad loser!" Dan remonstrated. "I was waiting for the right time." He rolled his eyes at Caro. "Honestly, this pair nag me more than my mother."

Avery punched his arm playfully. "As if we do! Just ignore him, Caro. He exaggerates."

Caro laughed. "I know. Don't worry, you seem perfectly harmless." She glanced around Happenstance Books. "I love your shop! I can't believe I haven't been in here before."

"By the sound of it, it's because Dan has been keeping you away from us." Sally's lips tightened as she glared at Dan. "Please come and visit us as often as you like!"

Dan had finally brought his girlfriend in to meet them, and Avery felt like she should be on her best behaviour. She was dressed in a long cotton skirt, loose t-shirt, and flip-flops, and hoped she looked as non-witchy as possible, whatever that meant. The shop, however, when she examined it with critical eyes, still had that vibe. Incense hung on the air, occult objects were placed around the space—tarot cards, angel cards, occult-themed bookmarks, and a small selection of gemstones, as well as the increasing selection of books on witchcraft that seemed to have crept out of the occult section and now appeared all around the shop. Plus, of course, the Lughnasadh decorations that Sally had recently placed around the interior.

Nothing, however, seemed to bother Caro. "I absolutely will. Unfortunately, most of the time I'm busy writing."

"You're a writer?" Sally's eyes lit up. "That's so exciting."

"Not really. Just endless hours spent procrastinating."

"What do you write?"

"Non-fiction mainly, for the university's paper, but I am working on some material for a podcast. Something me and Dan thought we'd do together."

"Really?" Avery was intrigued. "A podcast on what?"

"The supernatural and folklore around the world." She smiled at Dan. "Dan is helping me get the material together. We want to have a few episodes ready before we launch."

Dan looked a little smug, and a trifle embarrassed, too as Avery stared at him, surprised. "You kept that quiet!"

He shrugged. "Early days. We've only been planning it a short while. It's a summer project. Fun though, so far. We thought we'd take advantage of Ghost OPS's popularity and maybe interview them, too. Not right away, of course."

Sally raised her eyebrows at Avery, looking impressed. "I think that's a great idea, you two. Have you got a name yet?"

"Still thinking on it," Caro confessed. She raised up on tiptoes and kissed Dan's cheek. "Anyway, I have to go. I was just popping in. Great to meet you both." She beamed at Avery and Sally, before nodding at Dan. "See you in the pub later?"

"Absolutely."

Caro exited with a wave, and Avery settled back on the stool behind the counter. "Well, she's lovely. Did we pass?"

Dan rolled his eyes. "You weren't being inspected. But, yes, you didn't embarrass me too much."

"As if we would!" Sally still looked put out.

"Dan, while we have a few minutes," Avery said, glancing around the shop and realising it was still relatively quiet, "I need to pick your brain. Can you think of any type of supernatural creature that could kill someone without leaving a mark on them except for red, bloodshot eyes?"

Dan was still standing on the customers' side of the counter and he leaned against it, his cheerful expression disappearing. "You're thinking of those deaths, aren't you? The ones at the holiday cottage?"

"I'm afraid so. The post-mortem is today, but Newton says there was no sign of a break-in, and we didn't detect any magic there."

"Ugh." Sally groaned. "I can't believe you went there."

"We had to help Newton." Avery shrugged at the memory. "It wasn't a pleasant thing to do, but it felt like the right thing. Those poor people." She remembered the fallen bodies in the sunshine. "It could be a curse or something, but well, with no sign of magic..." She quickly summarised their thoughts from the night before, looking hopefully at Dan.

His hand rubbed his cleanshaven chin, his eyes staring at the wall behind her before coming to rest on her again. "Blimey, Ave. It's hard to say. Even if they had seen a ghost, it often doesn't scare someone to death! Especially two people. *Especially* at such a young age!"

"I know." She sighed. "We're clutching at straws. But maybe there is some weird, Cornish creature?"

"Like a malevolent piskie?" He looked incredulous.

"I'm serious!" Her voice rose, and a couple of customers looked over. She immediately lowered her voice again. "Is there anything that emits a scream that can kill?"

"A *scream*?" he was looking at her like she was mad, and so was Sally.

"The woman's hands were clasped around her ears. And I told you about Alex's horrible dream-visions. He had another last night, with more screams."

"You think they're connected?" Dan asked.

"Unfortunately, yes, I do."

Sally squeezed her hand. "What would have happened if you hadn't woken Alex?"

"I don't know, and to be honest, I don't want to find out, either. What if *I* don't wake next time?" She shivered, thinking of his shouting. "Although, to be honest, that's unlikely. He was making a racket."

"Sorry, Ave." Dan looked chastened. "I'll give it some thought while I make us a cuppa, sound good?"

"Sounds perfect."

Ben stood behind Cassie while she knocked at the door to the old cottage, and when no one answered, she knocked again.

"This is odd. It's the time we agreed on." Cassie checked her watch and then stepped back to look at the windows. "Maybe she's around the back, soaking up the sun."

Ben stepped onto the paved path that ran from the gate to the front door, and studied the house. The cottage was small and squat, and a little worse for wear. The front door had peeling blue paint, and the white-rendered walls were discoloured and cracked in places. The front garden, however, was lovingly tended, featuring a riot of colourful flowers, although it was wilting in the heat. Beyond the waist-height garden wall to his left was the moor, baking under a shimmer of heat. On the right was a line of cottages, all looking slightly battered by time. To the immediate right of the cottage, he spotted a side gate, almost disguised by the large shrub in front of it.

"Try once more," Ben suggested, shading his eyes with his hand and wishing he'd remembered to pick up his sunglasses. "If she doesn't answer, we'll try the side gate."

Cassie checked the address again on her notepad, and seemingly satisfied they were in the right place, knocked the door again. When there was still no answer, Cassie huffed. "Bloody hell. If she's forgotten and gone shopping..."

"Then we'll just have to come back," Ben said, reassuring her. "But she's probably dead-heading her roses around the back and is as deaf as a post."

He led them to the side gate and tried the latch. It was a bit stiff through lack of use, but it released, and Ben pushed it open, grimacing as an unpleasant creak and grating noise broke the silence. He led the way down the side of the house, seeking the welcoming sunshine that beckoned at the end. The garden at the back was as colourful as the one at the front, but this time there were raised beds too, a mix of vegetables and salad leaves amongst the flowers.

He gestured to Cassie, and she nodded and shouted, "Mrs Robertson! It's Cassie from Ghost Objective Paranormal Studies. We spoke yesterday on the phone!"

Only a bird call greeted them, but the back door was propped open.

Ben gestured Cassie behind him, a sudden flare of fear making him cautious, and he edged towards the rear entrance. But that's as far as he needed to go, because just inside was the sprawled body of an elderly lady in an old-fashioned cotton nightgown.

He stepped back, crashing into Cassie behind him, and he heard her sharp intake of breath as her hand clutched his arm. "Ben! What..." And then she stepped around him. "Oh, no..."

He licked his lips, his mouth suddenly dry, and was about to enter the kitchen and check her pulse when Cassie pushed past him and knelt at her side, careful to touch nothing but her wrist. Unfortunately, her expression said everything.

"Call Newton. She's dead."

Chapter Six

Newton wandered over to the garden wall while Mrs Robertson was being placed in the body bag and removed from the cottage, lighting a cigarette as he leaned his hip into the uneven bricks.

He lowered his sunglasses across his eyes and stared at the moor, wondering what was out there as he inhaled the smoke that, if he was honest, he no longer enjoyed as much as he used to. He continued to smoke more out of sheer bloody-mindedness than anything.

"I've got their statement, Guv," Kendall said, coming to stand next to him. A faint flush of perspiration was on her cheeks, and a bloom of freckles was beginning to show. "Shall I tell them to go?"

He noted her earnest expression, and the worry behind her eyes. "No, I'll have a chat with them first. Start the door to door interviews. I want to know if the neighbours heard anything."

She nodded, tucking her short hair behind her ear. An unconscious habit, more than a need to actually tidy up her pixie cut hairstyle. As she disappeared through the side gate, he beckoned to Cassie and Ben, both of them loitering by a vegetable patch, still chatting to Moore. In seconds they were at his side, and Moore disappeared into the house.

"Are you two okay?" They both looked pale, Cassie's eyes huge in her heart-shaped face, but she seemed more together than Ben.

Cassie shrugged. "Not really. Poor lady. I had hoped she'd just collapsed, but..."

"She might have died of a heart attack or a stroke," he pointed out, thinking of what Davidson had suggested. "Yes, her eyes were bloodshot like the others, but she was elderly, and there's no reason to think anything untoward happened. It could be an unfortunate coincidence."

"But we don't believe in coincidences," Ben reminded him.

"What is clear," Newton said, pressing on, eager not to dramatise what could be a perfectly normal death, "is that there's no sign of a break-in. It's possible she died on her way to bed. She was in her nightgown. Tell me again what she told you."

"She thought this place was haunted. Actually, no." Cassie paused as she corrected herself. "She said she'd heard odd noises lately, but that was as much as I got out of her on the phone. I explained to Kendall and Moore that sometimes you get more in a face-to-face interview."

Newton nodded as he scrutinised Cassie's face. "I hear that. She didn't say what noises?"

"Not really. She said they were unusual, and she was worried. She muttered something about foxes on the moor, or... It sounded like she thought the wind had got beneath the eaves, but there was no wind at all."

Newton mulled over her words, turning back to the shimmering moor, the grass golden in the light. "A wind or foxes. Does that mean she heard fox screams? Or the wind wailing?"

"I honestly don't know."

"Sorry, Newton," Ben put in. "We thought we'd find out more today. Why are you asking about screams and wails?"

He turned to face them again, stubbing his cigarette out on the wall. He saw Cassie's face wrinkle with displeasure as she waved the smoke away. "The bodies we found yesterday. The woman was covering her ears. It's a leap, I know..." *A big leap.* He was clutching at straws. Plus, this place was a good distance from the holiday cottage, and they might not be connected at all. "And Alex has been having weird, dreamlike visions again, and he hears screams."

"Has he?" Ben asked, shooting a nervous glance at Cassie. "Actually, it's strange you should mention screams. We have a new case. A woman has reported hearing screams on her estate. I suggested foxes, but she said it wasn't."

Newton immediately focussed. "When and where?"

"We went to see her yesterday. Dylan is there now, setting up cameras and recording equipment. It's called Stormcrossed Manor."

"Bloody hell. That sounds ominous."

"It doesn't look quite as bad as it sounds, but it is a wreck. She's trying to renovate it." He shrugged. "It's a complicated family history. I won't bore you with it all."

Typical civilian. "There is no such thing as a boring family history, Ben—not in policing, anyway. Where is this place?"

"On the edge of White Haven. It's an old manor house, but not nearly as well kept as Reuben's. Further out, too. In fact..." Ben frowned as he looked across the moor. "It's probably not too far away from here. This is on the edge of Mevagissey, and the manor is in that direction." He wafted his hand to the left.

Cassie's eyes widened as she followed his gaze. "Oh, wow. You're probably right, Ben. As the crow flies, it wouldn't be far at all."

Newton felt the familiar stir of unease as things aligned, but before he could ask anything more, Kendall came racing back through the gate, arriving breathless at his side.

"Newton, sorry, but there's more bad news." She straightened up, throwing her shoulders back. "The neighbour is dead, too."

Alex finished serving a customer and took his payment, offering a forced smile as the man carried the tray of drinks across the pub to the courtyard garden.

His head was pounding, and the Paracetamol he'd taken earlier was having zero effect. Fortunately, it was time for his late lunch, and checking that the bar was well staffed and under Marie's guidance, he headed to the staffroom to grab some food, passing the clatter from the kitchen as he did so. Despite his headache, he smiled. Jago was in full flow as he directed the kitchen staff. A tinny radio sounded in the background, and every now and again, Jago boomed out a song line, making Georgie giggle.

However, the small staffroom with its tiny window onto the courtyard was quiet. Zee was in there, watching the news as he ate his brunch sandwich, one of Jago's specials. He looked up as Alex entered, and then pointed at the TV screen. "You won't like this."

He dropped into the chair next to him, food forgotten as he stared at the screen. "Why?"

"There have been more deaths. In Mevagissey, this time."

Sarah Rutherford, the blonde news reporter, was stationed on a narrow lane at the end of a row of cottages talking to the camera. A line of police vehicles could be seen behind her, and the lane appeared to have been taped off.

Zee turned the volume up higher as Sarah said, "So far there is no explanation as to why several people who live in this row of houses have been found dead in their homes. Police are refusing to comment, but after the deaths yesterday of two holidaymakers in White Haven, surely we have to question if there is a serial killer in the area. Although," she paused and the camera zoomed in closer, "I have also spotted the van belonging to Ghost Objective Paranormal Studies on the lane, which suggests that maybe something paranormal is to blame. I will bring you more on this story as soon as I can. Sarah Rutherford, South Cornwall News."

"Oh, shit!" Alex leaned against the back of the saggy sofa, his energy leaching out of him, and then turned to see Zee watching him. "Did this happen last night?"

"Looks like it. And you had another vision last night, too. Anything of that place you recognise?"

He'd told Zee about his dream as soon as he'd arrived at work, and Alex shook his head. "No. The images were incoherent. It was the weird feeling and the noise I experienced, more than anything. I'd hoped it was just a dream, but now... How many people?"

"They haven't released numbers, or even said how they died yet." Zee's eyes were full of sympathy, but whether it was for Alex or the victims, Alex couldn't tell. *Both, probably.* Zee was a surprisingly empathetic guy. "Is there anything I can do to help?"

"No." Alex clambered to his feet, feeling nauseous, but knowing he needed to eat. He started to mechanically make a sandwich, until Zee hustled next to him, forcing him to sit again.

"Let me. You look like shit, and I don't want you collapsing again. Do you want Jago's brunch sandwich?"

"Bloody hell, no. They're huge. Just bacon and egg."

"Cool." Zee deftly started to cook, his huge frame leaving little room to do anything. "There must be something that gives you a clue about what's behind your visions."

Alex reached for the Paracetamol and knocked a couple back before he answered. "Unfortunately, no, but with these deaths, I need to start finding answers soon. I just need to figure out the best way to do it. I suppose the deaths, horrible though they are, give me something to focus on." He gave a dry laugh. "And I really can't pretend they're dreams anymore, either."

"You thinking of trying to scry again or something?"

"*Something*. If I could control my scrying better, I might see more details. Sunday's session, however, just swept me in. Trying to direct my visions would be good, too, but it's not always that easy."

"You're not connecting with a spirit, I presume?"

"No." Alex considered his experience again. "But I did feel the dread of being pursued. And loss again. Heart-breaking loss."

Zee flipped bacon in the pan, and then cracked an egg in next to it, before shooting Alex a sidelong glance. "You know, that's actually two things you're experiencing. You were being pursued, but you felt loss. I think your thoughts—or emotions—whatever you want to call them, are mixing with whatever is out there."

"Wow!" The shock of Zee's assessment made Alex's headache nearly disappear. "You're right! That is two things." Alex started to pace, running his hand through his thick hair that seemed to remain tangled no matter what he did with it. He continued to talk, almost to himself. "Yes, I'm being pursued, scared witless, but I also feel sadness. No, that's inadequate. Absolute grief and a heart-breaking loss."

"Maybe," Zee suggested, plating the sandwich up and handing it to him, "it's as if it was so close, you couldn't help but feel its emotions."

Alex sank on to the chair next to the table and took a bite of his sandwich, his thoughts whirling. "So," he said, swallowing, "something is connecting to me, but I don't know what or how. I'm piggybacking on it somehow." He flashed a smile at Zee. "I don't like it, but at least I'm getting a sense of what's happening."

"You didn't sense death, though? No malevolent intent?"

"No. Maybe the deaths are accidental."

"Accidental or not, that's several deaths in two nights."

"Surely there can't be any more?" But even as Alex said it, he knew it was a stupid question.

Zee jerked his head at the sandwich. "Eat up, Alex. You'll need all your strength with this one." He checked his watch. "I'll get back behind the bar and leave you in peace, but if you need anything, let me know."

Alex watched him go, continuing to eat and muse on his visions. *Something* had appeared suddenly, so *something else* had triggered it. He needed to connect to whatever was causing his visions and find a way to stop it. Knowing that he had a link to it had given him hope. He just had to find a way to manipulate it.

Dylan finished securing the video camera in its protective box to the old archway that roses scrambled over, and stepped back to assess the angle it would capture, wiping the sweat from his brow as he did so.

Rosa had given him free rein to roam around the garden, and he had spent the last couple of hours battling down overgrown, barely-there paths, hacking around towering hedges, and untangling himself from vociferous climbing plants. He had started close to the house where it was at least slightly more accessible, but when he realised the extent of the garden, he decided to be thorough.

It was a fascinating place. He'd found several small courtyards, some with cracked slabs and rusting benches, others containing all sorts of weird statues, and he'd also found the remains of an old wishing well, as well as a broken greenhouse and a crumbling potting shed. Despite the decrepitude and air of abandonment, the whole place was charming, and in the daylight, at least, offered no sense of threat. It was sleepy; soporific, even. He felt that if he lay down, he could fall into an endless, enchanted sleep.

He shook his head, and huffed at his fancifulness. The heat was addling his brain.

The archway was the entrance to another small courtyard, this one with a broken fountain in the middle—a mermaid bathing in a shallow pool. It was baked dry in the heat, a bloom of algae on its pitted surface. Dylan squinted, trying to imagine it at night. *What could be wandering these grounds?*

He checked the rudimentary map he'd made and added the courtyard and fountain, marking the spot where he'd put the camera. So far, he'd set up around half a dozen. He should probably call it quits, however, he wasn't at all sure that he'd found the edge of the property yet. He certainly hadn't found any large boundary walls, and Rosa had been uncertain as to how big the gardens were. In fact, at this point, even with the map, Dylan wasn't quite sure where he was. He couldn't see the house at all.

Satisfied with the camera, he checked the batteries, made sure it was set up correctly—it was triggered on with sound and movement—and decided that it was time to go. His stomach grumbled. He was starving, and he thought of the cake that Rosa had promised on his return.

Then he felt the prickle of unease that suggested someone was watching him.

He turned, slowly scanning the undergrowth, his hand gripping his backpack. He had no weapons with him, and if anything attacked him, no one would hear a thing. He squinted at the shadows around the tangled shrubs, and then realised he could see eyes watching him.

"I see you! Why don't come out and say hello."

For a few seconds nothing happened, and then the shrubs shook, leaves cascaded, and a skinny boy in shorts and a t-shirt wriggled free to stand in front of him.

"Took you a while," he said, belligerently.

"I've been preoccupied," Dylan shot back, hoping he hadn't been such a precocious little prick when he was a kid. And then he immediately felt mean. This kid was in the middle of nowhere, with no friends. "If you'd revealed yourself earlier, I could have shown you what I was doing."

"I know what you're doing! You're trying to find our ghost."

"Your mom has told you?" Dylan wasn't sure if his own mother would have discussed a ghost with a twelve-year old.

He shuffled and stared at the ground. "I heard her telling Gran."

"You were eavesdropping!"

"So?" He lifted his head and glared at Dylan.

Dylan shrugged. "I did too when I was your age." He stepped forward and held his hand out in a gesture of good will. "I'm Dylan, Ghost Hunter Extraordinaire. And you are?"

He eyed his hand warily, and then stepped forward to shake it. "Max."

"Excellent. So, Max, I was thinking I'd finished putting up cameras, but I hear you've been exploring the garden. Anywhere else you think I should check before I go?"

Max narrowed his eyes, his unruly blond hair tumbling over them. He brushed it aside, revealing cheeks smeared with dirt, the same as his t-shirt and shorts. He must have been grubbing about under hedges for hours. "I found a graveyard."

"In the garden? For pets, you mean?"

"No! People. Under a fallen tree. Over there." He pointed to his left. "It's old."

Dylan was intrigued. Perhaps this old manor house did have its own cemetery. This could put a whole new light on things. He hefted his backpack and swung it onto his shoulders again. "All right. Lead the way."

Chapter Seven

Today, El was thankful that her small shop, The Silver Bough, was on a tiny lane with little natural sunlight. It was hot enough inside without the sun slanting in and making it even hotter.

She turned the fan on and stood in front of it, enjoying the cool air blowing around her. It was late afternoon, and it felt as if all of White Haven had gone to sleep. She was alone, Zoey having gone for a mid-afternoon break and to get some coffee. Although, it wasn't really coffee that El wanted. She was ready for a cold beer.

The sound of voices made her turn to the door. A grizzled man in his forties stood outside looking up at her sign, and then he came inside, a younger woman with pink hair following him. He frowned as he approached the counter.

"This place is smaller than I expected."

El had no idea what she was supposed to say to that. She opted for sarcasm. "You can always leave if you're not happy."

"But I've just arrived! Do you not need the business?"

"Not from grumpy, insulting people, no."

"Dante sent me."

"Then you must be being ruder than normal. He generally has nice friends."

The man studied her for a few seconds and then stuck his hand out. "Sorry. The heat *is* making me grumpy. I'm Sam Clarke, and this is Ruby Townsend. We need a blade with special properties, and I hear you can make us one."

El bristled, ignoring his outstretched hand and his knowledge that she was a witch. She folded her arms, drawing her magic around her like a cloak. "Dante wouldn't have told you that. Who are you?"

He withdrew his hand with a scowl. "I've told you..."

"Not your name." El studied the weather-beaten man. He had a long, unkempt grey beard, a scar down one cheek, and broad shoulders that were hidden, despite the heat, under a heavy coat. "Why do you need a special blade?"

Sam grinned, revealing uneven teeth. "I hunt supernatural creatures. And from what I've seen on the news, there's a supernatural killer in White Haven."

El inwardly groaned. She'd seen the lunchtime news report on the deaths, and was looking forward to hearing the information from her friends first-hand, but this was unexpected. She turned her attention to pink-haired Ruby, who although younger, carried a belligerent, swaggering air about her, too. She was in her mid-thirties, perhaps, and although they were together, El thought it was a professional relationship, not sexual. But Sam was clearly in charge.

She addressed both of them. "If you have seen any news at all lately, White Haven always has interesting things happening. Why are you in my shop now?"

Sam leaned forward, his hands on the counter. "I told you, I've come to hunt the creature that's killing in White Haven, and I need a weapon." He raised his eyes, looking at the swords and daggers on the wall behind her. "Those look good."

"They are decorative, and as you can see from my main displays, I make jewellery. And besides," she leaned forward, staring the man down as she caught the scent of his sweating body, "what idiot hunter goes hunting without a blade?"

"I have many blades, but I need a *special* one."

Of course you do. "You've arrived in White Haven very quickly. Our most recent deaths were only announced at lunchtime."

"This is Cornwall, not outer Mongolia."

He leaned closer, trying to intimidate her perhaps. El was tall and slender, but this man was broad and powerful. He was also cocky and annoying, and she'd had enough of him and his companion. Her magic swelled out, subtle but powerful, repelling him, and he stepped back until he was standing in the middle of her shop, well away from the counter.

"You need to leave, Sam Clarke."

His eyes hardened. "I *need* a blade."

"If you're not careful, you'll have one, but not where you want it. Leave now—and don't come back."

Ruby was already at the door, eyes wary. El wasn't sure how much magic they could detect, but the air was thick with it, and Ruby clearly had more sense than her partner. "Sam, let's go."

He assessed El for a few seconds more, but she didn't budge, and her eyes never left his. If he did one wrong thing, she would hex him.

He must have seen the threat in her stare, because he stepped back, joining Ruby in the doorway. "Think on it. I'll be back." And then with one last, furious glance after his *Terminator* threat, he left.

El took a deep breath. *What the fuck was that? Was this the future of White Haven—aggressive ghost hunters?* When Ghost OPS had been

69

interviewed about the videos on their website, they had all known it would bring more attention to White Haven, but they hadn't considered the arrival of more ghosthunters. Well, *she* hadn't, anyway. *And what had Dante got to do with this?*

She rolled her shoulders, pulled back her magic, and reached for her phone. However, after spending a few minutes chatting with Dante, she was none the wiser. He knew nothing about Sam Clarke or Ruby Townsend, and he hadn't recommended her to anyone. He certainly hadn't mentioned magic blades.

When she ended the call, she looked through her mullioned windows to the quiet lane beyond. Someone had been talking in White Haven, and she wondered what else they had said.

Reuben settled at the end of the bar in The Wayward Son and sipped his pint, half an eye examining the crowd.

He didn't know most of the people in here today, but that wasn't surprising. White Haven was jam-packed with holidaymakers and paranormal lovers, and most of them looked uneasy. They clustered together around tables, and while the noise level was still high, there was no doubt an air of unease following the lunchtime announcement. He'd just left Greenlane Nurseries after locking up for the day, and the chatter about the bodies had found its way there, too, especially amongst the staff.

Alex joined him, taking a swift sip from his half pint. "You've seen the news?"

"Everyone's seen the news," Reuben answered. "It's all anyone is talking about. I wonder why Ghost OPS was there."

"I'm hoping they drop in here later. I'd like to get a few more details."

"Wouldn't we all. Do you think this has anything to do with Lughnasadh?"

Alex frowned. "Surely not. It's a harvest festival, nothing ominous. It celebrates Lugh! He's the God of light."

"Yeah, but these events have a habit of raising energies. Maybe it heralds something else."

"Let's hope Dan has some suggestions for Avery." Alex paused, his eyes lighting up. "I think I might have a had a breakthrough, courtesy of Zee."

Reuben glanced down the bar expecting to see him, but only spotted Marie, who'd served him, and she gave him a knowing wink. Reuben winked back, knowing she fancied him. He knew it exasperated Alex, so he liked to play along. "Where is he?"

"Gone home. He finished his shift. And stop winking at Marie! It disturbs me to hear the things she says about you."

He grinned. "I know. Go on. What breakthrough?"

"Whatever I'm picking up in my visions is linking to me, and that's why I'm experiencing feelings of loss. I'm hoping I can use that to make a connection—a stronger one."

All thoughts of flirting with Marie were instantly forgotten. "I'm not sure that's a good idea, Alex, until we actually know what we're dealing with."

"But it might help us find that out!"

"We don't want you put in danger."

"Several people are already dead!"

El sidled onto a stool next to them, wafting Chypre, her favourite scent, over Reuben as she kissed his cheek. "Are you two arguing? You're attracting attention."

"I don't care," Reuben said, glaring at his friend. "Alex has got a hero complex."

"Piss off. No, I haven't. I'm trying to use my powers for good."

"Bloody hell, you're not a Jedi!"

"Shut up, both of you," El said, unusually sharp. "I came in here for a pint and to calm down."

Reuben turned to her, frowning, while Alex swiftly pulled her a pint. "Why do you need to calm down?"

"I was visited by a bloody *supernatural hunter* who wanted to buy a 'blade with special properties.'" She held her fingers up in quote marks. "He was very rude!" She took her pint from Alex's outstretched hand and took a long drink. "Wanker."

"Hold on," Reuben glanced at Alex, who looked as worried as he felt. "How did he know you could even do such a thing?"

"Good question. He claimed that Dante had sent him, but that was bullshit. I think he's heard whispers around the town and concocted a bullshit story." She brushed her long hair off her shoulders, her dark purple nail polish immaculate. "But why bother? He must have known I would check."

El was simmering with annoyance, and Reuben had no wish to exacerbate that, but... "Back up, and tell us what happened. All the details!"

She took a deep breath and described her encounter in the shop.

"Sam Clarke and Ruby Townsend," Alex said, repeating their names. "I wonder what Newton can find out about them? I don't like the sound of them. He sounds arrogant, El. He probably thought he could bully you." He sniggered. "He clearly doesn't know you."

El was starting to calm down, and she smiled. "No. The gossips didn't tell him that much, obviously."

"He could have heard that information from anyone in White Haven," Reuben suggested. "You, Briar, and Avery all have a certain reputation because of your shops. I wonder how he heard Dante's name, though."

"I bet I know." Alex was staring over their heads at the windows, and turning, Reuben saw Rupert leading a group past the pub. "White Haven's very own occult tour leader."

Reuben groaned. "You're probably right. But how would he know about Dante?"

"It's no secret that I work with him," El said with a shrug. Her lips tightened as she stared at Rupert's back until he disappeared around the corner. "And Rupert likes to know everything about us. I might have even mentioned Dante's name to him once myself." She took another sip of her pint as she turned back to them. "At the end of the day, it doesn't really matter about Dante. I just object to someone using him as a reference. I'd have preferred a more honest approach by Sam—or anyone, actually."

"But even if he had approached you differently," Alex said, "would you have admitted that you could do magic?"

"Unlikely, considering that I don't know him. Of course, if he's a hunter, there's every chance he can pick up on magic, anyway. Like Harlan, or anyone else who's familiar with the occult."

Reuben studied the pub again, wondering who among the customers could be hiding something. "I don't like the idea that White Haven is going to be flooded with supernatural hunters. This place is unpredictable enough."

"I agree," Alex said. His eyes narrowed as they travelled across the room. "Unfortunately, I don't think there's much we can do about it, though. Of course, we could cast a spell to get rid of them, but that would be big and difficult. There are too many variables."

"Agreed," El said, nodding.

Reuben grinned. "We do this the old-fashioned way, then—get some background on them to use for leverage."

"And what about any others who rock up?" Alex asked.

"Them too." He drained his pint and pushed it to Alex for a refill, visions of lawless hunters prowling the streets like the Wild West. "I think they need to learn that White Haven is not a free for all. This is our town, and we look after it."

Chapter Eight

"This is a nightmare," Newton said, staring at Moore and Kendall. "Seven deaths in two days, and we have no idea what's causing them."

"Have you discussed it with our friends?" Moore asked, referring to the witches.

"Not today's deaths, no. But I will."

It was late on Tuesday evening, and they were gathered in Newton's stuffy office, surrounded by empty coffee cups and biscuit crumbs. Newton was starving, and he wanted a pint. And a smoke. He wished he'd never taken up the bloody habit again; he already stank like an ashtray.

Kendall gripped the black whiteboard marker like a weapon and stood again, staring at their notes. "Is there anything new I can add?"

They had discovered that of the four houses on the tiny lane, ending in a cul-de-sac at the moor's edge, only the two young women who lived in the end house had survived. They had heard nothing the night before other than a distant wail, and ignoring it, had rolled over and

TJ GREEN

gone back to sleep. Their board listed the names of the dead, their addresses, the manner of death—most of which were blank, pending the PM—and potential links. And the links were few. The circumstances of the deaths, of course. All seemingly non-violent and sudden, but leaving bloodshot, red eyes. None of them had been strangled—at least on cursory inspection, the most obvious cause of petechiae. Zero signs of a break-in. All happened at night. The fact that five of them were neighbours. And the latest, tentative link—the proximity to Stormcrossed Manor, where the owner had reported hearing screams.

Newton didn't answer her question. Instead, he said, "I want to check this manor out tomorrow morning."

"An official visit?" Moore asked, puzzled. "We've no grounds."

"No. I was thinking background checks. Who owns it, for how long, any news on it...anything at all. I want facts, gossip, everything. And Dylan says he'll share his footage."

"That's a shame," Kendall said, sitting down again. "I was looking forward to seeing that place after what Ben said."

"Me too, but Moore is right. There's no reason to go at the moment." He sighed, leaning back in his chair that creaked under his weight. "We'll go back to the cottages tomorrow, you and me, Kendall. I want to get a feel for them again. Moore, can you do background checks on the manor? And start them on the victims, too."

He nodded. "No problem."

Newton listed them off again, like a mantra, as if saying their names might give him more insight. "Mrs Robertson in the end cottage, aged ninety-one. Mr and Mrs Samson in the next. Sixty-eight and seventy-one, respectively. And then Mr Marsh and his mother. Fifty-four and seventy-nine." His fingers tapped his cigarette packet. "Five deaths! And initial checks suggest nothing links them, except that they were neighbours. This is insane."

"Are you going to the post-mortems?" Moore asked.

"Maybe a couple. I haven't got time to go to them all. Could you fit a couple in?"

"Sure." Moore nodded at Kendall. "You should, too. I think we should endeavour to see all of them between us."

"That's a good idea. Split them, like we did earlier." Only a few hours before, they'd had to contact the closest relatives and formally identify all of the bodies, always an unpleasant task, and they had divided those between them, too. Moore was a good officer and he felt lucky to have him, and Kendall was shaping up well, too. "You should go home, guys. We'll be fresher in the morning. And tomorrow will be busy."

Moore stood, stretching as he did so. "Cheers, Guv. You get a good rest, too. I know you'll be in the pub."

"I won't stay long, but I need to unwind. And they may have some news." And he wanted to see Briar. With luck she'd be there, and seeing her always cheered him up.

As if he'd read his mind, Moore nodded at the cigarette packet. "You'd have better luck if you gave those up again."

"Don't you start."

Moore grinned. "Just looking out for you. Come on, Kendall. Home time."

Kendall looked like she was angling for an invite to the pub. He knew she was intrigued about the witches, and although she'd met them all, she didn't know them well. He would ask her, one day. *But not tonight.*

What none of them had mentioned, he realised, as they all exited the office and headed to their cars, was the possibility that there may be more deaths tonight. Newton shook his head, banishing the horrible thought.

He needed a pint, a smoke, and then bed.

Briar stared at El, her white wine temporarily forgotten as El finished telling the group about her encounter with the hunters in her shop.

Newton had arrived not long before, and he and the witches were clustered around a table in The Wayward Son courtyard, lit up only by strings of fairy lights. The heat had eased with the onset of darkness, but not by much, and Briar knew it would be another sticky night's sleep.

Briar had arrived only a short while ago, after spending a few hours after closing making up more soaps, lotions and candles—especially candles. The woman who had visited earlier that day had bought lots of them.

"I think I had a visit from a hunter, too, early this morning," Briar told her friends. "Or rather, Eli thought she was one. I couldn't work out what was going on, although I knew there was something different about her." She recalled her brusque manner, the astute questions. "She knew what she was talking about. I presumed at first that she was a witch, but there were no signs of magic about her, so I went with very well-informed customer." She shrugged. "Some are. They take great interest in the herbs I put into my products, but she gave off a different vibe..."

El raised a plucked eyebrow. "Let me guess. Cocky. Arrogant?"

"Both. She was impatient, too. But she watched me like a hawk. Me and Eli. And what she said was quite unnerving." Newton leaned forward, the scent of stale cigarettes wafting around him, and Briar wrinkled her nose. "You're smoking again!"

"I'm stressed."

"That's no excuse."

He shuffled in his seat, his eyes falling to his pint briefly. "It's temporary. Describe this woman."

Knowing she had made her point, Briar said, "She's in her late thirties, maybe early forties. Shoulder-length brown hair, blue eyes, trim, muscular, tanned, with a no-nonsense air about her. And she knows her magic, but as I said, she isn't a witch. She was after a whole range of candles, and bought bundles of herbs. Unusual ones, too."

Reuben looked puzzled. "I didn't think you sold herbs."

"Just a selection of the most common ones that people use in spells or for household needs. But she asked if I carried any extras, and I didn't think to say no. Besides," Briar smiled, "I was curious as to what she'd ask for."

Avery laughed. "Good point. And what did she want?"

"Parosela, Mistletoe, Wolf's Bane, and Edelweiss."

Avery's laugh was quickly replaced with a gasp. "An unusual combination!"

"I know. I lied and said I had only small amounts of them. She knew I was lying, too. I could see it in her face."

Alex groaned. "Great. So we have a couple that we absolutely know are hunters, and another woman that sounds likely. I don't suppose you got a name?"

"No. She paid with cash, too, so no card receipts. But," Briar eyed the others, "Eli seemed to think she was bad news. That all hunters were. He said they didn't make distinctions between paranormal creatures. Anyone was fair game—including us and the Nephilim."

A stunned silence followed before Reuben scoffed. "You're kidding! We help people."

Briar shuffled in her chair, recalling Eli's uncomfortable truths. "Eli said we were all violent when we needed to be, and he's right, isn't he? Hunters could perceive us as a threat. Something to be dealt with to protect the *normal* population." She lowered her voice, not wanting anyone beyond their table to hear her. "He suggested they would hunt us, and that she probably wasn't alone. He's right about that. He could be right about this."

"Hold on!" Newton gripped his pint glass as he leaned forward, scowling. "How does bloody Eli know anything about hunters?"

"His brothers *do* work in the occult world now," Briar pointed out. "They hear all sorts of things. Plus, he's been around a long time. Maybe he's encountered them in his previous life."

El ignored Newton's scepticism, and just nodded. "Our visitors—*hunters*," she corrected herself, "came to us for help. Me for a blade, you, Briar, for herbs."

"And you turned him away," Alex reminded her. "I don't like this at all. We need to up our protection...on our houses, businesses, and ourselves. I don't like being targeted, even if we are able to protect ourselves."

Briar shivered, despite the warm night, thinking of Helena's horrible fate at the hands of an irate town and the Witchfinder General, and also the fact that she was alone at home. *She had powerful magic, and the Green Man nestled deep within her, but if these hunters were against them and whatever else they thought lurked in the town...* "Modern day witch hunters. That's awful. Terrifying, actually."

"Chill out!" Reuben instructed, rolling his eyes. "We're jumping to conclusions. Let's find out a bit more first. White Haven has been all over the news with Ghost OPS's activities, and now these deaths. Look at how Ghost OPS gets so excited about this stuff. Others will, too. It just annoys the crap out of us. And Newton, of course."

Newton rubbed his jaw, and in the low light, the shadows under his eyes were dark. "Bollocks. Seven deaths, and now bloody hunters. I don't like this at all. Although, Maggie mentioned that she has hunters on her patch...not surprisingly. She doesn't like them. Says they get in her way. I'll give her a call. She may recognise their descriptions."

"There's not much we can do about them, though," Avery pointed out. "People are welcome to come and go, even if they do hunt the paranormal. But perhaps," she looked sneaky, which was very unlike Avery, "we can try and get something personal from them, if any of us see them again. Hair is the easiest. We can track them, then. Even better, formulate a spell to get rid of them."

"Yes!" Newton pointed at her. "I like that idea!"

Avery saluted him. "Yes, sir! Now, you tell us what happened today. We're all dying to know."

"Don't say dying. There's been enough of that already."

"Sorry. Bad choice. Well?"

Newton pushed the remnants of his meal away, and sipped his pint. "There's not much else I can add, to be honest. Five people were found dead in their homes. Three out of the four in that row of cottages. All died at night. Some were in bed, others in front of the TV. Estimated time of death is early hours of the morning. And at this stage, all looked to have died through nonviolent means. Or should I say, non-invasive means?" He shrugged. "You know what I mean. It's uncanny, and weird, and I absolutely have no idea what killed them."

"Why was Ghost OPS there?" Alex asked. "We saw their van on the news."

"It seems the lady on the end, Mrs Robertson, had been hearing strange noises on the moor. Unfortunately, that's about as much as Cassie got from her on the phone. Ben and Cassie found her body when they turned up to interview her. A pre-arranged appointment. Kendall and the DC discovered the rest when they started the door-to-door enquires."

Briar's hand flew to her throat, her own concerns temporarily forgotten. "Poor Cassie. What a horrible thing to find."

Newton grunted. "She was holding up better than Ben. Not by much, admittedly. The surviving couple in the end cottage said they heard a distant wail on the moor last night. They assumed it was a fox and rolled over and went to sleep." He stared at Alex. "Did you have another vision last night?"

Alex nodded. "Unfortunately, yes, but I swear I didn't see deaths, or any people at all. Certainly not the victims. The only emotion I felt apart from my own fear was overwhelming grief."

"I'm hoping you have thought of something...or Dan has?"

They all shook their heads, and Avery said, "Dan is giving it some thought, but hasn't suggested anything yet."

He sipped his pint, looking at them speculatively. "What about Stormcrossed Manor? Have you heard of that?"

"I have," Reuben said, frowning. "It's on the edge of town. Why are you asking about that old place?"

"Ghost OPS haven't been in touch, then?" Newton asked, not answering his question.

"No. Why?"

"They have another job. A woman called Rosa says she's been hearing odd things there at night, and thinks the place might be haunted." He stared at Alex. "Since the storm, she hears screams at night."

Alex jerked in shock, almost knocking over his pint glass, and the rest of them froze. "She hears screams?"

"Apparently, yes. Dylan has been there today, setting up cameras around the house and grounds. Ben and Cassie were going to join him after their interview with the deceased. I'm not sure if they made it in the end. They were going to take measurements, do their usual thing. I'm wondering if it's related to your visions?"

Alex's grip tightened on his glass. "It could be. Screaming is the constant thread of every single vision, but I think I'm connecting to something, too. What's Stormcrossed Manor like?"

Newton shrugged. "An overgrown wreck, apparently."

Avery rested her hand on Alex's arm. "Your vision was about a wild, overgrown place. They *must* be connected."

Newton picked up his cigarette packet, playing idly with it. "So, three nights, three visions, two nights of death. That strikes me as an unholy coincidence. Are you sure you didn't see a creature, or person, o r *anything*?"

"Nothing specific," Alex insisted, before turning to Reuben. "What do you know about Stormcrossed Manor? I'm not sure I've heard of it."

"You must have. You're a local. And you, Avery! That place isn't as old as mine, though. Probably built in the 1800s."

"By that logic," Newton said, "I should have heard of it, too. But why should we? There are loads of old manor houses around. We can't know them all. Unless," he added, leaning forward, "it has a reputation."

"That's a fair point, I guess," Reuben conceded. "I suppose it's because it's one of my closest neighbours, and depending which way I drive, I can pass the entrance. I've always found it intriguing because of the way it's so rundown. Well, the drive is. You can barely see past the gate."

El looked at him, puzzled. "Have I ever passed it with you?"

"I'm not sure. Maybe. It's on that tiny lane that hardly anyone ever goes down. Like I said, unless you knew to look for it, you'd sail straight past it, anyway."

"Any weird rumours about the owners?" Newton asked.

"Not that I can recall. Well, other than the fact it was renamed Stormcrossed Manor, obviously. It used to be called Trevithick Manor. I think it was renamed after the death of the owner, sometime after the first World War. Sorry, I really don't know the details."

Newton finished the dregs of his beer, and pushed his seat back as if to leave. "That's okay. Moore will do some research on it tomorrow, and I'll get in touch with Ghost OPS. But I suggest," he turned to Alex, "that you call them, too."

Alex nodded. "I absolutely will."

"Right, I'm off." Newton's chair scraped back. "I'm knackered, but let me know what you find, and if you have any more visions."

Briar watched Newton go, a little regretful of the distance that remained between them. But that was to be expected, seeing as she was still seeing Hunter. *Sort of.* He was engaged in some sort of shifter-fight at home, and their conversations were erratic right now. She just hoped he was okay.

She dragged her attention back to the present, watching Alex's fingers drum the table as he said, "I should get a look at that place. Do you think they'd let me in?"

"It's not Fort Knox!" Reuben pointed out. "I'm sure Ben could get you in by explaining you are part of the team."

Avery nodded. "It's a good idea. You might recognise something. It could even trigger another memory."

"And while you do that," El said, tapping her polished nails on her wine glass, "the rest of us should try and find out about the hunters. I'll ask around. Maybe I should even talk to Rupert. Like you said, Alex, he could have spoken to them. And besides, they won't have left town yet."

A gnawing worry settled in Briar's stomach. "And what if we get more hunters arriving? With today's news, it's possible."

Reuben shrugged and winked, his usual *blasé* self. "Then we deal with them, too."

Chapter Nine

A very was making a very strong coffee in the kitchen of Happenstance Books the next morning when Dan swept energetically through the back door, carrying the scent of summer with him.

"I've been thinking about creatures that make strange noises," he said, slinging his messenger bag on to the kitchen table, "and I have a few suggestions." Then he stared at her, eyes widening in alarm. "What's happened? You look awful!"

Avery ran her hand self-consciously through her hair and added a waft of glamour to improve her appearance. She had slept intermittently and her head pounded, despite the herbal tea she had brewed for herself earlier. "Remind me how you have a girlfriend, again? I hope you don't say things like that to her."

"Sorry. But I'm serious—are you okay?"

"Alex had another vision last night. A strong one. He woke me up, yelling in his sleep." She rubbed the back of her neck, warming the muscles beneath her hand with a spell as she tried to ease the knot that had formed. "We both had trouble sleeping after that. The first thing

I did this morning was switch the news on. I'm terrified that someone else has died. Fortunately, there are no new reports. *Yet*."

"Shit. Sorry, Ave. How is he?"

"Okay, I guess. Frustrated. Worried. And knackered."

Dan perched on the edge of the table. "Interesting. So, the first vision was on Saturday night in the middle of the storm, then two more, both at night, and one at work. It's interesting he gets them more often at night. They have to be related to the deaths and whatever's causing them."

"I agree, but Alex doesn't see any deaths...thank the Gods." She turned to pour the coffee, and made Dan one, too. She was sick of thinking about Alex's visions and what they might imply. Now she wanted action. "However, we have to assume the visions and the deaths are linked. Tell me what you think could be behind them."

He took his cup from her. "I was thinking of moorland paranormal creatures, and thought, what about a Will-o'-the-wisp?"

"Do they scream?"

His nose wrinkled. "Not really. But they do lead people into bogs to kill them."

Avery knew he was trying to be helpful, but... "Seriously? None of the victims were found in bogs, Dan!"

"I know! But it could be a *metaphorical* bog. Like they were mentally taken there and died thinking they had drowned. That could explain the feeling of loss and panic."

"I suppose that's an interesting slant on it," she conceded. "Any other ideas?"

"Selkies. Seals that become human. I was thinking that what if one had found love with a human mate, and that mate had died. They could be wandering, lost and alone."

"Very romantic! I didn't think they were killers, though."

"Who's to say they're killing deliberately? It could be accidental. But," Dan sipped his coffee and grimaced at the heat, "ouch! I saved the best for last. Banshees."

"Banshees! I thought they were Irish!"

Dan rolled his eyes. "The supernatural do not have boundaries. Besides, Cornwall is a Celtic nation at heart. It's very possible."

"And they shriek—is that right?"

"Yep. It's a female spirit that cries over the death of a family member. Their appearance varies, but are generally tall, red-eyed, and weeping. Some myths suggest they're shorter. Anyway, they all wail."

"But the recent deaths aren't in one family," Avery reasoned, "so how does that work?"

"I don't know. But so far, it's the best suggestion I have."

Avery sipped her coffee, watching Dan over the rim of the cup, and with each sip, her thought processes sharpened. "What if it was centred on one family, but the effects encompassed the area around it?"

"I guess it's possible. What do you know, Avery Hamilton?" Dan narrowed his eyes at her.

"Ghost OPS are investigating a place called Stormcrossed Manor, and I'm wondering..."

"Stormcrossed Manor?" Dan's voice rose in alarm. "What's happening there?"

"You know it?"

"Sure I do. Well, by association. It's a long tale of death and mourning. The name says it all. But tell me why Ghost OPS are there."

Avery explained what had happened so far and asked, "What do *you* know?"

"Its original name wasn't Stormcrossed Manor, that's for sure. It was called Trevithick Manor, after the man who built it."

Avery nodded. "Yes, that's what Reuben said. Apparently, it's close to his place."

"Sounds about right. Anyway, just after the first World War, the owner of the manor, I forget his name, died—crushed by a fallen tree in a storm—leaving his wife to bring up their small children on her own. Grief-stricken, she renamed the place." Dan grinned. "I think it's a great name."

Avery could only think of the grieving woman. "That's so sad. Imagine grieving so much that you rename your house! And having to bring up your children without their father."

"She was rich! It's not like she'd have been completely on her own."

"She would have been alone in her heart," Avery said, thinking she was turning into a soppy romantic. "Anyway, what else do you know?"

"If I remember correctly, at some point a lightning strike took out one of the towers and set fire to it, and other storms over the years have felled some big trees on the estate."

Avery settled herself more comfortably against the counter. "And you know this how?"

He shrugged. "There are a few interesting places across Cornwall that have a reputation for hauntings—Pengersick Castle, Bodmin Jail, Jamaica Inn, and Prideaux Place, to name just a few. I'm interested in all of them. Stormcrossed Manor hasn't got a haunted reputation as such, but I guess this air of sorrow clings to it. Plus, it's local and therefore piques my interest. Screams, you say?"

"Apparently. I don't know the details." Another connection struck Avery. "But you mentioned storms..."

Dan nodded. "Perhaps the storm on Saturday stirred something up."

Avery drained her coffee. "We decided last night that Alex should visit there, but now it sounds even more intriguing."

"I'd like to go there, too," Dan admitted as he headed into the shop to join Sally, who'd already opened up. "I've always wondered what it's like behind those tangled hedges. I'll call Dylan and try to set it up – not today, obviously."

Avery trailed after him, and they joined Sally at the counter. She was dressed in a bright summer dress, and her hair was tied back in a ponytail. The front door was already propped open, and incense hung on the air, but the shop was empty at this early hour. Avery decided to take advantage of the quiet moment and update them on the other pressing issue.

After greeting Sally, she said, "It seems there are more hunters in White Haven, so just be aware. They seem...pushy."

Sally frowned. "Hunters? Like Ghost OPS?"

"Sort of." She described El and Briar's encounter, adding, "It's possible they may come in here today, or there may be others." She paused, uncertain of how much to say, and then decided that they deserved the honest truth. "Eli seems to think they might be targeting us, too. The Nephilim and us witches. I'm not so sure. We're powerful, but human. It's not like we're odd supernatural creatures, but his experience suggest they have no such boundaries."

Sally gasped. "Witch hunters! And the Nephilim, too? Surely no one would be stupid enough to target any of you."

"Eli is no fool," Dan said, "and neither would he spread panic for no good reason." He stared at Avery, arms crossed. "I know you're all strong and powerful, but I think you need to take this seriously. We have no idea why they might be here, but if there are a few of them, and they do this for a living, they'll have ways to hunt witches."

Dan and Sally were both staring at her, and Avery had to concede that they were probably right. "I've pushed it to the back of my mind with everything else going on, but that couple certainly pissed El off.

I guess if I'm not around and someone odd comes in, just be careful—although, you two should be fine. I'll see if Alex has organised things with Dylan. If he's going, I want to join him." The more she thought about the manor, especially knowing its tragic background, the more it fascinated her.

Sally exchanged a nervous glance with Dan, and he gave her a reassuring smile. "Don't worry, I'll be here all day."

Avery gave him a grateful smile, already reaching for her phone. Then a shadow fell across the window. All three turned to the street to see a huge man on the other side of the glass, staring in. *Hulk* was the word that sprang to Avery's mind.

In fact, he seemed less to stare than glower, his dark eyes almost lost behind the tangle of his hair. Sally visibly recoiled, but Dan straightened up. Avery summoned her magic, prepared for whatever might come their way.

"Woah! Back up!" Ben instructed as he stared at the screen. "Something moved there."

Dylan manipulated the mouse, rewinding the video, and then snorted. "It's a cat."

"Bollocks!" Ben leaned back in his chair, rolled his shoulders, and stretched. "Sorry. I'm enthusiastic."

"You're over-caffeinated," Cassie said, eyeing his cup. "That must be your third, and it's barely half-past nine."

"Wow, I'm slacking," he teased her. "I've normally had at least four by now."

Ghost OPS were sitting in their headquarters reviewing the overnight footage from all of the cameras Dylan had set up the day before, and it was slow going. The day before, he and Cassie had finally made it back to the manor to collect Dylan after finding Mrs Robertson's dead body at the cottage. Giving their statements had taken a long time. They hadn't been able to check for paranormal activity in the other cottages down the lane, but he hoped they might be allowed in them at some point.

When they had returned to the manor, Dylan had already started other baseline tests in the house—EMF and temperature readings—but Rosa had not wanted cameras inside the home. Understandable, but frustrating. But even more frustrating was her grandmother, Tamsyn's, refusal to let them in the wing where she lived. That certainly did pique Ben's curiosity.

He was still ruminating on the possible reasons behind that, as Dylan brought up footage of the cemetery's camera, saying, "Let's try this one."

Cassie shuffled forward. "I want to see the graveyard properly, rather than on screen."

"We'll be going back," Dylan said, distracted as he scrolled through the footage. "It had a *quality*. I'd be interested to see your reaction to it."

"Do you think," Ben said, leaning forward too, as he tried to distinguish the details, "that Tamsyn is hiding something? You know, a reason for not wanting us in her part of the house?"

"Maybe," Cassie answered, still staring at the screen. "But old people can be unnecessarily stubborn. She might just resent Rosa arriving and inviting strangers into her house. After all, she's been alone for years."

Ben wasn't really buying it, but with nothing else to go on, he didn't want to assume too much. Hard evidence was the key.

Dylan leaned even closer to the screen and paused the footage of the ruined grave. "I think I saw something." He took the footage back a few frames and let it play again, pulling the headphones over his ears as he did so he could listen to the audio. Dylan spent most of his time with his earphones perched on his head. They were like an extension of himself.

All three were now inches from the screen, the images rendered in dayglo blue showing the cold head stones of the graveyard, the stone walls, and gently undulating bushes in the sea breeze. And then something rose from the grave.

Goosebumps flared over Ben's arms as he watched, transfixed.

The figure was slender but shapeless, a suggestion of ridiculously long limbs. It hovered above the grave, drifted to the right, and then floated towards the camera. All three were now frozen, Ben barely aware of his friends on either side of him. The figure drifted closer to the camera, and an icy blue colour bloomed from what Ben construed as a head.

Suddenly, the video footage turned into grey static, lines erupting across the screen, and Dylan yelled, leaping to his feet and pulling his ear phones off in one swift movement. Ben was so shocked he spilled his coffee all over his lap, and Cassie jerked backwards as if she'd been shot.

As silence fell, a wail leaked from the discarded earphones—heartrending and horrifying.

"Holy shit on a blanket!" Dylan stared at the screen, his headphones, and then at Ben and Cassie. "That almost deafened me."

"What the fuck was that?" Cassie asked, in an unusual fit of cursing for her. She was white-faced, her arms covered in goosebumps, just like Ben. "Ghosts don't scream!"

Ben stared at them. "Did you see the blue colour in the face area? It looked like a mouth!"

"No argument from me!" Dylan said, shaking his head. "I need to get there...see it in the day."

"The ghoul?" Cassie asked, horrified.

"The graveyard, you tit! And it's not a ghoul!"

"It might be," she answered, indignant. "It really didn't look like a ghost."

"Hold on." Ben clung to reason. "Clean up the footage first. We need to try and work out what that is. You're right, Cassie, it didn't look like a ghost. Not the sort we've encountered, anyway. The only thing I can think of with a horrible scream is a banshee, but nothing about that makes sense, so don't ask questions right now." He pushed the thought to the back of his mind. "We need more evidence."

Dylan nodded, sinking slowly back into his seat. "Yes, of course. Clean up the footage." He smacked his ears as if clearing them. "Herne's hairy bollocks. That was chilling. You know, I watched some of this live last night, after you went to bed." He directed that at Ben. "But I gave up in the end. I was knackered."

"That's fair enough. What time did it happen?"

Dylan ran the footage back. "Ten to two."

"Has anyone checked the news yet?" Cassie asked, already looking at her phone.

"Not me," Ben confessed, knowing why she was asking, and still trying to blot warm coffee from his jeans. He'd have to change; he was covered in it.

Dylan's phone rang, and he strode across the room to take the call.

Cassie's shoulders dropped. "Nothing reported so far. Deaths, that is." She heaved a huge sigh and leaned back in her chair. "What *was* that, Ben?"

His thoughts jumbled, he said, "I don't want to speculate too soon."

Dylan soon marched back across the room, pulling his chair up purposefully. "Right. I'm going to see what else I can find, and then I'm going to meet Alex." He glanced over at them. "Alex is having visions of a place that sounds suspiciously like this. I'm going to take him to the graveyard in a couple of hours."

As much as Ben wanted to go with him, he decided that background work would be more useful. "Whose grave was disturbed by the falling tree?"

"No idea. The headstone was under the branches."

"Find out, and tell me. Whatever that was seemed to come from that grave. I'm going to do some research on that place. And in the meantime," he looked across to the telephone that was blinking with a red light, meaning they had messages, "we need to see what came in overnight, Cassie."

"I've heard a few," she said, rising to her feet. "More reports of strange noises. I'll check their locations, in case there's a pattern."

"There'll be one," Ben murmured, more to himself than the others. This was shaping up to be very odd indeed.

Chapter Ten

D S Kendall studied the living room of the cramped cottage, wondering how anyone could live there. It was oppressive. Some might even call it quaint. She did not.

Newton was prowling the small space like a caged animal, and she tried to take her mind off the size of the place and focus on what could have caused the deaths of the residents the day before. They were in the second cottage, where the old couple had lived; the furnishings were old-fashioned, and the kitchen looked as if it hadn't been updated since the 1950s.

"What can you see, Newton? I can't find a thing. It all looks absolutely normal."

"Bloody nothing!" He turned, a grimace marring his handsome face. Although Kendall really didn't want to call him handsome. He was her boss. But he was lean and muscled, and looked very good in his suit. Despite the trying last few days, he'd shaved and was immaculately turned out, and she appreciated that in a man. He paid attention to his appearance, which was more than could be said for

Alex and Reuben, the two witches of the White Haven Coven. They may be good looking in their tattooed, unconventional way, but they weren't her type at all. Although, Zee intrigued her, as did Eli, the huge Nephilim. She'd heard about the others, but hadn't met them yet.

She focussed on Newton as he said, "Nothing seems out of place. There's no sign of a struggle. I can't even detect magic."

Kendall blinked, confused. "You can feel magic?"

"Yeah. It has a certain quality. You'll get used to it when you've worked on this team long enough. I spend a lot of time with the witches, so that helps." He huffed and headed for the door. "Let's go next door. I think I'll get Ben to come here with his meter. Maybe he'll pick something up."

Within minutes they were in the next cottage, which Kendall was relieved to see was updated and more light-filled than the previous one. However, once again, it felt all too normal to say there'd been a recent death here. "So," she said, "this is where the guy, Mr Anthony Marsh, lived with his mother, Vera. She was in bed, he was watching TV, right?"

"Right." Newton didn't consult his notes as he said, "Anthony had moved in last year to look after his mother. I gather he modernised the place. It's a nice home."

"I thought that." Kendall headed upstairs and into the main bedroom, noting that SOCO had brushed for fingerprints in here, too. It was decorated with a cool elegance. No frills or flounces here, just good taste in light blues, but the bed was rumpled, and a terrible air of disuse had fallen over the place already. "This is horribly sad."

Newton had followed her up the stairs and he stood next to the window, looking out over the garden. "Whatever killed them had to be powerful. I mean, maybe whatever it was could have entered the house, but I'm inclined to think it—or *them*—was outside. Surely, we'd feel a residual something."

"But there's nothing outside, either. Just sunshine and pretty gardens."

Newton rubbed his face. "I thought I might get some insight by coming here today, but this is just a waste of time. I'm pretty sure SOCO will find nothing more, either." He straightened and fixed her with his pale, grey eyes. "There's something I'd like you to follow up on. El and Briar have encountered hunters in White Haven. They sounded aggressive, and I'm pretty sure the publicity has brought them here. I've got descriptions, so see if you can find anything out about them. Trawl through the town's CCTV footage. I doubt we'll get names, but..." He shrugged. "Whatever you can find. I'll give you Maggie's number, too."

Kendall nodded, pleased to have something else to do, and to have the opportunity to phone the notorious Maggie Milne.

She followed him as he stomped back down the stairs, and his phone pealed in his pocket.

He answered gruffly, stopping abruptly, and she banged into him as he said, "You've got to be kidding me... We'll be there in ten." He didn't even turn as he bounded down the last few steps. "Another dead couple, Kendall. This is turning into a right shitshow."

Despite the horror of it all, Kendall couldn't help but feel excited. This is what she'd joined the team for, and she couldn't wait to be more involved.

Newton virtually sprinted to his car, but she took one last look along the cottages before getting in her own, wondering what had happened here. She paused, frowning. There was a grubby, grey van at the end of the lane, just beyond the police tape. *That hadn't been there when they arrived.* She squinted, stepping closer as she tried to see who was inside it. *Press, perhaps? No. The van wasn't professional enough.* As she took one more step, the tyres squealed, and the van spun around and roared down the lane.

But not before she had seen the registration and committed it to memory.

Alex shuddered as he studied the small, overgrown cemetery. "This is where you saw the spectral-something? There's an odd feeling about this place."

Dylan nodded, his sunglasses pushed over his short dreads. "If you'd seen what we did, you would think it was more than odd. It was *freaky*! My ears are still ringing!"

There were perhaps a dozen graves, all with old stone markers, many of them plain. A low, crumbling wall encompassed the area, and old trees, bent and warped by wind and time, seemed to guard it. It was the first place Dylan had brought him to, weaving so swiftly through the overgrown gardens that Alex didn't have time to form any accurate impressions of the grounds. However, he was already sensing the uncanny resemblance to his visions.

Alex pointed to where the wall was damaged by a fallen tree, the roots upended and jutting into the air, stones tumbled around them. "That looks recent."

"It is. The young kid, Max, showed it to me. Unfortunately, it's damaged the end grave, too. It's what I wanted you to see." Dylan checked his camera that he'd fixed to a post. "That's good. It's un-damaged. Weird, though—the signal was interrupted last night."

Alex stood behind his shoulder. Dylan was right. There was nothing wrong with the camera. Alex looked back towards the grave. "So, that's where the spectral creature came from."

"Seemed to." Dylan gave a short laugh. "It looks harmless enough in the sunshine, but I swear that recording was as creepy as hell."

"And there was a scream?"

"Nearly shattered my bloody eardrums!"

Before approaching the disturbed grave, Alex cleared his mind, trying to feel for a presence. While the graveyard undoubtedly had an unusual air about it, a sense of abandonment, he couldn't feel anything magical or that resembled a presence. But the longer he focussed, the more he felt a sense of loss.

"Odd," Alex confessed, swinging around to survey the whole place. "I feel loneliness and sorrow, but it is a graveyard. They aren't exactly happy places, and I don't know whether I'm projecting my feelings here. You didn't see where it went?"

"No. The footage became distorted. I even watched for some time afterwards, but it didn't clear up."

"Did you say there was a live feed, too?"

"Sure." Dylan nodded, his short dreads bouncing. "I can watch it real time, but it records as well. I just need to tap into the feed. This place is more complicated because I put up quite a few cameras and have set up monitors for all of them. I watched them all for a bit, and then I went to bed."

"They're all outside?"

"Yeah, spread through the abandoned gardens. Rosa didn't want any inside." He smiled at Alex. "Yes, I checked them all this morning. Tried to track it. No luck."

Alex shrugged. "That's okay. At least now I have a place to connect my weird dream-visions to." Summoning his courage, he looked towards the grave. "Best look in it, then, Dylan."

"I guess so."

Up close, the ground was more disturbed than Alex had initially realised, the upended roots revealing several feet of churned earth, and the remnants of the rotten coffin below. They both stopped on the edge of the hole, staring into its depths. Fortunately, although they could see a portion of the ruined coffin, there were no bones visible.

"The destruction happened over the weekend?" Alex asked.

"Yep. During the storm on Saturday night."

"The night of my first vision."

"Sorry, dude. I wish I'd have known. I would have told you about this place sooner."

"No worries. I should have thought to ask you guys, but we've all been busy."

Dylan huffed. "Us, too. Nuts busy. There are more storms on the way, apparently."

"Let's hope they don't stir anything else up!" Alex crouched over the grave, eyes narrowed, and inhaled deeply. "In my vision, I smelled rich earth, you know, like when you're in a wood or a garden, but then I smelled something really rotten. Something decaying and disgusting. This grave is far too old for that." He turned to Dylan, who had crouched next to him, camera in hand as he panned across the grave. "However, the fact that you filmed something coming out of it says plenty. And the timing is right." He extended his magic, feeling for anything unusual, but there was nothing. And then something odd struck him. "Where's the gravestone?"

Dylan lowered the camera and pointed. "Half under the tree. I couldn't get to it yesterday. It's too big to move on my own, and Max was too small to help me. But we need to. Ben wants the details."

"Yes, so do I. Where *is* Max?" Alex looked around as he stood.

"Probably watching us." Dylan lowered his voice. "Nice kid, but a bit odd. I haven't met his sister yet."

Alex stepped around the grave, careful not to disturb the crumbling earth, and crouched at the head of it, trying to move the tree roots. They were heavy and unwieldy, and gripping the thickest roots, he used magic to help lift them. With a grunt, he thrust the roots out of the way, revealing the gravestone beneath, half hidden beneath the earth. He brushed the soil off to read the inscription.

"*Niamh Trevithick. 1888 – 1972. RIP.*" He looked across to Dylan, who was still filming. "Any idea who this is?"

"Trevithick is one of the original owners, that's all I know. Her grave is very close to another Trevithick, though."

Dylan was right. They were side by side, but the other grave was undisturbed. Alex checked the headstone, covered in moss. "*Jeremiah Trevithick. Beloved Husband and Father. 1883 – 1919. RIP.*" He ran his hand across the warm stone. "Her husband?"

"I'd say so."

"Any objections if I try a bit of psychic mojo?" Alex settled himself into a cross-legged position, the earth warm beneath him, and pulled his backpack onto his lap.

Dylan snorted. "Of course not.

Alex pulled out an amethyst and lapis lazuli to enhance his psychic abilities, cupping them within his palm. He was in a patch of shade, but it was hot, and the scent of the rich earth wafted around him. "I can already feel it pulling me."

"*It?*"

"This place. I might not be able to detect any spirits or magic, but the air seems thick with secrets."

"Can I film you?"

"Sure." Alex closed his eyes, and in seconds, the outside world had vanished.

"So," the huge man said to Avery from the doorway of Happenstance Books. "You're one of the witches."

"And you, I take it, are one of the hunters." She decided lying was pointless.

He grinned, and his face took on a feral, cunning appearance. "Word gets around."

"It's a small place. And I have good friends here."

"So do I."

"Ah, yes. Your pack," Avery said scathingly as she leaned on the counter, chin in her hand as if she hadn't a care in the world. "What are you hunting? Not us, surely? That would be foolish."

He eyed her up, not budging from the door, and then studied Dan and Sally too, quickly dismissing them. He looked above the door and around the shop, as if she had hunter traps waiting to catch him, and then he stepped inside, planting his legs a foot apart as if he would take root.

"Foolish? Is that a threat?"

"No. Advice. White Haven likes its witches. We protect it from people like you. I wouldn't upset the locals."

Avery studied him now that he was inside, noting his well-worn combat trousers, t-shirt, and big leather boots. He was powerful and tall. Over six feet. His shoulder-length, grey-streaked hair was tangled, and a scar ran down the length of his forearm, thick and knotted. Although Avery hadn't seen El's visitors, she wondered if they might be related. He sounded similar in appearance to Sam.

He stared into her eyes, his own a pale blue, almost grey. "We've come to *help* the locals. White Haven needs cleansing. It's become a centre for all things paranormal."

"There's no doubt this town attracts plenty of paranormal activities, but so do many Cornish towns. It's part of their charm—present deaths excluded, of course. You've come to join in the Lughnasadh celebrations? They're a lot of fun."

The stranger almost growled in response as he took another step into the shop. "We have not. We abhor such things."

"The old ways? Then I suggest you leave. White Haven is no place for bigots and haters."

"We'll leave when we've cleansed the town."

Avery subdued a shudder. The word "cleanse" carried horrific connotations. The witches had cleansed White Haven of negativity at Beltane, but she thought his words carried a different threat entirely. "And this meeting is what? A friendly warning? A threat? An assessment of the danger posed by a small bookshop that deals in the occult?"

"It's an assessment, all right. Just determining the scale of the problem. It's not so bad." He shrugged, a lazy grin spreading across his face. "Nothing we haven't handled before."

Avery laughed, taunting him. "And you're nothing we haven't handled before, either. As lovely as this has been, it's time for you to leave." Although she knew she was courting trouble, she cast a spell on the wreath made of summer flowers that hung on the inner wall above the door. Its tendrils stretched out, snagging in his hair. At the same time, she manipulated air to pull the door open a little wider, and gave him a gentle nudge through it.

He ducked his head in shock, and despite his wide stance, staggered over the threshold and onto the street, leaving some of his hair tangled in the wreath. He made to grab it, his eyes wide with alarm, but Avery spelled the door shut, and although he pulled on the handle with increasing fury, it wouldn't open again.

Avery walked across to the wreath and pulled the strands of his hair free, balling them in her palm as he watched her.

He slammed his hand against the glass, eyeballing her. "You'll regret that, witch!"

"So will you, if you threaten me again. Leave."

For a moment he hesitated, and then he spun and stalked down the street, not looking back, and Avery had the feeling that things were going to get even uglier in White Haven.

Chapter Eleven

"Bloody freedom campers," Newton said crossly, as he studied the old, brown, weather-damaged van. "If they hadn't camped here, they might have been okay."

Kendall rolled her eyes, seemingly no longer daunted by his grumbling. "You can't blame them for trying to find somewhere to sleep. The campsites are packed!"

"They should have booked, then, like organised people."

"They're dead, Newton!"

"I know! Why do you think I'm so pissed off?"

They were in a field edged by a narrow lane, a field that bordered the moor, and worryingly, that also edged the grounds of Stormcrossed Manor. He could see the wall and unruly trees that sprawled over it. He'd already checked the map, and knew he was right.

The van had pulled through the gate and was tucked under the hedge that bordered the lane. Only the fact that the field's owner, Joe Grant, had arrived that morning to check on his sheep meant he'd seen it.

Joe, who owned a small holding rather than a true farm, was sitting on the back of his old Land Rover that was also inside the gate, in obvious shock, the DC next to him. SOCO and Arthur were on the way. Newton ran through Joe's statement again. He had arrived an hour before to check on his animals when he spotted the van, and outraged, had hammered on the open door. When no one answered, he peered inside and spotted two bodies, unmoving, in the bed at the back.

Kendall disturbed his thoughts. "Do you think their deaths are linked to the others?"

"Sounds likely, doesn't it? But we better get inside and have a look." He scowled at the ground. "And don't step in the sheep shit."

He checked the outside of the large van that looked to have originally belonged to the army, wondering what on earth possessed anyone to drive around in such a heap, before stepping through the door. The smell of the great unwashed, as he liked to call hippies, hit him, as well as the stench of rubbish, and the lingering scent of death.

Newton examined the door first. "The lock is undamaged, and the door's been propped open. Probably to try to keep the interior cool."

"I hate to speak ill of the dead," Kendall said, her nose wrinkling in disgust, "but maybe so they didn't suffocate from the smell of rotten food, either."

"True."

Newton waited for his eyes to adjust to the light before heading to the bed, but when objects appeared out of the gloom, he froze. A crossbow lay on the table in the lounge area, and an array of magical objects were laid out on surfaces and on the tiny sofa. There was also a large map of White Haven tacked to the wall, with markings all over it.

He grunted. "Shit! This does not look good."

He walked carefully through the small kitchen, the remnants of the previous night's meal on the side, and stared at the bed, half expecting to see the couple El had described to him. But this couple were younger, the man with dreads, the woman with long, purple hair and a shaved scalp above her ears. An unusual carved knife was on the bedside shelf, covered in occult symbols, as well as a selection of intriguingly named books.

"I don't think these are ordinary campers, Kendall. I think they're hunters. And I think whatever they came to hunt has killed them."

"Hunters! More of them?" She crouched to study their bodies before looking over at him. "As we left the lane, I saw another van leaving. Old, like this. It sped off as soon as they knew I saw them, but I got the registration."

He stared at her, surprised. "I must be losing it. I didn't see it."

"You were on your phone."

He felt like an idiot, but he sighed, relieved. "Well done. As for this place, there are no obvious signs of violence, other than their bloodshot eyes. Their deaths have to be linked to the others." He spent another few minutes examining the space, taking in every grubby detail and occult reference before saying, "They didn't just travel in this. They lived here."

Kendall was in the living area, but she called back, "I agree. These hunters must be permanently on the road. Well, this couple at least."

Newton needed fresh air, and he suddenly couldn't get out of there quick enough. He clambered down the steps and took some deep breaths, and in seconds Kendall was next to him. He pointed at the boundary to Stormcrossed Manor. "I think it's about time we checked that place out."

"On what grounds? There's absolutely nothing that links it to the murders, other than proximity."

"I don't care."

"At least wait until you hear from Alex and Ghost OPS, and see what Moore finds out. Then we'll have something to base our visit on. The PM's will be starting today, too. We need to get to those."

Newton huffed, knowing she was right, but he still felt he should do something more. And then it struck him. "All right. You head back to the office; phone Maggie about hunters and start chasing that registration and this one. See if Moore has made progress on the manor. As soon as Arthur is finished here, I'll head to the first PM. But first I'll call Reuben and see if he can get here to check the scene. I have time."

Kendall nodded. "Of course. His house isn't far from here, is it?" She turned to go to her car that was parked on the lane, half in the hedge, but then pointed as a familiar, blonde-haired figure exited a car on the other side of the police tape. "Oh, shit, Newton. Sarah bloody Rutherford is here already."

"Ignore her. I'll deal with her later."

Alex emerged from his trancelike state, feeling like he'd been drugged. When he opened his eyes, Dylan was still filming him, sitting behind his camera that was mounted on a tripod.

"Did you see anything?" Dylan asked eagerly. "Or feel anything?"

"Sort of." Alex stretched, lifting his arms above his head, taking a moment to focus on the present and shake off the dark sense of loss he'd encountered. "I didn't see any spirits, but I did sense wild, turbulent energy and overwhelming sorrow." He took a deep breath and lifted his face to the sunshine. "Fuck. It was dark in there."

Dylan nodded. "I get it. But the storm is responsible for this, right? It must have disturbed whatever lurked in the grave."

Alex rubbed his neck, unwilling to commit himself just yet. "Maybe. I really hoped I'd communicate with something—the spirit, or whatever it is. Unfortunately, all I experienced were overwhelming emotions. Did I look any different, or say anything?"

"No." Dylan stopped recording. "You just fell into a deep trance."

Alex closed his eyes, feeling the strange energies magnify again. "It's not just the cemetery that feels odd, it's the whole place. Something ancient walks these grounds, Dylan, but I can't place it."

"I can show you the footage later, if you're interested."

"Yes, please."

A scream broke their conversation, and they both leapt to their feet, Dylan almost upending his camera. "That's Rosa! Come on!"

Dylan grabbed his camera, still fixed to the tripod, and ran to the house. Alex followed, his legs tingling because he'd sat cross-legged so long. As they ran, a young boy emerged from the bushes to follow them, and Alex presumed this must be Max, Rosa's son.

Alex quickly lost his sense of direction, but Dylan seemed to know exactly where he was going. Within minutes the house emerged ahead, and Alex's footsteps faltered as Max raced past him. Dylan hadn't brought him here earlier, instead taking him straight to the cemetery, so he'd only seen it at a distance. But up close, he realised that this was where the dark energies swirled, and the feeling of loss hit Alex like a b low.

Feeling like he was wading through treacle, he quickened his pace, and followed Max and Dylan into the house. Dylan was halfway along the hall, shouting, "Rosa! Where are you?"

Max raced past him, heading down a passageway to the left, knowing exactly where to go. Dylan glanced behind him to make sure Alex was there and then followed. Alex tried to keep up, fighting the tunnel vision that was magnifying with every step.

They were in an older part of the house that looked even more decayed than the main hallway. Max led them to a large kitchen-come-sitting room where he skidded to a halt. A woman was crouched over a small girl lying on the floor.

"Beth! Wake up! Wake up!"

Dylan crouched next to her. "Rosa, what happen—" He didn't finish his sentence, instead looking around at Alex. "Alex. Her eyes..."

Alex was struggling to focus, but he took a deep breath, blocking out the energy around him with a concerted effort, and pulled a protection spell around himself. To help the girl, he needed to concentrate.

Beth was prostrate, her arms outstretched, and Rosa had dragged her half onto her lap, as if she was a ragdoll. The girl was floppy and unresponsive, and even more unnerving were her eyes. They were wide open but completely white, as if they had rolled back in her head. But she wasn't having a fit. It was more than that. Alex had heard of this but had never seen it. The girl was in a seer state, and her lips were muttering soundlessly.

A woman stepped out of the shadows at the back of the room, unseen by Alex when he first ran in, and her voice was like ice in his veins. "I've told you, Rosa. Stop shaking her. She'll come right eventually."

Alex looked up in shock, almost recoiling. Here was the source of the feeling of loss. It was caught within the old woman. She was tiny, birdlike and frail in appearance, but her energy was huge. Her eyes shifted from Rosa and Beth to Alex, and a look of recognition flashed between them.

Without hesitating, Alex threw his protection spell over Dylan and the others, too. Something lurked within the old woman, and right now he couldn't decide if it was voluntary or possession.

Reuben entered the cramped van in his SOCO-issued white overalls that were already making him sweat.

"I can't believe you made me wear this, Newton."

"Do you want your face splashed across the news, with Sarah Rutherford reporting on you?"

"No, but now I'm sweating to death."

Reuben had been picked up from his house ten minutes earlier by the SOCO van en route to the scene. They were a small team of two, and were understandably bemused at having to outfit Reuben in one of their suits before they arrived at the site. Fortunately, he'd recognised both of them from when they'd examined the cave beneath Gull Island, and Tim, the older man of the two, asked, "More consultancy work, Reuben?"

Reuben had grinned. "Something like that. I have to go incognito."

The two were now working outside the van while Reuben and Newton were inside. It was suffocating.

"So," Newton asked impatiently. "Anything unusual here?"

"Apart from the dead bodies of two hunters, you mean?" Reuben was not usually so *laissez faire* in the face of death, but he could understand why so many policemen and nurses developed a black humour. It was the only way to deal with unending violence, illness, and death.

"Funny."

Reuben extended his awareness, feeling for any sign of magic. The van was a decent size compared to some, but even so, it wasn't as if there was anywhere for anything supernatural to hide. He checked the windows and door. One of the tiny windows was open, but it was ineffective in providing any air flow at all. "Herne's horns. It's stifling in here. I don't get how people like camping."

Newton stared at him balefully. "Forget the merits of camping. Check the bodies!"

"I'm getting there!" Reuben's attention was caught by the map. "They've got Ravens' Wood and the castle marked on here, as well as Gull Island and White Haven Museum." He frowned as he leaned closer. "And the girls' shops." He winced. They wouldn't appreciate him calling them *girls*, but it wasn't like they were there to hear him.

Newton was at his side in seconds. "Briar's too?"

"Yes!" Reuben stared at Newton, trying not to smirk. "You worried about her?"

"Don't start! Go and check the bodies."

Reuben headed to the bed, and studied the young couple who were barely covered by a thin sheet. "They've both got some great tattoos."

"What about the cause of death? There's not a mark on them, is there?"

"Other than their hideous bloodshot eyes, no." Reuben ran his hands across the bodies, inches from the skin, but just like the other day, he felt nothing. "Not a trace of magic, or anything remotely unusual." He moved closer to the man, spotting an unusual tattoo on his chest. "But that's a magical symbol of protection. It's a bit like the ones we got last year."

"Didn't save them, though."

Reuben pulled his phone from his pocket. "Some symbols offer specific protection. Mind if I take a photo?" Newton shook his head, and Reuben took pictures of some other unusual symbols he could see on their exposed limbs, on the woman as the well as the man. "I can't feel magic, but," Reuben looked around at the cramped space, his head ducked slightly so he didn't hit the roof, "it does feel heavy in here... Sort of gloomy. I'm not sure if that's the van, or something else." He closed his eyes, focussing only on his feelings, rather than magic. "Yes. Alex has been talking about a feeling of loss. I think that's what I'm feeling. Although, of course, that could be because it's depressing to be around two young people who've died in their sleep."

"Death does leave a residue all of its own," Newton admitted. "What about some of this magical paraphernalia?"

"The knife by the bed has some interesting symbols on it. Runes to enhance the blade and protect the person who wields it. The metal looks like silver." Returning to the small seating area, Reuben scanned the collection of objects, careful not to touch anything. "Rune scribed candles, a Ouija board, a selection of herbs, sigils inscribed on the walls, and a book on protective runes and symbols. I wonder if there's a standard hunter kit?" he asked, half-joking. "The crossbow looks m ean."

"Very. That didn't do them much good, either."

"There's nothing here that overly worries me," Reuben said, desperate to get out of the hot, smelly van.

"Good."

In seconds Newton hustled him out the door and around the back of the van, out of sight of the local news reporter at the gate with her cameraman.

Reuben took a deep breath of fresh air and pointed at the far wall. "That's Stormcrossed Manor's boundary?"

"Yep. All of the deaths are in a loose circle around the grounds. These two are definitely the closest. It has to be about that place—has to! There's no such thing as coincidences."

"Alex should be there now," Reuben said, suddenly worried. "With Dylan. Neither will have any idea about this." He was already reaching for his phone. "I'll let him know. I'd hate for them to blunder into something."

However, Alex's phone rang and rang, and Reuben shuffled on his feet, increasingly worried.

"He's not answering. Let me try Dylan." But Dylan didn't answer either. He looked at Newton, who was already smoking, a look of intense concentration on his face as he stared at Reuben. "No answer from either of them, and I'm pretty sure they're there! Alex phoned me earlier to say it was all arranged."

"Then we'll go there right now," Newton said, striding around the van. "Keep your head covered and your mask on until we get past Sarah. And say nothing!"

Avery strode through White Haven, wary for anyone unusual approaching her, and suspicious of everyone.

Knowing there were hunters in White Haven who classified anyone who had paranormal powers as a target was, despite her own impressive abilities, unnerving. Frightening, even. She'd placed herself in Helena's position before, imagining how it would feel to be dragged to the stake with villagers chanting for your death, but the threat this morning from the unknown man had made it all too real.

She reached El's shop and entered its dark, atmospheric interior, finding Zoey at the counter. Zoey, despite the heat, looked as immaculate as ever, with not a bead of sweat gathering on her brow, and making Avery all too aware of her own flushed appearance.

She was already lifting the counter. "El is in the back. Are you okay? You look...annoyed."

"I'm furious, actually. Some bloody huge hulk of a man threatened me in my own shop this morning. He reminded me of your visitor yesterday."

Zoey nodded, her dark red lips settling into a pout. "Unfortunately, I missed him and the woman. I don't like to think that El had to face them on her own—not that she needs me, of course."

"No, but support is nice. I hope they don't come back."

"We have added protection here, anyway."

"Good." Avery slid past her, about to open the door to the back room where El made her jewellery, but Zoey spoke again.

"Did you hear about the other two deaths?"

"What? *Two*?" She turned in the tight space, staring at Zoey. "When?"

"Overnight, in a field just outside of White Haven. It's been on the news already, but no details yet. Tell El, will you? I've just seen it on my phone."

Avery's mouth was suddenly dry. "Sure. Shout if you need us."

Zoey nodded, and Avery entered El's workspace, temporarily dazzled by the light. The courtyard beyond was bathed in sunshine, and El was caught in its glow as she sat at the long counter, her head bent over a piece of jewellery. She turned as Avery entered, and smiled. "Hey! Nice to have you visit."

"I wish it was a social call, but I wanted to speak to you about my visitor this morning." She flopped onto a stool. "I have other news, too. Zoey says there have been another two deaths reported."

El turned her back on the bench, the necklace she'd been working on forgotten. "This is terrible. Three nights of death! How long can this go on for?"

"As long as whatever's causing it is still out there, I guess. Let's hope Alex has found a clue this morning."

"Heard anything?"

"Not yet." She pushed those thoughts to the back of her mind for now, hoping he was okay. "However, Dan made a suggestion this morning. Well, a few, actually. He said he thought the most likely creature was a banshee."

"Really? I thought they were Irish and heralded deaths in a family."

"So did I, but Dan said something about supernatural creatures not having boundaries." Avery shrugged. "I guess we should consider it. Anyway, I really wanted to tell you that I had a visitor this morning. A hunter. A big guy with a swagger who accused me of being a witch." She related their encounter, getting more infuriated by the second. "However, I had the last laugh. I hustled him out the door with a nudge of magic, and snagged some of his hair with my door wreath."

El grinned. "Well done! Have you got it with you?"

"No. It's hidden in my attic until I decide what to do with it. I'm trying to decide if he really was threatening me, or just being a dick. Did Sam and Ruby threaten you?"

El took a moment to consider that. "No, actually. He wanted a magical blade and said he was hunting a supernatural killer. He certainly didn't extend that threat to me. He just lied about how he knew about me. And, obviously I pissed him off. Maybe I was a bit abrupt, but he took me by surprise."

"It's his own fault. You can't march into someone's shop, lie about your references, and then demand stuff." Avery leaned back against the wall, watching the play of sunlight on the glass of water on El's workstation before facing her again. "I initially assumed because of what Briar said that they were together, but maybe the bloke who came to see me was not working with the bloke who came to see you."

"Bloody hell. I don't know what's worse. One big group, or separate ones. And Briar's visitor? The woman?"

Avery shrugged. "No idea. But I doubt they're leaving yet, so I would like to find out who they are sooner rather than later. That way we can defend ourselves—if we need to."

"True. Or work with them. We may need their help with our supernatural killer."

"I'd rather not!"

"Me neither, but just considering all angles," El said. "I've also spread the word through the neighbouring shops, asking them to keep an eye out for Sam and Ruby. I'm hoping Newton can find out something from Maggie, too."

Avery stood. "Somebody has to know something, and White Haven is not that big. We'll see them again. I'm going to Briar's next to ask about her visitor. If we three have been identified as witches, then we might get more hunters. Especially once news of this morning's deaths gets around."

"How many hunters do you think there are, Avery?" El looked amused, a dimple creasing her cheek. "An army of them?"

Avery knew she was beginning to sound paranoid, but couldn't ignore what they knew. "Harlan is in The Orphic Guild, and they hunt paranormal and occult objects, and we know Gabe and Shadow have been getting involved in other areas of the occult, especially that ominous Black Cronos group. And remember that underground auction house that Newton and Caspian went to in London? I don't think we can be naive enough to think there isn't a lot more supernatural stuff going on than we're aware of. And White Haven is splashed across the news right now. There are bound to be more hunters, and they may well come here." She felt even more certain of it now that she'd said it out loud.

El nodded, her smile fading. "You're right. Be careful, Avery. See you in The Wayward Son later. We need strategies, and I think better over a pint."

Avery laughed. "Don't we all!"

Dylan couldn't quite work out what was going on with Alex, but he knew it wasn't good.

He'd locked eyes with the old woman, Tamsyn, who was like a wizened, dark bat in the corner of the room, and hadn't spoken for several seconds. For one horrible moment, Dylan wondered if he was having one of his psychic visions. He crept forward to watch him discreetly, but Alex was wide awake, his eyes searching hers. And then he blinked and sat back on his heels, turning instead to the girl, Beth, and Rosa, who still cradled her.

"How long has she been like this?" Alex asked.

"I'd just walked in to find her for lunch," Rosa said, fighting back tears. "She was on the floor, and—" she broke off, looking up at Tamsyn. Her gaze hardened. "Why didn't you call me? How long?"

Tamsyn grunted, a look of disgust on her face as she stared at Rosa. "You worry too much. It has been happening for minutes only. 'Tis the sight. But you know that—or should, if you'd remember your heritage."

"*Heritage?*" Rosa's voice rose to almost a screech. "It's a curse! What have you done to her?"

Dylan didn't have a clue what to say or do, but he felt a chill run through him at Tamsyn's expression. *The sight? The girl was a seer?* That was different to Alex.

Alex, fortunately, stepped in, laying a hand on Rosa's arm, while studiously avoiding looking at Tamsyn. "Tamsyn hasn't done anything. If it runs in your family, you must know that. It means your daughter sees the future—or things beyond our ken. It should pass soon."

Rosa dragged her gaze from Tamsyn to stare at Alex, before turning to Dylan. "Who's this?"

"My friend, Alex. The one I mentioned. He's been to the graveyard with me this morning. He's really good at this type of thing. You can trust him, Rosa."

Rosa's pulse was beating in her throat like a trapped bird, and he could see her wrestling with what to do. She was terrified, seemingly out of her depth, which was odd if the sight ran in her family. However, Dylan said nothing, and he waited, holding his breath, hoping she wouldn't throw them out. Finally, her shoulders dropped. "What do I do?"

Dylan looked to Alex, and he gestured to the old sofa under the window, bathed in the weak light that struggled through the grimy panes. "Let's put her there for now."

Without waiting for Rosa's permission, Alex lifted Beth and carried her across the room, placing her down gently. He brushed her hair from her forehead, and then placed his hand several inches above her head. Rosa crouched on the floor next to Beth, holding her hand.

Dylan watched from across the room, and then noticed Max hanging back by the door, transfixed by his sister. Clearly worried, he then stared at his great-grandmother. There was no sign of affection there. Just wariness.

Dylan watched Tamsyn, too. She was making a pot of tea, ignoring everyone—almost. She was keeping an eye on Alex out of the corner of her eye. Not Beth or Rosa. In fact, she seemed to radiate disdain for Rosa. And for all of her diminutive size and wizened appearance, Tamsyn carried power—especially in her flashing, beetle-black eyes. She was about five feet tall, her shoulders rounded, her hair an iron grey. It was pulled back in a tight bun on her head, but tendrils escaped, floating about her face that was as wrinkled as on old apple. Her clothes were ancient too, and despite the heat, a light knitted shawl was draped around her shoulders.

Dylan wasn't sure filming would be a good idea, as much as he wanted to, so he just studied the room instead. Everything was old and dilapidated, far more so than the main part of the house. An old, blackened range virtually filled one wall, and a chipped Belfast sink was set into a wooden countertop under the window. The kitchen cupboards were old, the paint peeling, and the floor was covered in cracked tiles, grimy in places. Herbs lined the deep windowsills, and hung from old macrame plant holders, placing the room in a murky green twilight.

Despite the stifling hot day outside, the room was cold. *No wonder Rosa was having problems. Stormcrossed Manor was...odd, and Tamsyn was even odder.* Alex, Rosa, and Beth seemed locked in a tableau under the window, and Dylan felt like he was in a snow globe without the snow.

A knocking sound from somewhere in the house disturbed his thoughts, and for one exciting moment, Dylan thought that spirits were manifesting, and then he heard shouts, and realised someone was at the front door. Relieved to have an excuse to leave the room, Dylan said, "I'll get it."

When he reached the front door and flung it open, Newton was standing with his fist raised, ready to hit the door again.

Dylan stepped back, allowing him inside. "Newton! Why are you here?"

Newton didn't answer at first, instead shouting along the front of the house, "Reuben!" Then he turned to Dylan. "There have been another two deaths, and I was worried about you and Alex."

"Were you? Why?"

"Because the deaths are in a field next to these grounds!" Newton stared down the hall suspiciously, sniffing like a bloodhound.

In seconds Reuben appeared at his side, huffing with relief. "Thank the Gods, Dylan! You had us worried." He looked over Dylan's shoulder. "Why aren't you answering your phone, and where's Alex?"

"Will you two chill out? I didn't hear you call! Maybe it's the reception in the old part of the house. It's a bit rundown there, and has thick walls."

"More rundown than here?" Reuben grimaced as he followed Newton inside, shutting the door behind him. "Holy shit! Look at this place!"

"Hold on, Newton!" Dylan said, restraining Newton, who was already pushing past him. "Listen to me. Something odd is happening, and you need to be prepared before we go in."

He quickly summarised Beth's condition and Tamsyn's odd behaviour.

Reuben immediately asked, "Is she a witch? Does she have magic?"

"I don't know, but Alex looked freaked out when he saw her. Now he's just focussing on Beth. Follow me."

Chapter Twelve

Briar was in her herb room making more candles, but she was feeling restless, wishing she was doing more than just topping up her supplies, especially when her customers that day had come in with news of two more deaths.

Panic was spread through the town, and there was nothing her coven could do to alleviate it. She kept running through types of paranormal creatures that might cause such unusual deaths, and when that was exhausted, she started reviewing spells that someone could be using. But all she was getting was a headache. What she wanted was a massage and to see Hunter again, but those things weren't going to happen any time soon, and once again she pondered how long their relationship could last. And when that happened, her thoughts always drifted to Newton.

It was with relief when she heard Avery crash through the door looking agitated, her red hair streaming behind her. "Another two deaths, Briar! We have to do something!"

"I know, but what?" She straightened up, placing the pan down on the counter, and then said a final spell over her candles, one that helped to calm and relax. She also sent it in Avery's direction, as well as wafting it over herself. "I think we both need this, Avery! Besides, we don't know if the two new deaths are connected yet."

"They better be!" Avery said, alarmed. "Or there's more than one killer in White Haven." Avery forced a laugh as she inhaled the calming scent. "I've let that man get to me. And the town. It has a vibe. Everyone's antsy!" She sagged against the counter, pushing her hair over her shoulder. "I'm trying to be positive, but failing. Perhaps Alex's visit to Stormcrossed Manor will answer some questions."

"Oh, good. He managed to get hold of Dylan, then?" Then she reconsidered what Avery had said. "Hold on! What man?"

"I had a visitor this morning, too. Another hunter—well, I presume that's what he was."

She described her encounter while Briar put the kettle on. It wasn't just a calming candle and spell they needed. One of Eli's amazing teas was also in order. The brew was finished by the time Avery had told her story, and Briar passed her a cup, hustling them both out into the tiny but sunny courtyard.

"So," Briar said, summarising, "you're wondering if the hunters have different agendas."

"I'm starting to." Avery eased back into the wicker chair, visibly relaxing. "Okay. As soon as I get back, I'll do a finding spell. I want to know where that bloke is and whether he's working with anyone."

"If you can. If they hunt the paranormal, they may have some level of occult protection that our spells can't penetrate."

"Maybe, but if I don't try, I won't know. El's put the word out to her neighbouring shops to keep watch for the new arrivals. I might do the same."

"That's a good idea. I'll speak to the shops next to me, too. And of course, Eli is keeping watch. But," Briar leaned forward, noting the determined set to Avery's jaw, "if you find him, don't go after him alone! These people are dangerous...whether they're after us or not." She thought about her encounter with the woman again. "My visitor had this air about her—power and knowledge. In other circumstances I might have liked her, but instead I'm just wary. And something else has struck me. Say they are here to hunt *anything* paranormal, what could that be? I mean, could they hunt for spriggans? Could they try to kill the spirit of giants?" Her thoughts flew to one of her favourite places in White Haven, and overwhelming despair flooded through her. Suddenly, her breath was shallow and rapid, and she felt she couldn't get enough oxygen. "What about Ravens' Wood? All sorts of things lurk in there! And also Shadow!"

"Is that tea not working?" Avery asked, sipping her own. "Shadow is more lethal than anything I know, and I doubt could be easily hunted by humans. And Ravens' Wood? It would swallow them whole!"

"Sorry. You're right. I don't know what came over me." Briar blinked away the sudden gloom that had descended upon her, suddenly aware of the bright sunshine again. She was normally positive, calm, and confident. *Where had that come from?*

She looked across at Avery and found her staring at her, cup suspended halfway to her mouth. "Are you okay, Briar?"

"Yes!" She gulped down her tea, almost scalding her mouth in the process. "I can come with you, if you find where he is. The hunter, I mean. I'm sure Eli can manage on his own for a while. Although..." As competent and strong as Eli was, she actually hated the thought of leaving him alone. *Who knew what these people were capable of?*

Her worry and uncertainty must have been obvious, because Avery reached forward and squeezed her arm. "Leave it with me. If I need you, I'll call."

Alex watched Beth, wondering how much longer she would remain in the seer state, and frustrated that he was powerless to do anything about it. Her lips moved as if she was trying to speak, but he couldn't hear anything, even though he lowered his ear close to her lips.

Rosa broke the silence. She was kneeling on the floor, Beth's hands in her own, watching her daughter anxiously. "I had hoped this wouldn't happen. That it would skip her, as it has skipped me."

Alex repressed a sigh. Rosa looked terrified, and she was clearly in denial about her family's heritage. "So, you knew this was a possibility."

Her lips settled in a thin line. "Of course. But she's so young..."

Alex decided honesty was best. "You know that the sight can skip generations. Sometimes it's stronger in the male line, others in female. And sometimes it starts very young."

Tamsyn's harsh croak interrupted them. "Like it did with me. She's a true McCarthy."

McCarthy? Alex barely had time to think about that before Rosa responded angrily, shooting Tamsyn an accusatory stare. "You shouldn't be pleased about this. It's a horrible thing to have to suffer."

"It's a gift."

"A curse."

"Not if she controls it. You are a fool to pretend otherwise."

Rosa stood up, facing her grandmother, her fists clenched. "How is it a gift? You have barely left this place in decades! It falls to ruin around you!"

"Not because of the sight. Because I choose to stay here."

Alex watched the women glare at each other, and wondered just what was going on here. Rosa clearly knew more than she was letting on, despite her attempt to appear otherwise. *And Tamsyn? Well, she was the key. And maybe Beth.* He'd come back to the name "McCarthy" later.

"Something happened here recently," he said to both of them. "Something that *you*—" he directed at Rosa, feeling his anger rise, "knew enough about to be worried, but did not fully disclose to Dylan and Ben." Both women dragged their gaze away from each other and glared at Alex; he could feel Tamsyn's stare like a weight in his chest. However, he forced himself to look at her now, stealing himself against her power. "And you, Tamsyn, *knew* this would happen, and you didn't warn Rosa. You might have even encouraged it."

"You can't change fate." Her black eyes bore into his, and he felt his soul wilt under her stare. "She's powerful, even though she's so young. The Gods have blessed her."

Before Alex could comment further, he heard voices at the door, and realised Dylan had returned with Newton and Reuben. He turned away from Tamsyn, eyeing the others with relief, especially Reuben.

Reuben strode across the room, covering it quickly with his long legs, and crouched next to him. "What's happening?"

"It seems that the sight runs through this family, and Beth has inherited it." He looked at the women. "This is the first time it's happened?"

"Yes!" Rosa answered straightaway.

Tamsyn huffed. "No. It happened on Sunday. After the storm."

Rosa rounded on Tamsyn again. "You should have told me! I'm her mother!"

"And you would have done *what*?" she sneered. "Things are in motion that you wouldn't understand."

Newton strode between them, forcing Rosa behind him. "Like what? Death?"

Newton towered over Tamsyn, but she glared up at him regardless, her sneer now directed at him. "The fates will have their way."

"Fate or you?"

"I am a conduit, and so is Beth, now."

"A conduit for what?"

Tamsyn fell silent, eyes on Beth.

Newton repeated the question. "A conduit for *what*?"

Tamsyn looked up at Newton, her lips twisting with dislike, but whether at Newton or the situation, Alex couldn't tell. "The past."

Alex exchanged an uneasy glance with Reuben, his thoughts reeling. *What the hell kind of an answer was that?*

Suddenly, Beth screamed and sat up, breaking the uneasy silence that had fallen, and Alex almost stumbled back in shock. She was hysterical, her eyes still white, her scream resonating around the room, and then she yelled, "She is coming! She is coming!" She sounded absolutely terrified.

Alex's skin prickled, and he saw Reuben recoil in shock, too. Rosa stepped back, staring at her daughter in horror.

But as soon as Beth finished shouting, the seer state ended. Beth fell backwards onto the sofa, eyes closed, unconscious.

Avery lowered a flame to the hunter's hair in her silver bowl, a selection of crushed herbs beneath it, and cast the finding spell.

The sharp, pungent odour of burnt hair filled the air, quickly followed by the scent of herbs, and for a few moments the smoke rose in a straight line. Then, as Avery repeated the spell, the smoke moved across the map of White Haven and the surrounding area.

Avery held her breath, hoping that it would work. The unidentified hunter knew she had his hair, but could he stop her finding him? Did he even want to?

The fine trail of smoke wound across the map like a sightless snake, passing across White Haven and its outskirts, until it pooled in West Haven, above an area she knew well.

The House of Spirits.

She yelled into the attic, "Fuck you, Rupert!"

Medea and Circe, who had been sleeping on the table and watching her through lidded eyes, leapt off the surface as she simultaneously jumped to her feet.

Damn it! Was Rupert responsible for the hunters arriving in White Haven? Did he know them all? Or just this one?

One way or another, she would find out.

She started pacing, trying to decide what to do next. Briar was right, though; she shouldn't go alone. However, she still hadn't heard from Alex, El and Briar were in their shops, and Reuben might well be at the nursery. But West Haven was close to Harecombe.

She'd call Caspian.

He picked up quickly. "Avery, everything okay?"

"No." She quickly summarised what had happened. "Everyone else is busy. Can you meet me at Rupert's? The spell suggests that the hunter is somewhere close to his house. Maybe even in it?"

"Of course. I'm at home right now. Why don't you fly to mine? We'll drive there together. That way we can talk about what to do."

"Perfect. On my way now."

Chapter Thirteen

El watched with disbelief as Sam Clarke, the grizzled hunter, entered her shop just after lunch, a wary expression in his eyes.

Two young girls were browsing the earring racks, but their presence didn't seem to bother him, and he walked to the counter, glancing briefly at Zoey before focussing on El. "I'm wondering if I can talk to you in private."

El kept her voice low. "And why would I want to do that?"

"I believe we got off on the wrong foot the other day."

"That's one way of putting it."

He ignored her sarcasm. "I need your help."

"With a blade?"

"Amongst other things."

El was reluctant to take this man into her workspace, but equally knew they couldn't talk there. Her shop was too small, and the two girls were already glancing over at them. Besides, he looked contrite.

She turned to Zoey. "Okay if I pop out for a bit? We'll go to the Seaspray Café."

Zoey ignored Sam. "Are you sure you want to talk to *that* man?"

"I think I should." She smiled to reassure her. "I'll be fine."

Zoey glared at Sam. "If she's not back in half an hour, I'll call the police."

Sam saluted her. "Scout's honour."

El couldn't help but smile as she lifted the counter and walked to the door. "Follow me."

In a few minutes' time they were seated in the corner of the café, surrounded by the murmur of locals and holidaymakers that would provide them with privacy.

"Where's your side-kick?" El asked, stirring sugar into her coffee. "Ruby, isn't it?"

Sam had ordered a pot of tea, and he was squeezing the tea bag to make it extra strong. She grimaced. He noticed her expression and grinned. "Not a tea fan?"

"Not a fan of the stewed variety."

"It's the best type of tea. I like it strong enough to stand my spoon up in. But you asked about Ruby. She's following up on some leads."

"That sounds official, like you're a professional."

"That's because I am. Or, I should say, we are. We hunt for a living, and I've been doing it a long time. I've been here a few times before, but that was many years ago."

"You've been to White Haven?"

"White Haven, Harecombe, Mevagissey. All along the coast." He poured his tea that was now almost black it was so strong, and dumped three sugars into it. "Cornwall has always had its supernatural side, but lately... Well..." He raised eyebrows that had clearly never, ever been groomed, and sipped his tea. *At least*, El reflected, *despite his unkempt appearance, he did wash his clothes and himself.*

"There's no doubt," she admitted, "that we've had a lot going on, but we dealt with it, and we'll deal with this."

He smiled like she'd walked into a trap. "Two interesting statements. You *are* used to dealing with the paranormal—proving my information about you was correct—and you said 'we'. I suspected that. But the most important question is, do you even know what *this* is?"

For all that Sam had pissed her off the day before, she was now extremely intrigued by him and the other hunters, and she was beginning to warm to him. But she was also over the cloak and dagger stuff. "No, do you?"

He wiggled his hand. "We suspect, but we don't know."

"Go on."

"So many dead in such a short time reminds me of something I encountered years ago—something other hunters were involved with, too. A banshee."

El stared at him as she recollected what Avery had mentioned, almost dismissively. "It's something we've considered, but it sounded improbable."

"Why?"

"We thought they announced the death of a family member. The banshee didn't kill them. Their scream was associated with their grief, not a method of killing."

"Traditionally, that *is* the case, but in that particular instance, the banshee's grief was so great, she killed accidentally."

"Accidentally? How?"

"It was something to do with its scream. It's so powerful that it affected the brain of those who heard it." He shrugged. "It sounds unlikely, I know, but that's the conclusion we came to, and it fit the circumstances."

"We know of someone who has heard it many times, but hasn't died."

Sam's eyes widened. "Someone has heard screams? I must be right, then. It is a banshee!"

El was still unwilling to commit to the idea. "Perhaps, although no one has seen it yet. And the person who hears the screams hasn't died, just loads of other people, who may or may not have heard screams. We obviously can't ask them—they aren't alive to report it."

"This witness hasn't died *yet*. Who is this person?"

"I can't say. This person sought help from friends, and I can't betray a confidence. Death is inevitable, you say?"

"Perhaps."

"Shit." El was suddenly fearful of the fact that Alex was having visions that might involve banshees and their screams, and was now at the manor with Dylan. *Could a vision-scream kill? What if they heard the screams in the day, too?* "Okay, say it is a banshee. What has triggered it now? Just the storm? An impending family death that has supercharged the creature? Some change in circumstances has to have manifested it!"

"Agreed, but I can't help you there." Sam topped his cup up with the strong brew and added more sugar. "I haven't heard the screams or seen the creature. It was just the reports that made me curious. Like I said earlier, Ruby is investigating now."

El wanted to trust him. He seemed sincere, and his previous experience was uncannily like their own, but she couldn't ignore what had happened to Avery. *Perhaps Sam had another agenda.* "Are you working with other hunters?"

His eyes narrowed. "No. I only work with Ruby. Why?"

"My friend was threatened this morning by one."

Sam froze. "Threatened by a hunter?"

"Yes."

"Got a name?"

"No. But he was big, apparently, with a long, knotted scar down his forearm."

"Fuck it. Titus is here already."

El felt suddenly cold, and hoped Avery was okay. "You know him?"

"Unfortunately. He doesn't differentiate between the vast number of paranormal creatures and those with supernatural abilities out there. He considers them all a threat."

"Unlike you, I hope?"

"Of course. I wouldn't be sitting here with a witch otherwise, would I?"

"I guess not. A witch you want to buy a blade from."

"Aye." Sam leaned across the table, lowering his voice. "We knew there were witches here. I have connections in London. You were mentioned by other witches I know."

"Me, specifically?" El asked, shocked.

"All of you."

"We don't know any witches in London."

"Well, they know you. You've impressed them. Anyway, I knew I could find you here, and it didn't take long to track down your shop. I shouldn't have mentioned Dante, because you're right—I don't know him, but I knew you worked with him. However, I *do* need a blade. If we are dealing with a banshee, they are hard to kill, but a silver blade mixed with copper and lead and a specific set of symbols would do the job—as well as be effective against other creatures."

El was becoming more and more worried. "You're sure it's a banshee?"

"As sure as I can be at this stage."

"But you don't know where it is?"

For the first time, uncertainty entered Sam's eyes. "No. We're trying to narrow it down, but so far it's eluding us."

El was pretty sure she knew exactly where it was, but was unwilling to share her knowledge about Stormcrossed Manor with Sam. The last thing any of them needed was him storming in and potentially making things worse. There were also other things she was curious about. "Why haven't you brought a blade with you? Or asked another witch to make one?"

"I hear your blades are the best. And this banshee is on your doorstep, and she is *strong*. I figured you'd want help."

"Perhaps, but I need to speak to my friends first. Trust me, whatever's going on, banshee or not, we will find out."

"Look, I should be honest," he said, shuffling in his seat. "The blade I need has other properties you may not like. It can cut through protection spells."

"Protection spells? Why do you need a blade that does that?"

"I don't. It just so happens that the sigils work against them, too."

"I don't like that at all!"

"Of course you don't. You witches like your protection spells."

"Which is why no one else would make it for you!"

"But no one else has a banshee running around town killing people, either."

He had a point, and it put El in an impossible situation. If they had no other way of getting rid of that banshee, they needed the knife. But it came with horrible consequences.

Sam shrugged, looking apologetic. "I promise I won't use it on any of you. At least I told you all of this. I could have kept it quiet."

"I suppose you could have."

He sipped his tea, looking amused. "I don't need your permission to hunt here, by the way. I will deal with the banshee, whether you help or not. I'd rather have the blade, but there are other options."

El didn't like the idea of hunters running around White Haven without knowing what they were doing, and had a feeling they'd have to work with them whether they wanted to or not. By the grin that was spreading across Sam's face, she knew he knew that, too.

He laughed. "You're protective of this place, and that's good. Maybe if more towns had a coven of witches protecting them, there'd be less need for people like me. Fortunately, that's not the case, or I'd starve."

Another thought struck El. "Is someone paying you to be here?"

"No. I accept paid jobs, obviously, but others I take on for the thrill of it."

"A banshee is a thrill?"

"I enjoy my work. And killing something that has already killed so many is a pleasure—and a necessity."

She sipped her coffee and wished she'd bought a piece of cake, too. "Look, I still don't understand, not really. Why are you here now? And why are so many other hunters? It surely can't be just about a banshee?"

"No, it's not. The group, Ghost OPS, has made everything here very public. News reports have made it to the national level. Things that might have passed under the radar before aren't a secret anymore. The events on Gull Island, the pirate treasure on the news... It's all fodder for the supernatural hunters. These deaths over the weekend went round the community like wildfire. And like I said about Titus...other hunters are not so discerning as us." His phone rang and he glanced at it, frowned, and said, "It's Ruby. I need to answer this."

"Of course."

He left the shop to take the call, standing just outside the entrance, and El studied his grizzled demeanour through the window. Now that she was talking to him, he felt genuine enough. He seemed earnest and determined, and she knew he and Ruby weren't going to just leave, so maybe making an alliance was the best thing to do. As for the blade, she'd never heard of one that could kill a banshee. But why would she? She'd never even considered having to deal with one before. She could make two—one for him and one for herself. Although, she did have the Empusa's sword. A banshee was a type of spirit, after all, so surely the Empusa's sword would work. She shook her head as she mulled over her options. *Best to play safe and make another blade.* She would hate to presume and find that she was wrong. She also wondered if she should introduce him to her coven. However, another idea struck her. It sounded like he knew who most of them were, but if he didn't and it was a trap to meet the other witches, then she'd put them all in danger... She shook her head, annoyed with herself. The events with Mariah had made her paranoid.

As she continued to watch Sam, it was clear that something was agitating him. He started to pace, his lips tightened and his eyes narrowed, and he swung around to stare through the window at her. In seconds he ended the call, strode back into the shop, and dropped into his chair. He leaned across the table. "The most recent two deaths are hunters."

"The ones in the camper van?" El couldn't keep the surprise out of her voice. "How do you know?"

"Their van is distinctive, and there was enough of a shot of it on the news for Ruby to tell."

"You knew them?"

"Well enough. So, what's it to be, Elspeth? Will you help us? Because it seems to me that with another two deaths added to the list, we are all running out of options."

Chapter Fourteen

Caspian stopped at the bottom of the road that led to Rupert's home, the House of Spirits, and studied the cars parked along the kerb.

"Did you see what vehicle the hunter was in?"

Avery shook her head, radiating annoyance. "No. He just walked in, swaggering like a bully boy."

Caspian grinned at her outraged expression. "He didn't swagger out like one though, did he?"

She twisted in her seat to look at him, allowing herself a smile for the first time since she'd arrived on his drive. "No, I guess not."

"That you managed to get some of his hair is brilliant, but how accurate do you think that spell was? Sometimes, the area identified can be broad."

"I know, but I used a detailed, local map."

"And," he added, voicing what he'd thought earlier, but not wanting to disappoint Avery, "the hunter could have been in this area for reasons other than Rupert."

Avery snorted. "Don't give me that coincidence bullshit."

"As if I would dream of it!"

Avery rubbed her neck as if to ease tight muscles, and once again, Caspian had the urge to touch her. *Damn it.* He thought he'd squashed those feelings, but clearly not well enough.

"Plus," she added, oblivious to his thoughts, "I literally did that spell fifteen minutes ago, tops. He must be close."

"Trust me," he said, putting the car into gear and cruising down the street, "I'm as anxious to find him as you. These hunters are worrying me, and I don't like my friends being threatened." *Especially you.*

They drove down the road in silence, loitering for seconds only outside Rupert's house, and then he turned the car around.

"I think he'd have an older car," Avery said, "although I know that's presumptuous."

"Let's head around the back. These houses all look over fields, don't they?"

He navigated the narrow lanes around West Haven, taking the wrong turn once, before he found the right one that led along the back of Rupert's street. He slowed down, trying to peer through the hedge to the field beyond. He had faith in Avery's magic, despite the unlikely link. However, there was also no getting away from the fact that Rupert had a *thing* about the White Haven Witches. Particularly Avery.

"There." He stopped and pointed to where there was a gap in the hedge. "That's the back of his place. A couple of vans are parked in the field. And," he squinted, not quite believing his eyes. "That looks like Rupert, talking to someone by the van."

Avery virtually leaned over him to see through the window, a waft of the herbs she'd used for the spell drifting from her clothes and hair. Her jaw tightened. "That bastard!"

"Hold on! We can't even see who he's talking to yet..." But then he trailed off as a brawny man with long hair stepped into view. "Is that him?"

Avery, however, was already halfway out of the car.

Caspian leapt out too, racing around the car to stand in front of her. "Avery! What are you doing?"

"I am going to ask him what the hell he thinks he's doing!" Her eyes blazed as she tried to push past him.

Caspian didn't budge, keeping his voice low and reasonable. "And then what? Can we at least discuss what we're going to do?" He glanced behind him at the high, thick hedge that protected them from view, hoping they were far enough away from the hunter and Rupert not to be heard, either. For added protection, he said a spell to muffle them. "You can't hex him! And you don't want to give Rupert the satisfaction, either."

She faltered, her shoulders dropping, although her fists were still clenched, and a wind was already whipping around her, lifting her hair, and swirling her long skirt. "I suppose you have a point."

"Why reveal that we know where he is? We keep that up our sleeve...and watch. And wouldn't it be nice to piss Rupert off?"

The wind dropped, and reason returned to her eyes. "Yes, I suppose that is a good suggestion."

Caspian smirked. He'd heard Alex talk very briefly of Avery's wild temper with the tone of someone who'd learned to cope with it. He could see what he meant.

"Don't smirk at me, Caspian Faversham!"

"Many apologies, madam. Can we get back in the car?"

"But I want to hear what they're saying!"

"Not now!"

At the risk of being hexed himself, Caspian grabbed her elbow and steered her back to the car. Fortunately, she didn't fight him, and he shut the door quietly as he repeated his spell. He'd left the engine running with the low purr of a well-maintained vehicle, and he drove a short distance up the lane before stopping again.

Avery was staring behind at the field as if she could still see them, but as soon as he halted, she glared at him. "I want to eavesdrop!"

"It's broad daylight, you twit! A shadow spell wouldn't work, and we can't fly to the van. Someone else might be in it. However," he confessed, also now twisting in his seat to look behind him at the offending spot, "I'd like to discover what they're plotting."

Avery grinned. "We could come back tonight!"

"Maybe. It looks like he's camping there. But he might be out hunting later."

"True. And he's likely to have his camp protected in some way." Avery slumped back in her seat, a look of intense concentration on her face. "There has to be another way!"

"How much of his hair have you got left?"

"Enough to do the spell once more."

"Well, whatever protection he might have over the camp, or himself, hasn't stopped your finding spell from working," Caspian mused. "Let's wait until nightfall and do the spell again. We can then follow him to where he is. He'll be local, and we may even be able to use witch-flight to find him."

"Of course! Sorry. I'm being thick-headed." She smiled ruefully. "Rupert just bugs me so much, I don't think straight."

"That's okay. I'll come to your place tonight, and then we can go wherever we need to together. What about the others?"

"I'm not sure what they'll be doing, and I haven't heard from Alex." She frowned and checked her watch. "He's been at the manor for a while now."

"Still busy, I'm sure. He'll be okay." Caspian wanted to hear everyone's progress, particularly what was going on at the manor. "What if I come to the pub later? You'll all be there, right?"

"You know us so well!"

"Excellent. See you then. You carry on home now—I can drive back alone."

She stared at him suspiciously. "Only if you promise you *are* going home! Don't do anything without me."

He smiled. "So paranoid. Of course I am."

In seconds, Avery had vanished, and Caspian sat in the car for a few minutes more, watching the field in his rear-view mirror. There was something very unsavoury about Rupert, and Caspian had every intention of finding out his connection to the hunters.

The question was, how?

Every fibre of Newton's body was bristling with anger. There was something completely off about this whole house, especially the tiny old woman with black eyes who stared at him implacably. Like he was a worm beneath her feet.

Why wasn't she more concerned about her granddaughter, who had just emitted an ear-piercing shriek? And who the hell was the *she* that was coming?

While the others tended to Beth, he squared up to the old woman, Dylan next to him. "You said you are a conduit for the past? What does that mean?"

She assessed him, from his toes to the top of his head. "You're a policeman."

"Detective Inspector Newton, to you. I'm here investigating two deaths on the doorstep of this house. Answer the question."

She sneered. "Exactly what it sounds like. The storm has stirred up an old presence. It is lonely. It searches for something."

Dylan added, "The presence that came out of the grave. Niamh's grave."

Newton turned to him, startled. "What presence? Whose grave?" He sounded like a jabbering idiot. *Why did everyone seem to know more about what was going on than him?*

Dylan watched Tamsyn while he spoke. "Rosa gave us permission to set up cameras yesterday, and I reviewed them this morning. Something came out of the grave the storm disturbed. It screamed. Nearly deafened me."

"A ghost?" Newton asked.

Dylan glanced at him, shaking his head, before staring at Tamsyn again. "No. Something different. We have theories, but they don't quite make sense."

"Like?"

"A banshee." A light began to kindle in Dylan's eyes as he said softly, "Niamh Trevithick." He addressed Tamsyn. "You said that Beth was a true McCarthy. She was born Niamh McCarthy, wasn't she? Irish?"

Tamsyn gave him a twisted smile. "And what of it?"

"Banshees commonly have Irish roots. Now it makes sense...well, sort of!"

Ever more impatient, Newton scowled. "Dylan! Explain."

"A banshee's scream heralds the death of a family member. The reason she has red eyes is that she weeps constantly, filled with grief for the impending loss of whoever's death she foretells. However, she doesn't kill people." He swallowed, his Adam's apple bobbing. "It doesn't explain why people are dying for seemingly no reason, and it doesn't explain why everyone here is still alive. If she did appear with the storm, why is no one here dead yet?"

Newton's blood ran cold. "A banshee! She's responsible for all those deaths! Those innocent people..."

"Traditionally!" Tamsyn spat. "What do you know of the banshee's ways? Sometimes, the fates have other ideas."

Rosa intervened, her voice full of fury, and Newton turned to see that she was standing, fists clenched and eyes blazing. "A *banshee*? *Fate*? Is this what this is? How does this affect Beth? I thought it was just the sight." She marched across the room. "Tell me!"

Tamsyn scowled. "The sight brings many things, Rosa, and most of it we have no control over. I cannot say what the banshee wants...or how she will achieve it."

Newton rounded on Alex and Reuben. "How do we stop it?"

Beth was now sleeping peacefully on the sofa, and Reuben and Alex had risen to their feet. Reuben shrugged. "We don't know, but we'll find out."

"Before tonight?" Newton asked. "Because otherwise, more people will die!"

Alex exchanged a nervous glance with Reuben, and then stared at Tamsyn. "We might be able to contain it."

"You may as well try to contain the wind," she muttered as she turned away to make a pot of tea.

146

"Well, we have to try." Alex addressed Newton. "Beth will be okay now, so I'm going home. Me and Reuben will work on a way to deal with this. But we'll be back."

"It would be unwise for you to return after dark," Tamsyn warned.

"We have to. Newton, you're coming with us."

"No. I want to look around this place." He studied the old kitchen, wondering what else Tamsyn was concealing.

Alex, however, grabbed his elbow, and then Dylan's, steering them ahead of him and out the door. "Nope. You're leaving. Reuben. Time to go."

Newton hated being manhandled and told what to do, and was about to complain—until he saw the expression on Alex's face. It held a warning, and instead he just nodded. "Fine. I'll do some investigating first, too." Dylan, he noticed, didn't complain at all.

Alex nodded with obvious relief, and then paused in the doorway, calling back to Rosa. "I'll get your number from Dylan and call you later. In the meantime, when Beth wakes, just make sure she eats and drinks."

In a few minutes they were all outside the house, Alex striding down the drive towards his car that was parked next to Dylan's van, and Newton chased after him, Reuben and Dylan on his heels. "Alex! What's going on? You couldn't get me out of that place quick enough."

"Yeah," Dylan said, his camera and tripod under his arm. "What's going on with you and Tamsyn? You looked at her oddly."

Alex wiped his hands across his face, and up close, Newton could see a sheen of sweat on his upper lip, and what seemed to be fear in Alex's eyes.

Reuben appeared to think so, too. He leaned against the side of the van, arms crossed. "You saw something in there. Or felt something?"

Alex looked as if he would deny it, but then he just sighed. "It's Tamsyn. I sensed something in her. A power or a presence or... I don't know right now. I don't know if it's by choice, or whether something has inhabited her."

Newton recoiled. "Possession?"

"Not exactly." Alex stared at the house, as if it would unveil its secrets. "She seemed to be in control of herself. Rosa certainly didn't seem to see anything different in her."

"Unless," Reuben suggested, "whatever it is has been there for years. Rosa only arrived recently, right Dylan?"

"Right. I'll check the date, but weeks only." He adjusted the tripod under his arm, looking back at the house, too. "Is it safe for them to stay?"

"That's a good question," Newton said. "There are two kids in that house. I saw a boy."

"Max," Dylan confirmed. "Nice kid. Lonely, I'd say. Runs wild around the garden. Damn it, Alex, I meant to show you so much more."

"Quite honestly, I've seen enough for now. I meant what I said—we need to contain whatever's here—and by that I mean in Tamsyn, too. Dylan, can you send us that footage of whatever came out of the grave?"

"The banshee, you mean?" Reuben clarified.

Newton remained unconvinced. "If it is one."

"I'd put money on it," Dylan said. "It's a name we all keep circling around. But sure. I'll flick it to you when I get back."

"And me," Newton added, not entirely sure he wanted to see it, but knowing he had to.

Reuben pushed himself off the van. "Alex can drop me home, if that's okay?" Alex nodded. "Great. We can talk possible spells."

"So that's it?" Newton said, disgruntled. He ran his finger along the inside of his sticky collar, cursing the fact that he had to wear a tie in this ridiculously hot weather. "We just leave them in there with a monster?"

"They're unharmed, for now," Alex pointed out. "Trust us. We're on this. But promise me, both of you," he glared at Dylan and Newton, "do not go back there again without us. Watch remotely, Dylan—and tell Ben and Cassie, too."

Dylan nodded. "If you insist."

"I do. Newton?"

"I'm investigating murders."

"Caused by something we do not understand. Newton!" he exclaimed at his protracted silence.

Newton huffed, but he'd be a fool to ignore Alex. "All right! But I'll call you in a few hours." He checked his watch, and then jolted with surprise. "Shit. I should be at the post-mortems."

Fuck it, he thought as he got in the car. This day was going to be extra shit.

Chapter Fifteen

C assie put the phone down and rubbed her eyes.

Her head was pounding from the non-stop phone calls and the beeping of the answering machine, and she leaned back in her chair and swung her legs onto the desk.

"Oh, no. That's a bad sign," Ben called over from behind the computer.

"What is?"

His head popped up over the top, and he nodded at her legs. "You with your feet on the desk. It's a sign that the day has been especially bad."

"Did you hear the endless phone calls and messages? Are you surprised?" She tried not to be resentful. Ben had taken a few calls before diving back into research.

He tapped his earphones that were currently pushed on top of his head, askew. "Not really. It was interfering with my work."

She poked her tongue out at him. "Lucky you. I am *not* on phones tomorrow. I am not a bloody secretary!"

"Of course you're not. Sorry." He looked chastened. "I'll do it tomorrow. Or we'll just put the answering machine on all day. Go on, give me the gist."

She pointed to the map on the wall, now labelled with bright red pins. "All of those are people reporting they've heard screams at night. They are super freaked."

"But not dead."

"I guess not, unless I was communing with their ghosts."

Ben stared at the map. "That's a fair spread around the east side of the moor. And the manor." He untangled himself from his head phones and strode over to the map. "Reuben is reasonably close. That's worrying."

"But you're right. Why aren't those people dead? Why is the scream killing some and not others? You mentioned a banshee earlier, but said it didn't make sense. I thought the banshee's scream was lethal."

Ben shook his head. "No, that's just urban fantasy and myths getting confused. It's a psychic creature that heralds the death of a family member. Its scream is a warning. The scream is supposedly chilling, terrifying even, but it doesn't kill...or shouldn't. And we certainly don't know whether the victims actually heard screams or not. That's pure supposition. Unless we talk to their spirits."

"No, thanks."

"You've got the callers' details, right?"

"Do I look like an imbecile?"

"Sorry." He sat on the edge of her desk. "Times?"

"All between midnight and two in the morning."

"Pattern?"

"Haven't analysed it yet, but I logged time *and* place."

"Good. I'll help you do that now." He checked his watch. "Where's Dylan? He's been gone a while."

"I'm sure he'll be fine. What have *you* found out?"

"On Stormcrossed Manor? Very bloody little, despite my very earnest attempts. The records really aren't accessible to the public. All I know is that it belongs to the Trevithick family, who also built it. The current owner is Tamsyn Pengelly, her married name but of Trevithick descent, and she's old. Rosa is her grandchild."

"Our employer. So, a lot of family history, and potentially no horrible secrets that Rosa is worried we'll discover, or why would she call us?"

The sound of the front door slamming had them both turning around, and Dylan burst into the office looking flushed with excitement. "You won't believe what I have to tell you!"

"So," Reuben said, grabbing two beers from the fridge, popping their caps, and handing Alex one. His old friend looked pale beneath his summer tan, and worry lurked behind his eyes. "I think you need to tell me what's going on."

Alex took a long drink of his beer before he answered. "I have."

"You've told me the basics. Come on. Tell me what you really think. What is lurking in Tamsyn?"

"I don't know!" Alex dropped onto a kitchen chair, looking exhausted. "I'm really not kidding. I can't work it out. All I know is that I sense something. It could be the power of the sight in her. I've never really met a true seer. But," he huffed and tapped his glass, "the sight shouldn't be a presence. It's a psychic ability."

"I get it." Reuben sat astride a chair and leaned on the back of it to stare at Alex. "It's not a *thing*." He thought about Tamsyn's tiny frame. "I suppose I didn't take much notice of her when I walked in. I just headed to your side and Beth. But thinking about it now, she did radiate a kind of dark power. It was sort of hypnotic."

"Exactly!"

"What's the difference between her abilities and what you do? Seers have different skills, right?"

"Yeah, and they can vary—that's my understanding. I have psychic visions. Flashes of the present or future. But they're incomplete, images only, that I have to try and interpret. They can be especially strong if I connect to something."

"And your abilities allow you to connect to someone too, right? Like you did with Gabe?"

Alex nodded. "Yes, and with Avery. But a seer is more of a prophet—they can actually foretell the future." He gave Reuben a lopsided grin. "Or maybe they're just more attuned to their visions than I am."

"But Tamsyn said she was a conduit. What does *that* mean?"

"I don't know. Maybe there's a powerful spirit that's trying to achieve change through Tamsyn. Or maybe it's a another supernatural being that she is a conduit for."

"Does that mean she's the killer? Is she carrying a murderer inside her?"

"Maybe." Alex leaned forward, seeming to throw off his tiredness as he came to a decision. "I meant what I said. While I'm not entirely sure what's going on, it does stem from that house—I'd put money on it. And while I know the word *banshee* is being bandied about, I'm not convinced yet. Whatever it is needs to be contained. We need to throw up a protection spell around that house, designed to keep things in, not out."

"Even though we don't know what that is?"

"Yep."

"That will need all of us, and we'll have to be onsite. It's a big place. That's going to be hard!"

"I know." Alex nodded, and drained his beer. "I need to go through my grimoires, decide what to use."

"You know what would be really good?" Reuben said, thinking of the night of the solstice and the type of magic they had used. "Gemstones. They pack a lot of power when used in the right way. They could enhance our spell. We could put them around the boundary, too."

Alex raised his empty bottle. "Mate! I am impressed."

"I know, I rock. Get it? Rock, gemstone?"

"You're painful," Alex said, laughing as he rose to his feet. "I'm going to pop into the pub, and then head home and consult my grimoire." He paused, his smile vanishing. "The thing is, I'm really worried about Rosa and the kids being in that house tonight. What if tomorrow morning they're all dead? That will be our fault!"

"Actually, it won't be, but I know what you mean." Reuben voiced the thought that had been circling at the back of his mind ever since they'd left Stormcrossed Manor. "I'm going to ask Rosa to stay here with the kids."

Alex dropped into the chair again, staring at him like he'd gone mad. "That's incredibly generous of you. And insane. You don't even know them!"

"I know. But Rosa looked terrified, and furious. Did you feel the tension in that room?" The room had crackled with dislike, and Reuben couldn't imagine how someone could live in that. He liked harmony in his life. Everything else was hard work.

Alex pushed his beer bottle aside and leaned on the table. "We don't know what's going on there...or with Beth. While I appreciate that you want them to be safe, it's risky."

"I know what you're saying about Tamsyn. I felt it, too—well, to a certain degree. But not Beth. Besides, we can keep an eye on her here. Monitor the situation."

"I'm not sure I like the idea at all."

"But you don't want to leave them there, either." Reuben laughed at his friend's worry. "I think them moving here is the safest suggestion out of the two. *If* they'll even come. Rosa doesn't know me and might refuse."

"Ask her with El. Although," Alex wagged a finger at him. "I reckon she'll tell you off and think you've gone mad, too."

Reuben winced, knowing Alex was right. She'd freaked when she found out that Mariah was imprisoned in his cellar, too, but that was for entirely different reasons. "I'll risk it. I'll call El now. When she knows the circumstances, she'll feel the same." Reuben glanced around his state-of-the-art kitchen, thinking there was nothing remotely magical about it. "I'll keep the attic locked. They won't know I'm a witch. I presume we say nothing about the protection spell?"

"No. We can work outside the grounds, so Tamsyn won't know, either."

Reuben felt uncomfortable with the subterfuge, but it was nothing new. He'd hidden his powers all his life. "All right. I'll call you later."

El could barely believe her ears. "You have to be joking, Reuben?"

"No. You know it makes sense!"

"Er, no! You don't know her! And we don't know what's going on in that house! I haven't even been there yet."

Reuben leaned against the wall watching her, arms folded across his chest, eyes wide with innocence. Furious with him, El started pacing around the back room of her shop, which was actually really hard to do because it was very small, and Reuben's tall frame seemed to suck up the remaining space.

She jabbed a finger at him. "You are exasperating!"

"I was rather expecting you to tell me I was a knight in shining armour!"

"You're a pillock!"

"El. Come on! A woman and her two young kids are stuck in spooky Stormcrossed Manor with some unknown entity, and—" he pointed outside at the increasingly cloudy sky, "another storm is coming. I feel it in my bones."

"Even better! A storm started this whole thing!"

"By upending a tree and disturbing a grave. There isn't a bogeyman in the storm." He sighed dramatically. "El! We're going to be casting a spell around that place tonight, trapping something in there. They're at risk."

"They've been at risk for the last three days, and have been absolutely fine."

He stepped forward and held her upper arms gently, making her stop pacing. "I'm not kidding. Once you go to the manor, you'll know what we mean. It has a dark vibe, and Tamsyn is uncanny. She unnerved Alex, and that says a lot."

El looked into Reuben's blue eyes. She always believed you could tell a lot about a person according to their eyes. They really were the windows to the soul. Reuben's were gentle, teasing, laughing, and when he wanted to be, very passionate. But mostly they were kind and generous, and she loved him for that more than anything.

She reached up and touched his cheek. "I'm just worried, and I hate how your home keeps being destroyed. It's only been weeks since your wall was repaired! And now you're inviting danger in again."

"Come to that house with me, and you'll see what I mean. If you say no, then I won't say another word about it."

El sighed. When he was being so reasonable, how could she refuse? Besides, she had something she'd need his support with.

"Okay. Fine. I suppose there's something I need to tell you, too."

His eyes widened and he gave a knowing smile. "Really? What have you been up to?"

"I met up with Sam Clarke, and agreed that we should all work together."

His arms folded across his chest again and hers felt suddenly cold after his warm touch. "Really? And did you discuss that with any of us? I don't think so. Let me check my messages." He looked at his phone, pretending to scroll through it. "No missed phone calls. How odd!"

"Piss off! It seemed the right thing to do. He made a good case. And he thinks it's a banshee, too."

He smirked. "I trust you, my love. It's a shame the trust doesn't go both ways. Do I get to meet this Sam?"

"Yes, actually. I was going to arrange a meeting for all of us, but time seems to be an issue now. Perhaps just you."

"How considerate! I'd suggest my place, but I'll have Rosa there..."

"Let's use my shop. I'll arrange it for tomorrow."

"In the meantime," he checked his watch, "you are about to close. May I escort you to Stormcrossed Manor?"

El couldn't help laughing and she jabbed him in the chest. "You are very bloody cheeky, Reuben Jackson!"

"Charming and handsome, actually." He grabbed her hand and kissed it. "When we have them settled, I'll buy you a curry."

"You're presuming a lot!"

He stopped teasing. "That's because I know you'll agree. Let's boo boo."

Chapter Sixteen

A very found Alex hunched over their grimoires in the attic room, the aromatic scent of incense curling like a djinn in the warm air.

All of the windows were open, but the room felt stifling, and no wonder. The air was getting stickier as the heat intensified with the cloud cover. Dark clouds amassed on the horizon, brooding over a flat, calm sea the colour of pewter. The sun had already disappeared behind them, and the atmosphere felt suitably ominous.

"Hey gorgeous," she said, kissing him on the cheek as she sat next to him. She hadn't spoken to him since he left for work that morning, and he looked at her, distracted. "How was Stormcrossed Manor?"

"A bloody nightmare." He proceeded to explain exactly why, and Avery sagged against the chair back, thinking that the whole situation sounded horrible. "So, here I am, trying to find the best kind of protection spell to seal in something decidedly Otherworldly. In theory, it's just like we use to keep out malevolent spells or people with ill intent."

"Any luck?"

He nodded, and pushed his original family grimoire across to her. "This one. It seals in spirits and," he squinted at the page, "*creatures that dwell on different planes of existence.*"

Avery studied the spell. It was towards the beginning of Alex's family grimoire, and as such the spells were written in ink, in a crabbed but ornate hand, and in middle English, which made it tricky to translate. Fortunately, all of the witches had become skilled with this type of translation, because so many of the really old spells were written in it. Later spells contained flowery phrases and ingredients that sounded terrifying, but were actually just odd names for plants. Eye of newt for example, was only mustard seed.

"It looks good. I presume we'll do it tonight?"

"Twilight, I thought. Dark enough so no one notices our witchy behaviour, but not late enough to put ourselves at risk." He winked, but his smile looked forced. "Especially with hunters around. They might even be circling Stormcrossed Manor."

"Okay. Then I need to speak to Caspian to discuss our plans."

As soon as she said it, she knew it had come out wrong, because Alex's face darkened. "You have plans with Caspian?"

"Sorry. That sounded odd. A hunter threatened me this morning—well, sort of. Either that or it was his weird idea of a joke." Alex's eyes widened, and before he could leap in, she explained what had happened. "So, I was very sensible, and didn't go alone! We found him at the back of Rupert's place...on a field, with another van."

"Bloody hell! Rupert is such a sneaky shit! What the hell is he thinking?"

As mad as Alex seemed, at least he didn't seem cross that she'd called Caspian anymore. "I don't know! It's hard to know what Rupert is really doing. I mean, does he actually know the hunter? Or, has he bumped into him in White Haven and seized the opportunity?"

Alex exhaled, and he suddenly looked tired as he pushed his hair back from his face and pinched the bridge of his nose. "Okay. Yes, Caspian was a wise choice. Better than going alone. So you were going back tonight, once you'd tried the spell again?"

"We were going wherever the spell said he was." Avery gestured to the silver bowl at the back of the table, charred with the remnants of the spell. "I did it in that. The remaining hair is in the cotton bag. Enough for one spell. You could come too if you're free. The only reason I didn't call you earlier was because I knew you were with Dylan." Alex and Caspian were friends now, but Avery knew Caspian still got under Alex's skin. Avery's fingers drummed the table at the thought of the hunter and Rupert. "I hate that they think they have one up on me—on us!"

Alex smiled finally. "Yeah, me too. *Idiots!*"

"Exactly. But now we have a new plan, and you need me for that."

"Caspian, too. The more the merrier. I'll work out the finer details." He studied her, worried again. "What exactly are you going to do with this hunter if you find him?"

"I'm not sure. I guess keep tabs on him. See where he goes and what he gets up to. And what Rupert has to do with all this."

"I haven't told you about Reuben's plans, either. I think once we've done this tonight, we all need to catch up and share information." His eyes were twinkling. "If El is still talking to him, that is."

Although Avery was pleased that Alex seemed to be returning to his usual, cheerful self, curiosity was eating her up. "Tell me!"

"Phone Caspian first, and then I'll tell you over a beer. I think tonight will be interesting, in more ways than one!"

By the time Newton returned to his office, it was late and he was exhausted. His day had been tiring, but intriguing.

In the end, only three post-mortems had been completed, and the rest were scheduled over the next couple of days. Moore had taken the first one, Kendall the second, and he'd attended the last. Now, all he wanted was a pint and a smoke. He settled for coffee.

As he eased back in his chair, he considered his strange day. Another two dead bodies, who on first impressions appeared to be hunters, a strange old woman in a strange old house, an unsettled Alex, which was even stranger, and a vulnerable woman and her two kids. Newton stared into space while he sipped his drink, wondering what it was about Rosa that seemed so familiar to him. *There was something about her eyes and her manner…* He was an observant man. He had to be; it was his job. *But what was niggling him?*

The post-mortems that day—the first couple who'd been killed and the old woman—had all shown the same thing. A brain haemorrhage and burst eardrums, as well as bloodshot eyes. Identical deaths. And that meant it had to be the same perpetrator. Now he was impatient to hear about the rest.

A knock on the door and Moore's voice had him focussing with a shock. "'Scuse me, Guv. Is this a good time?"

"Absolutely. Come in, both of you. I'm curious to know what you've found. Some success, I hope?"

Moore's expression was carefully guarded. "Yes, you could say that. Give me two tics to grab my papers."

In seconds, he and Kendall had returned, Moore with a bundle of handwritten notes, Kendall with a laptop. It wasn't that Moore distrusted computers, he just preferred paper. He said handwriting his notes committed them to his memory better, and Newton knew just what he meant.

Once they were settled, Moore said, "You first, Kendall."

"Cheers," she answered with a breezy nod. "Right. First of all, I tracked the number plate of the van I saw at the cottages. It belongs to a bloke called Titus Groves."

"Titus!" Newton groaned. "What sort of a bloody name is that?"

Kendall grinned. "His parents must have had grand aspirations. He's 55 and was born in Leicester, and his address is registered there, but that's as much as I could find. So, I called Maggie Milne to get details on our hunters. You're right, Guv. She's a handful! She's awesome!"

"Before you start imitating her by cussing everything and everyone," Newton said dryly, as he noted a bit of adoration creeping into her tone, "just bear in mind that she has a bit more experience than you, if you're planning on her being your role model."

Kendall grinned. "Yes, sir. Point taken. Let's start with Sam Clarke and Ruby Townsend. They are based, mostly, in London, but move around the country as required. She's come across them a couple of times, and says they have been generally friendly but keep themselves out of police work. They hunted a pack of vampires once, which was when she first met them, but then they disappeared up north for a while. She knows Titus, too. She called him Titus Groan after that book character from *Gormenghast*. She didn't know much about him, other than that he's tricky and headstrong. He hunts with his mate called Dave 'Apollo Indigo' Frobisher. He moves around a lot. She says," Kendall took a deep breath, "that there aren't that many hunters, really. The job doesn't pay, so unless you have independent means, you struggle. And it's a deadly job. They either die young, burn out, or give it up at a certain age—if they can. Sam does get paying jobs, but she says she doubts if he gets as many as he might boast. He spends most of his time in cities, but isn't surprised that the news of what's happening down here has caught his attention."

"Okay, so in Maggie's eyes, Sam is one of the good guys. Good." Newton sighed with relief, thinking of El's encounter with him.

"But," Kendall continued, "she says not to overly trust any of them. 'They're all dodgy buggers with a fucking point to prove.' Those are her words, not mine."

"No kidding." He exchanged an amused glance with Moore, who seemed uncharacteristically solemn. "I'll tell El and the others to be cautious. Any suggestions as to who Briar's visitor could be?"

Kendall consulted her notes. "Possibly a Leigh Evert. Known to associate with Titus and Apollo. That's only a maybe, though."

"Okay. And today's dead guys?"

"Jimmy Stanton and Carla Snow. Born in Manchester, attended school there—different schools. No idea when they met. Never attended university. The van is registered to him. That's about as much as I know. Unknown to Maggie. She says to check other cities. I'll try Manchester."

"No criminal convictions?" Moore asked.

"Nothing. But I have tracked down their parents in Manchester. I asked the local police to break the news and arranged for them to come here to ID them."

"Good," Newton said, thinking that was one more thing to cross off the list. "I don't even know how we prove that they are hunters, and does it even matter? They're dead."

"I guess," Moore said, "that unless we think other hunters did it, and we don't at this stage, then it's a moot point. We just need to confirm who they are."

Newton nodded, pleased that all of the cottage victims had been formally identified now, too. "Okay. What have you got on Stormcrossed Manor? I met Tamsyn today, the doyenne of the manor." He ran through his encounter in the decrepit kitchen. "She gave me the shivers."

"Was Rosa there?" Moore asked, edging forward slightly, eyes narrowed.

"Yes. Seemed like a nice lady. Odd kids. At her wit's end. Why?"

"I'll come to it. You asked me to find out about the woman in the grave—Niamh Trevithick."

Newton nodded. "Yes, it seems everything started happening when the storm brought that tree down and it disturbed her grave."

"She was born in Ireland, but came here as Jeremiah Trevithick's bride at the tender age of 18 in 1906. She bore him two children. Randwick was born in 1907, and Connor in 1909. Née McCarthy. Lived to a ripe old age. Died in 1972. Unfortunately, her husband died in 1919. She never remarried."

"Hold on," Newton said, as his tired brain started to fire. "McCarthy? Tamsyn said Beth was a 'true McCarthy'—meaning, she has the sight. Apparently, it skipped Rosa."

Moore heaved a heavy sigh. "I can't comment on the sight. It doesn't come up in county records. I can tell you, however, that Connor died in 1942 in the Second World War, he had no children, and wasn't married. Typical adventurous second son. Well, there are no identified heirs," he added, raising an eyebrow. "Randwick married Demelza Murray, a local girl. They had Tamsyn, their only child. Randwick died in 1943—also in the war."

Newton was struggling to concentrate, and Kendall was suppressing a yawn as he asked, "Okay, so nothing suspicious about Niamh so far. No local reports of black magic or being a social outcast?"

"Guv! County records, remember? We'd have to ask the locals about that," Moore said, clearly suppressing his impatience. "Bear with me. Tamsyn married a local man called Robby Pengelly, and they had two daughters, Merrin and Jennifer. Merrin had only one child, Rosa, who you met today. Rosa has two children, Beth and Max. Both born in Wales."

Newton nodded. "Yes, Rosa told Ben and Dylan she had been living there until she split with her husband. Merrin lives there too, I believe. Rosa went to her grandmother to look after her, and live there. Bad split, I gather. Beth is the one who had issues today—the sight."

Moore shuffled his papers, looking uncomfortable. "Well, this is where it gets interesting. Jennifer moved away from White Haven too, but further up the coast, to Devon, where she married Branok Ashworth. They had a child called Briar, who now resides in White Haven."

Newton froze, his mind seeming to turn to gloop. "Briar? Are you kidding me? *My* Briar?" And then he fumbled to correct himself. "*Our* Briar?"

Moore looked horribly sad as he nodded. "I doubted myself. I've double and triple-checked, but there's no mistake. I got one of the DCs to help me. It's taken me all bloody day. Briar's mom is a Trevithick. I have no idea why Briar doesn't know...unless she does and has kept it quiet."

"No. She would never keep *that* quiet, especially after all this."

"I know," Moore said, looking apologetic, "but I had to suggest it. Anyway, bottom line, she's related. I presume you'll want to tell her? I mean, she needs to know. After all, Rosa is her cousin."

Newton's mouth went dry and he swigged his now cold coffee, and then promptly spat it straight back into his cup. "Shit. That's disgusting."

Kendall leaned forward, utterly confused. "Hold on! How can she not know who her family is?"

"It's complicated," Newton confessed. "Briar's magical half of the family—her father's side, left White Haven years ago. She was the first to return. Her parents both concealed her magical heritage from her, and she only found out when she discovered their letters after they died, along with the family grimoire. The second one." Kendall looked more confused than ever, and he realised she had no idea about the witches' hunt for the missing grimoires twelve months earlier. "Sorry. Long story. I'll tell you over a pint one day. Anyway, she mentioned to me that her mother was estranged from her family, but never said why. Maybe she never knew."

She nodded. "I wonder if that house always had a bad vibe, and that's why both daughters left."

"You would have hoped," Moore said with a grunt, "that Merrin, Rosa's mother, would have warned her off going, then. Certainly not encouraged it!"

"Unfortunately," Newton reasoned, "not all families are so altruistic, especially if it meant Merrin could avoid going home again."

"Wow. Talk about throwing your daughter to the wolves!" Kendall placed her laptop on Newton's desk, and gave Moore her full attention. "What made you look up the family tree?"

"I was curious about who else may be local family, in case they were behind the deaths. You know—cousins, second cousins, disgruntled distant relatives. I also wanted to see if there were any colourful local characters we might know who were associated with that house." He shrugged. "It might sound easy, but going through records is a pain in the arse. I certainly didn't expect to find a connection to Briar."

Newton's mood darkened as his need to protect Briar kicked in. "I hope you don't think any of this could be caused by Briar, just because she's a witch? She's gentle. A good witch! She would never—"

Moore interrupted, looking like Newton had slapped him. "Of course not! I like Briar. I would never think she could do any of this!"

"No. Sorry, of course you wouldn't," Newton acknowledged, feeling like shit.

An awkward silence fell for a few moments, and Newton needed to get out of there. The room felt impossibly hot and stuffy, and he wanted to see Briar immediately.

"Oh, and by the way," Moore said, gathering his papers, "the manor was renamed by Niamh after Jeremiah died in a storm."

"Did he?" Kendall said, turning to him. "How?"

"He was flattened by a tree—hence, Stormcrossed Manor. Seemed she had a broken heart."

"And burdened the house with that name!" Kendall shivered. "It's like she placed a curse on the house. And with powers of her own, who knows what that might have triggered..."

Newton stood. "Do me a favour, Moore. Phone Ghost OPS and confirm Niamh's Irish connection—but not Briar! It may help them work out what's happening. I'll let the others know," he said, meaning the witches. "And then go home—both of you. Let's come back fresh tomorrow. With luck, our friends will ensure nothing else happens tonight." He only wished he felt more confident than he sounded.

"And Briar?" Moore asked.

"I'll tell her. I'm heading to her place now."

"I've got one more thing to share," Moore said, also rising to his feet. "I found out that Mrs Robertson's husband recently died. She's a grieving widow. *Was* a grieving widow."

"Oh, wow!" Kendall exclaimed. "That's another connection. The couple at the cottage were grieving the loss of their son! Perhaps the others were grieving, too?"

"Grief is the connection?" Newton shook his head. "That seems just plain weird, but we'll check tomorrow. Perhaps this is the lead we need."

Chapter Seventeen

Reuben knocked on the manor's front door in the deepening twilight that was hastened by the dark storm clouds gathering above, and realised he had not imagined the strange atmosphere that hung over the manor.

He glanced at El beside him, her lips tight as she radiated doubt about the whole endeavour. "Are you okay?"

"Not really. I feel we've both lost our senses. Although, I get what you're saying about this place. It has a creepy vibe."

"Wait until you get—"

But he couldn't say any more, because the door swung open and Max stood on the other side, his eyes wide and his face horribly pale. Recognition dawned as he said, "You were here earlier."

"I was." Reuben stuck his hand out, thinking he looked relieved to see that it was them, and Max tentatively shook it. "I'm your neighbour, actually. Reuben Jackson. I live just across there." He swung his arm behind him, gesturing vaguely over the unruly hedgerows. "This is my girlfriend, El."

El smiled, and Max's eyes widened even more as he took in her striking appearance. She shook his hand, too. "We'd like to chat to your mum, if that's okay?"

Max looked uncertain for a moment, but then stepped back. "She's with Beth in the living room."

"Is your sister feeling better?" Reuben asked, entering first, as if he needed to protect El from whatever lurked inside these walls.

Max shrugged. "She's awake."

That pale, wide-eyed expression said everything, and Reuben knew beyond a doubt that he was doing the right thing. One look at El's face as she peered down the hall said so, too. She mouthed, "*What the f...?*"

Reuben grinned. "Lead the way, Max!"

Max set off at a trot down the passage, and after a few turns that took them deeper into the house, he pushed open a door leading to a shabby sitting room overlooking the garden at the side of the house. *The furthest point*, Reuben noted, *from Tamsyn's wing*. It looked as if this was the room Rosa had done the most work in. Although the wallpaper was faded, the sofa looked modern, and a couple of older armchairs were covered with pretty throws. Good quality wooden furniture, gleaming in the lamplight, made the place cosy.

Rosa was sitting on the sofa, her arm around Beth, watching the TV that was on low in the corner, a kid's film playing. He had the feeling that Rosa wasn't watching it at all.

Her head whipped around as they entered, and she leapt to her feet, startled. She glared at Max. "Max! You can't let just anyone in!"

Reuben stepped forward, hand outstretched. "I was here earlier, Rosa. Reuben Jackson, from next door. I'm friends with Dylan and Alex, and the detective, Newton. And this is El, my girlfriend."

Relief returned to Rosa's eyes. "Yes, I remember. Sorry. Things were a bit weird earlier."

"They were more than that," Reuben conceded. "They were downright scary. Can we sit down? I'm here to check that you're okay." He shrugged and smiled. "I was worried."

"I guess so, but this really isn't a good time." She glanced at Beth, who was transfixed by the TV.

"I heard about everything," El said, moving around the sofa to study Beth. "Is she okay now?"

Rosa gave a strangled laugh. "She seems to be, but who knows?" She lowered her voice, moving closer to both of them. "She's barely spoken since. I'm worried sick." Tears sprang to her eyes. "And I'm furious with my grandmother!"

El nodded and started to chat about the day's events, and Rosa seemed to relax, finally taking a seat. El sat next to her, which allowed Reuben to get a feel for the atmosphere again. This part of the house didn't have such an oppressive feeling as the rest of the place, but even so, it felt like something was lurking, and when he moved to the window to look outside, the shadows seemed to contain all sorts of threats. And he would be out there later, with his coven, trying to contain whatever was here.

Max stood next to him, also studying the grounds. "Can you see something?"

"Just the storm," Reuben said, trying to be cheerful. He noted Max's rigid profile and asked, "Can you?"

His voice was barely above a whisper as he answered, "No. Not like Beth."

Reuben's heart faltered, and he crouched down so he was closer to Max's height. "What does she see?"

"A lady at night, with a long dress."

"And what about you, in the day when you explore the garden?"

"Nothing. No one."

It was impossible to say whether Max was relieved or disappointed. Or even maybe jealous of his sister. *Wow.* Reuben suppressed a shudder. *Things were weird in this house.*

He turned away from Max's bleak expression to look at Rosa, and saw that her hands were wringing her cotton dress as she said, "The thought of being here tonight, with another storm coming... I feel sick! I won't let Beth near Tammy, but I've no idea whether that will help or not. If I had got any other choice..."

El glanced at Reuben, and he seized his chance. He sat in the nearest armchair. "Actually, Rosa, you could come and stay with us. With Beth and Max, obviously. I have a big place, close by. You could have your own rooms and not even see us. El will be there, of course." He smiled, radiating calm. "I know you don't know us, but I'm serious. I don't like you staying here. It's unsafe. And it's obviously scaring you, or else why call Ghost OPS?"

Rosa faltered, her hands tightening in her lap. "It *does* scare me. I thought I was imagining things, but with Beth's..." she swallowed, "vision, it's even worse. She said something is coming."

"*She* is coming," Reuben repeated, her words echoing in his head. He wasn't going to repeat what Max said Beth had seen. Not now, at least. "And you've heard the screams. Did Dylan tell you what he saw on the camera?"

"He didn't specify, but he suggested it was a spirit that needed more investigation."

El squeezed her hand. "There have already been three nights of people dying, deaths that we fear could be linked to the screams you've heard. Reuben is right. I promise we won't harm you. We're just offering you a bed for a few days. Just you three. Not Tamsyn. We think," El looked to Reuben for confirmation, "that it would be better for her to stay here."

Beth suddenly looked around, losing her focus on the TV and saying, "Granny said the lady will come again tonight. She said she's too sad to stay asleep."

Everyone froze, but Rosa gathered herself first. "What lady, honey?"

"The lady from the past, who sleeps with Great-grandma Niamh. I saw her, too. In my dream. She's very upset."

Rosa looked at Reuben and El, and then back to Beth, her mouth working, but no words came out. She looked utterly frozen. She turned to Max, who was still by the window, solemnly looking onto the garden, and then seemed to make her mind up. She threw her shoulders back and stared at Reuben. "Are you serious? We can really stay with you?"

"Of course. We can go whenever you're ready—but the sooner, the better."

"Good." She jumped to her feet. "I'll gather some things."

"I'll help," El offered, and Reuben knew she was keen to explore the house, as well as make sure Rosa didn't change her mind.

Relief flowed through Reuben as he stood, too. "Great. Come on then, Max, I'll help you pack."

Briar grabbed Newton a beer and made herself some herbal tea before ushering him out to the veranda at the back of her cottage.

It was her favourite place, cosy at any time of year. It could be gloriously sunny, or moody in bad weather, like it was now with the storm clouds rolling in and the brisk wind stirring the plants in her garden.

She'd been seated at the wooden table when Newton arrived, studying her grimoires in preparation for the evening ahead. Although Alex had decided on a spell, she always liked to refresh her knowledge for special events, just in case. She was also trying to shake off the odd mood that had descended on her all day. A feeling of impending doom and worry. She felt foolish. She had enough faith in her magic to feel safe, so she wasn't sure what was going on.

She brushed it aside and focussed on Newton who'd taken a seat across the table, glad that he'd arrived to take her mind off her worries. However, he looked fairly preoccupied himself. He glanced around the room, taking in her vintage decorations and shabby-chic design that she guessed he found twee. *That was okay*. She loved it.

"Bad day, Newton?"

He focussed on her, looking guilty. "You could say that. These hunters that have arrived, plus the two dead ones, and that bloody Stormcrossed Manor... Creepy as hell, and that old woman looked..." He froze, face flushing. "Forget I said that. Are you okay? No other visits from that woman?"

"The supposed hunter? No." She tapped her grimoires, the familiar scents enveloping her as she leaned over them. "I'm just immersing myself in old family magic in preparation for tonight. It comforts me. You know what we have planned?"

"Yes. Alex told me. He invited me to the curry, too. Phoned as I was leaving work. At El's, I think, later."

"Yes, very late. Reuben and El are up to something." Briar considered his call. "He wouldn't elaborate, so who knows what that means!"

"That's okay," Newton said brusquely. "I'm sure we'll find out tonight. I wanted to speak to you alone first. It's important."

Briar's eyes widened with surprise, and for one ridiculous moment, a flash of hope ran through her that he might ask something personal, before she quickly squashed it again. *A date, perhaps? What was she thinking?* He'd rejected her, and she him, and now they were in this stupid friendship stalemate. Plus, she was seeing Hunter.

She forced a smile. "Now I'm intrigued! Go on!"

"You know we do all sorts of research on cases—background checks, bank stuff, family history, et cetera. Well, we did some on the family who lives in the manor, and we found something we didn't expect. It involves you."

Worry gripped her again, and Newton's concerned, grey eyes bore into hers. "Bloody hell, Newton. You're spooking me, now. Do you think I'm behind some of this?"

"Don't be bloody stupid! No. It's something else."

"Spit it out, then! The anticipation is killing me!"

"This is going to sound odd, but trust me, we've double-checked everything. It seems that Tamsyn Pengelly, the current owner of the house, is your grandmother. She had two daughters, Jennifer, your mother, and Merrin. Rosa, the woman who called in Ghost OPS, is Merrin's daughter. She's your cousin."

A dull buzzing filled Briar's ears as she stared at Newton, suddenly mute. *Grandmother? Cousin?* "What? Sorry, Newton, that makes no sense. My mother said her family were all dead. And that they were from up north. Not here in White Haven!" She shook her head. "You must be wrong."

Newton leaned across the table, eyes full of concern, and he took her hands in his. "No. Moore checked several times. Jennifer Pengelly married Branok Ashworth, your dad. It's all on record. Your birth is registered in Budleigh Salterton. It's definitely you, Briar."

Briar pulled her hands out of Newton's and leaned back in her chair, grimoires and spells forgotten. She trusted Newton, and knew he wouldn't lie, but... "I don't understand why my mum would lie about her family. Especially seeing as they kept my witch heritage a secret, too!" She started to get angry, her voice rising with confusion and anguish. "Why the hell would she lie? Both of them!"

"You haven't been to that manor house, Briar. For a start, the atmosphere there is plain creepy. Tamsyn—and I'm sorry to say this," he said, looking embarrassed, "is *very* creepy! She's lived alone there for years, and has let the place fall down around her. I don't know what's going on there, but it drove your mother and your aunt away." He swallowed. "There's something else, too."

Briar could barely take it all in, but she asked, "What?"

"You have Irish heritage. It seems Niamh McCarthy, who came to White Haven over a hundred years ago, had the sight. She was a seer. The skill has passed down through the generations, skipping some. Skipping you, I presume, and Rosa. But Tamsyn has it, and so does Beth, the youngest child."

"The sight? I had no idea." And then something else struck her. "Are you saying that my family is responsible for these deaths?"

She leapt to her feet, her chair scraping across the floor and hitting the wall behind her. Power flooded through her, balling in her hands as her energy surged. She slid out from the table and started pacing the room, taking deep breaths. She could feel the Green Man uncurling within her as if she'd summoned him, and she wanted to hit something—*anything*—just to release her anger.

Newton jumped to his feet too, trying to meet her eyes as she paced around the room. "Briar, something in that house is behind these deaths, but I'm not sure if it's your family! Tamsyn said she's a conduit for the past. I don't know what that means."

She finally looked up at him, and could feel tears threatening. "Does Alex? He knows about this kind of thing."

"Alex is baffled right now, too. But we'll work it out." His voice softened as he fumbled for her hands again. "I'm so sorry, Briar. This was no way to tell you, but I had to. Especially before you go there tonight."

Briar wasn't sure if it was Newton's sympathetic voice and his kind expression, or the overwhelming news, but inexplicably she burst into tears and Newton swept her into his arms, where she sobbed against his chest.

Chapter Eighteen

B en sat in the shadow-filled office, staring out of the windows at the gloomy twilight, trying to work out what was going on at Stormcrossed Manor.

Ever since Dylan had burst in and shared his news, it was like a veil had fallen on the group, and they had talked endlessly back and forth about what could be happening. Cassie and Dylan were still chatting quietly in front of Dylan's bank of computer screens, darkness thickening around them. No one had turned the lights on. It suited their mood.

"What do you think, Ben?" Cassie called over. "Could the banshee be causing these deaths? Or, is it another type of spirit involvement?"

He turned to her, the dull light from the computer screen highlighting her face. "Banshees are not killers. Normally. Maybe there is another spirit! It's all so bloody confusing. Maybe there are two things going on here, not one."

"Not so unusual though, is it?" Dylan suggested. "One paranormal event can sometimes herald another. But if this does stem from Niamh, she died a long time ago. I don't believe this storm has kicked up everything. That house has years of accumulated…" He shrugged. "How do you explain it? *Doom*?"

Cassie nodded. "Maybe her spirit has never left the grounds, or something was in her coffin? Something she'd trapped with her death, but the storm released?"

"And we know Niamh was Irish," Dylan added. "Her name alone told us that, but Moore's research confirms it. She was fresh off the boat! With the sight! A virgin bride for the Lord of the Manor, bringing her spirits with her!" A macabre grin lit up his face.

Cassie snorted with laughter. "Virgin bride with the sight! Have you been reading bodice rippers in your free time?"

"I'm trying to add some drama to the story. She would have arrived with her trousseau, excited, in love, and scared, perhaps! Plagued with demons from her homeland."

"Holy shit. Have you been sneaking drugs or alcohol in there?" Cassie grabbed his coffee and sniffed it. "Nope. Just your normal madness."

Ben laughed at their sniggers, and shuffled around in his chair to see them properly, swinging his legs off his desk onto the floor. "As colourful as that is, Dylan, we should check that there's been no history of unexplained deaths around the manor before her arrival. We could be laying the blame on Niamh, and she's innocent. And just because she had the sight doesn't make her a killer—or mean that she had a family banshee!"

"But," Cassie posited, still struggling not to smirk, "the fact she's Irish fits in with the banshee suggestion. Can you carry one around?"

Dylan snorted. "Like a bloody handbag? Are you nuts?"

"Not like a handbag!" Cassie cuffed him on the arm. "You filmed a lurking spirit. Alex also detected something odd. Maybe that's what's in Tamsyn right now!"

"I know it's impossible, and really dangerous," Ben said, "but I wish we could bring Tamsyn here. Hook her up to our equipment and ask her questions in a controlled way." Strangled cries from both of his colleagues had him holding up his hand. "I know. It's just a wish. I realise it would be far too dangerous. But maybe, when this is over, Rosa might consent to us investigating Beth."

"Her six-year old child?" Cassie sounded incredulous. "Ben! You're nuts. Besides, it's highly unethical."

"Not with her mother's consent. Come on. You know it would be useful."

"Forget it," Cassie said, her humour evaporating. "Valuable or not, she's too young. Let's focus on stopping this first."

Ben was about to argue, but decided not to antagonise Cassie further. He sat up and reached for his phone. "I presume you're both up for an all-nighter? We can watch the footage in real time as the witches do their thing. It means we can answer any phone calls that may come through, too."

"Of course," Dylan answered at once. His headphones were perched on his head, already keeping an eye on the footage. "But we need food. I think I'm delirious from hunger."

"On it," Ben said starting to dial. "Pizza is on the way."

Avery's drink sat at her elbow, forgotten, as she stared at Briar, and then Newton. "Are you kidding? This is unbelievable."

"I wish it was a joke," Briar admitted, clutching her wine glass so tightly that her knuckles were white. "I always wondered about my family, but I've learned to put it out of my head. My mother said her family were all dead, so I never thought to question it, and as you know, my parents kept my magical heritage a secret. I guess finding out about my father's family pushed all thoughts about my mother's to the back of my mind." She dragged her hand through her mane of dark hair as she stared at her coven. "Isn't that terrible? That I was so willing to ignore one whole side of me? They still make me who I am."

"But it's logical," El said, her face creasing with sympathy. "Finding out you're a witch and developing your magic skills was huge! And the last year has been nuts, really! So much has happened with our lost grimoires, and lately with the Cornwall Coven, why should you have thought about them?"

"That's true," Reuben said, still tucking into his huge bowl of curry. "I barely give any of my relatives a thought. We're not that close. They do their thing, I do mine."

"That's certainly true of mine," Alex agreed. "You guys are more like family to me than my actual relatives."

"As I know only too well," Caspian said, with a weary shrug, "family can be a curse, as well as a blessing!"

They were at El's place, sitting around her dining room table and eating curry. Avery was already there when Briar arrived with Newton, and as soon as she walked through the door, Avery knew something was wrong. Briar was distracted, despite trying to appear her normal self, and Avery wondered if she'd argued with Newton. But he stuck close to her side, keeping a careful eye on her, and for the majority of the meal they had discussed Ghost OPS findings and the video of the unnerving creature that could be a banshee. It wasn't until they had virtually finished their meal that Briar told them about being related to Tamsyn and Rosa.

"Well," Avery said, trying to be positive, "I think it's wonderful news! You have relatives now! A cousin and a grandmother! That's fantastic! And the kids, too—whatever you call them."

"First cousins, once removed," Newton advised her. "Although, they tend to be called nieces and nephews. It's easier."

She smiled. "Moore did great work to find all that history out."

"Took him all day, apparently," Newton admitted.

Briar huffed out a long sigh. "It *is* good, but my grandmother sounds loopy! The whole place sounds loopy! And dangerous. And why didn't *she* contact me?" She leaned back in her seat, trying to laugh. "I mean, they are literally living a stone's throw away!"

"You mean Tamsyn?" Alex asked. "If your mother left home and never went back, she probably doesn't even know you exist. And neither would Rosa."

Newton nodded. "It's true. When someone loses contact, it's hard to find them, unless they employ a detective or become a social media sleuth. Your mother obviously left for a good reason, and Merrin, your aunt, lives in Wales now. Despite her so-called worries about her mother being alone, she didn't come back. She sent Rosa, instead!"

El started to stack the plates, shaking her head as she did so. "I think that's unforgivable! Sending your daughter to that house, knowing something was deeply wrong there? Wow! Rosa should disown her."

Reuben winked at her. "I knew you'd see it my way."

El didn't even bite back. "You were right, Reuben. I admit it. They shouldn't be in that house. It gave me the creeps."

Newton rubbed his chin and stared at Reuben, who had updated them on Rosa moving in earlier. He'd removed his tie and undone his shirt's top button, but he didn't look remotely relaxed. "It's very generous of you, but what if something happens at your place tonight? You don't know what's going on with Beth."

"I'm convinced that she's not a threat," Alex said. "It was only Tamsyn that I sensed something off about. Beth might have had a vision, but I didn't detect a presence with her. Even so," he gave Reuben a wry smile, "I still think you're taking a big chance."

Reuben shrugged. "I'm okay with it. I've given them a series of linked rooms. They even have their own little kitchen area. And my house is heavily protected."

"I'm amazed they agreed to it," Avery confessed. "They don't even know you!"

"I radiate charm though, right? Besides," his grin disappeared as he admitted, "Rosa was terrified for her kids' safety. It was an easy choice."

"I want to meet them," Briar said suddenly. "After the spell, obviously." She looked at Newton. "She has no idea about me, though, right?"

"Right."

"That's okay. I reckon we both need some reassurance right now." She looked at El and Reuben. "You didn't say anything about us being witches?"

"No," El answered, heading to the kitchen with dirty plates. "That would have scared her even more. When all this is finished though, she might find out anyway."

Briar nodded. "Something to think about. And even if they don't stay in White Haven, she might want to keep in touch." Despite her earlier reservations, Briar looked hopeful, but then she shook her head and shrugged. "Anyway, let's move on. What's the plan tonight, Alex?"

"It's an enhanced protection spell, harnessing the power of charged crystals." He indicated a bag on the side of the table, atop his grimoire. "I have a selection that we can lay around the grounds. Essentially, this protection will be more physical than anything we've done before, trapping whatever is in that house—including Tamsyn. Only by constructing a magical doorway will we be able to get anyone in or out. Let's hope the postman doesn't call in the next couple of days." He looked at the startled faces around the table. "It will be invisible, of course. Apparently, Ben says they had a lot of calls from locals recording screams around the moors. We need to stop that. And the deaths, of course."

"We've had calls too, just to the local line, and some 999 calls," Newton said. "All reporting screams. A few were followed up, but nothing was found."

"Let's hope we're successful, then. There are enough rumours circulating the town as it is." Alex looked across to Caspian. "Thanks for coming. It's a big area to cover. I have a map, and we can split the area up between us, in pairs."

Caspian nodded. "That's fine. Honorary White Haven Coven member, remember? Are you sure we don't need more of us?"

"I'd rather not. The potential presence of hunters is making me wary."

"Speaking of which," El said, returning to the table. "I met with Sam Clarke today. He wants us to work together."

"*What*?" Newton said, voice rising with shock. "Did you tell him to sod off?"

She shook her head. "No, actually. He seemed genuine. He knew the two hunters who died today. Not well, but enough that he was upset. Angry, even. But I did say I needed to discuss it with you guys, first." She looked at Avery. "He told me who he thought your visitor was. A bloke called Titus. Said he's bad news."

"When the bloody hell were you going to tell me that!" Newton exclaimed, rounding on her.

"Sorry." El winced. "This afternoon went sideways. I did mean to."

"It's a good job I already found his name out, then."

"Titus!" Avery exclaimed, thinking how well it suited the bully hunter. "What a name! Do you know anything else about him?"

"Nothing that will be of use to you," Newton told her. "Although, he has a partner called Apollo, apparently. Stupid bloody names. Maggie doesn't like them, so be careful around them. Although, *you'll* be pleased to know," he glared at El again, "that Sam and Ruby check out. Apparently, Maggie calls them the good guys. Says they don't interfere much with police work, and get on with their own thing."

"See!" she smirked. "Good instincts!" El turned to her coven. "What do you think? I said I'd call him tomorrow."

"I trust you," Avery said, "In fact, I'm very curious to meet them. What did Sam say about Titus?"

"That he made no distinction between paranormal creatures and those with powers. He considers them all dangerous."

Newton interjected. "Kendall might have a lead on Briar's mystery visitor. Apparently, Titus has been known to work with a woman called Leigh who matches her description." He rolled his eyes. "Also bad news."

"At least we have a name," Briar said, smiling at him. "It's good to know they're not all bad, though. The way this is shaping up, I'm happy to collaborate."

"I guess that brings us to my news," Avery said, trying to suppress her renewed anger with Rupert and his meeting with Titus. "I used Titus's hair in a finding spell, and found him at Rupert's house."

"Rupert!" Reuben exclaimed. "That sneaky shit!"

"Exactly. I went with Caspian, and although we couldn't hear them, they looked very bloody friendly."

Caspian nodded. "There was another van there, too. Unfortunately, we have no idea how many people are there. We had to sneak around the back lanes." He turned to Avery. "Did you bring his hair so we can do the spell again?"

She gestured to her bag that she'd thrown on the sofa. "In there. I suggest we do it now, so we know exactly where he is before we start the spell at the manor."

"Absolutely," Alex agreed. "I don't want any surprises up there. Any more than we can help, anyway."

Newton perked up. "Good. You can tell me, and I'll track the bastard down."

"Tonight?" Briar asked, alarmed.

"Of course!" He checked his watch. "Kendall might want to help. She hasn't got kids to occupy her, like Moore. And she's young and keen. I reckon keeping an eye on a dodgy hunter will make her very happy."

"We were going to do that," Avery said resentfully, glancing at Caspian for back-up. "It might not be safe."

"You focus on that bloody house," Newton said, fixing her with a scowl that forbade any argument. "Leave Titus to me."

Reuben pointed outside. "Well, it's already dark, thanks to the storm clouds. I suggest we get a move on before it breaks and we all get soaked."

"Agreed." Avery headed to her bag to grab her spell ingredients, and started to set them up on the coffee table. Caspian joined her, and so did Newton.

"Have we got a plan if any hunters arrive?" El asked. "Titus or otherwise? I haven't mentioned the manor to Sam, but he might turn up because of his dead friends."

Alex gathered his grimoire and gemstones, bundling them into his pack. "I'm not concerned about Sam and Ruby. It's Titus I'm worried about, and whoever his cronies are. And Rupert, of course. To answer your question, no, I haven't really got a plan to deal with them, other than whatever springs to mind at the time."

"There might be other stragglers we don't know about, too," Reuben added, pulling a long-sleeved black t-shirt on over his surfing t-shirt. Avery suppressed a grin as she watched him don his ninja witch gear as he loved to call it, before she settled cross-legged on the floor, placing Titus's hair in the silver bowl.

"Are you still thinking this is all caused by a banshee?" Newton asked, half an eye on Avery's activities.

Alex shrugged. "Perhaps. I honestly couldn't tell what it might be earlier."

"Sam thinks our mystery killer is a banshee, as does Ghost OPS," El added, "but like you, I'm not sure yet. It doesn't make sense. However, if it is, Sam thinks a special knife could work. One I agreed to make."

"A banshee does seem a popular suggestion," Caspian said, frowning. "I gather that Dan suggested it, too. The Irish history, the screams, the sudden deaths—it all connects."

"I guess once we contain whatever it is," Alex said, obviously unwilling to commit, "then we try to work out what it is. I might even try to communicate with it."

Avery was about to light Titus's hair, but now she looked at him, alarmed. "Alex! That's too risky!"

He met her eyes, acknowledging her concern. "I know, but this can't continue indefinitely. We need to work out what this is and banish it, and right now, we have bugger all to go on. Tonight is step one."

"So, let's get on with it!" Rueben said impatiently. "Snap to it, Ave. Before we all get caught in a storm—and I don't mean the regular sort."

Avery nodded and focussed on the spell, the room falling silent as she uttered the words and burnt the herbs. The smoke drifted across the map, finally circling above a lane on the edge of the moor.

Newton almost growled as he leaned over the map, a fierce glare on his face. "Is that right?"

"It should be."

"Cheeky bastard. He's returned to the cottages." He straightened up, smiling grimly. "Good. I can arrest him for trespassing." And with that he stalked to the door, saying, "Be careful tonight. No heroics!"

"That applies to you, too, Newton!" Avery shouted after him, feeling she'd been denied the pleasure of challenging Titus. But he was already gone.

Alex stuck his hand out to help her to her feet. "Take your anger out on the manor, Avery. I have a feeling we'll need all the power we can get tonight."

Chapter Nineteen

The night air was thick and muggy by the time Alex exited Avery's van. She'd parked at the entrance to the field where the bodies had been found that morning behind Stormcrossed Manor. They were alone, the others stationing themselves around the perimeter. Reuben was with El, and Caspian with Briar.

"The van's gone," Avery said immediately as she joined him on the grass.

Alex nodded. "Newton had it towed away this morning." He pointed to some white blobs clustering at the far end. "The sheep are still here, though. Let's hope they're not averse to a bit of magic."

"I'm just glad Titus isn't here."

"Me too, although I want to meet the man who was stupid enough to threaten my girlfriend." He pulled her close and kissed her, and then nuzzled her glorious mass of hair that she'd unfortunately tied back. "I missed you today. You know—with you doing your thing and me doing mine. I wish you'd been at the manor with me. I would have liked your opinion."

"I missed being there, but no doubt I'll have my chance."

He nodded, releasing her reluctantly. He rummaged in his pack and handed her the cluster of gemstones that he'd prepared. "You start this end, and I'll start the other. We'll meet in the middle."

He tried to sound more confident than he felt. The manor's boundary was big, and although he knew their magic was strong, it was still a big ask. *Nothing they hadn't done before, though*, he reminded himself as he trudged along the old stone wall, hoping they weren't too late, and that the mysterious entity was still trapped inside. It was well before midnight.

The field was eerily quiet, the silence before the storm in more ways than one. The wind was picking up though, and he paused and looked out to the sea, noticing a flicker of lightning on the horizon.

Shit. The storm had started, and would be with them soon.

He started to bury the gemstones into the ground, pacing them out as he walked. They had already done the same along the wall edging the lane, and he trusted that the other witches had covered their areas, too. He'd almost reached the middle when he came to a break in the wall, allowing him a glimpse inside the grounds. He stepped closer to peer inside, and then jumped back in shock. It felt as if something was watching him.

Wary, he waited, magic balling at his fingertips, but nothing happened, and he took a deep, calming breath. *Shit.* He was jumpy. He buried a gemstone into the ground and picked up his pace. *Time to get started.*

El buried the gemstone in the centre of the rutted driveway just beyond where the drive met the lane, saying the words of power as she did so. She felt a flare of magic beneath the earth and stepped back, satisfied.

She turned to Reuben who was a few feet away, leaning against the rusted, wrought iron gate that was almost submerged by the hedge, watching the road. "I'm done."

"Good. Nothing going on out there." He gave her a lopsided grin. "I bet hardly anyone notices this entrance, and I would imagine Tamsyn discourages visitors." He pointed to the post box at the end of the drive. "Even the postman."

"No wonder Alex senses loneliness. How can she live here so isolated? I'd go mad."

"I think she has." Reuben faced the house that was invisible from the road. "I didn't see what Alex saw in her, but she was kind of like a vortex of loss. You didn't meet her, and I'm glad."

She walked to his side and kissed his cheek. "Are you trying to protect me?"

"I can't help it." He cupped her face gently in his calloused hands. "I might not be the most romantic man, but I need you to know that you mean everything to me. Never forget that."

El wasn't the most romantic person either, that's why her relationship with Reuben worked, but even so, she felt a rush of pure, unbridled pleasure rush through her. "I do know that, but it's still lovely to hear you say it. You mean everything to me, too. And lately, Reuben Jackson," she said before kissing him lightly on the lips, "you constantly surprise me."

He looked mock-offended. "In a good way I hope!"

"Of course. Twit." She pressed her hand over his heart, feeling his smooth, tautly muscled chest beneath his shirt. "You've got a big heart. I always knew it, but I think others are seeing it more and more now."

He winked cheekily. "I know. I'm a top bloke. And despite your reservations, I did the right thing with Rosa."

"As soon as I walked into that hall, I didn't doubt it. And the kids..." She shook her head at the recollection of Max's white, strained face. "Especially Max. He looked lost! I don't want to leave them alone for too long. We should get back as soon as this is done, with Briar. That's a shocker, I have to confess." She released him, needing to place her final gemstone in position, but her thoughts were with her friend. "We have to support her, Reuben."

He huffed as he buried his final gemstone on the left of the lane. "Duh! Big-hearted bloke, remember?"

El laughed and straightened up, scanning down the lane as she did so. Satisfied that no hunters were lurking around, she pulled her phone out. "I'll tell Alex we're ready."

Newton stopped at the end of the lane, headlamps off and engine idling.

There was only one lonely street lamp illuminating the cottages where the deaths had occurred, but there was enough light to see a large, grubby van parked outside Mrs Robertson's cottage.

"There he is," Newton said, grimacing as he recognised the registration. "I don't know whether to be pleased or annoyed."

"He's cocky," Kendall said. "He must have either been convinced that I didn't see him, or decided to risk it, anyway."

"I doubt he'll find much more than we have, but who knows what resources he may use." Newton hesitated, debating the best course of action. "What do you think, Kendall? If I park here, and he gets into his van and legs it, he'll have a head start. But if I get any closer..."

"He'll see us," she said finishing his sentence. Her expression was almost invisible in the car's dark interior. "You said you wanted to catch him in the act. I say, sneak up on him. If he legs it, we can arrest him later. Unless you want to block his exit with your very nice car."

"As much as I want to catch this renegade hunter, I also don't want my car wrecked, and I'm not convinced the sneaky bastard won't ram it. Or have firearms."

"Or even a supernatural weapon." Kendall unhooked her seat belt. "Stealth and possible escape it is, then. Besides, we don't want him to feel cornered with no way out. I value my life, not just your car."

Newton turned the engine off and exited the car, but pocketing his keys, left it unlocked. "Just be aware," he whispered as he reached her side, "he may have an accomplice."

"Good. There's a reason I pursue martial arts, Newton, and there's nothing better than using my skills on a perp."

Newton suppressed a grin, taking in Kendall's tall, lean, and muscular frame. "I've noticed you do like the gym."

"You should try it some time, Guv. It's a great way of letting off steam."

Newton wondered what that meant. Did he look permanently grumpy? Sex-starved, perhaps. Or just plain old. It might not be a bad suggestion, whatever the reason. Besides, if ever the damn *wolf* did get the push, he'd be competing with the memory of his lean brawn.

Ignoring those concerns, he focussed on Titus. "Let's loiter by his van. When he emerges from whichever house he's in, he'll have to explain himself. That way, I can search his vehicle, too."

Kendall nodded, and they strolled up the short lane, keeping to the shadows. Every single cottage was in darkness, even though they studied the windows for evidence of torch light. Newton knew the surviving couple had gone away for a few days to stay with relatives. Not surprising, considering recent events. When they reached the van, Newton tried the driver's door and, finding it unlocked, quietly opened it up and peered inside. It was a mess. Burger wrappers and old papers were strewn across the seats and the floor, and it stank of sweat.

Kendall wrinkled her nose in disgust. "The man's a pig." She peered over the seats into the rear of the large Kombi van, shining her torch across the mattress on the floor. "His bedding looks like a rat's nest."

Newton shined his own light beyond hers, seeing a small seating area. "There's a lot of paperwork up at that end. Maps, I think."

Easing out of the van and intending to circle around the back, he turned off his torch and looked towards the cottages first. The thud of a shutting door broke the silence, and as Kendall exited the van, he closed the door quietly.

Voices carried to them, two males, heading away.

Kendall leaned in, lips to his ear. "They must be going through the back gardens."

He nodded. She was right; it made the most sense.

She continued, "Shall we intercept them?"

"No. They'll be a few minutes yet. Let's check that paperwork. I want to see what they're up to."

The side door to the van was also unlocked, and a stale smell washed over Newton as he eased the door open. Leaving Kendall on watch, he gingerly stepped inside, trying to find a clear area of floor as he made his way to the cramped seating section. The table was strewn with maps and papers, but the uppermost one that caught his eye had Ravens'

Wood marked. A list comprised of magical terms was lying on top of it, and although he didn't really understand what most of them meant, he sensed it was nothing good. He took a few photos using his phone, and then exited again.

As he joined Kendall, a rumble of thunder rolled overhead. They both looked to the horizon, where a flicker of lightning illuminated the sky.

"Not long now," Kendall observed. "We could get caught in this."

Newton nodded, debating his best course of action. "We have every right to arrest them right now for breaking and entering, but I'd rather catch them off-guard here. Hear what bullshit excuse they pull." He showed Kendall the photo of the list. "This is what I need to check out. I have a horrible feeling that these are magical traps, or spells to work against the supernatural. I think he's planning something for Ravens' Wood."

Kendall scanned the list. "The witches would know what this means?"

"I hope so."

"It will be difficult for them to do whatever they're planning if we arrest them."

"Exactly." He grinned as he leaned back against the van. "I'm looking forward to this."

Caspian ended the call with Alex. "Everyone is in place. Are you ready?"

Briar had been staring at the manor's grounds from their position on a slight rise at the edge of the moor, frowning with a concentration that suggested if she stared hard enough, she would see through the wall and overgrown shrubs. However, she now turned to him, obviously forcing a smile on her face. "Of course."

"Are you sure you're up to this? You've just had a terrible shock."

She brushed off his concerns, waving her hand as if swatting a fly. "It's fine. No one's dead! In fact, it's just the opposite. I've discovered that I have family. That's a good thing. Even if my grandmother is a mad old woman, harbouring something weird inside her."

"It's okay to be upset. I would be. Your mother lied to you, and then died before you ever knew the truth. I wouldn't just be upset," he admitted, staring into her eyes that were ringed with green fire, "I'd be furious!"

Briar squared her slim shoulders. "Yeah, well, I'm feeling that, too. I'll use it productively." She faced the grounds again, wriggling her bare feet into the earth, a gesture that always instilled Caspian with confidence.

He took her outstretched hand. "I think we'll be a good combination, Briar. I'll gather the air, as you pull the earth's energies from below. We'll be the centre of our own vortex of power."

They intoned the spell Alex had taught them, repeating the phrases confidently, their voices getting louder and louder with each iteration. Caspian rocked on his feet as magic cracked through the ground and coursed through Briar. He added his own magic into the mix. The gemstones buried along the boundary powered into life, and although he'd been expecting it, the result still almost made him stumble back in surprise.

Essentially, they had created a magical fence, and the air crackled with power as a milky-white wave shimmered along the manor's wall. From their vantage point, he saw it roll outwards in a curve before it faded into invisibility, and he imagined it linking up with the other witches' efforts on the other sides of the grounds.

As they finished intoning the spell, a piercing scream shattered the silence, and Briar's hand gripped his even tighter. Ahead, the protection field flashed, as if something had hit it. Instantly, both of them raised their hands, power balling in their palms.

"What was that?" Briar asked, her breaths short and rapid.

Caspian hesitated, stepping forward to try to see better. "I don't know. It was just a flash of light—I couldn't see a shape."

And then the scream came again, long and drawn out, and utterly bloodcurdling. It pulled at his soul. He'd never known agony like it. *Desperation. Loss. Grief. Agonising, heart wrenching grief.* Briar fell to her knees next to him, tears pouring down her face, as another flash ignited the protective wall.

This time, he saw the shape of an unnaturally thin woman wearing long, tattered clothes that floated around her, buffeted by a wind only she could feel. Her spectral-blue face was gaunt, but her eyes were hideously bloodshot, ringed by reddened, almost blistered skin. She gripped the wall of protection with clawed fingers, as if clinging to a cage.

Caspian reacted instinctively, casting a spell around him and Briar, both to protect them and muffle her scream, and instantly, the sound muted to a plaintive wail. But the woman didn't move, her mouth a wide, dark void that looked as if it could swallow the world.

Then the storm broke. Thunder crashed overhead, and lightning split the sky. A white-hot fork struck the magical barrier, and it ignited like a supernova, searing Caspian's vision.

Unable to do anything else, he threw himself over Briar, hoping their spell would hold.

Chapter Twenty

"Holy fuck in a bucket!" Dylan exclaimed, averting his eyes as white light exploded across the screen. "What the hell happened?"

"I saw it. Her!" Cassie eyes were closed, her hands pressed against them. "That's all I can see. Her twisted body, climbing like a bat!"

Ben looked across her bent head to Dylan, mouth open in shock, before finally saying, "A bat? Who? The thing?"

She lifted her face and opened her eyes, blinking rapidly. "What else would it be?"

"But I didn't see a *thing*!"

"Shut up, both of you!" Dylan commanded, staring at his bank of screens that were now utterly black, and hoping his cameras hadn't fried. "Where has the feed gone? That damn blast has shorted everything out!" His fingers flew across the keypad, but now every screen dropped into static. "Shit!"

Cassie still looked dazzled, but like Ben, scooted closer to the monitors, panning them all for any signs the feed was coming back. "Was that their power? The witches?" she asked.

Dylan shook his head, knowing something was very wrong. "That first flash we saw on a couple of cameras was their magic. That second one was something very different."

"Lightning," Ben said, as thunder boomed outside. "Must have hit the manor."

"Or was it drawn by their magic?" Dylan ran through various scenarios in his head. "The witches' magic is elemental, after all. Perhaps it attracted the storm. Or their protective wall did?"

Another boom shook the house, and white light illuminated their office. All three looked at each other in shock, Ben saying, "That's huge, and we're a few miles away from them. Is it just bigger here?"

"Or," Dylan countered, "has their magic magnified it and turned it into a super-storm?"

Cassie leapt to her feet, her desk chair shooting backwards and hitting the wall behind her. "We should go. They might need us!"

"Are you nuts?" Ben grabbed her arm and her chair, forcing her to sit down. "We aren't going anywhere in this!" Another boom shook the building and Cassie meekly complied, although she looked torn with indecision. "Cassie, come on. We'll be the most help here. Which screen did you see the *thing* on? We'll try and pull it up." He looked at Dylan. "Even though they've shorted out now, we have the original footage, right?"

"Of course!" Dylan started searching through the files, hoping they weren't corrupted. "Did you say *climbing like a bat*? Are you sure?"

"I know it sounds weird, and it was seconds only, but I'm sure." After a moment's hesitation, Cassie added, "Camera six, I think.

Somewhere on the northern perimeter. A sort of flitty thing that was all long scrawny arms and legs."

They had originally split the monitors between them, but had ended up getting so distracted by the spell that they'd lost track of who was watching what, and Dylan huffed with annoyance. *Bloody amateurs*. "I presume it was seconds before the light?"

"Pretty much."

Dylan accessed the recording and scrolled back a few seconds. And then he froze—as did his blood. The feed showed a wild, clawing creature grasping the protective wall as if it was real. His mouth went dry with shock, and then disbelief. "Is that climbing the wall? That's impossible, right? It's pure energy! It doesn't exist as something to touch!"

"I told you!" Cassie said victoriously.

Ben grunted, transfixed. "You should tell her that. A bat is a good description, Cassie."

Cassie didn't speak, instead fascinated by the image on the screen. Dylan paused it, leaning in, revulsion rolling through him. It was unnatural, limbs twisted, clothing caught in a spectral flutter. But even with the screen paused, it was impossible to see any features, as they were filming her from behind.

Dylan played the recording back a few more seconds and shook his head, perplexed. "She came out of nowhere."

Ben nodded, focussed only on the screen. "Maybe the magic drew her out."

"Or the storm," Cassie suggested.

Frustrated, Dylan let the recording play. In a few seconds more, the screen exploded with light, and they shielded their eyes again. "And that's where it stops," he said with a disappointed huff, ending the transmission. He rolled his shoulders as he realised that he'd been so tense, he'd barely moved. "At least we caught it on camera—again! Damn, I'm good!"

"Er, how far does it go?" Cassie asked, ignoring his brilliance.

"How far does what go?"

"The protective wall they put up, dummy. The one she's scaling like a chimp in the zoo!" Cassie slapped her own forehead like they were imbeciles. "Is it a wall, or a dome? If it's just a wall, she could climb right over the top...to our friends on the other side."

Dylan fumbled for his phone. "No idea, but we better call them."

Then another huge flash of lightning illuminated their empty pizza boxes, coke cans, and coffee cups, thunder rattled the building, and the electricity went out.

The blast threw Avery onto her back, blinding her for a few awful seconds. She sat up, the stench of sheep dung emanating around her, and blinked several times, relieved when vague outlines of her surroundings reappeared.

"Alex! Where are you?"

He groaned. "Right here. What the hell happened?"

"It's your spell!"

"The exploding fence wasn't part of the plan."

A crash of thunder erupted overhead, and another jagged lightning strike hit the manor grounds. Avery averted her eyes just in time.

She staggered to her feet, the smell of ozone overpowering the stench of sheep. "Shit! Alex, we're going to get fried unless we move!" She grabbed his hand, pulling him upright, and they both stumbled backwards, studying the magical protection that was still holding along the manor's perimeter at a safer distance. It shimmered like a veil in soft, undulating waves, reminding Avery of photos of the aurora borealis.

"Wow! That's some spell, Alex!"

Alex brushed debris from his clothes, and then smoothed his frizzy hair down, too. It had been charged by the storm that crackled around them, and lifting her hand to her head, Avery realised her own hair was in a similar state.

"I have to confess," Alex admitted, "I wasn't quite sure how that would work, but it's better than I thought. However," he paused as both of them spun around again, shielding their eyes from the forked lightning that hit the spelled wall, "I think it's causing more trouble than I anticipated, too."

A crash of thunder made the ground shake, and the panic-stricken bleating of sheep added to the general cacophony. Avery studied the sky before turning to look at the sea. The storm was fully upon them, and huge. The whole sky seethed with clouds, backlit by lightning, and the sea churned like a maelstrom. Rain was imminent, and they would quickly be soaked.

"We need to get to the van," Avery said, grabbing his hand and pulling him across the grass.

He resisted. "Wait! My phone's ringing."

As he answered, her own phone buzzed within her pocket, and she fumbled for it as another fork of lightning hit their magical wall. She flinched, and for the first time, wondered if they should even leave it there. *Was it a conduit?*

"Avery!" A voice yelled in her ear. "It's Dylan! The thing is trying to escape over your wall!"

"The *what*?" The thunder was making it almost impossible to hear anything. "What on earth are you on about?"

"The creature! It looked like it was scaling..." Dylan's voice disappeared into static just as the rain fell—thick, heavy drops that drenched her in seconds.

"Dylan!" *Fuck it.* The storm had cut the connection. She whirled around to look at Alex, who was just ending his call. "Alex! Dylan said something about the creature scaling the wall. Is that even possible?" She waved her phone at him. "He couldn't even finish his sentence. It's dead!"

"It's doing *what*?" Alex shouted, slicking his hair back from his face. "Forget that for now. Caspian and Briar are in trouble."

Reuben pulled El out of the hedge that the blast had thrown them into, glad to see that other than being covered in scratches, she looked okay.

"Herne's horns, El. I think we've started Armageddon!"

"No shit, Sherlock." She flinched, her face contorted in horror, as another strike of lightning hit the magical defences they'd constructed. "We need to get out of here before we're killed!"

A distant scream cut through the air, curdling Reuben's blood, and he ducked as if something was about to swoop on him. "It's awake!"

They both covered their ears instinctively as he tried to narrow down its location. He scanned the shimmering wall in front of them. *Had trapping it inside woken it up?* He pointed to their left as the long, drawn-out scream continued to attract their attention. "It's coming from that direction." He looked at El, her face a spasm of discomfort. "That's where Briar and Caspian are!"

"But we've trapped it, surely?"

"Have we? Can we be sure of that?" He searched her face, but she exhibited the same doubt as he did.

He grabbed her hand and pulled her towards the car. They had to find their friends—now.

Newton spotted the bulky shapes moving away from the side of Mrs Robertson's house. They manifested into two tall men as they walked up the garden path, caught in the pale light from the street lamp. They had a swagger to them, and looked completely confident, their loud voices carrying to them easily, despite the thunder.

The storm had broken, and wind whipped across the moor as lightning shattered the sky. But Newton didn't care. He stepped into view, Kendall at his side, as Titus and his big, hairy companion stepped onto the lane, spotting them only at the last minute. They froze, eyes darting down the street, and then back to Newton and Kendall.

Newton recognised Titus from Avery's description and his driver's license photo. He was a bear of a man, with a long, unkempt beard and intense eyes. His companion was just as tall, but lean and wiry. Both were dressed in biker leathers, boots, and t-shirts.

"Evening, Mr Groves," Newton started. "I'm Detective Inspector Newton, and this is Detective Sergeant Kendall. Care to explain what you're doing out here, on someone else's property?"

After his initial shock that Newton knew his name, Titus didn't hesitate, his hard eyes raking over both of them. "Just on the grounds officer. No harm intended."

"It's still trespassing. Perhaps you didn't notice the police tape across it—although, you'd have to be blind not to see it. Besides, I heard slamming doors." His mouth twisted into a smile. "You were inside."

Titus straightened, his companion squaring up next to him, eyes darting to the van behind Newton, as if calculating how easy it would be to make a run for it. "The thing is, officer..."

"Detective Inspector," Newton corrected him, just to be bloody-minded. "Who's your friend?"

The man answered for himself. "Apollo Indigo."

"Otherwise known as Dave Frobisher," Newton said, resisting the effort to roll his eyes.

"That is not my preferred name."

"But it is your legal one!"

"DI Newton," Titus interrupted with a smile, revealing stained teeth. "We are actually trying to help your predicament. We specialise in the supernatural, and know that these deaths were caused by an as yet unknown creature." He stuck his hand out as he stepped towards Newton. "I suggest we work together."

Newton ignored his hand. "I don't like your methods so far, Mr Groves. Perhaps you should enlighten me as to what you intend to do?"

Titus withdrew his hand with a scowl. "Trap it and kill it, obviously."

"You're advertising the fact you're going to kill it? I'm pretty sure that's against the law."

Titus laughed. "I think we both know that no such law exists for the supernatural. In the normal policing world, no one even acknowledges it. The fact that you're here means you know more about this situation than most."

Newton ignored the crack of thunder that signified the storm was growing. "Tell me what you know so far, and I'll reconsider arresting you."

"You'll find that the houses are undamaged." Titus extended his hands, as did his friend. "Nothing is stolen. You'll have trouble proving we were even in there."

Newton was over his cocky attitude. "I'm a bloody policeman and I saw you, as did my colleague, so don't pull that shit with me. What do you know of the creature that caused those deaths?"

Titus hesitated only a moment, and then clearly thought better of arguing. "She kills swiftly and efficiently, not needing to touch her victims, but leaving their eyes bloodshot. Her primary method of killing is through her voice—shattering eardrums and causing brain bleeds. She carries death on her tongue."

"*She*?"

Apollo answered this time. "I suspect it is a banshee. A creature of grief and sadness."

Newton glanced at Kendall, who gave him a barely-there nod before staring at the men again. It seemed *banshee* was the general consensus. "My experts suggest that banshees are not killers by design, so why are people dying now?" Newton asked, impressed that the men knew so much. *Objectionable they may be, but they'd done their research.*

"So you know that much, policeman." Titus's sarcastic grin disappeared in a heartbeat. "Hard to say, but I've seen this happen before. I didn't ask questions before I killed her then, and I won't this time. And before you ask, I have no idea *where* she is, either."

Another huge flash of lightning ignited the sky behind them and an unearthly wail broke through the rumbles of thunder. All four of them whirled around, staring across the expanse of moor at a dancing white ribbon of light in the distance. A jagged bolt of light split the sky, igniting the ribbon and turning it incandescent. Newton shut his eyes, and when he opened them again, it looked as if the moor was on fire.

"Where the hell is that?" Apollo yelled.

"Stormcrossed Manor," Kendall yelled back, to be heard above the storm.

But Newton wasn't paying full attention. The scream intensified, and Newton's skin erupted in goosebumps, his stomach twisting into knots.

Briar.

Chapter Twenty-One

Briar struggled to her feet, Caspian's hand under her elbow, and stared at the creature scaling the magical wall.

She felt odd, almost disembodied, cushioned from reality in the bubble of safety created by Caspian. It kept the creature's scream at bay, as well as the storm that raged around them. She shivered uncontrollably, the now faint wail of the creature like something from a nightmare.

"By the great Goddess," she stuttered, taking in the spectral form glowing in blue and white, its mouth an endless void. "Is that it? A banshee."

"I guess so. And for some reason, it seems to be staring at you."

Briar dragged her gaze away from it to glare at Caspian. "No, it's not."

He didn't move, never taking his eyes off it. "Yes, it is. It seems to know you, Briar. Or at least sense something about you."

She stared back at the creature, her knees still weak from the unbelievable feeling of loss that had cut her down. "How is that possible?"

His voice was immeasurably gentle as he said, "Because you're family. Linked to that house, as the banshee is."

"I am not linked to *her*." A shudder of revulsion ran through her. "That harbinger of death."

"That's not what I meant. That creature, as horrendous as she is pitiful, needs something, and we need to find out what. At least it's trapped..." And then Caspian faltered. "Uh, it's climbing the damn wall, Briar! How is that even possible?"

He was right. The shimmering white wall that should be untouchable by any supernatural creature was sparking with every touch of her fingers. "But she can't get through. It's actually providing a barrier she can't cross."

Another lightning bolt split the air, striking the barrier once more, and the whole thing ignited. But if anything, it seemed to give the creature more power, and she scuttled higher, her bony limbs moving like a crab.

Alarmingly, the top of the magical wall wasn't that much higher than she was.

Caspian grabbed Briar's hand. "We need to raise the height."

"How? We don't even know where the others are." She felt all at odds, her thoughts scattered.

Caspian grabbed her shoulders and turned her to face him, his eyes boring into hers. "Briar! You can do this. You have immense power. You're just shocked right now, and I get that. But we cannot let that thing get out!"

Briar took a deep, cleansing breath. Caspian was right. What the hell was wrong with her?

"I'm ready. What's the plan?"

"We begin Alex's spell again, but focus on raising the wall, not extending it. Ready? I'm going to drop the bubble."

She nodded, bracing herself, and Caspian's protection suddenly vanished, leaving them exposed to the wild weather and the wail of the creature. Together they faced the manor, repeating the words of the spell. Briar's toes were still digging into the thick grass and soil of the moor, and she could feel the power of the storm rippling beneath her feet. The Green Man stirred within her, a well of pure energy, and she tapped into his magic, channelling it out through her fingertips.

It seemed that Caspian was drawing on the wind, because she felt it vortex around them, a different intensity to the storm.

But none of it was enough. They could only raise the wall's height by a few feet; the spell needed all of them to work together. And the creature was getting ever closer to the top. She could feel Caspian's desperation mixing with her own.

A shout distracted both of them, and Briar turned to see Avery and Alex manifest out of the storm a short distance away, Alex bent over his knees, retching. Avery had used witch-flight to find them. Just beyond them, a flash of lights along the lane and the screech of brakes announced the arrival of Reuben and El. She had never been more relieved to see her friends.

In seconds they were all together, drenched from the rain, wary eyes on the creature. The noise of the storm was immense, and Caspian shouted to be heard. "We have to raise the wall! It needs to be a dome, or she'll get out!"

"In that case, I have to get inside," Alex shouted back. "We need gemstones in the centre. They are what bind the spell and make the wall mesh together."

Avery was tight-lipped with fury as she rounded on him. "Are you insane? You can't go in there!"

"I have to!" He pointed at the banshee, still clawing her way to the top. "You can see what's happening, Avery! We've achieved this much.

The spell works!" Despite the desperate situation, Alex was clearly buoyed by success. "Once I place the stones inside, I can join you with the spell. It will work—I know it will."

"You have extra stones, then?" El asked him.

Alex patted his pack. "Absolutely."

Reuben interrupted, water streaming down his face. "Mate, I don't like this at all, but you're right. Are you going to the house? That will be the centre."

Alex nodded, and turned back to Avery. "Take me to the drive entrance and I'll make my way from there. You then go back to the van. Reuben and El, you go back to your position. Give me five minutes, and then we start again!" El and Reuben nodded and raced back to the car, but Avery was mute with fury and worry. "Avery! I have to do this. Don't make this harder than it is."

Briar had never seen Avery look so desolate, but she finally agreed, and without looking at either Briar or Caspian, she vanished in a whirl of air, taking Alex with her.

Kendall gripped the dashboard, eyes intent on the road, biting down on every urge to remonstrate with Newton about his driving.

He was driving dangerously fast, taking corners at breakneck speed, and she knew he was employing every bit of knowledge he'd gained on his advanced driving course. Every now and again, as they swerved around corners and accelerated up rises on the moor, a flash of the strange wall around the manor would appear as lightning struck it, but then it would vanish. Titus's van was a short distance behind them. Newton had accelerated like a madman to get in front of him after they had sprinted to the end of the lane. Once inside the car, Newton had given her a curt explanation of the witches' spell, but she still didn't really understand what was happening.

Eventually, although she didn't want to distract Newton, she had to ask. "Why does it keep vanishing? Is their spell not working?"

"You're not attuned to magic—that's why you can't see it properly. Magic isn't visible to most people. The bloody storm is affecting it."

"Can you see magic?" she asked, surprised.

"No. Although, I've been around the witches long enough to feel it. It's like I told you earlier. It's a skill; something you'll get used to when you've been on the team long enough."

Of course. He'd told her only that morning, but it felt like a million years ago. "But you can see it now? Their wall, I mean?"

"Of course I bloody can, and clearly so can you!" His face screwed up with concentration as he skidded into a tight bend on a narrow lane. "Which means if *we* can see it, then so can all of bloody White Haven! Fuck! It's a nightmare."

"But..." Kendall started to say before death flashed before her eyes and she bit back on rising nausea. Newton straightened and slowed as the manor boundary came into view. She tried again. "But this storm is atrocious. No one will see it. They'll think it's just lightning. And the manor is well above the town."

"Suppose so," Newton grunted. He skidded to a halt, stopping only inches behind Reuben's car.

The rain was torrential now. They were at the heart of the storm, the lightning shattering the sky into fragments, and striking the magical wall at an alarming frequency. Water streamed down the car windows, turning their surroundings into indistinct blurs. Kendall could see Reuben and El's drenched figures at the entrance to the drive, the wall a short distance ahead of them.

"Where the fuck is Briar?" Newton growled.

Kendall threw the door open. "I'll find out. Wait here."

She was soaked before she'd even shut the door, but she sloshed to the witches' side. Both turned to her, arms raised, power balling in their palms, and then relaxed when they saw her. El grabbed her arm and pulled her close, and with a shock, Kendall found herself in a protective bubble, shielded from the elements. However, they were as bedraggled as she was, and had obviously been exposed to the weather at some point.

"What are you doing here?" Reuben asked, face creasing with concern, and all sign of his usually laidback, surfer vibe vanished.

"We saw the explosion on the wall. What's happening? Where's Briar?"

El pointed down the lane. "Further along, on the moor with Caspian. You guys need to keep back. We have to raise the wall. It's not high enough."

Kendall's fear intensified. "Why not?"

"Because the creature is trying to climb over it." El was matter of fact, and seemed to be coping with that information far better than Kendall was. "Alex is inside. Now go. We're starting the spell again in seconds."

"Inside that?" Kendall stared at the rippling white energy with horror. "Why?"

"It's the only way to make a dome of protection," Reuben answered. "Now get in the car and go! This could get messy!"

He pushed her away, and she stumbled back into the storm, towards the car.

Newton was not going to like this. Not one bit.

Alex ploughed through the deluge, not even bothering to try and shield himself from the weather. He was already drenched, and it added to his mood.

He had used his athame to open a doorway in the wall with three swift slashes, and darting through it, had sealed it quickly before running up the drive to the house. He had thought the atmosphere inside might feel calmer, but he was wrong. If anything, it felt wilder in here. A current of energy rippled along his skin, and the air sizzled. Their spell was attracting the storm, and he needed to counteract that in some way, but that was a worry to address later. Now, he needed to focus on creating a dome.

He paused as he saw the house ahead of him, and assessing his position, decided he was in the centre of the grounds. The manor squatted like a troll, and he positioned himself so that he could see it in his peripheral vision. Tamsyn was still in there, and he had no idea what she might be capable of.

The part of the wall that the creature was climbing was impossible to see because of the storm-lashed trees that towered over him, but he knew the direction it was in, and he would remain wary of its approach. *Just in case.*

Alex slicked his hair back, the pounding rain obscuring everything, and with annoyance, realised he needed a shield around him just to proceed. He threw one up quickly, grateful for the reprieve, and then hastily buried the gemstones in the earth beneath his feet. He uttered the words of power over the stones, gripped his athame in his slick fingers, and then channelled his magic through its blackened blade and to the sky above him.

He had made good time, and only minutes had passed. He hoped his coven was ready. Drawing his intent around him like a cloak, he started the spell, determined to drag the wall higher, inch by inch.

In seconds, Alex felt the power of his coven join him, and he redoubled his efforts. The gemstones' magic coursed up his body like a fountain and along his outstretched arm, striking the storm clouds above him. His protective bubble shattered, the elements whipping around him once more. He ignored it all, focussing only on the spell.

Above him the clouds boiled, a churning mass at the centre where his magic pooled. Lightning flashed across the sky, and he gripped his athame even tighter. They were succeeding. He could see the wall creeping higher and higher, and buoyed by their success, he raised his voice, shouting the spell into the storm.

The scream of the banshee cut through everything, curdling his blood. She was frustrated. Incensed. And still grief-stricken. And her screams were getting louder.

Herne's balls. She was coming for him.

Avery was furious with Alex, but she used her passion to magnify her power.

How dare he disappear in there without her? Logically, she knew he was right, but even so... The thought of losing him was too much.

Maybe the cry of the banshee—she couldn't deny it any longer, that's exactly what it was—was exacerbating her own fury and worry. It seemed the creature magnified every dark emotion. It was exhausting. And maybe that was reason the creature was killing people, even if unintentionally. Or perhaps this was no ordinary banshee, and she had turned into a killer deliberately, demoralising and weakening her victims emotionally so that they would easily succumb to her supernatural power.

Avery strengthened her resolve. She would trap this creature and kill it.

Alex would be fine.

The magical wall kept rising, until, with a snap, there it was! A beautiful dome of magic that trapped the creature. Avery stood for a few moments longer, making sure the spell held, and then eased her magic down, feeling her coven do the same.

The storm, however, showed no sign of abating. It still raged on. The storm clouds churned, the thunder cracked, lightning flashed, and the sea was a towering mass of waves. Behind the sound of the thunder, she heard the crash of waves against the cliffs.

She summoned air, and moments later appeared behind Reuben and El. She ran to their side. "Any sign of him?"

"None," Reuben said, staring up the long, dark driveway.

"I'm going in," Avery announced, her mouth so dry with fear for Alex's safety that her tongue felt thick. She pulled her athame out of her kit, and started to march past them.

Reuben pulled her back, his hand an iron clamp around her arm. "Don't be stupid, Avery! Wait. He'll be here soon."

"And if he's not?" The banshee's scream punctuated her words. "He's in there with that thing!"

She wrenched her arm free and stomped past him, a warning in her eyes not to stop her again, and she felt his stare between her shoulder blades.

But when she reached the shimmering wall and started to cut a doorway, nothing happened. She tried again, repeating the words of command. Again, the wall remained stubbornly sealed. She tried variations of the spell, growing more and more frantic with every iteration. She turned to Reuben and El, distraught.

"I can't get in! And that means *he* can't get out! Alex is trapped!"

Chapter Twenty-Two

Newton slammed on the brakes when he saw Briar and Caspian on the moor, and almost skidded into the hedge. He leapt out of the car, leaving the door open, and stumbled through the storm to Briar's side. He had no idea what Kendall was doing, and he didn't care.

He was breathless when he reached Briar, horrified to see her crying. Outraged, he looked at Caspian, thinking he should have protected her more, and then focussed back on Briar. "Are you all right? Injured? What the hell happened?"

Briar wiped her face, which was pointless. The rain was relentless, and they were all drenched. "I'm fine, Newton. That thing is doing weird things to my mood, but I'm okay, honestly. I'm just worried about Alex."

"Alex? Oh, of course." He swung around to stare at the wall of protection, relieved to see it was now a dome. "You did it."

"Yes, we did. Finally." Caspian looked exhausted as he hustled them back to the lane. "We need to join the others. There's nothing else we can do here. The spell is complete. And besides," he flinched as lightning forked overhead, "we're in danger of being killed."

They arrived back at the cars and found Kendall still inside Newton's, watching the shimmering dome with wide-eyed concern. Newton grimaced. *The storm better start abating soon, or the whole bloody town would see the hillside lit up like a bloody stadium.* With luck, most people were already tucked up in bed, or at least at home, warm and dry.

Briar turned to Caspian. "See you at the gate. I'll travel with Newton, and get them up to date."

It was only then that Newton realised Titus and Apollo were no longer behind him.

Where the hell had they gone?

Alex waited for the creature to arrive, his hands outstretched, magic at his fingertips, his athame still ready to conduct his power where he guided it.

The illuminated, spectral figure of the banshee swept through the trees as if they didn't exist, and swooped in front of him, her mouth wide-open as she emitted her ghastly scream.

It took all of Alex's power not to drop to his knees. But he knew his life depended on staying alert.

He was just about to blast the creature, when seemingly out of nowhere, Tamsyn appeared at his side, speaking some unintelligible language. She stepped in front of him, her head held high, and thrust her hand out.

Immediately, the creature vanished, and she seemed to take the storm with her. The strange feeling of super-charged air vanished, the wind dropped, the rain reduced to a drizzle, and the glowing, silvery dome faded into invisibility.

"What did you say to her?" Alex demanded, as Tamsyn turned her beetle-dark eyes on him.

"I told her to rest. That you were not her enemy. She'll go for a while. You better leave."

Alex still sensed a dark power within her, and it confused him. "You control her? Are you behind the deaths?"

"Don't be foolish! You're but a boy. What do you know of loss?"

Alex's anger rose like a cobra, thinking of Gil. "I know enough. What are you to her?"

She shook her head. "You would not understand." She grabbed his elbow, her fingers like claws as she marched him down the rutted drive, muddy from the rain. Alex didn't object. As much as he wanted to ask questions, he wanted even more to return to Avery and his coven. But they had barely progressed more than a few feet when the creature appeared in front of them again, snarling and spitting.

Tamsyn spoke in her incomprehensible language, and Alex took the time afforded him to study the creature. She was undoubtedly female, despite her unnatural height, long, spindly limbs, and shapeless body that was draped in rags. She had a bony, cadaverous face, framed with long, wispy hair, and her eyes were red and bloodshot, glowing with a hideous crimson light in the darkness. But it was her gaping maw that was the most terrifying part of her appearance. Her jaw seemed unhinged, so that when she opened her mouth, it encompassed her whole face. Flesh clung to her bones, but it was dry and shrunken, no blood beneath. Instinctively, Alex stepped back, despite the fact that

Tamsyn stood between them. Even at a distance, he could smell rotten flesh, and bile rose in his throat.

Tamsyn's words were commanding, but this time, the creature refused to move, and once again her wail filled the air. Tamsyn turned, her lips pinched with fury, and tugged him back to the house with her.

"What's going on?" Alex asked, now utterly confused as he stumbled in Tamsyn's wake.

"You're trapped, boy. For some reason, she wants you here." She stared up at him. "You're staying with me."

El watched as their shimmering wall of protection vanished, leaving only the vibrant feel of their magic behind. It was still there, but at least now it was invisible from most people's sight.

The storm had abated, but the rain still fell steadily, and she had long-since given up trying to protect them from the elements. Now, she welcomed it. Being drenched suited her mood.

Avery still stood in front of the protective field, athame gripped in her hand, looking both desolate and furious. Reuben was trying to reassure her, but seemed to be having no luck. El wanted to comfort her, but knew that right now, Avery wasn't in the mood. She wanted results, not platitudes.

The sound of car engines made her turn around, and with relief, she saw Caspian pull to the side of the lane, Newton behind him. Newton and Kendall stayed in the car talking with Briar, but Caspian joined her. He was also soaked, his hair slicked back, revealing his strong cheekbones.

He nodded towards Avery. "What's going on? Where's Alex?"

"Trapped inside. I'm sure he's okay, but we haven't seen him, and Avery can't get in."

"She can't create a doorway?"

"No." Despite her assertion that Alex was fine, she still felt a tremor of worry. "The creature must have trapped him."

"Let's call it what it is, El. She's a banshee. We've suspected it, but seeing her tonight has confirmed it for me."

"Then what does she want with Alex?"

He met her eyes finally. "I don't know. But talking about it here won't do us any good. Let's head to Reuben's. I'd like to meet this Rosa woman."

She glanced back towards Avery. "She won't want to leave Alex."

"Well, she can't stay here all night. Have we phoned him?"

"It just rings and rings. I think the protection is blocking it. Or the banshee's power."

"There's probably a landline at the manor. We'll get the number from Rosa. With luck, he's in the house. That's the most logical place for him to be."

El shuddered. "I hope so. He'll be dry, at least. But it's an odd house, Caspian. I wouldn't want to stay there."

"Rosa and her kids have been there for months. It can't be that bad." He smiled confidently. "Come and help me get Avery to leave. I think we'll need all of us to talk sense into her."

When they reached her side, it sounded as if Reuben was already exasperated. "Avery! You can't stay here. You've tried all manner of spells, and none of them work. And we're drenched. We could get pneumonia."

Avery glared at him, and then at El and Caspian. "Don't you two start! Alex is in there, and I'm not leaving without him!"

"You don't trust him to look after himself?" Caspian asked straightaway.

Avery faltered. "Of course I do! He achieved this!" Her arm waved outward, encompassing the spell. "It's amazing. So strong. *He's* strong!"

"In that case, why are you so keen to stay? Reuben is right. If you can't get in, and he's trapped, he'll have found a way to protect himself. He's no fool, Avery. We need to regroup. At Reuben's."

Reuben nodded in agreement, and El watched Caspian with admiration. He'd found the perfect way to reason with Avery—by focussing on Alex's abilities. It gave her no room to argue.

Although, she still tried. "Yes, but..." She stared up the long driveway.

"But nothing, Avery. You know I'm right."

El touched Avery's arm. "Come on. The temperature's dropping, and I'm cold. I need a hot shower. There's only so much my magic can do." Images of Reuben's warm snug was already filling her thoughts. "And I'm not leaving you here."

Avery finally nodded, her shoulders dropping with disappointment. "All right. But I want to try again tomorrow."

"We all will," Reuben said, shooting Caspian a grateful glance over her head as he steered her towards his car. "We'll drive you to your van. No more witch-flight for you tonight. You've expended enough energy."

"I'll take her," Caspian offered. "You open up the house, and we'll be with you soon."

Briar sipped her herbal tea, watching the flames twist and dance in Reuben's fireplace in the snug.

Almost an hour had passed since they had left Stormcrossed Manor. An hour in which they had either showered or just towelled themselves dry, sometimes using magic to speed things along.

Briar still felt hollowed out, as if her encounter with the banshee had scoured her insides—physically and emotionally. And now she was preparing to meet Rosa, her cousin, and she had no idea how she felt about that.

El was busying herself in the kitchen, preparing snacks with Caspian, while Reuben was somewhere in his enormous house, locating Rosa. Avery was outside on the terrace, still trying to reach Alex. The storm had abated, leaving the sky washed clear and the air cooler, but the heat was already building again, mixing with the damp aftermath of the storm.

Kendall was conferring with Newton, and they were also in the kitchen. She could hear them debating what to do about Titus and Apollo, who had vanished in the storm. *They couldn't have gone far.* None of them doubted that.

A knock on the door that connected the snug to the hall made her turn, and Reuben stuck his head in. His blond hair was sticking up on his head from where he'd towel dried it, and his bright blue eyes were full of concern. "Is now a good time? Rosa is with me."

She smiled at his compassion. "Of course. I'm not an invalid."

He grinned and threw the door open, ushering Rosa inside as he made the introductions. "I'll leave you two alone."

Briar stood to shake Rosa's hand, feeling strangely formal as she took in Rosa's appearance. She was slim too, but taller than Briar, and her hair was light brown rather than dark. She was also older than her, and right now looked tired and undoubtedly confused.

"Sorry," Briar said, leading Rosa to a seat by the fire. "I bet you're wondering why Reuben is being so mysterious."

Rosa's eyes flitted around the room before settling on Briar. "Sort of. I hardly know him, so this is all very strange. And..." she faltered. "I couldn't help but see that some odd things have been happening at my home, Stormcrossed Manor. I was watching out of the window. You're a good friend of Reuben's, I gather. He said you had something to share." She was staring at Briar as if she had two heads, and Briar realised how brave she was to be sitting here, her two kids asleep in a strange house, after seeing the manor lit up like a snow globe.

Briar had debated how to start this conversation, and in the end decided that speed was better than some long, drawn-out history. There'd be time for that later. "My friend Newton, the Detective Inspector, has been doing some research on your manor and family, because of the screams you heard and the recent deaths in the area, and has found something unexpected. Your mother, Merrin, is sister to my mother, Jennifer. We're cousins." She shrugged apologetically. "I didn't know I had an aunt, let alone a cousin, so I'm a bit shocked, actually. I'm sure you are, too. I am excited too, of course," she added, in case she sounded more horrified than pleased.

"Oh, my God! You're Aunt Jennifer's child? My mother tried to find you after we heard that she died, but she couldn't find a thing! You just disappeared."

Briar blinked with surprise. "You knew about me, then?"

"I knew she'd had a child, that was all." Rosa leaned forward, drinking her in. "She hid you and your father from us. Oh, my God!" she repeated. "You even look like her! And my mother."

"My mother kept you a secret completely. I never knew about Stormcrossed Manor, or Aunt Merrin, or Tamsyn! None of it." Resentiment rose up in Briar. At least Rosa had known *something. She had known nothing!* "Why didn't she keep in touch?"

Rosa eased back in her chair, her fingers gripping the arms. "For the same reason my mother left the manor. I understand now that I've been living there a while with Tamsyn, and have seen the full horror of the family curse. The sight." Her voice was bitter.

"It's not a curse," Briar said automatically. "It's a gift. But one that must be controlled, before it controls you."

Rosa's eyes narrowed, her gaze sweeping over her suspiciously. "You have it, too?"

"No, but I know of such things." Suddenly, Rosa's declaration to Alex and Reuben that she knew little about the sight struck her as a lie. "You lived with your mother, and are obviously still in touch with her. You told Alex that she told you to come here, and that your grandmother was struggling! *Our* grandmother," she corrected herself, feeling weird about it. "You must have known about the sight!"

Rosa bristled with annoyance. "Only that the ability ran in our family. I have never experienced it, or seen anyone have a vision. I certainly didn't know Beth had the ability, or that it would strike so young! As for the house, my mother just said it was odd and that she didn't really like living there. I thought it was just an excuse to leave home. In fact, it's been so long since it's ever been mentioned that it has become a myth. I didn't actually believe it!" Her eyes filled with tears. "Now poor Beth has this burden."

Briar took a deep breath. Antagonising her wasn't going to achieve anything, and Rosa was just as shocked as Briar. "Sorry. I had an encounter with the banshee tonight." Rosa flinched at that word, eyes widening with shock, but Briar carried on before she could ask any questions. "It's left me feeling weird...as well as finding out about everything else." Briar gestured to the teapot, saying a silent spell to reheat the tea steeping inside. "Why don't you join me in a cup, and tell me about Beth?"

Briar would bring up Tamsyn later. She was the key, and they all knew it.

Chapter Twenty-Three

Newton accepted his tea from El, but eyed Reuben's whiskey enviously. That looked so much better.

Reuben saw him and lifted his glass. "Are you sure you don't want one?"

"Positive. I have to drive home."

"No, you don't," Kendall intervened. She was sitting at the kitchen table in jeans and a t-shirt, her short hair tussled after she'd rubbed it dry with a towel. She looked none the worse for her experience, and actually seemed quite at home in Reuben's kitchen. No doubt she was just glad to be part of the team. She sipped her tea, and then said, "I could drive you home. I don't like whiskey, and promise I won't crash your car."

Newton was about to protest, feeling it would be unprofessional in front of his new sergeant, and then thought that's actually what sergeants were for. When Reuben wiggled the bottle and Caspian raised his own glass, he relented. "Fuck it. Yes, please." He tossed his tea outside the open French doors that shared the same terrace as the snug next door. "Sorry, El. I'm sure your tea is lovely."

El laughed and raised her glass of wine. "I'm not offended. After tonight's events, I also needed more than tea."

"The thing is," Newton said after taking a sip of the fiery liquid, "we should be looking for Titus and Apollo." He'd already updated them on their frustrating encounter. "They're lurking out there, somewhere."

Kendall just shrugged. "But they know we're on to them. And even though they know about the manor now, they can't do anything. Not unless they have more magic than the witches, and I doubt that."

Reuben dropped into a chair next to her, his usual, breezy manner on show. "I doubt it, too. That was some spell we just cast. Now we just need to work out another way to get Alex out." He looked up as Avery entered. Her hair was thick and wild after the rain, rubbed dry into waves. "Any news?"

"No." Avery walked to the kitchen counter and poured herself a large glass of red wine before sitting at the table. "The mobile number just keeps ringing out, and the landline is dead."

"He'll be okay," Newton said, sitting next to her and trying to keep her spirits up. "He had his pack with him, right?"

"Yes, with plenty of magic supplies and his grimoire. That's something, at least. I just wish I knew what was happening in there." And then her eyes widened. "Ghost OPS!"

"Already tried them," Reuben said. "I can't get through. That storm was huge. It must have knocked everything out. We're running on the generator now, or we'd have no power, either."

Newton had forgotten that. That was why the lights seemed dimmer than normal, and they were managing with only a couple of low lamps rather than the bright overhead kitchen light. And why the food El had prepared had taken longer than normal to cook.

Kendall groaned. "Shit. That means Alex will be in darkness, too."

"He has witch-lights," Caspian told her, "and hopefully some candles. I imagine he's not hiding his magic any longer. Especially if he's with Tamsyn."

Reuben grunted in agreement. "It's not like our spell will have gone unnoticed! And she strikes me as a smart cookie."

"Yes!" El said as she finally produced the meal with a flourish and placed it on the table. There was a large bowl of fries, and a tray of nachos slathered in melted cheese. She sat down, gesturing for everyone to help themselves. "I've had rather a brilliant idea. I think I know of a way we can get in."

"How?" Reuben asked through a mouthful of food.

"Sam told me about a blade that will kill a banshee. It's a combination of metals, spells, and magical symbols. I said I'd make him one, but actually, I'll make two. One for me, too. Anyway, he gave me the specs, and I was intending to make it today, but well, that didn't happen. It has another ability, one that I'm uncomfortable about, but that will potentially be just what we need. It can penetrate protection spells. Sort of cut through them."

"That *is* worrying," Caspian said, eyes narrowing with alarm.

"I know, but what choice do we have? Sam is coming to the shop tomorrow, and I'll work in my courtyard."

"You have your own smithy?" Kendall asked, surprised.

El nodded. "It's small compared to Dante's, but big enough for a short blade. It also means I can use magic in there freely." She looked sheepish. "I don't like to expose Dante to it. It doesn't seem fair, although I know he suspects me."

Reuben sniggered. "He does, but he has no idea of the scale of your power."

"And it will stay that way," El said firmly. "Anyway, I'm hoping that the blade will break through the protection spell on the house."

Avery leaned forward, her mood palpably lifting. "While I hate that you're making a knife with such properties, right now I think that's a great idea. Like you said, we have little choice. How long will it take you?"

"If I start on it first thing, I could have the basic blades done by midday, and start the spell work soon after. It depends how complex the symbols are."

"So, we can try tomorrow night?"

El squeezed her hand. "Absolutely."

"And we can investigate spells, too," Reuben added, looking to Caspian for confirmation. "We can focus specifically on banshees. And Avery, you should check with Dan for specific banshee myths. He might have new information we can use."

"Sure." Avery was becoming more animated with every word. "And I'll think about Alex's spell. Really take it apart for clues as to what else might have changed the parameters."

"Good." Newton nodded, pleased at their progress. "Me, Kendall, and Moore will continue to do background checks on the victims. So many people have heard the banshee's scream now, and yet so few have died. The only thing that links three of the victims are bereavements, but we haven't investigated them all yet. That will be tomorrow's job."

"And track down Titus and Apollo," Kendall added, a glint of determination in her eyes. "They pissed me off. I intend to find out what they're up to. I'm sure they're here for more than just this issue. And also the woman who visited Briar. She must still be here somewhere."

She was right. Additionally, there was the map of Ravens' Wood to consider. Newton needed to share that with the witches, too.

Reuben leaned back in his chair, raising his arms behind his head as he stretched like a satisfied cat. "Sounds like a plan. I'll chase up Ghost OPS, too. Hopefully, they have some good footage. And with luck and cousinly love," he glanced towards the snug, "Briar has some useful information, too."

"And Alex?" Newton asked, his gaze returning to the window. Despite his faith in his friend's abilities, he was worried for him. "Is there anything we can do for him now?"

Avery followed his gaze too, her earlier animation gone as her lips tightened. "Nothing except hope that he's safe."

Alex stepped into Stormcrossed Manor, and as soon as he was through the front door, he felt a creeping dread seep into his bones.

Any feeling of hope he'd entertained as the spell took hold had been ebbing away since he knew he was trapped, but now despair threatened to overwhelm him. He paused, taking deep breaths while he threw up a circle of personal protection.

Tamsyn's voice sounded hollow next to him. "You'd do well to keep that in place while you're here. She senses your power."

Alex froze as he tried to focus on Tamsyn's shadow-draped figure, unwilling to use witch-light. He wasn't sure he'd like to see the weight of knowledge and darkness she carried. The night was dark enough. "You know what I'm doing?"

"I can feel it. The sight makes me sensitive to magic and the power of that which we cannot see. We are alike, you and I. You see what I carry. I know it. I see it in your eyes."

Alex hated the comparison. "We are nothing alike. You carry something dark within you. I seek only light."

"You think I carry this by choice? Fool. I carry it because I must. It is my duty. I thought it would protect my girls, but instead it has driven them away. Until now."

"You mean your daughters? And now Rosa, Beth, and Max?"

"Who else?" She sounded scornful. "I had hoped *she* would rest until my death, but now the storm has awakened her and she has grown too strong for me...almost."

"*Almost?*" Alex's annoyance and incredulity overcame his fear. "You're deluded. People are dead because of that thing! We are trying to stop it. Her! You know who she is?"

"Of course. The banshee has been with us for generations. Now she oversteps her boundaries. But you..."

She paused, and Alex threw a witch-light up above them, suddenly needing to see her expression. Then he wished he hadn't. Its pale, blueish-white light threw her features into sharp relief, her wrinkles now deep crevices on her face. Her beetle black eyes, so intense, looked possessed. It took all of Alex's willpower not to step back in shock.

"What about me?" he asked, not sure if he wanted to hear the answer.

"I foresaw it. All of it. I hoped I was wrong, that I could control her myself, but the sight is never wrong. It is just our interpretation that can muddy the waters. You know this, too. You have the sight."

Alex didn't say anything to that. His heart was beating loudly in his chest, and there was a drumming behind his eyes that threatened his vision. And his sanity. It was as he had foreseen. *The tangle of branches, the feeling of being trapped. The presence of grief and loss.*

Tamsyn stepped closer, lifting her head to look up at him, her gaze searching his. "Events are now in motion. You are meant to be here, Alex Bonneville, White Haven witch. You must help me control her, or we will both die trying."

Chapter Twenty-Four

When Cassie woke up the next morning, the sun streaming in through the blinds and onto the sofa she'd slept on, she wondered if the night before had been a dream. The terrifying image of the creature at Stormcrossed Manor, the thunder, the lightning, the loss of power, and the torrential rain. It had felt like the end of the world, for a while.

However, when she sat upright, easing the kink out of her neck, the mess in the office confirmed the reality of the night before. It was strewn with empty pizza boxes, coffee cups, beer cans, and crisp packets.

It had been impossible for her to drive home, and actually, she hadn't wanted to. Her flatmates were away, and the thought of staying on her own filled her with dread. Plus, the power had gone out. Ben had offered her his bed, even volunteering to change his no doubt grubby sheets, but she declined, preferring to sleep in the office.

After the other two went to bed, she had listened to the ebbing storm, hoping the witches were okay. It was the thought of their safety that made her get up and check her phone, turning the computers and screens on as she did so. *Was seven in the morning too early to call Briar? No. She'd be up, despite their late night.*

Briar answered quickly, and Cassie headed to the corner of the room where the kettle and a selection of cups were stored in a small cupboard with tea and coffee supplies. She put the kettle on as they talked, relieved to hear her friend's voice. But by the end of the phone call, Cassie's mood had soured.

She hung up as Dylan entered the office, his short dreads sticking up on his head and sleep in his eyes. "Are you talking to yourself?" he asked, squinting in the sunlight. "Ooh, great! Power!" He sat at his desk, pushing the detritus from the night before out of the way, and Cassie rolled her eyes. It was as if he didn't even see the mess.

"No. I was talking to Briar. There was a problem last night. Alex is stuck at the manor."

Dylan had disappeared behind the row of monitors, but now his head popped up over the top. "You're kidding!"

"Why would I kid about that? Moron. Coffee?"

"Yep, strong. How is he trapped? Weren't they all supposed to be outside of the circle?"

"He went inside to place the gemstones in order to make a dome. That was the only way to stop the creature from getting out."

A mixture of relief and concern flashed across Dylan's face, and Cassie knew why; she'd experienced the same mix of emotions herself. Relief that the creature was trapped, and horror that Alex was trapped with it. She handed him his coffee, and sat next to him as he tried to access the cameras again.

"Worrying as that is," Cassie continued as she watched him access the files, "the worst thing is that they can't speak to him. Neither his phone or the landline work."

"Shit. That is worrying," Dylan said, pausing to look at her. "We don't know if he's okay, or..."

"He *is* okay. He has to be!" Cassie refused to entertain the thought of anything else. "If we could get the feed going, we might be able to see him."

Dylan exhaled heavily as the first of the screens flickered to life. "I wouldn't hold your breath. Camera number one's feed is fuzzy. And so is that one." They watched as camera after camera displayed a flickering, grey screen. "Bollocks. That's all of them."

Cassie wasn't a tech whiz like Dylan, but one thing did seem obvious to her. "But the screen isn't black. Does that mean that the cameras are still working, and just the feed is interrupted?"

Dylan looked at her, eyebrow raised. "Very good! Yep, that's exactly what it means. Their dome of protection must be interfering with the signal, which is why Alex's phone won't work."

"Is there any way to try to clean it up?"

"No. It's the interference on their end. The only thing we can hope for is that Alex can do something...if he's free to roam the grounds. For all we know, he's being held captive in the house."

Cassie was grateful Dylan hadn't suggested that Alex was dead. There was still something to hope for, at least. "Good idea. I'll tell Avery. You never know...she might have another way to communicate with him."

Dylan nodded, already scrolling through the previous night's footage. "Good plan. And I'll search what we have recorded. Hopefully, something in here will tell us what's really going on."

Avery marched into her shop the next morning just after opening time to find Sally behind the counter, and Dan putting on some music. Blues notes filled the air, and it seemed like a good soundtrack for her mood.

She had slept badly after using witch-flight to get home from Reuben's house, despite his offer of a bed. Part of her wanted to remain in his house, knowing that Stormcrossed Manor was only a short distance away. However, another part of her couldn't bear to be so close and yet not be able to see Alex, or even talk to him. She decided to return home, seeking the comfort of her cats and familiar surroundings. She drank two large glasses of wine in the hope that the alcohol would help her sleep. It hadn't. Instead, she'd suffered through a terrible night of light sleeping mixed with tossing and turning.

"Dan! I need as much information on banshees as possible. I've done some reading of my own, and it seems that they are attached to a family, sometimes for years! Like a bloody pet!"

"Well. Good morning to you, too," Dan said breezily. "What's set you off?"

"Alex being trapped in Stormcrossed Manor with a devil woman!"

Dan and Sally both took a sharp intake of breath. Sally spoke up first. "Oh, no! Is he okay?"

"How?" Dan asked. Then his eyes widened. "It was you guys, wasn't it? Up on the moor last night? The lightning struck that area several times."

"You saw it?" Avery asked, growing more alarmed and ignoring their other questions. "Did you see the dome?"

Sally and Dan exchanged worried glances, as Dan said, "No dome, but I saw the top of the hill glowing. Well, *we* did, actually. I was staying at Caroline's flat, and it has a decent view of the moor. It's still above us, though."

Avery sighed, relieved. He was right. That part of the moor was above town, and no one would really be able to see it from White Haven. "Thank the Gods for that. It was huge, actually."

Sally placed her hands on her hips, a grimace twisting her lips. "Avery, you're making no sense. What happened?"

Avery took a deep breath and relayed their night's activities and Briar's family connection. "As you can see, we had great success on one hand, and utter disaster on the other. And ever since Alex went inside, I can't speak to him! It's a nightmare!" Avery realised her hands were shaking, and she placed her coffee cup down before she sloshed it everywhere. "I've been trying to remain calm, but I can't focus!"

Dan moved her coffee behind him. "A restorative, calming tea for you, Ave. Coffee is not your friend right now."

She fumbled for a stool and sat down. "I need to be sharp today. Not an empty noodlehead."

Sally hugged her. "You are not a noodlehead. You're worried. But Alex will be okay. Let's be practical. Dan, tell us about banshees."

He glanced around the shop to make sure it was empty, and then settled on his own stool. "As I mentioned the other day, the banshee is primarily a creature attached to Celtic myth and the Celtic race, but not exclusively. However, your news that an Irish woman married into the Trevithick family pretty much seals the deal. It must have come with her. What did you say her name was?"

"Niamh McCarthy. Her husband, Jeremiah, died quite early into their marriage. She was a young mum, and never remarried."

"Interesting. It's hard to know, of course, but if it had been a love match, then she could have been grief-stricken for years. According to myth, a banshee is often devoted to a family, sticking with them for generations. Traditionally they are not violent, and don't cause deaths, but they do appear to warn of the death of a family member.

They are so upset about this impending death that they weep and wail. Their screams are said to be bloodcurdling, and their eyes are red from c rying."

Avery recalled the horribly reddened eyes of the creature as she clambered up the wall. "Yes, I can confirm her red eyes, and her wail was just awful. It contained so much loss. But hold on," she said, confused. "She *predicts* death? Not causes it?"

"Yes. It's one of her special abilities—her main ability, actually. The power to divine future deaths."

Sally cut in, "But why do some families have them and not others? Where do they come from?"

"Good question," Dan said warming to his subject. "There are a couple of theories. The first one suggests that it's the ghost of a female relative who had either been murdered or who had died in childbirth. Their grief and rage transform their spirits into the banshee, and henceforth she stays with her family for generations."

Avery nodded. "Okay, so this particular banshee could be one of Niamh's—and I guess Briar's—long-deceased ancestors." She shook her head, still unable to believe that Briar was related to the Trevithicks. "And that's also interesting, because it seems the family have the gift of the sight. Or rather, the female line does."

Sally frowned. "But Briar doesn't have the sight, does she?"

"No. Not unless it's been latent up until now, but that's unlikely," Avery said. "It skips generations. Rosa, Briar's cousin, doesn't have the ability either, but Beth does." She turned to Dan. "Could Niamh's spirit be the banshee? It seemed to rise from her grave."

"I guess it's possible. Did she die violently?"

"I don't think so. I think she died of old age."

"But," Sally suggested, "if she mourned her whole life, could that have changed her spirit? I mean, how does it transform?"

Dan shrugged. "Another great question. I have no idea, and from what I've read, no one else does, either. Perhaps strong emotion of any sort can warp the spirit, but only those of Celtic ancestry will become a banshee?" He raked his hand through his hair that had up until that point looked a little tidier than usual. Because of Caro, perhaps. "I'm just guessing."

"You said there were a couple of theories," Avery reminded him. "What's the other?"

"Ah! Some people believe they are faery queens, deprived of their land, and cast out from their people, and they have nothing to do with spirits at all."

"A malevolent fey?" Sally said with a snort. "We should ask Shadow about that!"

Dan grinned. "And I would imagine she would say that fey queens have better things to do than mourn the deaths of humans."

"But if it is a fey spirit," Avery said, feeling like she was clutching at straws, "Shadow might be able to help."

"Do you really think that's what it is?" Dan looked at her dubiously, arms crossed over his chest.

Avery huffed. "No. I think she's a grief-stricken spirit of some sort. But if you say it's not violent normally, and foresees death rather than causes it, why are people dying around it?"

"Perhaps she's not responsible. Maybe she has foreseen their deaths too, and that's what the wailing is about."

"She's trying to warn them, not kill them?" Sally asked, looking even more confused. "Then why did those people die?"

"I don't know. Sorry," Dan said. "I'm just telling you what I know about banshees—which still isn't much, I admit."

"Last night her wail demoralised me so much," Avery admitted, "that I wondered if that had contributed to the deaths in some way, but I think I'm grasping at straws. We're all suggesting so many things that I don't know what to think anymore. However, you've told me more than I knew before, and I feel a bit more positive. Perhaps she senses Alex's psychic abilities, too, and thinks he can help her. Maybe that's why he's trapped?" Avery wasn't sure she liked having more questions than answers, but she felt more positive than when she woke up. "I need to get my van out of the field behind the manor. Are you two okay here?"

"Of course," Sally said shooing her off. "Just be careful, Avery. There's still too much happening that we don't understand. And say hi to Reuben and the others—I know you'll visit them!"

Avery suppressed a grin as she headed to the back room. *Sally and Dan knew her far too well.*

Stormcrossed Manor felt gloomy despite the daylight, and Alex sighed as he stood on the threshold of the front door, wondering how safe it might be to wander the grounds.

He had seen nothing of Tamsyn after her ominous words the night before. As soon as she had made her proclamation, she had disappeared to her wing, instructing him to make himself at home. *Some hope of that in such a creepy house with the banshee prowling outside.*

Despite the fact that he insisted he had lots of questions, she waved him away imperiously, saying, "I'm old and I need to sleep. It can all wait until morning."

Part of him was relieved. Alex wasn't easily unnerved, especially by psychic phenomena; it was something he was confident with. However, Tamsyn's strong presence made him very uneasy. There was also no doubt that she had zero fear of him, despite the fact that she knew he was a witch.

What exactly had Tamsyn foreseen? All night, Alex had been pondering that comment. It had preoccupied his dream-filled, fitful sleep on the sofa in the living room he had found at the far end of the house. Clearly, Tamsyn thought he was there to help her, even though she'd tried to escort him off the grounds the night before. It was a surprise to learn that she wanted to banish the banshee. He'd actually thought she was helping it. *Perhaps the banshee also wanted help, and that was why she had blocked his escape?* And that posed another question.

Was a banshee sentient? Did she know of the deaths she was causing? Did she want to stop?

He groaned. *So many questions, and so few answers.* At least one thing was certain. He was trapped in the grounds with no way out. Only working with Tamsyn seemed to offer a solution, and the banshee seemed to know it. And if Tamsyn had foreseen it, maybe the banshee had, too. After all, she also had the sight. *Perhaps she was feeding off his magic in some way? Or rather, all of their magic. Maybe the spell that trapped her inside also enhanced her strength.*

Alex leaned against the doorframe, watching the shadows retreat as the sun crept higher into the sky, revealing the torn branches, leaves, mud, and other detritus scattered across the grounds—the only evidence of the huge storm and the crazy events of the night before. It seemed like a nightmare now. However, one thing was certain. If the banshee had wanted him dead, she would have already killed him, and with that in mind, he set out across the grounds.

The crackle of magic from their protection spell was palpable, to him at least, but fortunately it was invisible to the human eye. As he walked, he tried to phone Avery, but again the call failed. Something he had not planned had made his spell block all communication. He would try to contact Avery telepathically later, but for that he would need a quiet, safe space.

Without a clear destination in mind, he meandered through the overgrown courtyards, their cracked paving strewn with shredded leaves and petals. With a lot of work, this garden would be stunning, and he smiled to think that hopefully Briar would come here and enjoy it. She would treasure this place. Return it to its former glory, if she wanted to. If she liked Rosa, or Tamsyn when she finally met her, and wanted to maintain her link to the family.

He found himself at the graveyard, his feet guiding him subconsciously, and he saw the video camera mounted on a wooden stake. He hurried towards it. As usual, Dylan had placed it in a waterproof box, and with relief, Alex saw that it was still working, the blinking red light steady and regular. *But was the feed leaving the grounds? If it wasn't, was there a way to manipulate it?*

He spent a few moments studying it and smiling hopefully into the camera before abandoning it. For now, he would set himself up by Niamh's grave. If the banshee was here, he was going to communicate with her, and with luck, the camera would record it all.

Newton scowled at Kendall and Moore. "What do you mean, they've disappeared?"

"Their van has not returned to the field behind Rupert's house," Moore told him from the chair across Newton's desk. "And without any address to go on, we don't know where they are."

"They're not around Stormcrossed Manor?"

"Not that I could see," Kendall answered. "I drove all the way around there this morning. The only van in the neighbouring field was Avery's."

"CCTV?" Newton suggested hopefully. "There are cameras at all sorts of places."

"In the centre of town, yes," Moore agreed. "Not so much on the lanes."

"Bollocks! Then where have they gone?" He thought for a moment, and then, "That bloody map of Ravens' Wood! They must be there."

"Guv, it's not an offense to be in a wood!" Moore pointed out.

"I know that! But what are they doing there? They are hunters!" Newton exclaimed. "They searched those cottages, and I knew I should have arrested them. Titus has more or less threatened Avery, and now they know about Stormcrossed Manor!"

Kendall shrugged. "But they can't get in there. No one can."

"No, but," Newton said voicing his fears, "Ravens' Wood is a weird, supernatural place. What if they know that, and try to...I don't know... Catch a dryad or something!"

Newton suddenly realised he'd probably said too much. No one except those who had been there on the night of the fight with the Empusa at Crossroads Circus had witnessed the sudden birth of the ancient forest now called Ravens' Wood. A gift from the Green Man and the Raven King. Everyone else believed it had been there for centuries. *Crazy, powerful magic.*

"A dryad!" Kendall shot up in her chair. "There are dryads in Ravens' Wood?"

"No there aren't," Moore remonstrated, glaring at Newton. "They exist in some kind of liminal state, only visible at certain times of the day, or even year. It's a fey borderland. And if you think Titus or Apollo could harm a fey, Guv, then you've lost your marbles."

Newton was struck dumb. *Fey borderland.* Where was Moore getting it from? He didn't think he knew anything about the ancient forest.

Moore shook his head, amused. "I talk to Shadow, and I hear things. That wood has been a source of wonder and terror since its inception hundreds of years ago. I got lost in there as a child, and thought I was stuck there forever. I got out eventually, obviously. I have had a deep respect for it ever since. In fact, that place is one of the reasons I became interested in the supernatural in the first place."

Now Newton was even more dumbfounded. First, it was clear that Moore had some kind of implanted memory of something that had never actually happened, since the wood had been around for less than a year. Secondly, did everyone have such memories? Thirdly, was that the most Moore had ever said at one time?

Newton, always a master of his composure, recovered swiftly and just nodded. "Of course. You're right. And if White Haven knows about its unusual tenants and occasional wildness, why shouldn't our visitors?"

"Dryads!" Kendall repeated. "Fey borderland! I never knew!"

"It used to be a closely-guarded, locals-only thing," Moore told her. "I suppose with recent events, that knowledge will spread. But my point is, hunters or not, I doubt they will have success in there."

"I'm not so sure," Newton mused. "They had all sorts of magical paraphernalia in their van. They might have some black magic tools that could do real harm." Newton ran through what they needed to do. "Kendall, cruise around Ravens' Wood, check the laybys for their vehicle, but don't go in. They won't act in the day, anyway. Moore, keep following up on any connections with the victims, specifically recent bereavements. That appears to be a likely angle, considering what we've found so far. I'll head to the post-mortems. I doubt there'll be a variation on cause of death, but you never know."

Kendall was already heading to the door. "If they are at Ravens' Wood, what then? The witches are busy."

Newton grinned. "But Shadow isn't."

Chapter Twenty-Five

E l lowered the blade into the barrel of water, and steam hissed from it like a dragon, making her already hot smithy even hotter.

She winced and turned her face away, holding the blade at arm's length, the heavy-duty, long leather gloves that reached to her elbows protecting her skin. She then placed it on the bench and examined it with a critical eye, pulling her gloves off as she did so.

Sam stepped to her side. He'd arrived an hour or two earlier, and had been standing at the back of her small workshop, leaving every now and again to get some fresh air. Normally El hated having anyone around while she worked, but she was so focussed that she'd almost forgotten he was there.

"That looks pretty good," he said, admiring her metalwork. "You've made it quicker than I thought you would."

"Courtesy of a little magic, of course. I wove it into the metal as I worked. It speeds up the process, as well as imbuing it with special properties."

Sam nodded. "I could feel it. You're a fire witch?"

"It's one of my strengths. A family trait. I like working with metals and gemstones. They sing to me."

Sam raised an eyebrow. "Sing? I've never heard that before."

"Perhaps I'm exaggerating it, but that's how it sometimes feels to me. All metals have special properties, and some are stronger than others. I can feel them. When several of them are mixed together," she told him, trying to describe how her magic made sense of metals and their powers—their correspondences, some would call it, "it really does sound like a song. They harmonise."

"Wow! A symphony of metal." Sam smiled, clearly impressed as he stared at the blade again. "That must be quite something. I use magic, of course, but more prescriptively. Not like you do."

"My magic is in my bloodline. You buy your spells?"

"I have learned to use sigils and certain words of power, but others I buy from an old friend." He cocked his head at her. "You disapprove?"

"Of course not. We make spells for our friends, too. But I trust them to use them responsibly."

"And you think I wouldn't?" A challenge was in his eyes, and annoyance. "I've learned the hard way to respect magic."

"I'm glad to hear that." El smiled and shrugged. She liked Sam and didn't want to offend him. Besides, he had shared knowledge they needed. "Sorry. Not all are so discerning."

"Of course not. Titus being one of them."

Mention of his name reminded El of Newton's encounter the night before, and she told Sam about it. She had already told him about the events at Stormcrossed Manor. "He and his friend, Apollo, followed Newton and Kendall to the manor, so they know where this particular issue has its centre."

Sam folded his arms across his broad chest, repeating his earlier complaint. "I wish you'd have shared that with us."

"I told you! Last night was about containing it. It was dangerous, and you didn't need to be there. This blade is about ending it. Ending her."

El ran her palm along the now cool blade, eager to get on, but Sam had turned away from her as he studied her smithy and some of the metals she had stored there, as well as some rudimentary pieces she'd been working on. Small sculptures she was thinking of selling in her shop, and perhaps Greenlane Nurseries, Reuben's business. Sam picked one up now. It was the basis for a Green Man metal plaque.

"And this? Does it have a purpose?"

"It's only decorative, but I have woven in some protection spells. Now," she said, bringing his attention back to the blade, "I need to etch the sigils." The blade was dull at present, but she would polish it later, make it shine. The blade itself wouldn't be too sharp. It was a ritual weapon, like an athame, despite what they would use it for. "Where are they?"

Sam rummaged in his pocket, and extracted a dogeared notebook. When he found the pages he needed, he handed her the book. "Those three, please."

El studied them, trying to work out the combination of shapes. Sigils were made from combining runes and other powerful shapes together to make symbols of protection, binding, or other powerful uses. She sighed as she noted their complexity. "These are unusual, and complicated. Where did you find them?"

"I visit many places, and find all sorts of rare things. I found these in an old grimoire and tucked them away for a rainy day."

"Very fortuitous, but their complexity means this will take a while." One thing was certain. El needed to focus and having Sam watching her wasn't going to work. She needed time to make the second blade, too. "You need to come back later."

He looked disappointed. "I was hoping to observe."

"You'll disturb me." She checked the time on her phone. "Come back at three, and bring Ruby. I'd like to meet her."

"An order?"

"You can call it what you like." She smirked. "At least I'm letting you come back."

He grimaced. "Fair enough. Later, Elspeth."

As soon as he left, El shut the door, sealing herself in the hot, airless room. This would require all of her concentration, so she cast a cooling spell. Time for the tricky part.

Reuben pushed his grimoire aside with frustration. "There's nothing in it of use. Nothing!"

Caspian looked at him across the table in the attic spell room. "Are you sure? We've only been looking for an hour!"

"Two hours! Have you found anything?"

"No, actually, but banshees are not uncommon. There must be something in here!"

Reuben stood and stretched his tall frame, reaching his hands upwards so he touched the rafters above his head. "Maybe not. Banshees are Irish. Perhaps our ancestors never encountered them."

"Celtic," Caspian corrected him. "And Cornwall has a Celtic past."

"Yeah, well, maybe we missed the banshee part."

Caspian had arrived very early, as promised, just after breakfast, and looked as well-groomed as usual, despite his casual clothing. Reuben hadn't seen him wear a suit for a while, and he was glad of it. Shedding it seemed like Caspian had shed the weight of a CEO's responsibilities, and consequently, he looked younger. Reuben knew only too well the pressures of running a business and keeping his employees happy, although he had no doubt Caspian's business was far bigger than his. That was fine. Reuben wasn't competitive over money, and the thought of wearing a suit and rocking up to business meetings had him breaking out in hives.

Knowing Caspian was arriving early, Reuben had risen even earlier to surf. Now, especially after the late night, he felt like he'd barely slept, and the energising effects of his surf had worn off. But he shouldn't complain. Caspian had become his research buddy, and his calm, collected approach was a welcome one. Reuben wasn't good at researching, and he wondered why he'd even suggested it in the first place.

"Come on," he said, suddenly eager for fresh air. "Let's get some coffee, and speak to Rosa."

"Okay. Caffeine sounds good, but then we come straight back here. El may be making the weapon, but we need to have more in our arsenal that just that." He tapped the spell beneath his fingers, releasing a waft of magic. "This one is a binding spell for resistant spirits. A binding to a grave. A banshee is a type of spirit. This could work, especially if we combine it with the sigils that El is inscribing in the blade."

"Some bloody spirit! She was scaling a magical wall!"

"Even better that we bind it, then," Caspian said rising to his feet. "Any news from Alex?"

"Nothing." Reuben led the way downstairs. "Even more reason to speak to Rosa."

They arrived in the snug, and found Rosa and Briar standing at the open doors to the patio, watching the children soak up the sunshine. Rosa looked more relaxed than when Reuben had first met her, and he hoped that the change in location had helped. Briar just looked anxious, and when she swung around to greet Caspian and Reuben, there was a wariness behind her eyes that worried Reuben. She had stayed the night, and had phoned Eli to cover her first few hours at work, but he knew that she would be leaving soon.

Unexpectedly, Max was in the garden playing at sword fighting with Zee, both wielding slender branches instead of actual swords. Beth was playing with her dolls on the lawn, watching them shyly.

"Hey, ladies. You've met Zee, I see, Rosa?"

Rosa turned to them, startled. "Sorry. I didn't hear you come in. Yes, he arrived about half an hour ago, looking for you. He's enormous! It was a good job Briar was here, or I would never have let him in. However, I have to confess he's unexpectedly charming..." Her eyes slid to him again.

"Yeah, charming." Reuben wondered what she'd think of Eli. "Why are they pretending to sword fight?"

"Max was moping. I think Zee took pity on him."

Caspian leaned against the doorframe, his gaze drifting between the playfight and Rosa. "Why was he moping? I thought being here would cheer him up."

"It's terrible, really. He's only twelve, and yet he sees himself as the man of the house. His great-granny scares him a little, but he misses her. He's worried about her being there on her own."

"But Alex is there," Briar said. "Did you tell him?"

She nodded. "And that made it worse. Now he's worried about both of them." She turned back to watch her son. "He didn't used to be so serious. I should never have brought him here."

Reuben exchanged a worried glance with Caspian and Briar. "You thought you were doing the right thing. In fact, you have. That's your family home. These events are just a hiccough. We'll sort it out."

Briar smiled at him. "That's what I said. We've dealt with worse."

"But I confess, that's worrying me, too," Rosa said. "Why? How are all of you equipped to deal with whatever's going on there?"

Briar shook her head almost imperceptibly, and Reuben knew she hadn't told her they were witches yet. Another hurdle to climb.

Caspian answered smoothly. "Just as you have the sight running through your family, we have special skills that run through ours."

"And," Reuben added, "White Haven is our home. Enough people have died."

"My fault."

"Actually, probably not," Briar said. "It seems the storm has a part to play in this. Anyway, Reuben, Zee wanted to know about Alex, and to have a chat about a few things..." Her eyebrows raised expressively, and Reuben's heart sank. *What now?*

"In that case," Caspian said, a rueful smile on his face, "I should take over sword fighting. I don't think I'll be as good as Zee, but I'll try."

Briar rested a hand on his arm. "No, you stay. He wants to speak to you, too. I'll take over."

And without another word, she walked across the lawn to relieve Zee.

Ben watched the banshee flit across the screen, and then turned to the next monitor, seeing it appear on another feed.

"Nice one, Dylan. You've managed to film her a few times."

"It's not helping us much, though. I don't know where she rests. She certainly hasn't been near the grave."

"She's not a bloody vampire!" Ben pointed out.

"Thank the Gods," Dylan muttered. "I do not want to meet one of those again!"

"Perhaps," Cassie suggested, ignoring both of them, "she feels trapped there."

"Or maybe she never rests," Ben said with a sigh. "Maybe she just endlessly roams."

Dylan accessed another camera feed. "I doubt that. She'll go somewhere. You haven't seen those grounds like I did. The place is huge, with lots of places for spirits to lurk. Old potting sheds, fake temples, rusting fountains, courtyard after courtyard. It's madness."

They had been searching through the previous night's recordings for a couple of hours with some success, but so far nothing they had done had made the cameras work again. The witches' spell was blocking the signal.

"Do you think she would be closer to the house?" Ben asked.

Dylan shrugged, still staring at the screens. "It depends on the connection she has with Tamsyn. She was so bloody mysterious the other day, I have no idea what's going on between them."

Cassie picked up her coffee cup and turned to Dylan, settling back in her chair as she did. "Tell us what she said again. It might give us a clue."

Dylan huffed, staring into the distance as he recalled his memories. "It was gibberish. Tamsyn said the storm had stirred it up and she said something about not knowing what the banshee wanted, but she also said she—Tamsyn herself—was a conduit to the past. What the hell does that mean?"

"Well," Cassie mused, "we know the storm stirred something up, because we saw the creature rise from the grave. The fact that Tamsyn said she is a conduit for the past could mean that she links the present to the past, or allows the past to work through her."

"Still gibberish," Dylan insisted. "A past experience or event? That could be anything!"

"Not if we consider what a banshee is," Ben said, feeling like he might be making headway. "Banshees predict deaths in the family. What if that's just it? Maybe someone's going to die, and she has seen it. Tamsyn, Rosa, Beth, or Max. Those are the four family members that we know of. And Rosa's mom, of course, but she's miles away. The banshee's grief is affecting others and killing them. She's hanging around because no one has died yet." He shuddered. "Sorry. That's gruesome, but that is essentially what banshees do."

Cassie jerked upright and her cup fell to the floor. "Oh my God! Briar is a family member, too! What if she's predicting *her* death? We've been obsessing all this time about the creature escaping the grounds and killing people as it crosses the moors and circles the manor like it was a random, unplanned event, but what if she was looking for the person she knew was going to die? The one person she hasn't met yet!" Cassie froze, eyes wide. "The person she was climbing over the bloody magical wall to see—Briar! That's what she told me this morning. She was at the exact place where the banshee was. Briar said her scream made her fall to her knees!"

Ben leapt to his feet and grabbed his phone off the table. "Fuck! You're right. We've tried to be too clever. The banshee is doing what it always does. Delivering her message. We have to tell the witches."

Chapter Twenty-Six

"How long has she been missing?" Caspian asked Zee.

"Since about nine this morning. That's when she was due back after taking Kailen for a ride. She was meeting Gabe and Niel to talk about a case, so we know she wouldn't have been side-tracked by anything else." Zee, normally so calm, looked unsettled. "Shadow is amazingly resourceful, we all know that, so I have to trust that she'll be okay, but even so..."

"It's worrying," Reuben agreed, thrusting a mug of hot coffee at him. "She loves risk, but it's always tempered with a high regard for her life. She wouldn't court danger if she thought she'd lose."

"Which is why it's all the more worrying that she's not home."

They were in the kitchen, having left Rosa in the snug while Briar played with Max. Caspian accepted his own drink from Reuben, strong and black, which was just what he needed. "Who's looking for her?"

"Gabe, of course, with Niel. Nahum, Ash, and Barak are away at the moment. Guild business. Eli is covering Briar's shop, and I've popped into the pub. Everything's fine there. Simon is in today and the place is under control." Caspian knew that Simon was the manager of The Wayward Son. Zee rolled his shoulders and neck. "I'll start searching now, but I thought you should know. I'm sure we'll find her soon, if they haven't already." Zee forced a smile. "Gabe is like a bear with a sore head."

Caspian exchanged a worried glance with Reuben. "Zee, did you know there are paranormal hunters in town?"

"Eli mentioned a woman who'd visited Charming Balms, and that Avery had been threatened by a big guy." A frown creased his brow. "Do you think this could be something to do with them? Eli didn't seem overly worried."

"It's possible," Reuben said. "Newton found Titus last night, the bloke who threatened Avery, with his sidekick at the cottages. From the maps Newton saw in his van, they might be targeting Ravens' Wood."

Zee had been slumped against the counter, but now he stood upright, his dark eyes turning stormy. "Targeting how?"

"Hard to say. Newton saw some occult images he didn't recognise. They could be magical traps. We didn't even end up looking at them after the night that we had."

"Yeah," Zee said, nodding absently. "We presumed that madness on the moor last night was your handiwork. We had a good view from our place. That was an impressive spell. Well, apart from the fact that Alex is now trapped, of course."

Caspian grimaced. "We're working on a solution."

"I wish I could help, but now..."

"You need to search for Shadow," Reuben finished for him. "Look, there's nothing we can do right now regarding our problem, other than wait for El to make a new weapon. I'll get Newton to send us those images and see if we can work out what the magical traps are—*if* that is what they are."

"But," Caspian added, suddenly feeling guilty, "we honestly didn't think they would be strong enough to do anything of significance in Ravens' Wood. That place is soaked in ancient magic, and Shadow is too strong. So are you! I don't think they have a clue what they're up against."

Zee finished his drink. "I'd like to think you're right, but they're an unknown quantity, and could be far more dangerous than we know. Potentially, they took off last night knowing you were completely preoccupied and couldn't stop them." He strode across the kitchen to the door. "I'll keep you posted, and if you find out anything, let me know."

Zee left, and Caspian turned to Reuben. "Great. Shadow has vanished, Alex is trapped, and we have hunters on the loose."

"We have a worse problem than that," Avery announced, taking them both by surprise.

"Holy shit, ninja witch!" Reuben exclaimed. "Where did you come from?"

"The garden, you twit!" Avery stood just inside the patio door, glancing back towards Briar. Avery looked untamed, which, to Caspian, was her natural state. Her porcelain skin was framed by her wild red hair that Caspian doubted had seen a brush that morning, but it suited her. Combined with her hippy summer skirt and top, she looked like she'd spent the weekend at a music festival, not battling a banshee for half the night.

"What problem?" Caspian asked, summoning her attention.

She dragged her gaze away from Briar and hurried to their side, lowering her voice. "I've just spoken to Ben. He suggested something we should have thought of much sooner. The banshee predicts deaths in the family—we know that. It's her primary function. *But that's why she's here*! She has predicted a death! What if it's Briar's?"

Caspian's heart missed a beat and his blood seemed to slow as he looked over Avery's head to where Briar played on the lawn, looking like a woodland sprite. She was like a sister to him. "No. Surely not. I don't believe it."

Avery touched his forearm, and he looked down into her green eyes. "That thing was clambering over the wall to you two! Not me and Alex, or Reuben and El. You and Briar. Briar was devastated by her arrival. I saw it!"

Caspian blinked and swallowed, feeling suddenly nauseous. "Her scream cut through all of Briar's defences. I had to throw up a protection shield. It affected her far more than it did me."

"Exactly." Avery turned away, appealing to Reuben, too. "What if Ben is right? What if the thing she's been searching for is Briar? What if the deaths were secondary to that search?"

"Can a banshee be wrong?" Reuben asked with a rising panic that Caspian hardly ever saw. "I refuse to believe it's inevitable. If it's an accident, then we can protect her, warn her. Or if it's the hunters, we will keep them away from her. I will not let Briar die!"

"Hold on," Caspian said, desperately trying to keep hold of reason. "Why has it trapped Alex, then? What's going on with Tamsyn? There is still more to this, there has to be!"

Reuben banged the counter with his fist. "Right. I need to do something. I'll ask Newton for his photos to help Zee find Shadow, and then search for more information on banshees. We'll surround Briar with protection spells, and we won't let her out of our sight!"

Caspian nodded. "And tonight, we get in the grounds and find out what the hell is going on."

"Do we tell Briar? Avery asked.

"We have to," Caspian said. "She needs to be forewarned."

"Then I'll do it," Avery said, marching resolutely across the kitchen and out to the grounds.

Alex felt like he was drowning in sorrow. Everywhere he turned was inky blackness. The air was thick around him, wrapped so tight he could barely move his limbs. *But he had no limbs or body here*, Alex reminded himself. *This was the realm of the spirits.*

He forced himself to be calm and focus on the presence of the troubled spirit that drew him here, because that's exactly what the banshee was—a spirit hounded by loss and grief. Behind it all was a person.

As his mind stilled, the thick, turgid atmosphere around him thinned, and he reached out, looking for a presence. All he wanted was to make contact, to try and find out who the spirit was. Then perhaps guide her to safety, or at least ease her sorrow.

Suddenly a presence loomed in front of him, seemingly emerging out of nowhere. Without warning it encompassed him, and he felt he was falling into an abyss. He couldn't breathe. Despair flooded through him. There was no way out. No chink of light. No hand in the darkness. He was going to die. He was unloved, unwanted. No one would miss him. His soul would forever tumble in nothingness.

He screamed, the sound harsh in the void. *Or was it his scream?* It couldn't be. He had no voice. He was a vessel of endless sadness. And then eyes appeared in the darkness. Hellish, red-rimmed and bloodshot eyes that crushed his remaining spirit.

Let me die. At least then it would be over.

Briar stared at Avery, incredulous, her heart hammering in her chest. "She's coming for me?"

"It's horrible, I know, but it's also logical." Avery took a visibly deep breath and lifted her chin. "We'll protect you, Briar!"

"From what? The banshee doesn't *cause* death. She predicts it! You don't know what's going to kill me!" Briar's emotions swung from being scared to being incredibly angry. "It's true, then! All of these deaths are caused by that awful creature, searching for me! She wields her sorrow like a bloody axe, felling everything in her way. This is my fault!"

She turned away from Avery and stared at the sea, clenching her fists. Herne's horns, she was furious. She had never asked for any of this. Her life had been just fine without any family. She had friends, good ones! A life, her work, her magic. Hunter. Newton. *Damn it!* Now was not the time to be thinking of him.

The Green Man uncurled within her, and suddenly she saw her surroundings through his eyes. The verdant greenery of Reuben's garden, the feel of plants growing around her, the deep, gentle sensation of the breathing earth beneath her feet, and the sea stretching out to the horizon where it met the sky in a shimmering haze. His wildness comforted her as he wrapped around her, and her magic responded. It surged upwards like tree sap until she felt it at her finger tips.

Fuck this.

She was not going to die. He wouldn't let her.

But then Briar remembered how the banshee had made her feel. Her sorrow that had felled her, weakening all resolve.

A battle was raging inside her.

"Briar!" Avery's alarmed shout brought her back to the present. "Look at me!"

Briar took a deep, shuddering breath she hadn't known she needed and looked into Avery's clear green eyes. "I'm okay."

"No, you are not. Holy cow. Your eyes are glowing. He's woken up, hasn't he?"

Briar nodded, unclenching her hands. "Yes. My anger called to him."

"Good. You'll need him. This is far from over, Briar. There's more going on here, I'm sure of it."

Briar turned to look at Max and Beth, still playing on the smooth lawn, Rosa now with them. "I think I need to get into Stormcrossed Manor. What if," she mused, as she turned back to Avery, feeling her equilibrium return, "this is about the past. Perhaps something needs resolving. Maybe this is about my mother."

"We all need to get into that manor. And we need to get Alex out."

Briar's natural empathy returned, and pushing her own fears aside she hugged Avery. "He'll be okay."

"Yes, he will be. And so will you." Avery pulled away, steely determination in her eyes, and pulled her phone out. "I'll call El and see how she's getting on with that blade."

Briar turned to look at Rosa again. "And I'll have another chat with my cousin. There's so much I don't know about my family that I need to, and frankly, there's no time like the present to learn."

Kendall drove slowly along the lane bordering Ravens' Wood, and finding a shallow layby, pulled into it and stared at its murky green interior.

There were no high hedges here to prevent access. Instead, the trees ran right to the edge of the lane, and it was hard to see anything beyond the first few feet of tangled branches. Even so, it was captivating. Almost unwillingly she exited her car and stood at the wood's edge, breathing in the verdant greenery. The heat had returned after the storm, and the air felt oppressive. However, the tantalisingly cool scent of leaf mould carried to her, caressing her cheek as if beckoning her in.

Something stirred in the shadows beyond the first few feet of filtered green sunlight.

She focussed, stepping closer and holding her breath. *There it was again*. A bobbing shadow a short way ahead. It was tempting to follow it. She hadn't been in Ravens' Wood before, and until Moore and Newton had mentioned it that morning, had no idea of the rumours that circulated about it. She had been scared earlier, but now she was just curious. *Dryads? Fey borderland?*

The cracking of branches and the caw of ravens shattered the peace, and Kendall stepped back, alarmed, the noise bringing her to her senses. She was searching for Titus and Apollo, not Otherworldly creatures.

She returned to the driver's seat, the feeling of being watched prickling between her shoulder blades, and she quickly drove away, refusing to look back.

Something yanked Alex upwards, the fierce shout of an unintelligible language shattering the wallowing, soporific feeling that had enveloped him. He felt a sharp sting on his cheek, and a bright, yellow light beat against his eyes.

"Open your eyes, you damn fool!" a harsh voice shouted.

Alex felt drunk, his head throbbing. Something hard was beneath him, and his limbs were twisted and uncomfortable.

"Alex Bonneville. Return to the world of the living! I command you."

His eyes flew open and Tamsyn's wizened face loomed over him, her beetle-black eyes inches from his own.

"Fuck!" He tried to retreat, but there was nowhere to go with the hard earth beneath his back.

"Watch your language!" Tamsyn pulled back, scowling at him.

Alex immediately tried to sit up, but his limbs protested as pins and needles revealed how long he had been out. "Ouch! Fuck. What happened?"

"Stop swearing, you foul-mouthed idiot." Tamsyn glared at him, her mouth twisting with disdain.

As his senses returned, so did Alex's awareness of the darkness Tamsyn carried within her, a burden in her intense eyes. Now, instead of retreating from it, he explored it. Perhaps it was because he still had part of himself in the spirit world, but he seemed more attuned to it than he had been. *Was it a spirit? Or maybe just the knowledge of past events that she carried like a wound?* Whatever it was, Tamsyn bore him no ill will, that was for sure. She'd just saved his life.

"Sorry." He eased upright, finally looking away from her intense gaze to take in his surroundings. The sun was far higher in the sky than when he'd entered the spirit world, and the patch of shade he'd sat in was now in full sun. He felt hot, his skin tight, and he realised he'd fallen back, sprawling across the upended gravestone. "I was surprised. I feel drunk."

"You were lost. I had to pull you out. Idiot," she repeated. Her wrinkled face was scrunched up with annoyance.

Alex grinned despite her attitude, grateful to feel the sun on his face. "I'm not an idiot. I'm actually quite good at that. I would have found a way out."

She grunted, moving from her crouched position to sit on the baked earth. "Maybe so, but you'd have been burnt to a crisp out here, and your magic would be drained."

"Thank you. Although," he touched his face and felt the heat in his skin, "I think I'm already burnt."

"You're a good-looking boy. You'll survive." A smile crept across her face, and Alex thought he saw a twinkle in her dark eyes. "You need water, and some food. We should get you inside."

"In a moment. I want to soak up the heat for a bit longer. It was dark in there. Cold. I found her. The banshee."

"I suspected as much. Very risky."

"She's not entirely alone, either," Alex said, remembering what he'd felt just before Tamsyn pulled him from the darkness. "I sensed other souls in there with her. They were confused, and just as despairing as she is." He shuddered. "What a hideous place."

"Her recent kills, surely. Or perhaps all of them. 'Tis a terrible place she walks in, and nigh on impossible to get her out of it. That is the fate of the banshee."

"You knew what was happening here all along."

"Of course I did!" She huffed. "I haven't lived here for all these years only to not know what sits on my own land."

"Why didn't you do anything?"

"You saw her last night. You felt her! I can't control her that much. I just try to take on some of her grief. It means that I keep her calm...for the most part."

Alex felt dull-witted. "This doesn't make sense. A banshee rises to warn of a death in the family, right? She predicts the death and mourns it. I presume seeing as that doesn't happen every day, why do you need to keep her calm? And why is she killing others?"

"She mourns for more than just the impending death of a family member. Loss comes in many forms." She struggled to her feet, extending her tiny hand to Alex. "Come. This heat is boiling my brain. It's time for some tea."

Chapter Twenty-Seven

Engraving the complex sigils into the blades had left El drained. Leaving them on her workbench, she threw the door of her smithy open and took a deep breath.

She was bathed in sweat, and her concentration had been so intense, she hadn't even realised how hot she was. Now her skin prickled with heat, and she uttered a spell to cool herself down. *By the Goddess, it was hot.*

But she'd done it. The blades were complete, etched with the sigils and bound with magic. *The question was, would they work?* The weapon was designed to wound a spirit as if it was made of flesh and bone. It also pierced general protection spells, and that was playing on her mind more than anything. She'd always considered their protection spells inviolate. It was unnerving to think that something could penetrate them. Even more unnerving to think she was handing such a weapon to a hunter. *Was she being duped?*

She phoned Reuben, heading inside to inspect the Empusa's sword, which she had on the workbench for comparison. She picked it up, feeling its weight and the strong magic it contained. The copper blade felt very different to the ones she'd just crafted. She hadn't lied when she told Sam that the metal sang to her. This metal, ancient and mysterious, whispered of strange lands and even stranger people that she longed to see. Not just Gods, but the fey; Shadow's race. It was the same feeling that helping Dante with Shadow's armour had given her. Her own blades, carefully crafted and imbued with her powerful magic felt weak in comparison. A candle's flame, compared to the sun. It strengthened her resolve to improve her craft.

"Hey you," she said when Reuben answered her call. "Sam will be here in another couple of hours. Want to come and meet him? I just need to know that I'm not making a big mistake."

Kendall pulled onto the crowded car park that served White Haven Castle, cursing herself for not trying this place sooner.

She had cruised the lanes that skirted Ravens' Wood several times, finding a couple of cars pulled into small parking bays, but there was no sign of Titus's van, or the van registered to Apollo Indigo. She had even driven along White Haven's streets, cursing the crowds that sprawled off the pavements. It hadn't helped that some of the roads had been closed off, partly to prepare for the impending Lughnasadh celebrations, and partly to accommodate the abundance of tourists. It was only when she'd paused to look up to the wood on the hillside that she saw the castle and remembered that it also edged the forest.

When Kendall pulled into a parking spot, she immediately saw Titus's van, parked alongside Apollo's. *Damn it. What now?* Newton had told her not to venture into the wood, but right now, she didn't even know if they were in there. She'd head to the castle first. There were plenty of people around, and it wouldn't hurt to look. *Perhaps the hunters were sightseeing.*

Knowing she was deluding herself, she threaded through the cars baking in the heat to the path that led to the castle. En route, she spotted a large, imposing figure she recognised, and she approached him, calling out, "Zee!"

Zee was locking his helmet to the seat of an old, battered motorbike, his dark curly hair currently plastered to his head. As he heard his name, he turned, flashing Kendall a big grin, and ruffling his hair as he did so.

"Kendall! Day off?"

"Funny. I'm searching for our hunters. We have reason to believe they are planning something for Ravens' Wood."

His grin disappeared. "Yeah, I heard. I saw Caspian and Reuben, and they told me what was going on. Unfortunately, Shadow had vanished." He pointed to the tangled wood above them. "Somewhere in there, we suspect. Now I'm doubly worried."

"How long has she been missing?"

"A few hours. Gabe and my brothers are in there now."

"Are you sure she's in there?"

"That's her favourite place, and we've searched most other possibilities. The moors, the coast, the castle." While he talked, Zee took off his leather jacket, revealing his sinewy, muscled arms, and locked his jacket in the pannier. "The worrying thing is, now I can't get hold of *them*, either."

"But the castle is busy, as is the wood, I bet. Surely Titus and Apollo can't be doing anything untoward in broad daylight?"

"You haven't been in the wood before, have you?"

Kendall shook her head. "No."

"Then trust me, anything is possible in there, at any time of day. It has its own rules." His gaze travelled around the car park, studying the people milling about. "I said I'd approach the wood from this direction the last time we spoke, but now I wonder if that's a mistake."

"No, it's not." Kendall pointed to the hunters' vans. "Those belong to them. And if you're going in, then I'm going with you."

"Are you sure?" Newton asked Moore, searching his face as if he were lying.

"Of course I'm sure." Moore clenched his jaw, and Newton knew he was trying his patience. "Every single victim has experienced a recent bereavement, be it family or a friend. I can only presume that their grief is what draws the banshee."

Newton knew he needed to make amends. "That's excellent work, thank you. I'm not sure how that helps us stop the damn thing, but at least we have something to go on."

He opened his canteen-bought sandwich packet with a frown. *Wilting lettuce and bacon.* He was starving though, so it would have to do.

"What about your morning?" Moore asked as he dropped into the opposite chair. "The post-mortems?"

"Same cause of death. Again, good to know, but doesn't help us stop the creature. At least the damn thing is trapped. Now we have to trust that our friends can deal with it."

"And Alex?"

"Still no word." Newton bit into his sandwich, and then scrolled through his phone. "Or from Kendall, actually. Have you heard from her?"

"No, but that's not surprising. I've been on the phone all morning. I'm going mad. I wish I'd have been outside in the sunshine." His voice held the slightest recrimination, although his eyes, when Newton looked at him, were resigned.

"Sorry, Moore. I thought it best to leave you chasing this up, as you had such a great start. Oh, hold on. She left me a message."

Newton hit play and turned on the speaker so Moore could hear, too. However, by the time they'd heard her message, both of them were on their feet.

"Bloody stupid, impetuous woman!" Newton roared, throwing the rest of his sandwich into the bin. "I told her explicitly not to go into the wood!"

"She is with Zee," Moore pointed out.

"I don't care! They might get separated, and then she'll be on her own in that damn place, with God knows what weird creatures running around. And hunters!" he added forcefully. He strode across the room, Moore trailing after him.

"So, we're going in, too?"

Newton stared at him, alarmed. Moore sounded hopeful. "I am, but I'm not sure you should. You have kids."

Moore glared at him. "Don't start that bullshit. I'm a bloody policeman!"

"Fair enough." Newton was actually relieved that he didn't have to go alone. Moore's calm, no-nonsense attitude in what he called the *fey borderland* was exactly what he needed. "But maybe you should warn your wife that you might be late home. And tell the witches about the link. It might help them in some way."

If they became trapped or lost in the wood, who knows how long they might be out there.

Avery settled on the lawn close to Briar and Rosa, half watching them and half watching Beth, the child seer. Max was across the lawn, still swishing his branch like it was a sword.

Beth was a pretty child, her hair a darker brown than her mother's. In fact, she looked like a smaller version of Briar. She was making daisy chains, her small fingers splitting the stalks to weave them together, concentration etched on her serious face. She seemed unaffected by the vision she had received the day before, which was a relief. From Alex's account, it had been severe.

Briar's voice rose with agitation, and Avery turned to her instead, watching as she said, "Rosa! I know this is scaring you, and that you are worried about Beth, but that *thing* is a banshee, and it's possible that it has predicted my death! Anything you can tell us is important!"

"But I don't know anything!" Rosa said, a challenge flashing in her eyes. "I have lived in Wales my entire life. My grandmother visited us there; we hardly ever came here. I visited a few times when I was really young, between about Beth and Max's ages, but that all stopped when I became a teenager." She smiled, a hint of regret in her eyes. "I loved it, actually. The gardens were still wild and unkempt, and the house certainly not as dilapidated as it is now. Although, perhaps I wouldn't have noticed that. The whole place seemed enchanted. My mother, however, hated that place. Looking back, I can see how on edge she seemed. There was tension between her and Grandma."

"Perhaps your mother sensed the darkness that you couldn't," Briar suggested, "and that's why she moved away. My mother did the same."

"Maybe. Although, I certainly feel it now. I should never have come here, but I was desperate to get away after my marriage ended. Financially, I had little choice, to be honest. Memories of my childhood made it seem like a safe place to be."

Avery couldn't help but interrupt. "I don't understand your mother. If she stopped coming here when you were small, why let you return with your children?"

Rosa watched Beth before answering. "I think she knew Beth had the sight, and wanted her to get guidance from my grandmother."

"Beth had visions before you arrived here, then?" Briar asked, her voice low so it wouldn't carry to Beth.

"Not really. More like absences, and she'd say the odd unusual thing, occasionally."

"Like what?" Avery prompted when Rosa fell silent.

She sighed. "Well, when my marriage collapsed, I told the children we would find somewhere special to live. Beth said that Great-grandma needed us. That the lady who lived with her was coming back, and she was very upset."

"The lady who lived with her?" Briar asked, exchanging an alarmed glance with Avery.

"I know. Weird, right? I told her that Great-grandma lived alone, but she wouldn't have it. I guess that, along with my mother's suggestion, sealed the deal. So I came here. And then, when we first arrived and I realised how bad the house was and how unwell Tamsyn seemed, I assume I would have looked worried. I tried to hide it, but clearly didn't. Beth told me that Great-grandma needed help, but the man with the long, dark hair would help her."

Briar gasped. "Alex!"

"It seems so."

Avery kept silent as she studied Rosa. She didn't know what to make of her. On the one hand she said she knew little of the sight, on the other she didn't seem overly concerned by her daughter's odd suggestions. From what Alex had told her too, she seemed furious that Tamsyn had seen Beth have visions but hadn't told her. None of it made sense. Maybe she was in denial. Or maybe Tamsyn's confession had confirmed her fears. Worried mums sometimes behaved irrationally, but it irritated her, and with every passing second, her anger intensified.

Rosa continued. "Where is Alex?"

"With Tamsyn, at the manor," Briar said. "As Beth foretold, he's helping her with *the lady*."

"The thing that's responsible for the deaths. The banshee." Rosa shuddered. "I can't believe I'm even saying such a thing. I feel my whole world has turned upside down."

Avery couldn't help herself. "Just stop it! You keep feigning ignorance, but it's all bullshit. You knew the sight ran in your family, you knew Beth was showing signs of it, and you even returned here because you had nowhere else to go! My boyfriend, the man I love, is trapped in that bloody place with that harbinger of death. She has predicted Briar's death! Her grief has somehow killed others! And you sit there, a ll, 'I don't know. It's so odd. I'm so scared!' What the fuck is wrong with you?"

"Avery!" Briar interjected, looking appalled.

Avery ignored her, unleashing all of her pent-up frustration at Rosa, and a wind whipped up around her. "What else do you know? We have to stop this! Stop her!"

Rosa froze, eyes wide as she stared at Avery. And then her gaze fixed on Beth, her eyes opening even wider. "Beth!"

Avery turned, knowing exactly what was happening.

Beth was sitting motionless, the daisy chain in her lap, daisies strewn all around her. Her eyes were white. The seer state was upon her. Suddenly, words were tumbling from her mouth, her childish voice even more chilling with the message she delivered. "The lady will walk again tonight. She will take the soul she has come for. The darkness beyond is too great to bear alone. She comes. She comes..."

And then Beth screamed and collapsed on the grass.

Chapter Twenty-Eight

Alex sipped the tea that Tamsyn had placed in front of him, and then grimaced at the amount of sugar in it.

Tamsyn saw his expression and frowned. "Drink it. Your journey has weakened you. You'll need your strength later. Have one of these, too." She placed a plate of home-baked biscuits in front of him, and the rich, buttery scent of oats and honey wafted towards him.

He nodded and took a biscuit, slumping against the chair back as he did so. "I'm shattered. I've journeyed into the spirit world before, and talked to spirits many times, but I have to admit, nothing felt like she did. I wanted to die just to escape the horrible pit of depression."

Tamsyn sat opposite him, taking a biscuit and dipping it into her tea. "Her grief is overwhelming. It sickens me to see her suffer, so I do what I can. It is little, in the scheme of things."

Alex stared at her, identifying what he'd seen earlier. "You have somehow taken a share of her grief. I can feel it... I see it in you. How did you do that?"

Tamsyn swallowed her bite of biscuit and then sipped her tea, gesturing at Alex to do the same before she answered. "Like Beth, I am a seer, but it went further than that. Years ago, in a particularly strong vision, I connected with *her*. It almost killed me. But, it also showed me what I must do. I accepted a part of her burden to save my girls."

Alex crunched his biscuit, feeling the rush of sugar energise him, but it didn't aid his understanding. "She *is* a banshee, right?" Tamsyn nodded, and he continued. "So that means that she predicts family deaths, not causes them. Why did you need to protect your girls? Why is she killing people now?"

"She is displaced from her homeland, brought here by Niamh McCarthy—not on purpose, you understand. She piggy-backed after making a strong connection to Niamh. That sometimes happens. The banshee belongs to that side of the family. Has done for hundreds of years. She had a tragic death of her own. She lost so many babies before she finally had her family. And then she tried again. It killed her."

"She died in childbirth?"

Tamsyn nodded. "Childbirth was a killer before modern medicine—still can be. Her grief was so great that upon her death, her spirit was warped into the banshee. They are tragic creatures, and should be pitied, not feared."

Alex shuddered. "Hard not to fear them when they look as they do. How do you know this?"

"We talk, she and I, on the occasion when our paths cross."

"The language you speak to her?"

"Gaelic. I learnt it specifically. It took me a long time."

"Does she have a name? It might help me to connect to her later. Reason with her."

"Orla. Old, like she is."

Alex nodded, tucking it away for later. "Was she a seer, too? You said it runs in the McCarthy family."

"It skips generations, but yes, she was. She saw her own death." Tamsyn said it matter-of-factly, but it chilled Alex's blood.

"That's horrific."

"I know." Tamsyn took another biscuit. "It added to the trauma of her death. No wonder she became such a creature. My seer abilities have faded, a consequence of shouldering her grief, I suspect." She gave a dry laugh. "I exchanged one burden for another. At least my daughters didn't have to put up with it. Not that it stopped them from leaving, of course." Her voice was bitter, resigned. "It was for the best. At least I'm still in touch with one."

Guilt raced through Alex, and his hands jerked in shock. Was it possible she had no idea about Jennifer's death? He needed to tell her.

"And now Rosa is here," Tamsyn continued, her expression softening. "And Beth and Max. I was hoping to guide Beth through her first visions, help her deal with them as she grows up. For her to be experiencing them so young means she will be very powerful as she grows. She will need help if it is not to consume her. You know that."

Alex nodded. "Only too well."

"Now, however, I regret them coming. The storm released Orla, and she walks the grounds freely. I fear for them."

"You think she would hurt them?"

"She hurts everyone, eventually."

A horrible thought struck Alex. "What about your husband?"

Tamsyn's eyes suddenly blazed, and it took all of his willpower not to shoot back in his chair as he took in the anger and grief there. "She took him."

"She killed your husband?" It was as if ice ran through Alex's veins. "How? Why?"

"Like I said, she is lonely. She took Niamh's husband, too."

"I thought a tree struck him in the middle of a storm?"

"Orla likes storms. Their energy matches her own. It was a tool. Niamh knew it, too."

"And yet you still pity her? Help her? Carry her grief?" Alex didn't know whether to be appalled or admire her. "I don't know how you can."

"I didn't want her to take the rest of my family. Over the last few days since she reappeared, it has taken all of my control to keep her from them. But now…"

"Now you can't control her."

"No. It's as if by denying her my family, she has sought out others. She cannot grieve alone."

Alex was confused, his thoughts blunted by his earlier experience. "Let me get this straight. A banshee attaches itself to the family, her descendants, predicting their deaths, and mourning that eventuality. This one, Orla, not only does that, but she kills, too. It isn't enough to wait for a natural death? Is that what you're saying?"

"I'm afraid I am. And yet, I still pity her."

"You shouldn't. She's still here. All those deaths haven't been enough, or she would have already gone, right?"

Tamsyn nodded. "Yes, normally she would retreat to her own world again, with encouragement from me. Now, she will have none of it. You did well to seal her in. I saw it all last night. You and your coven are powerful. I'm glad my family left with the blond man, the other witch, last night. He's kind."

"You saw them go?"

"I was glad of it. And Rosa left me a note."

Recalling their first conversation, Alex said, "You said you were a conduit for the past. You meant Orla, I understand that now, but how is Beth connected?"

"We are three seers, connected by our abilities and bloodline, linked over the centuries. I have learned to control the banshee's needs. Beth has not." Tamsyn looked older now, her face etched with worry. "She is susceptible to Orla's demands, her depths of grief. That is partly what I sought to teach her."

"You wanted Beth to take over your role here. To take your place when you die." He was horrified. "For a start, she's too young, and secondly, how can you even think about subjecting her to this?"

Tamsyn clucked in annoyance. "Have the events of the past few days shown you nothing? I would subject her to this for the same reason as I have myself—to protect others! But as I said, recent events have made me question that. Now I have no idea of what to do!"

Alex finally understood the terrible burden that Tamsyn had subjected herself to. A lifetime bonded to a creature with an insatiable appetite for death. He needed to think of a way to deal with this. But first, he had to share his other news.

"I have something to tell you, and please excuse my abruptness. Your daughter, Jennifer, is dead. She died years ago. I'm sorry."

"Dead?" For the first time since Alex had met her, he saw Tamsyn's guard tumble down. "How? She's too young!"

"An accident. I don't know the circumstances, not fully."

Tamsyn was shaking. "How do you know this?"

"Because she had a daughter, and I'm friends with her. Good friends. She's a witch, too. Her name is Briar."

"Briar? I have another granddaughter? Here in White Haven?"

"She didn't know about you, either."

"Can I meet her?"

"When this is over, yes. But there's more," Alex said, as last night's events finally shuffled into a coherent pattern. "I think Orla was after Briar last night. She was scrambling over our protective wall to get to her. *Damn it*. I feel such a fool."

"No." Tamsyn's small hands clenched into fists. "*No*. I will not allow it."

"Neither will I." New resolve flooded through Alex. "I don't know whether all of those deaths are because she somehow knew about Briar and was searching for her, and she killed them as collateral damage, or whether she was just looking for more spirits to fill her lonely void. Either way, she knows about Briar now. If I know my friends, they are doing all they can to get to me, even though they have no idea if I'm alive or not. What if Orla trapped me here just to get to Briar? *Briar* is who she wants!"

"I would offer myself in her place, but she won't have me."

"I'm not suggesting we trade her for you!" Alex said, horrified at the idea. "Hold on! You've already tried?"

"Many times. You think I would stay here all alone, in this cursed place for all these years, burdening my soul with her grief, without trying another way?" She gave a dry laugh. "I thought that by offering myself, I could tie her to my spirit, and we would both find rest. But, no. She doesn't want me. She likes me sharing her pain."

"Then she's a twisted psychopath who no longer deserves your pity, but rather your anger. We're here alone with her, Tamsyn. Just you and me. If we are to save Briar and Beth, we are ending her today. As of right now, her reign of terror is over. Are you with me?"

Tamsyn leaned forward, her hands clasping Alex's. "You really think you can do this?"

"I will give it my best shot." He gestured to his pack. "I have my grimoire, and my tools. I *will* find a way."

"Then I will help you any way I can."

Chapter Twenty-Nine

K endall followed Zee into Ravens' Wood, wondering with every step what she'd got herself into.

Initially they progressed in an uneven sweep of the wood's periphery, passing people walking with friends or family, walking their dogs, and chatting and laughing in the soporific heat beneath the green canopy. Every now and then they paused to examine their surroundings, checking the ground, tree trunks, and branches above for any traps, signs, sigils, or anything out of the ordinary. However, finding nothing untoward, they plunged deeper into the wood, following the winding paths that left Kendall disorientated.

If there was anyone else in here, she couldn't hear them. Deep, watchful silence muffled every step, and every shadow seemed threatening in the murky green light that resembled dusk, despite the fact that it was nowhere near sunset. Perhaps, here in the fey borderland, the wood had its own time zone, too.

"I still can't see anything unusual," Kendall complained, thrashing a branch aside to progress down the narrow path. "Well, apart from the fact that I feel we're the only people left on Earth!"

"Yeah, this place does make you feel like that." Zee paused at a crossroads, debating which way to turn. "I suspect they will be further in."

"Have you a destination in mind?"

"Not really, but I want to be thorough. I know Shadow favoured the centre, but she said the paths to it change every time."

"The hunters are in here too, though. What if we find them?"

"There's no law about walking in a wood, and if they attack, I'm pretty sure I can handle them."

"I'm not entirely useless," she retorted.

Zee gave a small bow. "My apologies. We will handle them together."

Kendall followed Zee down another narrow path, the ground baked hard beneath their feet. She tried to find landmarks—unusual trees, twisted branches, or forks in the path so that she could find her way back—but it was impossible. She was sure the castle was still to her left, the coastline beyond it, but she couldn't even hear the sea breaking against the cliffs in here.

Zee relentlessly headed inwards, pausing occasionally to sniff at the air like a dog before progressing. Just as Kendall was thinking this was a big fat waste of time, he froze and gestured Kendall to a crouch.

"I feel magic."

"How can you tell the damn difference? Everything feels weird here."

Zee grinned, his face striped with shadows. "Ravens' Wood has wild, earthy magic. This is different. Darker. More structured." His grin vanished as his eyes narrowed and fixed on a point beyond them.

"There." He pointed to a strange, swirling sigil carved onto a tree trunk. "They won't like that."

"Who won't?"

"Tree spirits, of course. They don't appreciate wilful damage. You know, you may fare better than us in here. You're human, and their spells are not designed to trap you."

"That sign is a trap?"

But Zee didn't answer, because as he took another step forward, the trees literally shimmered between them, and in a split second he'd vanished, leaving her on her own.

"Another vision?" Caspian asked Avery, crouching next to her.

Beth was spreadeagled before them on the lawn, eyes closed and daisies strewn around her, while Rosa sobbed next to her. Briar was being more practical, her healing hands hovering above Beth's head. He and Reuben had been in the attic when they heard the shout that had pierced their quiet conversation, and they had raced down the stairs, thinking they were being attacked.

Avery stood up, drawing Caspian and Reuben aside. "Unfortunately, yes. It seemed to come out of nowhere. One second she was making daisy chains, the next she announced that 'she was coming.' The banshee, I presume."

"Poor kids," Caspian said, looking from Beth to Max, who was standing at the edge of the lawn, watching silently. "We can't control Beth's visions, but we can help Max. And we have to stop this creature."

"Any luck with your research?" Avery asked.

"Nothing in particular," Reuben admitted, "but after last night's success with gemstones, we're charging a bunch of them to take tonight. We thought the best thing was to plan for every and any eventuality. Especially seeing as Alex is inside. We have to trust that he will have found a way to deal with her."

Caspian nodded in agreement. "We're Alex's support crew. And don't forget El's blade."

"And the Empusa's sword," Reuben reminded them. "We're taking that tonight, too. The banshee is a type of spirit, after all."

Relief flooded Avery's face. "Of course! The Empusa's sword! That makes me feel so much better to know we have options."

"We always have options, Avery," Caspian said, certain that Avery's worry about Alex had clouded her normal perception.

Reuben checked the time. "I have to go and see El. She's worried about giving Sam that blade, so I'm heading there now to suss him out. I'll catch up with you guys later. What time are we heading to the manor?"

"Dusk again," Caspian suggested. "In the meantime, I'm going to speak to Max, and then I think we just need to gather ourselves for tonight. We can't afford to be tired." He looked at Briar, remembering how the banshee's cry seemed to have cut through all her defences. Her vulnerability had terrified him. "Especially Briar, if our suspicions are correct. Maybe she shouldn't come."

Reuben snorted. "Like she'd agree to that."

Caspian sighed, knowing he was right. Despite all the risks, Briar would never abandon them. He resolved that he would stay at her side all night.

"Any news of Shadow?" Avery asked. "Did you have luck with the photos Newton sent you?"

"Of Titus's plans?" Caspian shook his head. "Nothing conclusive there, either. A selection of runes and sigils that could be used for anything."

Reuben voiced the concerns he'd discussed with Caspian earlier. "Part of me thinks we should help to search for her, but none of us can afford to be stuck in Ravens' Wood. We have to be at Stormcrossed Manor later."

"Agreed." Caspian closed his eyes briefly, images of the previous night flashing across his mind. So far there was no sign of another storm, but if one started brewing, they all needed to be there to counteract the energies it would manifest. "We have to trust that the Nephilim will find her."

"Okay, I admit that I cannot get these feeds back up," Dylan declared, standing and stretching, utterly frustrated. "It is impossible!"

It was now late afternoon, and Dylan had been struggling to retrieve the feed all day, as well as reviewing the footage. The only thing they had determined was that in addition to the grave the banshee had emerged from, there was one more place she seemed to favour: the courtyard with the dried-up fountain. That may help them later.

"You gave it your best shot," Cassie said, shooting him a sympathetic smile from across the room. "The good news is that other than a few panic-stricken calls about unearthly lightning strikes around White Haven, there were no reports of anyone hearing ghastly screams in the night. Well, no one called us, anyway."

Ben was at his desk, munching on a packet of crisps. "And they would have, considering the flood of calls we had before. Which means the witches were completely successful."

"Except for Alex being trapped inside, of course," Dylan said sarcastically. "*So* successful!"

Ben shrugged. "That could work in our favour."

"So, what now?" Cassie asked. "There are other things to follow up on, but right now, I can't focus on anything other than Stormcrossed Manor. We have to help them."

"Agreed." Dylan studied the screens again. "The cameras can't help now, but once we're in there, if the creature is being elusive, we might be able to track it using the EMF meter."

"If that even works in there," Ben pointed out. "The protection spell might well block everything electronic. Not that it should stop us from going, though!" he added hurriedly.

Dylan grinned. "Good. In that case, let's pack our kit up, grab some food, and head to Reuben's place."

Newton virtually abandoned his car on a layby at the edge of Ravens' Wood, after having driven like a madman to get there in the quickest time possible.

Moore looked green as he exited the car. "Bloody hell, Guv. I feel sick."

"I do not intend to let another one of my sergeants die!" Newton declared, glaring at him. "We are going in there and finding her—and Shadow. All of them!" he added forcefully.

"Great. Just killing us both in a car accident doesn't matter, then?"

Newton grunted as he led the way into the wood. "Sarcasm is not your friend."

"You should have thought of that before you drove like a lunatic."

"Moore!"

"Fine. Get on with it." Moore gestured ahead. "What if we get separated?"

"Let's try not to."

Furious with everyone and everything, Newton marched down the path, eyes darting everywhere. They had tried to call Kendall several times, but she hadn't answered, and Newton hoped that it was for safety purposes, rather than anything untoward.

She was with Zee, anyway, and that meant she would be fine. He hoped.

"Nice blade!" Reuben said, admiring El's handiwork. "You've outdone yourself." He balanced the dagger on his palm, admiring its balance. The magic it contained made his skin tingle. "It must have taken a while to engrave the symbols."

"Ages." El looked hot and bothered. Sweat glistened on her skin, and black marks were smudged down her arms and across her face. "They're so bloody complicated."

"I see what you mean, though. The sigils do make a threatening combination."

"I know!" El looked exasperated. "I can't believe I agreed to it, to be honest. Giving this to Sam is potentially hazardous, to us and all witches."

"But it's really for killing banshees, right?" Reuben studied the sigils again, the complexity of them giving him a headache. "Because they aren't normal spirits."

"No, apparently not." El wiped her hands across her face, smearing dirt over her cheeks even more. "And maybe our powers have added to that—along with the storm. Alex's spell was a double-edged sword. Excuse the pun."

Reuben picked up the Empusa's blade, swishing it around. "You think this will work, too?"

"For the banshee, I think so. To get through our spell, no."

"Have you finished the second blade yet?"

El pointed to her workbench where a plain, dull, metal dagger lay, partly engraved. "I've made a start."

Banging on the door to the smithy interrupted them, and El said quietly, "That's Sam. Just see what you think of him."

Reuben walked into the courtyard, taking in Sam's grizzled appearance. A woman with red hair—Ruby, he presumed—was with him. Reuben shook their hands and introduced himself as El joined them.

She gestured to the chairs around the tiny wrought iron table. "Grab a seat."

They sat, but Sam looked beyond her to the smithy. "Have you made it?"

"I have," El said. "But I confess, I have reservations."

Sam's eyes darkened. "Why?"

"Because it's a dangerous weapon. It can cut through protection spells, and that makes me nervous."

"You don't trust me."

El shrugged. "I'd be insane not to worry."

"I told you about this blade as a favour."

"No, you didn't," El said patiently. "You needed a weapon to hunt a banshee, and a witch to make it. You *had* to share this with me. And I admit, we need a blade, too. Of course I'm grateful, but you can understand why this blade's properties worry me."

Sam stared at El, and it was hard for Reuben to read him. He was just as El had described. A grizzled, middle-aged man whose eyes were weary with his experiences. He was burly, not losing muscle despite his age, and although generally unkempt, he was clean. Ruby was, as El had told him, younger, and clearly intelligent. She had lively brown eyes that took everything in. They roved around El's courtyard and then settled on Reuben, studying him with open curiosity before her gaze settled on Sam and El again.

Sam huffed with impatience. "I don't know what to say. We are hunters who kill dangerous paranormal creatures. I don't hunt witches—unless they deserve it. There's nothing I can say or do to make you trust me, but I swear I'm being as honest as I can."

"He's right," Ruby added unexpectedly. Her voice had a regional accent that Reuben couldn't quite place. "I've had run-ins with other hunters—Titus, included—and they can be an unprincipled bunch. But not us. And you'll need help with the banshee tonight."

Reuben looked at her, alarmed. "You're intending to come with us?"

She lifted her chin. "That's why we have a blade, dummy! You'll need our help." She tapped the table, eyes darting between him and El. "We've assessed Stormcrossed Manor. It's a big place. Plenty of space for her to roam. You'll need a team."

"We *have* a team!"

"Is it big enough?"

Reuben looked at El, whose face wrinkled with uncertainty. He knew exactly what she was thinking. *Yes, they may well need their help...if they could trust them.* "We don't know you."

Sam leaned forward, staring into their eyes. "If we betray you, I fully expect you to attack us. Spell us in some way. Hell, you just might anyway, for the fun of it. We don't know *you*, either. That is also the risk we take. You're powerful. Do you think getting into bed with a coven of witches is an easy choice for us? We normally work alone, and prefer to. But I know we can't in this case. May I at least see the blade?"

"Sure," El said, heading to the smithy. In seconds she had returned, handing the blade to Sam. He turned it over, examining it carefully before passing it to Ruby.

She scrutinised the sigils, and then nodded. "It's excellent work."

Sam nodded, pulling cash from his pocket and placing it on the table before leaning back in his chair. "So, what's it to be?"

El looked at Reuben, a question in her eyes, and he studied Sam and Ruby for a few moments more. He could see why El liked Sam. He was open and upfront. There was something guileless about him, despite his world-weary demeanour. Reuben liked him, too. Sometimes they *were* too suspicious. Sometimes people were just what they said they were. Plus, they had already been endorsed by Maggie Milne. Reuben also had to admit that Sam was right. They were asking *him* to trust *them*, and it made him horribly uncomfortable to think that they were feared as witches, and as a coven.

Reuben sighed. "All right. You keep the blade, and you can come with us tonight. I guess we all need to have a little faith in each other."

Sam grinned, and the mood around the table lifted. He shook El's hand, then Reuben's.

"Deal."

Chapter Thirty

A lex used salt to put the final symbol in place around Niamh's grave, and stepped back to examine the circle. It wasn't as detailed as he would have liked, but he had limited options.

"Took you long enough," Tamsyn grunted next to him.

"Any other words of wisdom you'd like to impart?" Alex asked tartly.

She looked up at him, her eyes squinting against the sun that dropped behind him. "Tetchy."

"Of course I bloody am. I'm knackered, and pissed off at being trapped within this bloody bubble like a fly in amber."

"Stop swearing. Will it help if I tell you I'm impressed?"

"Not really. You don't even know what it does."

Tamsyn cackled like a crone. "I know enough. It's a trap."

Alex nodded, smiling enigmatically. "Of a sort."

Tamsyn was growing on him. The darkness he sensed within her before had terrified him, but now that he understood what it was, and the sacrifice Tamsyn had made, he admired her. He was able to separate the darkness of the banshee, Orla, from Tamsyn herself, which meant he saw her own character within.

He explained, "This is the place she rose from. I'm hoping to send her back to it."

"It makes sense. But it won't be easy. She hasn't been back here in days."

Alex's heart sank, wishing he'd discussed this with Tamsyn sooner, but she'd disappeared a few hours earlier, saying she had her own plans to make. "Where is she, then?"

"Everywhere and anywhere. I can't pin her down."

"I thought you could feel her? Talk to her."

"I can, but it's easier at night. Even so, she evades me sometimes. Last night's storm made her stronger. As does your magic." Tamsyn surveyed the edge of the manor's grounds. "It feels funny to be surrounded by a protection spell. You say my granddaughter's magic is in there?"

"Absolutely. She's very strong." Alex studied Tamsyn's profile. The determined set of her jaw, the fierce intelligence in her eyes, and the strength that radiated from her. "She's much like you. Small, petite in build, bloody-minded when needed. She's gentle though, for the most part. A healer, and gardener. A green witch." Alex suddenly choked up. "We can't lose her. I *won't*. I will not let her become one of those lost souls swirling in Orla's pit of grief."

Tamsyn squeezed his hand. "You're a good boy. Have you finished your preparations?"

Alex took a deep breath, feeling like an emotional fool, and focussed on what he needed to do. "I have a few more gemstones I'd like to bury at strategic locations, and then come dusk, I'm going to sit there, at the grave again. I'm planning to draw her in."

"What are the gemstones for?"

"They contain a combination of properties that I will release at certain times to try and herd her to me."

"Interesting. Then you are better on your feet than sitting there. Besides, she almost sucked you in last time."

"I'll be better prepared tonight."

Tamsyn shook her head and marched across the graveyard, back towards the house. "I have a better idea. Come with me."

For several horrible moments, Kendall thought she was lost.

After Zee disappeared, she had run around searching for him, convinced he was pulling some terrible prank on her, until she'd had to accept that he would never do such a thing. Then she pulled herself together. Zee had said before he vanished that she would stand a better chance than them. She was human, after all. The traps were not designed for her. Plus, she was a police officer.

Although Titus knew only too well there were no laws about killing or trapping paranormal creatures, he also knew there were very clear rules about hunting and killing humans. None of the hunters were stupid enough to do that.

Filled with renewed positivity, she studied the sigil on the tree that Zee had spotted before he vanished. On a hunch, she started searching for other signs, and was rewarded moments later when she found another, and then another. She smiled with grim satisfaction. *There was a pattern*. After that, she found the other signs more quickly. They were etched on the old oak trees that were prolific in this part of the wood, their huge, gnarled barks knotted and twisted. The oaks they had chosen formed a loose, curving line.

An invisible boundary.

For a long time Kendall stood on it, trying to feel for any difference between the sides. *Was there magic present?* Apart from the wild magic of the wood, she couldn't feel any, but the sigils had to mark something. Frustrated, she poked around in the undergrowth and found more signs carved into the earth. *What did these mean?* There was still no trace of the hunters yet. *Were they further in, or would they come back at dusk? And where had Zee gone?*

She still had more questions than answers, but she was on to something. However, she couldn't do it alone, and she had to work quickly before the hunters turned up. She needed Newton and Moore. She reached for her phone, but there was no signal. *Fuck it.*

Satisfied that she had done as much as she could at present, Briar stood and smoothed her skirt down.

Beth was now in bed, sleeping naturally, her energy levels stabilised after her psychic experience less than an hour before. It had been an intense period of time after Reuben had apologetically left them to see El. Rosa had been in tears, panic-stricken and frustrated, and Max had retreated into his shell. Caspian, after a few moments of deliberation, carried Beth to the bedrooms Reuben had set aside for the family, leaving Briar to work her healing magic, and Avery had taken charge of Max. Briar hadn't told Beth that she was a witch, but she had to suspect that she was some kind of empathetic healer. She was happy to leave it that way. Rosa was not.

"Where are you going?" Rosa asked, jumping to her feet. She had been sitting next to Beth's bed, watching her anxiously, but she hustled Briar across the room.

"I have to go to the manor. Alex is stuck there."

"But what if something else happens? Another vision. You did something to her!"

"Nothing bad!"

"I know that." Rosa's voice was a harsh whisper. "You did something with your hands, and you whispered something."

Briar drew her closer to the door. "I am a healer. That's the easiest way to explain it. I can't stop her visions. It's probably better that Tamsyn helps her deal with them, or Alex, my friend. You just have to make sure she's safe during them, and let her sleep it off. Plenty of food and water later is good."

Rosa stared at her, uncertain. "You're going to deal with that *creature* at the manor. The banshee. What will you do?"

"Stop it, any way we can, and rescue Alex."

Rosa swallowed. "What are you, other than my long-lost cousin?"

"Someone you can trust. Can we talk about this later? I have to go."

"But you'll come back?"

"Of course, but probably not until late."

At least I hope I will return, Briar thought as she marched down the hall to find Avery and Caspian.

Just as Newton was ready to explode with frustration, his phone rang, and he snatched it from his pocket and hit the speaker button.

"Kendall? Where the hell are you?"

"Up a tree."

"What?" He paused on the leaf-dappled path, staring at Moore. "Why?"

"To get a bloody signal. Just listen!" He bristled at her peremptory tone, but kept quiet. "Zee has vanished, and I've found loads of sigils in the wood. The Nephilim and Shadow must be here somewhere, hidden or trapped. I need help!"

"Where are you?"

"I don't bloody know. Somewhere in the middle of the bloody wood! Just look for sigils and follow them. I was thinking Ghost OPS might be able to help. They read magical energy, right?"

Newton stared at Moore, eyebrows raised. "Yes, they do. That's actually quite a good suggestion...if they can get here." He was aware that they were caught up in the banshee investigation.

"Well, if they can't, you'd best think of a better idea, because right now I'm going in circles."

"Leave it with me, and don't move. We'll find you."

Newton ended the call, sighing with exasperation as he stared into the thick undergrowth. "I should have arrested them last night. Then we wouldn't be in this mess."

"You couldn't have held them for long," Moore said in his usual, reasonable tone. "Besides, the events at Stormcrossed Manor happened, and you couldn't ignore those, either. It was, quite literally, the perfect storm. They took advantage of that."

Newton swatted at a branch, wanting to take out his frustration on something. "I resolved not to have my hands tied anymore. To fully exploit my own agency when dealing with the paranormal, and within weeks, I'm stymied again."

"Because they're human. But," a smile crept up Moore's face, "if they are targeting Shadow and the Nephilim, they are generally seen as being human. You might get something to stick."

"Not without it all getting messy, and exposing our friends to scrutiny." Newton gestured around him. "This place, and their abilities, are the answer, and I'm happy to turn a blind eye. Hunting killer creatures is one thing. Hunting the innocent is something else entirely."

"The Nephilim and Shadow are innocent?"

"You know what I mean!"

Moore sniggered. "Yes, I do. Are we going to get on with it?"

"Yep. I'd better call Ben now, and while I phone him, keep your eyes peeled, Moore. Those bloody hunters are here somewhere, and we have to find them."

When El finally arrived in Reuben's kitchen after completing the second knife, she was tired, but pleased with her achievements.

The coven was seated around the kitchen table, half-eaten pizzas in boxes spread across the surface, and a virtually untouched bowl of salad next to it. Reuben had left her earlier to finish her task undisturbed, and was sitting with the others, deep in conversation.

He grinned when she arrived. "Here she is! Our hero of the hour!"

"Funny." She slid into a seat, and reached for the closest slice. "This is heaven," she muttered through a mouthful of food. "I'm ravenous."

"I hear your blade is going to be very effective," Caspian said, also reaching for a pizza slice.

"I hope it is. It certainly has some unusual, and frankly quite disturbing, abilities. If I've done it right."

Briar huffed. "Of course you have." Briar looked preoccupied, as if she was forcing herself to concentrate. Not surprising, considering she'd been told the banshee was most likely searching for her. El would be side-tracked, too.

"You look tired," Avery told her. "Are you sure you're ready for later?"

"I just need food." She slid the knife out of her bag and onto the table. "Here it is. Sam has the other."

"I hope we can trust him," Avery said, her eyes hooded. "What if he goes in before we arrive?"

"He won't. I feel confident we can trust him. So does Reuben."

He nodded. "I get good vibes from both of them. We need to get there soon, though. Less than an hour now."

"I'll be ready." El took another bite, and pointed behind her. "The Empusa's sword is in my car. We're weaponed up, and ready to go." As the food hit her stomach and she could think of other things, she realised the atmosphere around the table was tense. "Has something else happened? I mean, I know the situation is tough, but there seems to be more..."

Reuben shuffled in his chair, looking guilty. "I neglected to tell you about Shadow. I didn't want to distract you earlier."

"Shadow? What's happened to her?"

"She didn't come back from her early morning ride."

El threw her remaining pizza crust at him. "You shit! You should have told me!"

"And what would you have done? We needed the knife for Alex. You would have been distracted."

"I'm not a bloody child!" El was furious. Shadow was her friend. A good friend. She didn't care if she was making a scene in front of everyone. "You're an infuriating, male arsehole! I'm not here to be managed!"

"I was trying to be thoughtful!"

"Wanker!"

"I'm going to clear the table," Caspian declared, grabbing the pizza boxes. "Give you some space."

"I don't need space. I need another boyfriend."

Reuben winced. "Sorry." Wide-eyed and pleading, he mouthed, "*I love you.*"

"Piss off!" El took a deep breath, wrestling a box from Caspian's hands, and he sank back in his seat. "I need more food. Is there any news of Shadow now?" She glared at all of them. "I can handle it!"

"Of course you can," Avery said, shooting Reuben an impatient look. "No. Unfortunately, Gabe and Niel went looking for her, and there's been no news from them, either. The last thing we heard was that Kendall was searching for them all in the wood with Zee. Then Zee disappeared. Newton and Moore are trying to find her—and the others—and they've asked Ghost OPS to help. Cassie and Ben are joining the search. They thought their EMF meter might help detect magical signatures, because the hunters must have set something up."

El's mind whirled with shock. "Shit! Some kind of trap." Mouth dry, she placed her half-eaten food on the plate. "We've underestimated Titus and Apollo. They're cleverer than we thought if they've captured the Nephilim and Shadow. We need to help, but... Fuck."

Avery nodded. "Titus is a wily old goat. He saw what was happening last night and took full advantage. Even if he doesn't know the details of what's going on, he knows we're distracted."

"That's too polite. He's a sneaky, underhanded bastard." Fire danced along El's palms. "If he hurts anyone, I shall shrivel his balls to raisins."

"My love," Reuben said, suddenly serious as he took her hands in his. They were cool thanks to his water element, extinguishing her elemental fire. "I shall force-feed them to him, too. But can we focus on Alex and the banshee first, before we address Ravens' Wood?"

El took a deep, cleansing breath, saving her anger for later. "Yes, fine."

She looked around the table, realising how strange it felt without Alex there. An empty chair seemed to mock them. As her jumbled thoughts settled, she asked, "What about Dylan?"

"Meeting us at the manor, any time now," Avery said, rising to her feet. She stared at Briar, who had been silent for a long time. "Are you sure about this, Briar? You could stay behind and tend to Beth. You might be safer here."

Briar looked up, startled. "Absolutely not. If somehow that damn creature escapes, she might find me here, with the rest of the family. I won't risk that. Besides, I'd like to get some revenge." She stood too, her eyes sparking with the green fire that always gave El a thrill. "Let's go and slay a banshee."

Chapter Thirty-One

The whine of the EMF meter almost jolted Cassie off the branch she was perching on. Cursing herself for being so jumpy, she continued to study the sigil in front of her.

It was small and crude, but certainly effective, and the trunk was blackened beneath the scar, as if it had been scored in by fire. Unfortunately, many of the trees here had the same sign, and they were different from the larger ones below that made up a magical barrier.

She and Ben had met up with Newton and Moore almost an hour ago, not sure whether she was excited to be in Ravens' Wood tracking hunters, or disappointed not to be going to Stormcrossed Manor. They had trudged through the dusky green light beneath the thick canopy, searching for Kendall, whilst keeping a wary watch for the hunters. This place had an Otherworldly quality, but you could argue that many ancient woodlands did. They seemed to carry the distant past in their sap, their roots digging into the layers of time beneath their feet. Cassie found the place both fascinating and unnerving.

Once they'd found the sigils, they worked their way along the trail, discovering Kendall loitering on a narrow track.

While Ben used his EMF meter, constantly adjusting the frequency as Newton and Kendall followed his every move, Cassie suggested to Moore that they search for other signs. He had enthusiastically agreed, and they had clambered up surroundings trees to examine the bark, and quickly had success. *Perhaps these simpler sigils were another type of trap for the tree spirits.*

She called over to Moore in the neighbouring tree, just about visible through the thick leaf cover. "I've found another."

"Me, too." He stuck his head out, pushing a branch aside. "Same as the others. That's all of the big trees in this vicinity marked."

"And there will be more we haven't seen." She gestured to the ground below. "I have an idea. I'll speak to you down there."

Glad she'd been working out, Cassie climbed back down the gnarled, knotted trunk, feeling guilty about even climbing these venerable trees. The thought that someone had carved horrible, controlling symbols into them made her blood boil. She loved the paranormal and Otherworldly. Yes, it was scary, and yes, some troublesome things had to be vanquished, but it could be beautiful, too. These hunters were evil.

Moore fished twigs out of his hair as he approached her. "How do you know so much about these signs?"

"It's part of the job. Especially since Samhain, when that horrible witch used them at Old Haven Church. I borrowed a book from Briar, and bought a few of my own. You can look at them, if you like."

Moore nodded, appearing impressed. "I think I might, thanks. And your conclusion?"

She pointed behind them to where the others were clustered, Ben's EMF meter now whining incessantly. "The hunters have made some kind of trap, obviously, presumably to trap dryads and other paranormal creatures—if they exist." Cassie, like everyone, had heard the rumours about Ravens' Wood, especially from the witches, who had a very unnerving experience at Beltane. To date, despite the fact that Ghost OPS had also done some research here, they were yet to find anything conclusive.

Moore gave a dry laugh. "Oh, they exist all right."

Cassie looked at him, startled. Although Moore was on the paranormal police team, he had seemed prosaic. Now she reassessed that view. "Anyway, the other sigils that—I think—have been branded onto the trunks—"

"I agree."

"Well, I think they're incomplete. Why would you want to trap tree spirits inside if you wished to do them harm?"

"You wouldn't. You'd want to trap them *outside*."

"Exactly. So, if we presume the spirits will leave their trees at night..."

Moore groaned. "They will complete the spell and stop them from returning to safety."

"Exactly. And the other trap, where Zee and the others seem to be, maybe that's like a compound. Potentially, they spent last night setting it up, ready to finish their plans tonight."

"A killing compound?"

Cassie shuddered. "Don't say that."

"Also potentially, they don't know who they have trapped in there." Moore's eyes lit up. "They might not know anything about the Nephilim or Shadow. It could be a shock."

"Let's make it a bigger one. I have a plan."

Vibrating with her magic, and desperate to get onto Stormcrossed Manor's grounds, Avery watched El pull the sigil-engraved knife from her backpack.

They were standing on the drive before the magical wall that surrounded the gardens. *Alex was in there somewhere, possibly hurt, and she had to find him.* She had repeatedly phoned him all day with no success, and was imagining all sorts of scenarios that she was desperately trying to push to the back of her mind.

The tension in their group was palpable. Dylan was with them, carrying a shotgun loaded with salt shells, as well as a selection of spells in his backpack. He was standing next to Sam and Ruby, also packing rune-inscribed weapons. The rest of them carried gemstones, and of course, their own magic.

The general plan was that they would try to immobilise the banshee, so that either El or Sam could attack it with the blade. Avery and El would head left, Sam and Ruby would go to the right, and Briar and Caspian would go up the drive to the house. Reuben and Dylan had volunteered to move between the groups in a sweeping pattern.

Dylan had shown them the crude map he'd made of the grounds, and they intended to drive the banshee to the graveyard area at the edge of the property. They hoped that if Alex had a plan, it would somehow involve the grave the banshee had emerged from. It seemed logical—as much as anything could, in this weird situation.

"If I breach this wall, I may not be able to close it," El warned them.

"Then one of us will have to guard it, to stop her getting out," Caspian said. He eyed Briar, his jaw clenching. "I suggest I do it, with Briar. You should stay on the periphery."

Briar glared at him. "I don't appreciate you nannying me. Besides, if she senses the breach, which is highly possible, this is the first place she'll come!"

"Can we just get in there first?" Avery asked, voice rising with exasperation. "I suggest we all prepare for the fact that the banshee might appear in seconds."

Reuben grunted with derision. "Like we'll be that lucky. Anyway, I have an idea for the breach. Just get on with it."

El flexed her fingers and jabbed forward with the blade, puncturing the wall. At the first touch of the knife, the magical boundary lit up, and progressing quickly, El created a doorway within the shimmering mass. Without waiting, El darted through it, the rest of them on her heels.

On the other side they all paused, weapons raised, but the silence was thick and heavy.

"Okaaay," Reuben drawled, looking at the gaping hole in the wall. "That worked, but as suspected, the whole damn door has vanished. However, perhaps one of my carefully prepared crystals will work." He rummaged in his pack. "Go find Alex, and I'll deal with this before we follow."

"I'll wait with you," Dylan said, sweeping his gun around. "You shouldn't be alone."

Avery didn't wait. "Good luck, guys, and be careful! El?"

"Right with you."

Avery started up the long drive, quickly finding the path that led to the gardens on the left. She ducked beneath the overhanging branches, aware that El was right behind her, but they hadn't gone far when a piercing scream shattered the night.

The banshee was back.

Alex shivered as the banshee's wail shattered the quiet dusk, and looked at Tamsyn, who stood next to him. "She sounds close by."

Tamsyn nodded. "She's active earlier than normal. I presume *that* has something to do with it." She pointed at the wall of protection that shimmered with a bluish light. "I think your friends are back."

"Trying to get in, perhaps."

"Or they've already succeeded."

"I hope so." He laughed, despite their grim situation. "They're a stubborn bunch. Especially my girlfriend."

"Good. Friends like that are valuable. Let's hope they don't get in our way." Tamsyn closed her eyes. "I'll try to find her."

Tamsyn and Alex were in an overgrown courtyard that Tamsyn had suggested would be the best place for her to try and detect the banshee's path as she crossed the garden. They intended to drive her to the grave, where Alex would seal her in and then attempt to banish her forever.

He had placed gemstones in strategic positions, imbued with magic that he would release as needed in an attempt to herd her in the right direction. Unfortunately, he didn't have a lot of faith in his plan. The grounds were large, and there was only he and Tamsyn there at the moment. As he had observed the night before, the banshee moved quickly, flitting in and out of his vision, and she was horribly strong. The depths of her despair were also overwhelming, making it hard for Alex to concentrate. It was an uphill battle.

But, if somehow his coven had got in...

"There!" Tamsyn pointed to where the banshee clung to the wall like a bat, screeching at the outside world.

Alex's blood curdled. The sound was horrific. Worse, he had no gemstone in place there, or close by. He couldn't risk damaging the wall, even though she seemed to have strengthened it somehow. He needed to get her back on the ground. Tamsyn called to her in Gaelic; a command. The banshee ignored her, head whipping to the left as she surveyed along the wall before vanishing again.

"This way," he called, heading in the general direction she had looked in.

"The drive!" Tamsyn shouted. "I can feel her there."

Damn it. That was the place furthest from the grave. *This was going to be impossible.*

Dylan's eyes widened with horror as the banshee manifested with an ear-piercing wail, right on top of Reuben, who was burying the gemstone in the earth beneath the gap in the wall.

"Reuben! Duck!"

Dylan was only feet away, and he fired his shotgun with shaking hands, unable to control the shudders that the scream had triggered in his body.

The shot went wide, the salt catching only the side of her body, but the boom was enough to have her spinning around with fury as she fixed her red-eyed stare on Dylan. Immediately, he fell to his knees as her despair and loss overwhelmed his own emotions. He couldn't think straight. *Shit!*

Reuben, however, had rolled out of the way and was back on his feet. He yelled a spell, and a blinding white light exploded from the ground, obliterated the banshee, and blocked the hole in the wall.

"You did it!" Dylan yelled. "Have you killed her already?"

"Nope! Incoming!"

Dylan spun on his knees, shotgun lifted again, just in time to see the banshee manifest and race at him. This time he was prepared for her. He fired the second round, and it struck her in the chest. She shattered like glass and vanished.

"Bullseye!" Reuben yelled, racing to Dylan's side and pulling him to his feet. "Nice shot, mate."

"Where's she gone?" Dylan fumbled for more shells and reloaded quickly.

"Fuck knows, but she can't get out now."

"Neither can we!"

"It's do or die, my man. Crystal magic rocks. Get it?" He grinned.

Dylan groaned. He loved Reuben's humour—when he wasn't in fear of losing his life. "Now is not the time for puns!"

"Spoilsport." Reuben started running up the drive. "Come on. I've got many more of those."

Briar skidded to a halt as the dilapidated house appeared in front of her. *Stormcrossed Manor.* The family home she never knew she had. *This was surreal.*

The banshee's cry, however, didn't allow time for introspection. Despite her knees feeling wobbly, Briar spun around, hands raised, but the creature was nowhere in sight. However, a flash of light exploded on the boundary, and the boom of the shotgun rang out.

"Dylan!" Her heart was in her mouth.

Caspian was next to her, fire balling in his palms. "And Reuben. Let's hope they've kept her from leaving."

311

A second scream that sounded much closer made Briar nauseous, and a wave of despair rolled through her. "Sounds like she's still here. Good...I think."

"You're as white as a sheet!" Caspian glared at her. "You shouldn't have come."

"Don't start! I'm seeing this through." Her gaze swept over the small portion of the overgrown gardens that she could see, her heart lifting despite the closeness of the banshee. She took deep breaths, savouring the rich scent of loam and garden flowers, and with every breath, her equilibrium returned. "It's so odd! To think I lived so close by and never knew. I like this place. It calls to me, even through its melancholy. It needs love."

"The garden?"

Briar threw her arms wide. "*Everything*. I feel it. And so does he." The Green Man uncurled within her, responding to the wildness of their surroundings. Hope flooded through her, as did a fresh resolve. "This is where I'm meant to be."

"For the banshee, you mean?" Caspian's head was cocked to the side. "You're baffling me, Briar!"

Briar ripped her shoes off, throwing them towards the house. "I don't need those. I need the earth beneath my feet. This is her earth, too." As soon as Briar's bare feet touched the soil, she felt the creature, and thrusting Caspian aside, she waited. "Don't do anything until I do! Trust me!"

In seconds the banshee appeared, a hideous, spectral hag hovering only a few feet from them. Briar opened herself up to it, throwing her arms wide as she allowed the creature to access her emotions. But only for a second. As soon as she felt the banshee's despair pierce her core, she blocked it, closing herself off again. She knew what to expect now, and that was a weapon in itself.

Bundling her positive thoughts into a ball of magic, she hurled it at the creature, and Caspian followed up with fireballs. With another ear-piercing shriek, the banshee vanished.

He stared at her, a smile curling the corner of his mouth. "You felt her arrive."

"I did. And I felt something else, too. She hates feeling love. *Hates it.* She despises it because she can't win against it. She wants to crush me even more now."

"That does not fill me with hope, Briar."

"It should do. It means she'll follow me—right to the graveyard. I'll stop occasionally and draw her in."

"That's a dangerous game."

"But the others will hear her screams and follow *her*. Follow us. We'll have her exactly where we need her."

"You're going to be the bait." It wasn't a question.

"If she gets too close..." Briar hesitated, knowing this would get harder. The more she opened up to tempt the banshee, the more despair she would feel. "I just have to remain positive."

"I'll help you out. Don't worry about that."

Briar nodded, and without another word, raced across the grounds towards the graveyard, Caspian next to her, hoping they wouldn't get lost in the garden's wilderness.

Chapter Thirty-Two

"You want us to do *what*?" Ben asked Cassie, incredulous. "Sit in the trees?"

"Yes! It's a perfectly good idea."

"You're nuts!"

"Actually," Moore said, intervening, "it's a great idea. I think Cassie is right. And even if she's not, have you got a better idea?"

Ben huffed and fiddled with the EMF meter. "No."

Newton's hands were on his hips, his face dappled in shadows as the dusk thickened. "Let me recap. You think that come night fall, as the sprites leave the trees or whatever it is they do, the hunters will cast some kind of spell that prevents them from going *back* into the trees?"

"Yes." Cassie's hands were also on her hips as she stared at Newton defiantly. "That's what the sigils signify. I think, anyway. But it makes sense!"

"Nothing about this whole thing makes sense!" Newton complained. "I suppose at least we know the weird barrier isn't that big, thanks to that." He eyed the EMF meter that had identified the perimeter.

"They can't afford for it to be if there's only three of them," Ben reasoned. "If we include Briar's visitor."

"But where are they?" Cassie wondered. "They might even be doing something right now, further along the path."

"I've been thinking about that," Ben said, looking at Kendall. "You said their vans were here?"

She nodded, staring into the undergrowth. "They were. Perhaps they're waiting somewhere for nightfall."

Cassie nodded. "That makes sense. We have to find a spot to wait and keep quiet."

A deep, amused voice spoke from behind them. "I agree, and I'm more than happy to help."

They all spun around and found Eli grinning at them.

"Fuck's sake!" Ben said, heart pounding. "Did you have to approach so quietly?"

"You're all making enough noise to rouse the dead. Where's Zee?"

"Beyond that!" Ben said, turning on the EMF meter so Eli could tell what he was talking about. "We think that's where they all are. Trapped in some kind of prison." He quickly summarised Cassie's theory.

"Clever. Good enough to trick my brothers and Shadow." He studied their pensive faces. "You have a plan?"

Cassie shrugged. "We were just discussing it. But we need to decide quickly, before the hunters appear."

Eli stepped closer, lowering his voice. "I saw the woman who visited our shop by a van in the castle grounds with two men. I think they are waiting for the visitors to leave, and most have by now. They won't be long."

Kendall sighed with relief. "Just the three of them?"

"In that car park, at least."

"What about Ruby and Sam?" Ben asked.

"With the witches," Newton said. "I hope. To go back to our earlier issue—what's the plan?"

"I suspect," Cassie said, "that they will have to lower that barrier to get in, or at least a portion of it. We'll follow them in. I have the witches' shadow spell with me. It's very effective. We get up in the trees, watch for their arrival, wait for them to act, and tail them."

Newton grunted with disapproval. "I think we should just demand that they stop. We are the police, after all. I can arrest them."

"And if they resist? Or attack us using magic that we have no answer to?" Kendall argued. "They might escape, and then the barrier stays up. What if the witches can't help us? Our friends will be stuck!"

"I agree with Newton," Moore said, looking exasperated. "We're the police! I'm not cowering from them."

"I won't cower from *anyone*!" Eli declared. "Attack is always better than defence—"

"Said the Nephilim!" Ben said, eyeing up his ridiculously impressive build. "Kendall is right. If we get this wrong and they leg it, we are stuffed!"

"I have a better idea." Eli pulled his t-shirt over his head and thrust it under a thicket of bushes, extended his wings, and pulled his sword from his scabbard. "We wait in the trees, then I swoop down on them, take one hostage, and threaten to cut their throat if they don't open up the damn barrier. You lot can tackle the rest. Better?"

They all nodded, even though Ben was still thinking it was insane.

"Good," Eli said in response to their nods. "Now, get up in the trees and wait. It won't be long now."

As another scream resounded across the grounds, El changed direction and ran, branches thrashing at her face and arms before she tumbled into a small courtyard. "Bloody hell! This sodding place is like a maze!"

Avery stopped behind her, hands on her knees as she took deep breaths. "She's moving away from us!"

"Chasing someone?"

"Alex, or maybe Tamsyn?" Avery's eyes widened. "Oh no..."

"Briar!"

Another blood-curdling wail, a blistering flash of light, and a yell had them running again, and the next thing El knew, she smacked straight into Alex and a small, wizened woman who looked like a raisin in human form.

"Shit! Alex!"

"El! Avery!" Alex swept Avery into his arms. "You're okay!"

"I thought you might be injured, or dead!" Avery exclaimed, eyes sweeping over him. "I'm so relieved to see you!"

The elderly woman rolled her eyes. "We haven't got time for this! Reunions will have to wait."

"Ladies, this is Tamsyn," Alex said. "Briar's grandmother."

"Later! This way!" Tamsyn ignored the introduction and marched across the courtyard surprisingly quickly. "She's hunting something. And she's close. I haven't felt her so furious in a long time."

As they hurried along behind her, Avery said, "We think she's after Briar."

Tamsyn called over her shoulder. "Right now, I think she'll take anyone."

"Herne's balls," Alex said, frustrated. "I've put spelled gemstones around this place to try and trap her, and I couldn't have got it more wrong. She's too quick!"

"What about the grave?" El asked, following Alex and Tamsyn through the tangle of overgrown paths.

"I've put a salt circle—incomplete, for now—around it. I don't think that will work, though."

"Don't worry." El flashed her new knife at him. "Hopefully, this will. In fact..." she broke off as the banshee's desolate scream shattered the twilight, sounding surprisingly close. Her knife began to vibrate in her palm. "Shit. The blade feels her, too." She pulled the Empusa's sword from its scabbard. "Someone else should take this. I don't need both."

"I'll have it," Alex said, wresting it from her grip.

Then another scream made them start running.

Briar.

Caspian watched with horror as the banshee appeared before them, blocking off their route, much closer than she had been before.

She was right on top of Briar, mere feet away, and Caspian knew Briar had overstepped her ability to resist the creature's cry. She fell to her knees, face wracked with pain as the hag advanced, her horrific mouth that seemed to open to a void, wide with longing.

Caspian hurled spell after spell at her, feeling his own power weakening as her cry curdled his blood. The banshee disappeared with every blast of his magic, but she returned just as quickly, her red eyes fixed on Briar. He threw himself over his friend and raised a protection spell, just as a knife whizzed past and embedded in the banshee's chest. Twisting around, he saw Ruby and Sam skid into the small, paved garden, their other weapons raised.

Was that it? Had they done it?

But the banshee screamed again, pulled the knife out, and hurled it at Caspian. *Shit.* Remembering that it could penetrate protection spells, he used witch-flight, transporting him and Briar across the courtyard and behind the banshee. Wondering why the blade hadn't worked, he uttered a banishing spell, and with a screech, the creature disappeared.

Sam raced over to them, while Ruby retrieved the knife from the bushes where it had landed. "Are you two okay?"

"I've been better," Caspian admitted, his head ringing with the creature's cry. He turned to Briar, who was still huddled on the ground. "Briar?"

She sat up, as if every part of her body ached. "I'm fine, but by the Goddess, she's strong. Help me up."

Caspian pulled her to her feet, then turned to Sam and Ruby. "Your knife didn't work."

Ruby shook her head. "I disagree. You didn't see her properly, but I did. It left a hole in her chest. We've wounded her."

Sam almost growled as he lifted his head and looked across the grounds. "We can't afford for her to retreat. Not now."

"Then I'll draw her out again," Briar said, lifting her chin as green fire flashed in her eyes. She dug her feet into the earth in studied concentration, and then pointed. "That way."

As shouts resounded through the grounds, Reuben changed direction. "Over there."

"That sounds like Alex!" Dylan lifted his shotgun as he ran. "I can't tell whether it's good or bad, though."

"At least we know he's still alive," Reuben said, relief running through him. Not that he'd really doubted it, but in his darkest moments, he had wondered. Now he increased his speed, slapping branches out of the way.

Dylan pointed. "The graveyard is over there. We're close!"

The shouts grew louder, and then another wail echoed across the grounds. Reuben winced. The effect of the banshee's cry seemed to magnify every time he heard it. The good thing was that adrenalin was keeping him moving. Fear for Alex and Briar, in particular. And El, of course, who had insisted on carrying the knife herself, despite his protestations.

Without warning, the banshee manifested in front of them, her eyes wild with spite. Reuben fell backwards in shock, sprawling on the ground, but Dylan didn't hesitate, and he fired the shotgun, both barrels. She vanished, but reappeared seconds later, only a few feet further back.

Reuben could feel her fury now. They were thwarting her, and she didn't like it.

Then Briar appeared out of the undergrowth behind her, yelling, "It's me you want! Come on!"

Caspian, Ruby, and Sam emerged next to her, a mixture of horror and worry on their faces, but Dylan pointed beyond them. "That way, Briar! That's where the graveyard is!"

She gave him the briefest of nods and then turned and ran, the banshee vanished, and in seconds, the others were following.

Newton heard Titus before he saw him. He was laughing in that cruel, arrogant way of his, and Newton clenched his fists. He didn't consider himself a violent man, but right now, he just wanted to punch him repeatedly.

He couldn't hear what Titus was saying, but that's because he was perched on a branch surrounded by leaves, feeling like Robin Hood. He couldn't believe that he'd even agreed to this mad plan, but without a better one, here they all were. Moore was close by on another branch, while Eli was further along with Kendall. Cassie and Ben were together in another tree.

He quickly texted the group to tell them that the hunters had arrived, and waited until Titus drew closer.

Peering through the branches, Newton saw Titus walking with Apollo and the woman he presumed was Leigh. All three carried blades. He was just about to warn the others, when Eli soared through the canopy like the Angel of Death, swooping on Titus and knocking the blade out of his grasp.

Newton scrambled down the tree, arriving on the ground at the same time as Moore. Eli hovered above them, gripping Titus to his chest. He was a big man, and he squirmed in Eli's grasp, but Eli had wrapped a powerful arm around him, and the other held a blade to his neck. "I'll slit your throat right now if you don't release that trap."

"Who the fuck are you?" Titus grunted, eyes furious.

Apollo and Leigh had both taken a defensive stance, knives raised and back-to-back as Kendall, Cassie, and Ben arrived.

Eli was grinning. "I'm your worst nightmare. Get your friends to release the trap, or I'll kill you!"

"I don't know what trap you're talking about."

"He's not lying," Apollo yelled, wide-eyed. "You've got this all wrong!"

Newton gestured at the wicked blades they carried. "Then why are you carrying weapons? Why are there sigils on the trees? And why did Zee vanish in front of Kendall's eyes?"

"I don't know! Who the fuck is Zee?"

"A very good friend." Newton stepped closer. Both hunters were covered in sweat, eyes darting everywhere. "I suggest that you drop the knives. You're now threatening the police. It's not a good look."

Apollo waved his blade at Eli. "Get your freak friend to put Titus down!"

Eli pressed the blade to Titus's throat, and blood trickled onto his chest. "Release the trap. I *will* kill him. I'm not kidding."

Newton nodded. "Yes, he will. Now drop your knives!"

It was getting dark beneath the dense green canopy, and without warning, the air seemed to shift around them, as shapes manifested in the shadows.

Leigh screamed. "They're coming! You fools! Let us go!"

She lunged at Kendall, who was closest, but Kendall was ready for her. With lightning-quick reflexes, she knocked the blade away and wrestled Leigh to the ground.

A strange, green-skinned creature appeared out of thin air behind Apollo and dragged him backwards. He screamed and dropped his blade in surprise, before both vanished behind the magical barrier.

In seconds they were all surrounded by the most unearthly creatures Newton had ever seen, and he quickly realised he didn't have the upper hand anymore. They did.

Chapter Thirty-Three

A lex sprinted into the graveyard, but quickly skidded to a halt, El, Avery, and Tamsyn at his side. In seconds, Reuben and Dylan arrived.

Briar was next to the disturbed grave, her feet planted in the earth. She was right beside the incomplete salt circle, her arms raised, green fire raging in her eyes. Caspian stood only a short distance away. Two people Alex didn't know but suspected to be the hunters were on the other side of the grave.

The banshee was in the middle of the graveyard, and she spun around to face them. She wasn't screaming anymore. Instead, she paced like a caged animal, and if anything, that was worse. She looked calculating. Evil.

Tamsyn froze next to him. "Is that my granddaughter?"

Alex nodded, his mouth dry. Tamsyn scowled and stepped forward to intervene.

Briar yelled, "No! Stay back!" She directed her anger at the red-eyed hag. "Come on! It's me you want! What are you scared of? I'm waiting!"

The banshee lifted her head and keened. Everyone winced, hands flying to their ears. The sound was horrific, and it cut through Alex's defences. The banshee advanced towards Briar, and Sam threw his knife at the creature. It ripped straight through her, leaving a ragged tear in her spectral body, and landed only a few feet from Reuben. He swooped to pick it up and took aim. But then she vanished, and in seconds was even closer to Briar.

Briar, however, had now stepped into the salt circle around the grave, and she retreated, calling the banshee closer. "Come on. You need me. I know you do!"

The banshee moved a tentative foot forward, staring at the ground, as if she knew exactly what the circle was.

Caspian had the container of salt in his hands, waiting, but the banshee didn't move any more.

This time, El released the blade, positioning herself so it wouldn't hit Briar. Again, it ripped through the creature and left another ragged hole, but it didn't seem to weaken the banshee. Briar goaded her again, the rest watching and wondering what to do. They didn't want her to disappear completely, they were so close to ending her, but the blade wasn't working. Alex itched to use the Empusa's sword, but was wary of getting too close.

And then he had an idea. "Tamsyn! You need to release the grief that you carry. *Her* grief. It will overwhelm her—weaken her, I hope!"

Tamsyn looked at him, confused. "But it might make her stronger!"

"Not if you do it quickly. She won't be expecting it! Then," he eyed his companions, "we attack together. Blades, gun, magic. Get her into that circle. Avery, take this." He thrust the Empusa's sword at her. "Tamsyn! Do it now!"

Tamsyn nodded, threw her arms wide, and released all of the pent-up emotion she had carried for years. Alex felt it roll out towards the banshee like a tidal wave, hitting her so quickly that she staggered.

He yelled, "Now!"

As his friends attacked, Alex conjured the fiery runes he had used on her before, hoping that now she couldn't fight them off.

The banshee faltered under the onslaught, and with every thrust of the blades and blast of the shotgun, she grew weaker and weaker. Using the rune bindings, Alex finally wrestled her into the circle, and as Briar leapt out, Caspian sealed it.

Alex called the witches to him. "After me!" He started the spell he had prepared, the others repeating and strengthening his words with every iteration. The banshee howled, and goosebumps raced across his skin. But she was weaker now, her voice unable to do the damage it had caused before. She sank into the earth, twisting and writhing, arms outstretched, as if imploring them for help.

Alex started to see who she really was under all of that warped and twisted grief. The young woman who'd lost so much, and whose spirit had transformed so horribly. But he couldn't sympathise with her now. Not after all of the damage she had caused. He threw his shoulders back and repeated the spell, and he felt the renewed intent of his coven. They didn't stop until she had vanished.

Blissful silence fell and Alex heaved a sigh of relief, but it didn't last long, as Dylan shouted behind him. "Tamsyn!"

He whirled around, and saw that Tamsyn was motionless on the ground.

Kendall had never been so excited or so terrified in her life.

The air shimmered around the willowy, ethereal creatures that manifested out of the trees. Their skin was green and brown, dappled with markings like tree bark, and their eyes were a liquid brown that promised timeless knowledge. All were absolutely stunning. Shadows seem to slant through them, and yet for all of that, they still seemed very real.

Leigh struggled in Kendall's grasp, clearly terrified, and well she should be. She had been planning to kill these beautiful creatures, and it seemed they knew it. The others had frozen, watching the events unfold.

Eli, however, still imprisoned Titus several feet above the ground; he wasn't struggling any more. "Titus, open the damn barrier, or you may never see Apollo again."

Titus nodded, swallowing loudly. "You need to put me down."

"Sure. But don't think for a second that I'm going to let you go." Eli lowered them both to the ground, still grasping Titus firmly.

He grunted and eyed the dryads warily. "I need Leigh's bag. She has the spell ingredients."

Kendall rolled Leigh to the side as Moore leaned in and took her bag, which had landed beneath her. He searched through it, lifting out a selection of herbs, a bowl, a dark red glass bottle, and several candles. "These?"

Titus nodded. "Just place them on the ground and light the candles."

Eli tightened his grip. "No tricks."

"None, I swear. Put the herbs in the bowl."

Kendall tried not to smile. Titus had lost all of his bluster, and she could feel the fear rolling off him while Moore quickly did as he asked.

"Okay, now you need to add the mixture in the bottle, and blend them together."

Moore pulled the cork out of the bottle and tipped the thick liquid into the herbs, mixing them together with his fingertip.

Newton eyed Titus warily, and said to Moore, "Be careful!"

"I'm all good, Guv." He looked up at Titus. "Next?"

"Smear it over the sigils on the closest two trees."

Newton glared at him. "Why these two? There is a whole row of them that you've desecrated."

Leigh answered him. "It's how we designed it. Any two sigils, if triggered correctly, will create a doorway. Just do it!"

"Had enough?" Kendall asked, amused.

Leigh didn't answer and Moore did as instructed, smearing the thick, sticky mix on the sigils before he stepped back.

Titus uttered a few guttural words that Kendall struggled to hear, and then the barrier shimmered and a doorway opened.

Apollo's lifeless body was thrown through the door first, earning a squeak from Leigh. It was quickly followed by Shadow, her sword raised. She looked magnificent without the usual glamour disguising her fey otherness. Despite the fact that Kendall had met her and knew she had nothing to fear, she shrank back instinctively. Gabe, Niel, and Zee, were right behind her, their own weapons raised. A few other ethereal creatures followed them.

"It's just us!" Newton yelled. "Lower your weapons."

They looked none the worse for their experience, other than the fury that radiated from them, particularly Shadow. Her gaze raked over them all, finally settling on Titus clasped within Eli's grasp.

She extended her sword to Titus. "*You* did this?"

He nodded, as much as he could with a sword at his neck.

Shadow didn't hesitate. She plunged her sword into his guts and twisted. "You're a bastard, and deserve to die."

Titus dropped to his knees as Eli released him, and Newton shouted, "Shadow, no!"

But he was too late. Another quick slash of her sword left Titus dead at her feet.

Cassie yelped and turned away, and Ben looked green next to her.

A strange, horned creature with the face of a deer reached for Leigh, and Kendall retreated as Leigh was hauled to her feet, screaming. It pulled her through the doorway, and her scream was suddenly cut off.

Kendall felt sick. She had expected retribution. She wasn't sure she had expected *this*.

In seconds, the Otherworldly beings melted back into the shadows, leaving the group alone, and for a second, Kendall wondered if she'd imagined them.

Newton was glowering at Shadow. "I was going to deal with this!"

Eli sheathed his sword. "You did."

"I was going to arrest them."

Shadow took a deep breath, her anger dissipating as she took in the two dead bodies at her feet. She pulled a cloth from her pocket and wiped the blood off her blade with practiced efficiency. "I saved you the trouble. Did you really expect me to do otherwise?"

Newton exhaled heavily. "No, I suppose not. Are you all okay? Everyone? Any injuries?"

"Just my pride," Gabe virtually growled. "Tricked by some bloody hunters. I'm absolutely mortified."

"To be fair," Ben said, "they were good."

Cassie still looked away from the dead bodies on the forest floor as she said, "Really good! Very clever use of sigils."

"Can we discuss this another time?" Niel asked. "I'm over this bloody place, and I want a drink."

Zee spotted Kendall. "I'm glad to see you're okay."

She grinned. "Glad to see you are, too. You gave me a fright when you vanished."

He grimaced. "Not my finest moment."

Moore had collected the candles, bottle, and bowl, and returned them to Leigh's backpack. He straightened up, peering through the doorway into the space beyond. "What *was* in there?"

"A hideous warping of magic, time, and space," Niel said, glaring at it. "I thought I'd been in there for weeks. Have I been gone that long?" he asked, alarmed.

"Less than a day," Eli reassured him, clapping him on the shoulder. "Let's get these bodies cleared away and get out of here."

Avery raced across the graveyard, surprising herself with her burst of energy after everything that had just happened, and landed in a heap next to Dylan and Tamsyn, the others crowding around them.

Dylan was already feeling for a pulse in Tamsyn's birdlike wrist, and he immediately heaved a sigh of relief. "She's alive! Out cold, though."

Briar reached her hands above her grandmother, feeling across her head and then along her body. "She's very weak."

"She's in shock," Alex said. "She was carrying some of the banshee's grief for so long, I imagine releasing it was overwhelming." He glanced behind him to the grave. "You should get her out of here. I just want to finish off a few things here first."

Avery nodded, giving Briar's hand a squeeze as she did. "I'll stay. You go back to Reuben's, Briar. Take Tamsyn with you, and look after her. You both need to rest."

"I agree. You scared the crap out of me." Caspian's eyes were almost unfathomable as he stared at Briar, forcefully reminding Avery of just how close he was to her.

She smiled at him. "Sorry. Thanks for looking after me, though. It was the only way, and you know it."

"It doesn't make me feel any better, though."

El snorted. "I think you scared all of us, Briar. Honestly, for such a small person, I think you're the scariest one of us."

"You and your grandmother," Alex said. "She packs a punch for such a little thing—metaphorically, of course. You're incredibly alike."

"Don't be silly." Briar looked embarrassed. She focussed on her grandmother instead. "I knew the banshee wanted me, and I used it."

"Well, now it's time to rest," Caspian told her. "You go, and I'll stay here and help secure this place. Make sure everything's okay. We'll meet you at Reuben's house."

"I'm not sure Tamsyn will thank us for taking her out of her home," Alex said, standing and stretching. "But she will be glad to see Rosa. And you, of course, Briar." He flashed her a grin. "I've been telling her all about you."

"Awesome. Whiskey all around?" Reuben suggested, lifting Tamsyn effortlessly. "Herne's horns. She's like a little bird."

"Does that include us?" Sam asked, looking hopeful as he picked up the blade and placed it carefully in his pack. "I must admit, that was harder than I thought. She was nothing like the last banshee I encountered."

"Of course it includes you," Reuben said, already striding across the graveyard, the others trailing behind him. His voice was fading as he said, "And the rest of you, make it quick! El, call Newton. I'm hoping they're okay, too."

Dylan hung back with Avery, Caspian, and Alex, already pulling his camera from his pack. "Any objections?"

"You and that bloody camera," Avery said, shaking her head. She looked around at the deserted graveyard that felt suddenly desolate after the madness of the previous minutes. "Hopefully there's nothing left to film now."

"There better bloody not be," Alex grunted, heading back towards the grave.

"Any final spells you want to say?" Caspian asked.

Alex pulled a couple of spades out of the long grass and handed Caspian one. "We're going to fill the grave in, and then yes, another spell."

"And a blessing," Avery added, feeling it would be appropriate. She spun around, taking in the dilapidated grounds. "This place feels so sad. So unloved. And it has experienced so much sorrow."

"Like you wouldn't believe." Alex was already shovelling soil into the grave, Caspian doing the same. "I had a very enlightening conversation with Tamsyn."

"She's not as scary as you thought, then?" Dylan asked. "I must admit, I was worried sick when I heard you were trapped here with her."

"I didn't sleep at all," Avery confessed, already feeling her energy ebbing. "If I'm honest, only adrenalin is keeping me going right now."

"Last night was a challenge for me, too," Alex told them. "But then I realised what was going on. At that point, I only felt sorry for Tamsyn. She sacrificed a lot for her family. But that story can wait for a whiskey. The thought of that is the only thing keeping *me* going right now."

Avery took a deep breath, inhaling the rich, earthy smell of soil, plants, and the breeze from the sea, and underlying it all the sense of loss and loneliness. This place needed healing, and there was no better person to do it than Briar.

Chapter Thirty-Four

Reuben picked up the whiskey bottle to refresh everyone's drinks, and alarmed to see it was almost empty, headed to the cupboard for a new bottle. He extracted an expensive one reserved for special occasions. He might have a lot of money, but that didn't mean he threw it around.

Tonight, though, it felt like he was hosting a party, not just celebrating the defeat of the banshee and a few malevolent hunters. Newton's group had arrived about an hour after he had carried Tamsyn up to the bedrooms where he'd settled Rosa and the kids. He'd left Briar with them, carried up a tray of drinks and snacks, and after making sure Briar didn't need any help, left them to it. She needed time with her family, he could tell, and he was happy to give her the space.

Newton's team had turned up bearing what he called the thousand-yard stare. Well, some of them had. Kendall and Moore, in particular. He knew what that meant. They'd encountered something unusual in Ravens' Wood. Moore looked delighted, like the cat who got the cream, while Kendall was more circumspect. Cassie looked like she wouldn't sleep for a week, Ben was scribbling in a notepad at the kitchen table, and Shadow and the Nephilim bristled with resentment at having been trapped in the first place. Some of his guests were in the snug, some in the kitchen, and others were seated on the patio, enjoying the cool night breeze.

Reuben headed to Moore's side, and topped his glass up. "I'm glad to see you here. You always usually go straight home."

Moore grinned at him. "I like to tuck my kids in, but I called my wife. After tonight's experience, I needed to let off some steam. The dryads…"

"Ah, yes. Interesting, aren't they? Not that I've seen much of them, really. Just a glimpse at Beltane."

"We had more than a glimpse of them tonight. We were surrounded! It was amazing. It was probably the greatest experience of my life."

"And the most terrifying," Kendall added, sidling next to them.

Moore stared at her, astounded. "But that's the beauty of them. Creatures from another world, who are actually here!"

"*I'm* here!" Shadow said scathingly. "Is that the beauty of me? I am fey."

Reuben rolled his eyes. Some things never changed.

"You're terrifying, too!" Kendall said, eyeing her sword nervously.

"You have nothing to fear from me. As long as you never take me hostage, of course." She gave Kendall a feral smile that wasn't the least bit reassuring.

"I swear, I never will. But, do you think we were really needed? Would the dryads have stopped the hunters on their own?"

Shadow shook her head. "Never. They are shy, peaceful creatures. They were scared tonight, and curious. Your help made them a little bolder than usual. Hence, the one that pulled Apollo out of the way."

"But the creature that dragged Leigh inside…"

"Was not a dryad." Shadow looked amused. "And that's as much as I'll say about that."

If anything, that news seemed to excite Moore even further, and a dreamy look filled his eyes as he murmured, "It really is a fey borderland. Amazing. Wait 'til I tell my kids."

Trusting that Moore would leave out the very bloody end of the hunters, Reuben circulated, finding Gabe and Niel deep in conversation as they leaned against the kitchen counter, muttering something about Black Cronos. He topped their drinks up and moved on, finding Zee and Eli on the patio chatting with Dylan. All three of them were stretched out on the loungers, gazing either out at the garden and the sea beyond, or up at the stars.

"Gentlemen! Top up?" Reuben asked.

"Don't you ever get sick of hosting these things?" Zee asked, holding out his glass cheerfully.

"Not in the slightest. For a start, when you all bugger off, I can just roll into bed. Plus, my lovely cleaners will make all the mess disappear tomorrow." He didn't tell them that he would also help. He didn't like to impose too much on their goodwill. Plus, they mothered him and made him breakfast, which he always liked. "Besides, the last big party was at your place."

"True," Eli said, nodding. "I had a big hangover after that one."

Dylan frowned. "I didn't think you guys got hangovers."

Zee huffed. "I wish. No, we ache after battle, get hangovers after drinking too much, and suffer if we eat too much. The good thing is, we recover quickly. Anyway, finish telling us about the banshee. Was she tricky?"

"Tricky? She was nuts! My ears are still ringing."

Reuben left them to it, and found El in the snug, talking to Caspian, Newton, Alex, Avery, Sam, and Ruby. The latter two looked comfortable enough, despite not really knowing anyone. He headed to them first, freshening their drinks before he dropped into the armchair.

Newton looked sneaky. "We've decided how we'll discover the two dead hunters without compromising ourselves. Kendall volunteered to go out for a morning run. That way, some poor bugger won't have to stumble across them." He shrugged. "She's the running kind. No one would believe me." He stared at Sam and Ruby, as if suddenly aware of them. "Shit. You're hunters, too. Did you know them?"

Ruby glared at him. "Do not compare us to *them*! They were a very different breed to us. Right, Sam?"

Sam nodded, his hands stroking his thick beard. "Their deaths are no great loss. I've never liked Titus. No one will miss him, or Apollo. Leigh, I'm surprised about, I admit."

"She's always been slippery," Ruby said darkly. "I'm not surprised at all."

"You said *two* gutted hunters. What happened to Leigh?" Reuben asked.

Alex looked at him, alarmed. "Don't start him off again!"

But it was too late. Newton rolled his eyes and muttered, "Only the Gods know where she is! Some bloody Otherworldly something dragged her off and we never saw her again."

"Oops. Sorry. Sounds like she deserved it, though," Reuben said. "All of them did. It was a night for retribution."

"Yes, it bloody was," Newton said forcefully. "I don't care if I have to lie to my boss, either. He should stop asking so many bloody questions!"

Avery laughed. "Crikey, Newton. You surprise me all the time, lately."

"What the hell else can I do? That bloody woman causes me all sorts of problems." *Shadow*. He glared through the wall. "That deadly nightmare is relentless."

"At least she's *our* deadly nightmare," Alex reminded him.

Newton sighed, leaning back in his chair, his whiskey glass balanced on his armrest. "True. And I'm glad she's okay. All of them. I'm especially glad that Ravens' Wood is okay. Not only do I hunt paranormal creatures, but now I feel like I have to protect some of them. Unbelievable."

"Is there anything we can do about Rupert?" Avery asked. "We saw him talking to the hunters. He has to be held responsible in some way!"

"Conversation is not a crime, Avery," Newton said. "I know you dislike the man, and I agree he's unpleasant, but we have no idea of his involvement. For all we know, it was nothing more than a chat about the weather in a field."

Avery looked as if she was about to argue. Of all of them, Avery disliked Rupert the most, but moments later, she shook her head. "No, you're right. It's dealt with now. Over."

Reuben grinned at Caspian. "And now we can resume our plans for a gig team."

Caspian groaned. "What in the Gods' names have I agreed to?"

"Being bugged every second of the day by Reuben, that's what!" Alex raised his glass to Caspian. "Thanks for saving me from that!"

Everyone laughed, including Reuben. "You, my friend, will regret missing all the fun!"

"I bloody won't."

Newton interrupted them. "How is Briar doing? I was hoping she'd come downstairs..."

El shook her head. "I doubt she'll be down tonight. She's got some catching up to do."

"I hope she'll rest," Caspian said. "She overdid it tonight. Green Man or not, she struggled."

"She can stay here if she wants," Reuben suggested. "I'll keep an eye on her, although I have a feeling she'll soon be heading back to Stormcrossed Manor with her family."

Alex huffed and drained his glass. "As long as Tamsyn is honest with her. That's some history she has to share. Long, dark, and tortured."

Briar sniffed and wiped a tear from her eye as she listened to Tamsyn—*her grandmother*, she corrected herself—relay the story of Orla, and how she became a banshee.

"That's so tragic," Rosa exclaimed. "I can't believe you never shared that!"

Tamsyn shrugged. "It seemed a cruel thing to share. And what could anyone have done?"

"She was a monster. She killed your husband. Our grandfather."

"And drove away our mothers," Briar added sadly.

Tamsyn shook her head. "Oh, no. I think I did that."

The three of them were gathered in Rosa's private sitting room on the second floor. With a little magical healing from Briar, Tamsyn had recovered from her ordeal, and was now drinking tea. The windows were wide open, allowing the sound of the sea to carry to them. The lighting was low, and all three sat close together, their voices hushed. The two children were sleeping in the next room. Briar still couldn't believe that she was with her family.

"You carried a weight of grief that no one should!" Briar exclaimed, studying the tiny woman. "A supernatural burden of grief. I'm surprised it didn't crush you."

"I think it did. When your friend, Alex, told me to let it go, I thought I would float away with the shock of it all. I still feel as light as a feather now." She gave Briar a shy smile. "He's a good boy, although he swears too much. Single?"

Briar giggled. "Are you matchmaking? No. He loves Avery, and they're a lovely couple!"

She sighed. "That's right. The redhead. Never mind."

Rosa leaned forward and held Tamsyn's hand. "You look different. I can actually see that your burden has gone. You even look younger—it's astonishing! I'm so sorry. I was terribly cross with you, but I didn't understand. You must think I'm just awful. But Beth..."

"Beth." Tamsyn sighed and leaned against the back of the sofa. "The fact that the banshee has gone doesn't change Beth's abilities. She is still a seer. She will need to be trained. It is both a gift and a burden, and I should have talked to you about that. I can teach her, but I'm old, and she'll need more. I'm hoping Alex will help."

Briar nodded. "He will, and so will I. As much as I am able to, anyway. My skills are different."

"So, you'll come to the house?" Tamsyn asked. "I want you to visit."

"Of course I will." Briar remembered the thrill that had raced through her when she set foot on the land. "I want to help you restore it. Especially the gardens. That's where my passion lies."

Tamsyn's smile was radiant. "Lovely. But now you need to tell Rosa the truth about yourself. There are no secrets among us anymore."

Rosa turned to her, wide-eyed. "I *knew* it! What secrets? Oh, God." She groaned. "I don't think I can take any more bad news."

"It's not bad news." Briar was starting to realise that Rosa had a flare for the dramatic. "It's just different. I'm a witch."

Rosa squealed and shot back in her chair.

Tamsyn rolled her eyes. "Hush, child. Listen."

Briar laughed. "It's time for you to hear about the other side of my family. I suggest you settle in. It gets quite twisty." Then something else struck her. Rosa didn't seem like someone who paid much attention to the news. "You're new to White Haven! Do you know anything about this place?"

Rosa still eyed her with concern. "Not really. Why?"

"This place celebrates the old ways, it always has. Magic is strong here. It's the Lughnasadh festival at the weekend. There'll be drummers marching through the town, fire jugglers, and a bonfire on the beach. You have to come. The children will love it. It's the best way to get a feel for your new home. You are staying, aren't you?"

Rosa smiled. "I guess I am."

"Then you have to join us, I insist."

Briar realised she was going to enjoy having a family again, despite their differences. Or maybe even because of them.

Thanks for reading *Stormcrossed Magic*. Please make an author happy and leave a review. There will be another book in this series coming soon.

Midnight Fire, White Haven Hunters #5, is on pre-order now, out in November 2022.

If you enjoyed this book and would like to read more of my stories, please visit my website at tjgreen.nz. You will get two free short stories, *Excalibur Rises* and *Jack's Encounter*, and will also receive free character sheets for all of the main White Haven witches.

By staying on my mailing list you'll receive free excerpts of my new books, as well as short stories, news of giveaways, and a chance to join my launch team. I'll also be sharing information about other books in this genre you might enjoy.

Read on for a list of my other books.

Author's Note

Thank you for reading *Stormcrossed Magic*, the tenth book in the White Haven Witches series.

After the events of *Chaos Magic*, I thought it would be interesting to introduce another supernatural creature causing havoc. I knew I wanted to explore Briar's family at some point, and one thing led to another... I love old houses and whimsical secret gardens, and really enjoyed writing about the manor with a dark past. You can be sure we'll be seeing more of it, and its residents, in the future!

There are more White Haven Witches stories to come, and although I'm not exactly sure what the next one will be about yet, there are still plenty more English and Cornish myths to explore. The next book should be released in February 2023.

Please visit www.tjgreen.nz, where I blog about the books I've read and the research I've done for the series. In fact, there's lots of stuff on there about my other two series, Rise of the King and White Haven Hunters, as well.

Thanks again to Fiona Jayde Media for my awesome cover, and thanks to Kyla Stein at Missed Period Editing for applying her fabulous editing skills.

Thanks also to my beta readers—glad you enjoyed it; your feedback, as always, is very helpful!

Finally, thank you to my launch team, who give valuable feedback on typos and are happy to review upon release. It's lovely to hear from them—you know who you are! You're amazing! I also love hearing from all of my readers, so I welcome you to get in touch.

You can get a free short story called *Jack's Encounter*, describing how Jack met Fahey—a longer version of the prologue in *Call of the King*—by subscribing to my newsletter. You'll also get a free copy of *Excalibur Rises*, a short story prequel. You will also receive free character sheets on all of my main characters in White Haven Witches series—exclusive to my email list! To sign up, visit www.tjgreen.nz/landing

By staying on my mailing list, you'll receive free excerpts of my new books and updates on new releases, as well as short stories and news of giveaways. I'll also be sharing information about other books in this genre you might enjoy.

I encourage you to follow my Facebook page, T J Green. I post there reasonably frequently. In addition, I have a Facebook group called TJ's Inner Circle. It's a fab little group where I run giveaways and post teasers, so come and join us.

About the Author

I grew up in England and now live in the Algarve, in Portugal, with my partner, Jason, and my cats, Sacha and Leia. When I'm not writing, you'll find me with my head in a book, gardening, or doing yoga. And maybe getting some retail therapy!

In a previous life I've been a singer in a band, and have done some acting with a theatre company—both of which were lots of fun.

Please follow me on social media to keep up to date with my news, or join my mailing list—I promise I don't spam!

Here are all the places where you can find me:

Website: http://www.tjgreen.nz

Facebook: https://www.facebook.com/tjgreenauthor/

Twitter: https:/twitter.com/tjay_green

Pinterest: https://nz.pinterest.com/Mount0live/boards/

Instagram: https://www.instagram.com/tjgreenauthor/

BookBub: https://www.bookbub.com/authors/tj-green

Contact: tjgreennz@gmail.com

344

Other Books by TJ Green

A Young Adult series about a teen called Tom who is summoned to wake King Arthur. It's a fun adventure about King Arthur in the Otherworld!

Call of the King #1

King Arthur is destined to return, and Tom is destined to wake him.

When sixteen-year old Tom's grandfather mysteriously disappears, Tom will stop at nothing to find him, even if that means crossing over into a mysterious and unknown world.

When he gets there, Tom discovers that everything he thought he knew about himself and his life was wrong. Vivian, the Lady of the Lake, has been watching over him and manipulating his life since his birth. And now she needs his help.

The Silver Tower #2

Merlin disappeared over a thousand years ago. Now Tom will risk everything to find him.

Vivian needs King Arthur's help. Nimue, a powerful witch and priestess who lives on Avalon, has disappeared.

King Arthur, Tom, and his friends set off across the Otherworld to find her. Nimue seems to have a quest of her own, one she's deliberately hiding. Arthur is convinced it's about Merlin, and he's determined to find them both.

The Cursed Sword #3

An ancient sword. A dark secret. A new enemy.

Tom loves his new life in the Otherworld. He lives with Arthur in New Camelot, and Arthur is hosting a tournament. Eager to test his sword-fighting skills, Tom is competing.

But while the games are being played, his friends are attacked, and everything he loves is threatened. Tom has to find the intruder before anyone else gets hurt.

Tom's sword seems to be the focus of these attacks. Their investigations uncover its dark history, and a terrible betrayal that a family has kept secret for generations.

White Haven Hunters

The fun-filled spinoff to the White Haven Witches series! Featuring Fey, Nephilim, and the hunt for the occult.

Spirit of the Fallen #1

Kill the ghost, save the host.

Shadow is an overconfident fey stranded in White Haven after the Wild Hunt is defeated on Samhain.

Gabe is a Nephilim, newly arrived from the spirit world, along with six of his companions. He has a violent history that haunts him, and a father he wants answers from—if he ever finds him.

When they get into business together with The Orphic Guild, they're expecting adventure, intrigue, and easy money.

But their first job is more complicated than they imagined.

When they break the fey magic that seals an old tomb, they discover that it contains more than they bargained for. Now they're hunting for a rogue spirit, and he always seems one step ahead.

The fight leads them in a direction they never expected.

Gabe can leave his past behind, or he could delve into the darkest secrets of mankind.

Shadow has no intention of being left out.

Shadow's Edge #2

As Shadow and Gabe become more involved with The Orphic Guild, they find out that the occult world is full of intrigue, and far more complicated than they realised.

Especially when it seems that someone wants the same thing that they do—The Trinity of the Seeker.

Cause for concern?

Absolutely not. If anything, Shadow is more committed than ever, and relishes pitting her wits against an unpredictable enemy.

And Gabe? When they find instructions that could enable him to speak to his father, he and the Nephilim are more than ready to fight.

Join Shadow, Gabe, and Harlan as they race against an occult organisation that is as underhand as they are.

Dark Star #3

A race against time to find a stolen arcane artefact turns out to be far more dangerous than they ever expected.

When an ancient relic is stolen from the Order of the Midnight Sun, Shadow and Gabe are hired to track it down, pitting them against a new enemy.

The search leads them across the country and tests their resources—and their faith in each other, as fey and Nephilim discover that this world is as tricky as the life they left behind.

Harlan, desperate to help, finds himself at war with JD, and suddenly alliances are under pressure. No longer able to trust The Orphic Guild, Harlan is faced with a dilemma that forces him to make choices he never envisaged.

Enjoy magic, mystery, intrigue, and the occult? Then you'll love the White Haven Hunters. Buckle up for the ride!